A GATHERING
OF DOORWAYS

OTHER BOOKS BY
MICHAEL JASPER

Gunning for the Buddha, Prime Books, 2005
Heart's Revenge (writing as Julia C. Porter), Five Star Books, 2006
The Wannoshay Cycle, Five Star Books, 2008
Maps and Legends, Prime Books, 2009

A GATHERING OF DOORWAYS

∽o∽

MICHAEL JASPER

PRIME BOOKS

A GATHERING OF DOORWAYS

Prime Books

www.prime-books.com

ISBN: 978-0-8095-7315-8

ACKNOWLEDGEMENTS

Special thanks for inspiration and assistance go to Kathy Sedia, Carolyn Jasper, Sarah Smith, Michael Kelly, Shawn Scarber, Mahesh Raj Mohan, Lee Capps, Oz Drummond, Greg van Eekhout, Sarah Prineas, Samantha Ling, Tim Pratt, Garry Nurrish, Sean Wallace, my wife Elizabeth, and of course our two sons, Drew and Mitch.

For Drew and Mitch

PROLOGUE:
A REMEMBRANCE OF DREAMS

This all began a while back, when Noah was just out of diapers, and I started having these fucked-up dreams. Got so I wasn't sleeping much anymore, big surprise there, thanks to my dreams of that place. I'd wake from one of them panting and dry-throated and disoriented, staring up at the ceiling until the blackness turned to blues and grays, and the world took shape again. I would listen to the whisper of my wife's breathing next to me and wait—as I'd done ever since his birth—for my son to stir or cry out in his bedroom down the hall, shaken from sleep by bad dreams of his own.

I didn't dare get up and risk waking Melissa, a painfully light sleeper. She'd want to know what was wrong and then probably try to come up with some sort of assessment or treatment for my insomnia. No thanks. I had enough on my plate as it was, with her and Noah, the farm and the water. The fucking polluted water.

So I'd lie there—aching to return to that place from my dreams, that almost-familiar city—but afraid that if I did, I'd keep searching its endless side streets and abrupt dead ends and déjà-vued neighborhoods until either my car or I broke down.

The dreams always started off the same way: me driving in my old puke-green Ford Escort, two hundred thousand miles on it and still rolling, just the slightest tang of burnt oil coming from under the hood. The tired engine shuddered like an irregular heartbeat as I made my way up steep hills on tire-blackened streets four lanes wide, traffic slicing past me, all gray sedans with black-tinted windows and motorcycles with faceless helmeted riders, with the occasional out-of-place blue pickup rushing past in a burst of color and a roar of muffler.

I spent all my time squinting through the windshield at this shifting city unfolding in front of me, watching the buildings slip back out of sight when I turned my head this way or that, rearranging themselves like a kid's oversized set of blocks. I always felt like I was just two or three synaptic firings away from remembering the exact path to get to my destination. The place was a mash-up of all the cities I'd ever been to, sketchy neighborhoods right next door to grand squares and restored mansions. I had no maps. Each dream I'd go a bit deeper, but never arriving anywhere in the Undercity.

The Undercity. What the hell kind of made-up name was that?

Sometimes I'd make it to the upper reaches of the city, up impossible inclines that led to blocky unpainted houses with shuttered windows, houses built into the sheer purple rock of the mountain range that somehow cut through this sprawling metropolis. Sometimes down to the inner neighborhoods ringed with green parks and lined with pink pedestrians. At other times, I'd be stuck creeping through stop-and-go traffic in the bustling downtown, the road a valley between sharp concrete towers without windows. I could never get where I needed to go. My frustration grew, night after night, accumulating layers like a pearl, or a tumor.

I'd wake from those dreams with the smell of rot and car exhaust in my nose, body thrumming with the muscle memory of traveling by car. I'd lay there in the dark, aching to remember more, wishing I could wake Melissa, knowing I didn't dare. Our lives had been enough of a nightmare ever since Sophie.

If only I could blame all that happened that day on the damned Undercity.

CHAPTER ONE:
STRANGE FRUIT

You were supposed to be watching him, Gil.

Her words created a backbeat to each step he took, his boots pounding on the sun-baked trail that lead to the forest—the last place he wanted to go. But his son was in there; Gil knew it. His boy, Noah. And he was lost. Gil kicked at the dry, scarred ground and scrambled over blackened tree roots reaching up to trip him. Each step took him farther from the farm, but closer to Noah. Gil knew where his boy was, knew the name of the place. He just had to find it and *get* there.

Noah. He'd already wandered off twice this summer, a typical spacey, curious five-year-old. And Melissa was right—Gil had been responsible. Three times now. The world turned white as the late-morning sunlight beat on Gil's bare head, the smell of dust and dead vegetation sharp in his nose.

Not even an hour ago, Noah had been sitting on his lap, squirming with impatience as he waited for Gil to continue telling him the latest story about Prince One-Eye and his band of Black Hoods. An eternity ago. Now the boy was gone. Lost.

Gil pushed through the trees, ignoring the dull jabs of pain in his bad hip as he walked, grabbing frustrated fistfuls of leaves dried by the sun. He hadn't been up here on the trails adjacent to the farm in weeks, and the lack of rain had started frying the trees already. Nothing wanted to grow this summer; even the pines looked parched.

Sometimes the forest eats you, Gil thought, sometimes you eat the forest.

Pushing his way through the trees, he let the elastic, dust-covered limbs snap back before realizing that the man walking behind him might catch one in the face.

Ray, Gil's sixty-five-year-old neighbor, was already chuffing air, sounding like he'd been running all-out with a pack of rabid dogs at his heels instead of just walking on the trail for the past fifteen minutes. Ray lifted his bullet-shaped head as he fiddled with the translucent cord that ran from his nose back up his shoulder and into the hissing pack of oxygen on his broad back.

Supposed to be watching him, Melissa's voice reminded Gil. He winced and picked up the pace.

Next to Ray walked his fawn-colored greyhound Bullitt, straining against his leash. Ray had shown up a few seconds after Gil had broken the news about Noah to Melissa, and Gil had been stung by her response. Twenty steps outside their farmhouse, knowing where he had to go to find Noah, he had simply detoured around the unexpected appearance of Ray in his gravel driveway. Gil had avoided the black leash attached to Ray's skittish yellow dog and figured that was it—he was free of the old man and anyone else foolish enough to want to help.

But Ray and Bullitt had decided to follow Gil up here, and Gil didn't have the energy to tell them to back off.

"Forget calling the cops," Ray said now. He exhaled a crackly breath. "They wouldn't even . . . give us the time of day. Not after that . . . false alarm last month."

Already he was making himself part of this, Gil noticed, saying "us" instead of "you." But with Noah out there somewhere, trying to find his way back home—*can't think about that, can't think about that*—Gil figured he'd take whatever help he could get.

"Cops don't matter, Ray," he said, all confident voice and no hesitation. Fooling exactly no one. He touched the cell phone in his jeans pocket, wondering if he might have missed a call from Melissa. "Noah can't be far off, I tell ya. He's okay, probably just exploring, as usual."

Melissa's reaction still baffled him. After he'd realized Noah had slipped off, and he'd done his best to find him on his own, Gil had found her orchestrating the day's activities in the kitchen with Julio, Mariana, and Herschel. When he asked her if she'd seen Noah, she rushed toward him with this look of intense—what? Fear? Hatred?—on her face.

"What happened?" Her voice had a dull clang to it, like a doorframe echoing after the door it holds has been slammed. Not waiting for a response, she pushed past him on her way outside. Gil knew she wanted to have their discussion away from the hired help. Melissa hated showing that anything was wrong. Ever.

"You were supposed to be *watching* him, Gil," she said over her shoulder as soon as he was outside, crunching over gravel.

"He was just playing outside, on the swings," he began, moving closer to her only to be pulled up short by fresh pain in his injured hip. "He was right there . . . "

His words dried up when she showed him her back, once again, and put both hands to her head. He could tell without seeing her face that her eyes were clenched shut, that she'd be claiming another migraine soon. Gil wanted to grab her, turn her around and wrap her in his arms the way he used to. She was too quick to turn away from him lately. What he wanted to do was hold her and feel her heart beating as madly as his own, giving them both the strength to face this together.

But he didn't dare reach for her. Instead, he started walking away from the house, her words stinging like cold sleet thrown by the winter wind. He swallowed his anger and turned his gaze south, to the old trails leading up to the forest at the edge of their property. A heartbeat later, Ray and his dog had arrived.

Ray and Bullitt and Gil trudged over the uneven ground rising up on the last few acres of Gil's land. He had no idea who owned the forest looming ahead of them (it certainly wasn't Ray), but he needed to move faster, had to get in there sooner, even though his feet grew more heavy and his hip more sore with each stride.

"I think Noah was here," Ray said. Somehow he'd gotten ten steps ahead of Gil. "See that?"

Ray stood up straight, one hand resting on the back of his head to open up his lungs. His other hand pointed downward, at an intersecting trail. He'd dropped Bullitt's leash and was now standing on it with a booted foot to keep the jumpy dog from darting off like a pup chasing squirrels and rabbits.

In the bit of softened dirt, Gil saw the crescent shape—*so small!*—of what had to be the toe of one of Noah's sandals. The rest was obscured by a flat rock embedded into the earth.

He fought he urge to break away from Ray and plunge down the trail after his son. He could almost taste the musky air of the trees and dirt, surrounded by the stink of rot in the shaded coolness. Air so thick you could feel it on your skin, a moist jacket of guilt and decay. Gil remembered it all too well.

But he couldn't move forward. A memory had snagged him, sharper than any thorn-filled bush or low-hanging tree limb.

"Hold up a second," he mumbled. "Just hold up."

Moving like a dead man, shambling and dragging his leaden feet, Gil slid off the trail and pulled the shovel from behind the big boulder where he'd stashed it last time he was here, in the early spring.

Touching it made his head spin, just for a moment. What went down last time he was here was now coming around to snap him in the ass. The blade of the shovel looked slightly black, stained somehow. Ray could probably see it from where he stood.

Let him ask, Gil thought as he returned to the trail. If he wants to know more, I'll tell him about the squatter and how I got rid of that skinny, snooping bastard. See how he likes that.

With the shovel in hand, Gil's guts stopped roiling and churning and instead filled with ice. He knew what this feeling was. He'd experienced it countless times before in his nightmares, night after night for the past few years.

"Something is *amiss*," he muttered, gripping the shovel in both hands as the sun crept ever closer to its daily zenith. "Something is *amiss* because of the Undercity."

౭౦౦

Gil and Noah sat perched behind the counter of the store. Gil had one heel hooked on a rung of the creaky old stool, Noah balanced on his knee. At ten a.m., the sun was already pre-heating the store's tin roof like an oven, overpowering the window AC unit next to them and the three ceiling fans whirling on high above them. Billie Holiday crooned "Blue Moon" on the radio as Gil rested a hand on his son's back and continued making up a new story to while away their lazy morning together.

Noah gazed at the fan closest to them, listening hard. This story was one of those constantly evolving tales that never truly ended. Gil just picked up from where he left off the last time, usually with help from Noah—the boy recalled the details much better than his dad.

But as luck would have it, after not even five minutes of spinning out the latest adventure of the outlaw Prince and his secret band of Black Hoods, down in a dungeon chasing trolls, to be exact, two women from up the road walked in and interrupted them.

"Foiled again," Gil whispered, annoyed. He slid Noah down to his shin until Noah's sandals slapped the scratched and dust-tracked hardwood floor, his body all wiry little-boy muscle capped by a blonde moptop. "I'll finish this later, 'kay, bud?"

Soon as I come up with a plot twist or three, he thought, biting down on a sudden yawn trying to escape. Another sleepless night last night. Gil's eyes felt like they'd been smoothed down with fine-grit sandpaper, and he felt a not-unpleasant head rush as he got to his feet, favoring his bad hip.

"All right," Noah said, disappointed but distracted already by the various magnets on the humming dorm fridge Gil kept behind the counter. Gil could tell he was still inside the story, plotting what would happen next. With his imagination, he thought, the youngster could probably tell the stories better than me these days.

"Stay close to the store," he called as Noah turned and disappeared down one of the aisles without a sound.

Gil could still smell Noah's kid scents of baby shampoo, sweat, and dirt on his clothes, already missing his son's wriggling forty-five pounds on his knee.

"Hel-*lo* ladies," he called out with the best fake enthusiasm he could muster as another yawn came on. "Just got some new apricots off our trees this morning, along with the last batch of some killer cherries."

His hand on his bad hip, he threw a smile at the two thirtysomething women wandering through his store, stay-at-home moms with nothing better to do all day but shop and take aerobics classes to entertain themselves. At least these two took care of their own kids; Gil had heard that many of the housewives up there had nannies to watch their kids for them. The women were from the new neighborhood up the road—*Estate homes starting in the mid 800s!* the sign along the road shouted at him whenever he drove past—and Melissa had made him vow to be nice to all of them, reminding him that their patronage would help pay for a large chunk of the bills on the farm in the coming months.

It wasn't easy. People like them were convinced they had to eat all the forests before the forests ate them.

The screen door leading out to the fenced-in playground whined open and then slammed shut with a shot. Noah had made it outside. Gil grinned, picturing him meeting up with Mrs. Peterson's twin girls and Ms. Harrison's surly little boy, the hint of a smile on his face as he called out a "Hey" to them.

Still grinning, Gil closed his sore eyes for longer than a blink and was rewarded with a nightmare image of an endless smooth road surrounded by oversized concrete curbs that protected twin rows of twisted gray houses from a trio of night-blue pickups that were now roaring down the road at him.

His eyes snapped open when he heard the shudder of air brakes on Jones Ferry Road, barely fifty yards from the store. A sudden stab of fear passed through him, a sensation not unlike the sliver of pain still embedded in his hip months after he'd first injured it in the forest.

Remember the fence, Gil told himself. Noah knew the boundaries of the farm. Even if he did like to wander off sometimes, he knew not to leave their land. The kid was safe.

The two women chatted and walked up and down the six narrow aisles of the store, the squeaking wood floor announcing each footstep they made in their pricey cross-trainers. Gil could almost smell their sweat after their walk here to cap off their workouts at the two-story health club next to the Olympic-sized pool that now sat where a dense stand of loblolly pines, kudzu, and other bushes and weeds had once held reign.

Now, everything was dying. Even their pool had been closed, due to some issues with the water, some sort of contamination, from what Gil had heard. He just hoped it wasn't spreading to his land.

Eat the forest before it eats you.

Gil gazed at the scuffed floor, recalling the days when it was just him and Melissa, building their dream farm together, the place they'd gotten for a song from the previous owners, a pair of diehard Chapel Hill hippies.

The therapy farm. The recovery ranch.

We'd been happy then, Gil thought, in spite of the stress and hard labor. Maybe even *because* of it.

Once they got the place up and running, then hired some help, Gil's role went from farmer and fix-it man to shopkeeper, and now he was mainly a babysitter. No complaints, there. Beat cubicle work and corporate life any day. What killed him was how the women coming into the store always gave him that "so-sweet" look whenever they saw him with Noah, as if a father spending time with his son was cause for adulation.

Gil also caught the look given him by some of the men who saw him with Noah, a squinty look, as if he were half a man for allowing himself to sink to the level of a child's caretaker.

Half a man, Gil thought, arms prickling with goose-bumps. He shot a look at the two windows opening onto the playground. That was something else from my dreams, wasn't it? The ones about driving through an almost-familiar city, on the cusp of being utterly lost. Glimpses of half a man, someone who disappeared if you looked at him head-on.

A half-man.

As if on cue, the radio played more Billie—"Strange Fruit" this time. Surrounded by crates of fresh fruits and veggies, Gil had to smile at the irony, even if technically, Billie wasn't singing about fruit at all. His goose flesh faded.

Fluttering the neck of his faded Apple Chill Street Fair T-shirt for a breeze, he squinted at a trail of dust in the last aisle and the unsprung mousetrap strategically placed under the shelving there. Time to get back to Prince One-Eye and the Black Hoods, back in the Forbidden Forest, running from tigers and hunting trolls and searching for the Humming Sword of Peace. Such heavy thoughts were the current stresses of Gil's life: he was on deadline to a five-year-old.

"Say, Gil, where these mangoes from?" called out Mrs. Peterson, pulling him back to reality. "Are they local?"

Or had it been Ms. Harrison? They always remembered *his* name, using it at every opportunity, like a farmer prodding a slow cow.

"From the McGinley farm just up the road," he said, turning again toward the big windows looking out onto the playground, opaque with morning light. Stifling a yawn, he put a hand to his forehead and wiped away a line of sweat. He wished it would rain soon—over a month had slipped by without so much as a drop. Their plants and trees were going brown, dying from the heat. At least, Gil hoped drought was the cause of the crops going bad.

"*Southern trees bear strange fruit,*" Billie sang as Gil tried to locate Noah out on the old, uneven merry-go-round or the monkey bars. Never should've put up those damn monkey bars. "*Blood on the leaves and blood at the root . . .*"

Was that another truck thundering up Jones Ferry? Those maniacs never slowed down for the curve.

"Just up the road," he repeated, looking through the window at just the right angle to see what looked like a dark blue pickup truck pulling into the gravel parking lot, and then he was running around the counter and down the aisle of granola and hemp products, sore hip screaming from the sudden call to action, booted feet drumming on the squeaking wooden floor.

"Gil?" said Mrs. Peterson or Harrison. "Are you all right?"

Gil ignored her. He could barely breathe in the hot, close air of the store.

"Noah!" he called out even as he put his hand on—and then through—the rusty screen of the spring-loaded door. Melissa's going to kill me for that, he thought, and then he was shouting out his son's name again. He could've sworn he saw a second, then a third blue pickup pulling into the driveway.

But when Gil stepped through the ruined door of the store and put his feet on the top step leading downward, the playground and the parking lot in front of him were empty.

⌇∘⌇

Ray either didn't hear what Gil had said over the hiss of his portable oxygen tank, or he was ignoring Gil. He'd give the old guy the benefit of the doubt. Ahead of them, the dark green expanse of the forest loomed like a leafy thundercloud, replacing Gil's thoughts about the Undercity with mingled sensations of guilt and gloom.

Still gripping the stained, rusty shovel tight, he ended up walking right through an unexpected stream and soaking his boots. With Melissa's voice still repeating its ugly, condemning mantra in his skull, he looked down at the water and sniffed its sulfurous odor. The stream was no wider than a trickle of piss, but dark and thick as syrup, and it flowed north, downhill toward his farm. More bad water.

That stream hadn't been here yesterday.

Something's amiss in the Undercity . . .

Up here, the hard, dry ground supported only scrub brush, pines, and sun-baked, clay-stained rocks big as your head.

Thought you were watching him . . .

Ray trudged and splashed past Gil, oblivious to the bad water below them, though Bullitt made sure to leap over it. As if moving of its own volition, Gil's hand shot out as Ray trudged by, and Gil ended up snagging Ray's tank of oxygen.

What the hell? At the cool touch of the metal tank, Gil felt a sudden out-of-body rush of dislocation. The events of this day—a day that had started out so peacefully, so normally—caught up to him like an elbow to the nose.

Something was amiss? *Everything* was amiss. He was standing outside the forest with Ray, for shit's sake. The guy was on oxygen. With twenty-percent lung capacity, Melissa had told Gil.

"Gonna . . . let go of that?" Ray gasped.

With a start Gil realized the old man's nosepiece had come loose. He looked down and saw his hand still gripping Ray's slim oxygen tank, its cords dangling to the ground.

"Jesus, I'm sorry, Ray!" Gil scrambled to get Ray's breathing apparatus attached again. He ended up bumping into Ray's greyhound and getting tangled up in the leash, tottering closer to the diseased stream at their feet. Ray just laughed and took the cords and tank from Gil, leaving the younger man to get free of the leash on his own.

"You've got a pretty . . . healthy respect for these woods." Ray inhaled, coughed, and spat. The stuff hit the trail with a slapping sound. "So," Ray hissed, nodding at the trees without ever taking his eyes off of Gil, "what makes you think . . . your boy would go in there on his own?"

Because, Gil wanted to say. *Because of the Undercity. Because something's amiss there.*

"We don't have time to go into that now, Ray," he said instead, trying to get around Ray. He thought he saw another sandal print there amid the rocks and gnarled tree roots. "I can tell you later."

"No." Ray stepped in front of Gil until they were face-to-face. Even though Gil was six inches taller than Ray and had full use of his lungs, he felt like the smaller man here. Ray still hadn't reattached his nosepiece, and his breathing was like wind throwing hail against a tin roof every few seconds.

"No, we get this . . . hashed out *now,*" Ray said, rubbing Bullitt's narrow head. He pointed off to the southeast, and through a gap in the trees Gil could see the rest of Ray's dogs. Ray had often told him that he'd lived on his place next door all his life, and how he collected former racing greyhounds the way a kid collects baseball cards, or a college kid collects debts. All of his dogs, easily three dozen of them—brindle, fawn, white, and a couple black ones— were racing in a wide, tightly packed circle across the short grass of his four-acre-long field. Coursing at top speed, chasing after some invisible prey, so fast they seemed to blend together as they circled and circled in ever-widening ovals.

Ray sucked in a painful breath as two of them collided and hit the ground. It took a good two seconds for their yelping to reach them, as if they were ghost dogs moving out of synch with time and space.

"I won't *have* that anymore," Ray said through clenched teeth. "Talk to me now or you go in there by yourself, no guide. My dogs've been going nuts like that all morning, and something's going on that

I want taken care of." He looked at Gil, watery blue eyes unblinking. "Now."

"Damn it," Gil muttered. Not now, old man.

Something rustled through the forest ahead of them, and Gil fought the urge to run after it like a wild man. He needed something tangible, something he could pin down and beat into submission. He fought back the urge to pursue, but only barely.

He could hear Ray breathing next to him. Waiting.

Gil rubbed his face and stepped back, wishing he were still in the store with Noah on his knee, a story spilling from his lips. Noah's kid odor was still on his hands and shirt, while the forest was a hulking bully, arms crossed, ahead of him.

When Gil blinked, he could've sworn he saw movement inside the forest from the corner of his tired, sleep-deprived eyes. An image from his dreams—a pale slice of a dangerously thin man's face, in profile, the trees leaning away from his presence. A partially digested fragment of memory. Yet another deal gone bad.

Herschel, one of the old men who worked on the farm with Melissa, would've had a theory or two about this. Herschel was always talking about probability and coincidences: "What are the odds of this happening? What is the likelihood of that?"

Now Gil was wondering the same damn question.

Then he blinked again and the image of the man inside the trees disappeared.

When he did, Gil knew what he had to do. He gritted his teeth, got his feet under him, and punched Ray as hard as he could in the jaw.

As Ray reeled backward, Gil pried the leash off Ray's thick wrist and threw it. Bullitt panicked at the sudden commotion and skittered off down the trail they'd just walked up, picking up speed. Ray went gasping to one knee, fumbling for his oxygen, and Gil turned on his heel, hip muttering a warning.

"Sorry, Ray," he said. "I've got to do this on my own."

He half-ran, half-walked away from his old neighbor, his knuckles aching from where he'd connected with Ray's jaw. He hadn't expected so much resistance from the old guy.

Hold on, Noah. I'm coming for you. Finally.

Gil was three steps away from the entrance to the forest, a gap formed by two oaks whose upper branches had grown together, when something slammed into the backs of both his legs. He toppled forward, bad hip screaming back to life with a vengeance. His hands sank into the cold, wet earth inside the darkness of the forest. The black dirt smelled sickly sweet, like overripe compost. Good, rich soil, he thought foolishly.

Then he turned. Towering over Gil was his neighbor, standing up straight with his thick arms folded on his chest. His lanky, fawn-colored racing dog stood next to him, and his oxygen tank sat on its side ten yards behind him, cords streaming away from it like torn guts.

Ray wasn't wheezing. For the first time since Gil had met him over six years ago, he couldn't hear the old man's tortured breathing.

"I think you forget," Ray said in a low voice, "that I've lived here a *tiny* bit longer than you, Gil."

Ray bent off to one side, put a finger to the side of his nose, and did a long farmer-style blow out one nostril, then the other, shooting strands of ropy snot onto the red-clay ground like an offering to the forest.

"God, I hate having that plastic tube up my nose all the time. And you punch like a girl. Let's *go*, Gil."

Fingers numb, Gil pulled himself up on the nearest tree trunk. He tried putting as much of his weight on his bad hip as he dared. A few feet away, resting blade-down next to a tree as neat as if he'd placed it there, sat his trusty shovel.

What were the odds of that? he thought, and nearly began laughing hysterically. He risked a quick look at Ray, the neighbor he thought he knew, and hobbled forward to grab the rough, splintery wooden handle of his shovel. It was all coming full-circle, here at the forest's edge once more.

Holding the weather-beaten shovel like a crutch, Gil took a deep breath and without another word limped into the first rank of old-growth trees at the edge of his land in search of his son, with Ray and Bullitt at his heels, and together the three of them left the rest of the world behind.

CHAPTER TWO:
NOT ON PAUSE

Noah Anderson usually listened to what his dad told him. Usually. Dad talked so much, and made up so many stories, it sometimes got tricky keeping up with *everything* he said. With Mom, yeah—Noah always followed every word she said, because she backed it up with grumpy eyes or a timeout or the death of a cookie. Dad tried to be strict, but he didn't always follow through.

While Noah never would've been able to put all this in words, he felt it on the inside, like a stitch he'd get after running too fast for too long. So when Dad told him to stay close to the store on their farm that morning, Noah knew that the words "staying" and "close" had a good bit of stretchiness to them.

After leaving Dad's store, Noah had right away gotten stuck on the swings with the mean kid who lived in one of the big new houses up the road. As the two boys kicked and swung on the creaky old swing set next to Dad's store, the bigger boy kept making up stupid songs with annoying rhymes ("Who likes to eat yellow snow-ah? It's Noah, Noah, Noah! He's a dirt-eating boa, baby Noah! Fee-fi-foah, Noah!").

The kid's name was Eric, and Eric had learned how to punch. That punching made the twins go and hide next to the big oak next to the store while their mom was inside shopping for vegetables. Noah wished they would've stuck around to play and teach him another one of their home-made twin games.

So it was just Noah and the singing, punching kid on the swings. Above them, the sun broke free of the row of pines in front of them, heating the top of Noah's head until he felt like he was wearing a frying pan for a hat. He started kicking hard as he could on the swing, pumping his legs just like Dad had taught him. When he reached what felt like the highest height he could get, he tried the trick that Dad had told him to never show to Mom. Noah let go.

The earth tilted as he continued rising in the air off the swing, and the ground rushed away from him, and Noah felt like he was flying straight up into the hot white sky. Then, for the tiniest moment, he *stopped* in mid-air. This was the best part. He felt everything just freeze, and he couldn't even breathe.

I'm on Pause, Noah thought, just like Dad's CD player.

And then the ground shot back up at him as he dropped. He caught himself on both feet—a nice trick to not fall over—and turned his back on Eric's silliness and meanness. Time for a walk, he decided, all by myself.

He'd made it about twenty steps down the rutted driveway before he heard the grumble of engines and the loud crunch of big wheels on gravel. Noah looked back as two blue pickups pulled into the parking lot behind him. Back on the swings, Eric stopped singing. He must've run out of Noah rhyme words.

The people inside the two pickup trucks never opened their doors to get out. Another truck pulled up beside them. Noah had seen those trucks a couple times before, and they weren't anything interesting. Not really, even if they did all match. But if the people inside them weren't even going to get out, what was the point? With a shrug, he kept on walking, the rumble of the truck engines fading with each step he took.

The best thing about the farm was that he always had someplace new to explore. Now that Noah was five, Dad had been letting him go off on his own more and more, and he loved the adventure of finding a new place or discovering new details about places he'd already been. It gave him a thrill almost as good as Dad's stories about Prince One-Eye and his band of heroes. Almost.

If I stay on this side of the gravel lane, Noah thought, I could go up to our house next to Dad's store, see what Mom was doing, maybe cool off a bit in the air-conditioning. But her old-folk clients were probably there, doing their busy work, and they'd want me to sit next to them and answer their questions about how and what I'm doing today. Not fun.

He thought about trying to get Mom's old pottery wheel turning again in her little art shack next to the lake, but he remembered her warnings not to touch anything in there when she wasn't with him. Her mean eyes, as always, drove the point home.

The little shack was probably hot inside, too, he figured, feeling proud of himself for the grown-up thought. Dad would say it was "hot as Hades" in there.

"Hot as Hades," Noah muttered, trying out the words as he walked toward the lake. The store and its parking lot and playground were behind him now, the big white two-story farm house coming up on his left. He wished he had someone else to talk to other than himself, someone close to his age who didn't punch or sing annoying songs. Most days Noah didn't mind being an only child, but today he felt an unfamiliar emptiness inside. A little brother, even a little sister, might be nice.

Leaning forward and balancing on the balls of his feet, Noah kept walking up the smooth gravel lane. The machine shed next to the barn looked nice and dark and cool, but with a shudder of memory he decided not to bother.

Ever since he'd gotten stuck in there a while ago, something had really bugged him about that shed. Maybe it was all those sharp tools or the old pieces of lawn mowers and other machines in there at the back, all waiting to snag the finger or the hand of a curious five-year-old. Noah was convinced that the door to the machine shed had closed and locked on him that day. He had screamed himself silly until Julio let him out of the shed. He'd felt like the walls were closing in on him, dragging him down under the ground.

And now he was almost at the edge of the stinky lake, with the big hay barn next to him, across from the house. All around the lake shore was a ring of brown where the water used to be. Noah remembered taking their canoe out on the little lake, but now the canoe was red with rust, sitting upside-down like an empty peanut shell next to the shrinking circle of pond. The mud at his feet had dried up into big puzzle pieces that were now pulling up from the ground.

Not enough rain this summer, Dad had said. Maybe that was why the water that was left in the lake looked so black and smelled so bad.

Noah stood in the shadow of the hay barn, wiping sweat out of his eyes. He could go all the way through the barn and watch the goats chew on the fence posts, or maybe walk into the orchard and pick a green apple and some peaches.

Too much work, he decided, and turned back to the big farmhouse.

He looked at the three old people sitting on the front porch of the house—snapping peas, cleaning potatoes, writing down something on a clipboard next to a stack of boxes—and thought about all the times he used to sit there, caught up in one of Dad's stories, or just listening to him and Mom talk.

He loved it when they'd chat there on the porch at the end of a day and he could follow along like a big boy. When the sun started going down, he'd close his eyes and rest his head on the railing and let the sound of their voices lull him to sleep. He'd always be in the middle of a dream when they woke him and brought him into the quiet, dark house.

Those talks didn't happen much any more. Noah could barely remember the last time Mom and Dad both sat here, together. Maybe it was a year ago. Maybe even two.

Now all he could hear was old Mr. Dun, complaining in his loud voice about the spots on the fruits and veggies in his bucket, and how little they all were. The fruits and veggies, not the spots. "Bunch of diseased-looking sons of—" Mr. Dun was saying, before Mr. Herschel cleared his throat to tell him to shut up and watch his language.

Noah was thinking about going up on the porch, saying hello to the old folks, and then finding Mom. The thought of her made his lower lip suddenly tremble for some reason. He'd tell her about Eric the bully and his new punching skills, and she'd explain why the boy was that way and make it all better.

Yeah, that sounds good, Noah thought. Maybe I could get a hug or two.

With the sun still pressing down on his head like the hand of one of the store ladies that Dad was always fake-nice to, he trudged across the gravel toward the porch. He glanced back at the store and its parking lot, but the blue pickup trucks were gone.

I could go back there and see Dad again—

Noah was halfway through the thought, ten steps from the front porch, when a tiny black and green creature skittered out from the hay barn and across the gravel in front of him. He stopped walking for a second, worried it might be one of the rats Mom had warned him about, and then he gave a tiny whoop.

"You!" he whispered. "You again!"

It was the tail-less salamander he'd been trying to find for the past week. The salamander was as long as Noah's hand, as thin as two of his fingers. Ever since their first encounter under the porch of the house, Noah had been carrying around the critter's bright green tail in his pocket.

"Come here, you sucker," he muttered, breaking into a trot as all of his worries about how to spend his day disappeared. He was going to catch the salamander and give him back his tail.

But he still hadn't caught up to the salamander by the time it had left the gravel driveway, and it was now scrambling across the front lawn, making a beeline for the clump of browning magnolia trees between the store and the house, in front of Julio's trailer.

Noah knew he could catch the critter in the magnolias. But instead of stopping and hiding in the waxy-leaved trees, the salamander kept going. It was aiming for the bigger group of trees farther up the hill.

Noah followed the tail-less salamander, bottom lip caught in his top teeth, hands clenched into small, determined fists. He passed Julio's trailer, smelling the spicy food Mariana was cooking up for the kids and her and Julio, and slowed down.

No, he thought. I got to move faster. I have to get the critter before it reached the dark, cobwebby place that Dad called the forest. The place that, at the beginning of the summer, Dad had made me promise never to go into by myself.

Dad needn't have worried. Noah figured he'd be crazy to go into that creepy place all alone. Not after what he'd seen and heard inside those trees back on that cold, dark morning not that long ago. The forest gave him the serious creeps.

∽o∽

Most days Noah heard Dad get up early, though Dad always said he did his best to be quiet. But Dad always managed to bump into something—the coffee table or the overstuffed bookcase in the living room—or he'd knock something over while he was making coffee in the dark. Instead of rolling over and catching some more Zs like he usually did, Noah slid out of bed, sneaky as a king's one-eyed son, and tiptoed, barefoot and still in his pajamas, after his father. As far as Noah could tell, Dad never knew he'd been following him that day.

Dad was walking fast in his old clompy boots, already headed down the gravel lane toward Jones Ferry Road. Noah stayed on the front porch until Dad's messy head of hair disappeared around the corner of the store. Then he jogged after him on the grass, his bare feet kicking up cold dew. Past the store and around the fenced-in playground, Dad headed down the path between the fence and the ditch toward the trails.

Noah thought about running ahead and surprising Dad on the rocky paths lined with weeds and bushes, but he was enjoying spying on his father, watching him from a distance. It was like having a secret that nobody else knew, not even Dad. Plus, Dad's head was down, and he was chugging along like a train on a hill. Noah would never be able to head him off at the pass.

Noah had to rub his eyes when he looked at Dad again, squinting. Dad had stopped next to a big rock and bent over to pick up something from behind it. For some reason, he'd left his good shovel out here, the one with the long, skinny metal head.

Watching Dad put the shovel on his shoulder like a soldier and then lower his head again, Noah started to wish he'd stayed in bed. His feet and the pants of his pajamas were wet and cold, and his teeth kept wanting to chatter.

But that shovel had grabbed his curiosity like nobody's business. Dad was now about half a football field away, Noah guessed. Mom was always trying to teach him how to judge distances, saying it would help as he worked on the farm and for when he "grewup." Mom loved teaching Noah things like that, though he preferred learning from Dad's stories and from having adventures of his own before it was too late and he "grewup" too.

Panting for breath now, one hand over his mouth to muffle the sound, Noah watched Dad with his shovel and his hunched back disappear into the darkness of the trees. These trees were different from the ones on the farm—their leaves weren't green all the time, and the trunks were much fatter. There were a lot of them. So many that they created a darkness inside them that couldn't be chased off by the red light now filling the sky. The sun would be poking up its head any minute now.

Noah couldn't make himself enter the forest. Stepping into the shadows made by those leafless trees would've required more courage than he could muster that morning with his cold, wet feet and dew-soaked pajamas. He had a cocklebur between the first and second toes of his left foot, his lungs were stinging from the cold air, and he was pretty sure there were snakes in there. His bed was sounding better and better all the time.

Before he could turn back home, however, he heard angry voices inside the trees. Dad was talking to someone in there. Arguing, it sounded like.

Noah held his breath as long as he could, leaning forward, then he heard Dad say the biggest of the bad words. The sound of it shocked him into motion. He spun on his sore left foot, all his air stuck in his lungs, and ran back down the trail, away from the forest and the dark, fat trees.

F-word, he kept thinking. Dad was saying the F-word. And he was saying it a *lot*.

So Noah ran.

He made it a good football field away before his vision began to go gray for lack of air, and he nearly fell down when he stumped his big toe on a rock. Hopping on one foot as he rubbed his injured toe, he took a couple of quick, shaky breaths. He almost stepped in a dark puddle of black water that had gathered in the hole left by a fallen tree. The tree itself was gone except for half a dozen rotting roots poking up from the ground like broken teeth. Noah's nose wrinkled at the foul smell from the puddle. He'd never seen water like that here on the trails.

Something skittered behind him, and he bit down a scared shout as he let go of his big toe and ran again. He wished the wind whistling in his ears would drown out the angry words he'd heard in the forest. But he just couldn't run fast enough.

In his dreams that night, and on occasional nights since then, Noah would sometimes hear that second voice in the forest again.

It sounded like dozens of big bugs, crawling up his bedroom wall. He'd wake up from those dreams trying to call to his mother, but his own voice would always fail him.

From then on, Noah would insist that all of Dad's stories take place inside a forest of dark, tall trees like that one. He and Dad even had a name for it. They called it the Forbidden Forest, and Noah couldn't stop thinking about it, as hard as he tried not to.

ᴄᴏᴄᴏ

Today, Noah decided as he wiped more sweat from his forehead and rubbed it onto his shorts, what was happening today was turning into was one of those . . . *things*. One of those things that Prince One-Eye always did in Dad's stories. What was it called again?

Going on a *kest*.

Or something like that. Noah remembered that heroes did lots of walking like this on a kest. He was now hurrying along a trail after the salamander, jumping from one rock to another.

I'm on a kest to give this salamander back his tail.

And maybe I can tell him the ending to the story Dad was telling me today. Probably he could help me figure it out. Prince One-Eye and his band of Black Hoods could run into a dragon that had lost its tail, and the dragon could be their friend. They could use the dragon's flame to light up the darkness to help them out of the black-as-tar dungeons of crooked King Smoot.

It was all going to make one very nifty story to tell Dad.

Noah was puffing for air now as the land began to gradually rise. He was glad he had sandals on this morning—he saw lots more rocks this time around than he'd seen that morning he'd followed Dad in his bare feet. He didn't need another toe-stumping on his salamander quest. Every time he'd get close enough to pounce on it, the shiny critter scrabbled faster over the rocks, its little knobby butt wagging at Noah as if he still had a tail.

Capture the dragon, Prince One-Eye. Grab it and wrestle it to the ground with your bare hands if you have to.

Gritting his teeth with determination, Noah chased the salamander in zigzag fashion, passing tall, skinny pine trees creaking in the breeze. He hoped those sky-scraping trees wouldn't fall over on him or the salamander. At one point he jumped over a tiny river that must have popped up since the last time he was there. The dark water smelled like bad eggs, and it made its determined way toward their farm, as if it were stretching out to connect up with the lake next to the house.

Something about that tiny stream made Noah pause, only for a second. He thought he could almost *hear* the water flowing, and it sounded like somebody crying. A sad sound. Noah shrugged to himself and continued tailing the salamander. The water became part of his story—the Sad Black River outside the Forbidden Forest. Nothing to slow down a Prince on a kest.

Noah was so focused on the salamander and the story he was telling to himself about the Prince that he didn't notice until too late that he was already a good half-a-football-field inside the shadowy forest, the last place he'd ever want to be, alone.

And the salamander was nowhere to be seen. Just wide tree trunks, poking branches, a musty smell of rot, and wet darkness. Everything went silent in here, and Noah's sweat turned cool on his skin.

"Crap," he whispered, then clapped a hand over his mouth. He thought of Dad with his shovel, talking to that other person inside these trees, and he felt suddenly small and weak.

"Stay the eff off our land," Dad had said.

The stranger had answered in a laughing, teasing, skittery voice: "This land ain't your land, this land ain't my land. Nope-nope."

Noah shuddered at the memory of that voice and wished he'd brought along his wiffleball bat. Or a big stick.

I don't even have a sword. No shovel, no nothing. Unless . . .

He stopped next to a barkless tree and dug both hands into the pockets of his shorts. In the left pocket he could feel three bottlecaps, a couple pennies, some string, a crumpled piece of paper, some wrapped mints from the store, and the thick magnet he'd plucked from Dad's fridge that morning. All he had in his right pocket was his dad's old pocketknife and the rubbery green spike of the salamander tail.

He thought about his options for a moment, and then he went for the tail instead of the pocketknife. It felt like the right weapon for the job. With the tail held tight between the thumb and first finger of his right hand, he started walking again, slower now.

The dead air in the forest was so different from the outside world. There were no chirping birds or rustling wind or, every now and then, the reassuring groan of a car creeping up the hill on Jones Ferry, headed for Chapel Hill. In here, the only thing making any noise was him.

Noah was holding his breath again, tiptoeing. He didn't want to look behind him to see how far he'd walked into the trees.

"Stay close to the store," Dad had said that morning.

"Stay the eff off our land," he'd also said, before.

Noah walked until he came to a clearing in the trees. At his feet was a round bump in the ground, like an oversized anthill. Inside the mound of dirt was a hole that reminded him of his dog Daisy's butthole when she lifted up her tail. He crept up close to the tiny opening and caught himself reaching a finger into it.

"No, kiddo," he told himself, hearing Dad's voice instead of his own as he spoke. "Be smart. Use a stick and be ready to run if you stir up some bees or a hornet's nest."

He found a stick, poked it inside, and ended up getting it stuck inside the strange hole. Something rumbled in the air around him when he tugged hard on the stick. It was a sound he could feel in his teeth and at the pit of his stomach. It sounded like a growl.

Noah froze, his sweat turning cold in the heavy air.

"I want to go home," he whispered. "I want my Daddy."

But his feet didn't seem to care anymore what he wanted. They remained planted in front of the hole, as if he were a tree too, putting down roots. When he leaned forward again to try to pull out the stick, the earth gave way under him.

For a heart-stopping second, the world froze, as if someone had hit a gigantic Pause button.

And then the hole opened like a giant mouth, and Noah fell downward. It felt just like getting hit by a wave and knocked off his boogie board. He could almost hear the roar of water in his ears. A gulp of air was all he could manage, not even a scream, as he fell.

Above him, more orange-brown clay slid forward, obscuring the hole, the mound of dirt, and all traces of the blonde-haired little boy who, just a second earlier, had been standing there in the clearing, looking down at the ground.

CHAPTER THREE:
BACK HOME ON THE FARM

Melissa knew she needed to be doing some sort of meaningful work instead of just sitting there on the back porch of Julio and Mariana's trailer, staring out at the trees and waiting for the shakes to stop. But with Mariana's soft singing coming from the trailer's kitchen, the smells of spices and frying meat and onions in the air, and Anna sitting close to her, shucking corn, Melissa didn't feel much like getting up.

The wind rustled the dry brown leaves of the trio of magnolias guarding the back porch of the narrow trailer. The trees looked as thirsty and worn-out as Melissa felt, but she wasn't ready to ask for any water just yet. She'd keep this situation under control, and she could get started on something meaningful.

That was what her training and years of experience were telling her. People need work to find a purpose in life, otherwise they start stagnating. Dying. She knew she'd feel better if she helped Julio and Mariana's ten-year-old Anna clean the recently picked corn. But before reaching for one of the undersized, slightly curved ears from the paper bag sitting between them, she touched Anna's shoulder and sat back, feeling the sweat slide down her neck.

Just sitting here was meaningful enough for me right now, she decided, basking in the glow of Anna's smile. At least until my hands stop shaking and the pounding in my head goes away.

The headache had arrived as soon as Gil burst into the kitchen that morning, announcing to her (in front of Julio and the others, no less) that he'd lost Noah again. The pain had only intensified after he left. That was when Melissa had taken it upon herself to find Noah before Gil did, one of those nasty little competitions between husband and wife that neither would admit to taking part in, but both were intent on winning.

She'd started with the farm house, going first under the front porch, where she'd found Noah's collection of two dozen action figures, a pile of comics in English and Spanish, some Nabs wrappers, a trio of what looked like spiderwebby maps of places she couldn't recognize, and a metal canister full of coins, nails, and rocks. But no Noah.

While she was down there, she'd been tempted to lie down on the flattened piece of cardboard that lined the little cave and savor the cool dampness of her son's hideout, pretending she was a kid again. She did hunker down so she could look up through a crack at the world outside.

Thinking of Noah using that opening to get a look at what was happening above him, sudden tears had filled her eyes. As big as he'd gotten in the past five years, he was still *so* small. She nearly brained herself on a wooden beam on the way out in her hurry to get back to her search.

From the porch she left the heat and humidity and went inside, tearing through all twelve rooms and three bathrooms in the rambling old farm house, even checking the upstairs bedroom next to Noah's that they always kept closed up. Then she hurried downstairs and charged out through the kitchen to her art shack. The place was empty, smelling slightly of dust and turpentine.

Unable to believe he wasn't in here, Melissa had wasted a precious handful of minutes moving untouched canvases and boxes of old pottery, saddened by the fact that she hadn't worked in here for so long. When did I have time for art these days? Or anything else, for that matter?

But Noah wasn't in the shed, nor was he sitting on the buckling wood of the pier overlooking the murky lake, or hiding out in their grounded canoe. Should do something about that water, she thought, as always, when she looked at the sludgy lake, but she kept going, saving *that* migraine for another day.

By this point, she was practically running as she hurried through the hay barn, passing the goats and Mr. Dunleavy on her way to the orchard and its shriveled fruit, then circling back past Herschel and the goat pasture and into the barn. Legs shaking so badly she thought she'd fall at any second onto the dirt floor, she gave the machine shed a good once-over, but the dark, cluttered, cramped little building was empty, too.

Melissa had paused for a moment then, remembering how just two weeks ago, Julio had found him there. Poor Noah had been screaming for who knew how long, and when Julio brought him up to the house, the little guy's face had been a mask of dust and dirt, held together with tears. No way would Noah go back to the shed again any time soon.

That left the playground and Gil's store. And the trails leading up to the forest at the end of their property.

Her headache took root, possibly for good, when she saw the empty playground. The hard-coded panic of a mother without her child began setting in. Thanks to the shade thrown from the thirty-foot-tall pines stationed between the playground and Jones Ferry, the playground was a popular place for kids to escape the summer heat; it should not have been deserted.

Even if the store was now closed—Melissa had wanted to kill Gil for that, with the finances in such a sorry state this past year—there should've been kids on the swings or merry-go-round or monkey bars. Not today. Not even a couple of the rich kids from up the road digging in the sand box, accompanied by their doting mommies in their expensive cross trainers and perfect hair.

Melissa noticed the ruined screen for the door leading into Gil's store, but she could no longer muster the energy to get pissed at Gil about that. Her temples were throbbing, as if someone had stood behind her and clapped his hands like cymbals against her head.

"One last place," she told herself.

Hurrying past the abandoned swings, she bent down to the crawlspace door wedged into the bricked foundation of the store. Thanks to all of Gil's stories, Noah had probably thought this would make a cool dungeon for exploring.

The half-door leading into the crawlspace was closed and bolted shut, but Melissa threw open the bolt and the door anyway. She leaned in and immediately got caught in a sticky cobweb. She flailed at her face and hair to get it off her, feeling small creatures crawling over her cheeks and into her hair. The whole time she kept calling Noah's name.

She paused for a moment, thinking of Gil down here a while back. Determined to put a stop to the squeaking floors in the store aisles above, he'd armed himself with a big bag of wooden shims. With Noah and Melissa above him, walking around and stepping on the squeaky boards, Gil had scuffled along on the cold wet ground under the converted schoolhouse, jamming wedge after wedge of wood in the gaps made between the two-by-four supports and the plywood floor. Gil had emerged muddy and bedraggled, red-faced and coated in cobwebs. She'd made a big fuss over him, calling him her hero as she and Noah brushed him off and led him to the house so he could clean up and get warm. So long ago—

"You got a spider on your shoulder, Missus Anderson."

Melissa jumped at the sound of Anna's voice next to her.

"Got it," Anna said, holding out her cupped hands to Melissa. Melissa caught a glimpse of tiny legs inside the girl's fingers. "Hope it's not a brown recluse."

"Put it down, honey," Melissa said, too sharply, still thinking about Gil, not even a week later, going back under the store and pulling all the shims out, claiming the silence in the place was making him crazy.

When had that been? She remembered being big as a house then with Sophie, which would've made it a little over two years ago. Where did those two years go? Time had gotten all distorted and unreliable after Noah's birth, and grew worse after Sophie.

Melissa looked at her hands and willed them to stop shaking, just as she willed her brain to stop thinking about Sophie. She had no success with either attempt.

Anna gave her another smile as she came back up the steps, rubbing her spider-free hands on her baggy jeans shorts. "All better," she said.

"*Gracias*," Melissa said.

I didn't mean to snap at you, she tried to say, but her throat had tightened up as she looked at Julio and Mariana's beautiful daughter. Anna had long black hair, tied up as usual in a ponytail and sticking out of a battered baseball cap, and her brown eyes were bright and always curious. Her long fingers plucked the corn silk from another small ear of corn, and Melissa couldn't help but watch her work, thinking about the bedroom upstairs, untouched, the crib still made up and waiting for its occupant. Stuffed animals lined the dresser, staring blankly at Melissa when she had thrown the door open, calling her son's name in the stuffy air.

"I'd better go," she said, standing up, hands clenched at her side. All the blood rushed to her head, and the world spun for a second. She forced herself to relax. She was no good to anyone if she passed out from the heat.

Anna's big eyes went serious, and Mariana's singing stopped in the kitchen behind them. She paused and swallowed, glancing behind her before speaking again.

"Missus Anderson," Anna whispered. "Have you looked in the forest yet?"

"Not yet," Melissa said, her skin suddenly cold despite the noon sun beating down on them. "Do you really think he went up there? We've always told him not to go there by himself."

Anna shrugged. "I saw his daddy go that way before, with Ray and one of his crazy doggies. I just thought . . . "

"What?" Melissa said, too quickly, without thinking, using what she always thought of as her bitch voice. She never knew when that was going to come over her. "You thought what?"

"Just thought he might be up there," Anna muttered, pulling another husk free from the ear of corn in her hand, her face shaded by the brim of her cap. The kernels on this ear were all brown and runny, and Anna tossed the whole works into her garbage bag.

"Right." Melissa sighed. Time was passing, and she was wasting it. "Look, I've got to go. Thanks for helping with the corn. You can have your daddy bring the ears up to the house when you're done, okay? The good ones, that is. If we have any."

Anna nodded, and Melissa walked down the steps of the back porch and onto the dirt path, looking from left to right, hoping to catch a glimpse of her missing son. She walked past the magnolias, their flowers drooping and turning yellow already. Heading for her own kitchen again, she inhaled the scent of the magnolia blossoms, but it seemed too sweet today. And underneath that perfume was the odor of rot, possibly from the compost pile behind the house, or maybe the bad pipes in Julio's trailers, or even the bad water of the lake, giving off its unique stench.

It was all enough to give her a fresh headache, a pain that started right behind her eyes, slowly pressing inward. Melissa breathed through her mouth and pounded her fists against her upper thighs as she walked back to the big farm house.

Someone needed to stay here, she told herself, in case Noah came back. What would happen if he wandered back from wherever he'd gone, the dusty adventurer all scared or shaken up, and nobody was there to greet him?

It was up to me, she decided, to stay home on the farm.

All these years, Melissa had carried on a love-hate relationship with the farm. Mostly love for the lifestyle it provided for her and her family, all fresh air and living off the land and making up their own schedules. But what earned her hatred was the unending work, the constant upkeep, the hard labor she did here with her patients to get them back on the road to recovery while also keeping the farm running and profitable. The enormity of this place threatened to overwhelm her on a regular basis.

She trudged up the steps of the front porch, wishing the sweat on her sleeveless blouse would dry faster.

It had all seemed so simple back when they were just beginning, those reckless first years when the loan money started rolling in. As a female business owner, Melissa had been amazed at the number of special "minority" loans she could qualify for, so long as she put the farm and the land in her name only, against Gil's bitter protesting. She'd ended up taking on quite a few of them to get the place operational after buying it from the F-Ts.

The F-Ts. Mister and Missus Finley-Thompson. What a great pair of hippies they were.

Back in the house, unable to avoid the work piling up for the day, Melissa began directing traffic in the kitchen. Herschel and Julio were cleaning and primping the latest batches of vegetables for the store, Julio whistling a fast Mexican tune, and Dun was arranging a new sampler platter for customers that afternoon. Dun did nice work—this collection of ragtag veggies looked fairly presentable. Melissa winced and averted her eyes when she saw the stack of bills in today's mail on the counter next to her.

As she washed carrots and apples in their oversized sink, she tried not to think about Noah and instead focused on that slightly surreal night of barbecue and wine with the previous owners of this place that Gil had happily exclaimed was "sixteen miles from everywhere."

Gil had been drinking that early autumn night, of course, but not her. She'd been barely eight weeks pregnant with Noah and constantly nauseous. So Gil "took up her slack," with the wine consumption as well as with the talking.

He was actually pretty enjoyable to see and hear in action, she had to admit. He had his confidence back then, or at least the appearance of a confident man. Or a *confidence* man.

He told her later that night, in bed, still chattering away as the last remnants of his wine wore off, how they'd practically stolen the house and land from the older couple. How he hoped the F-Ts didn't wise up overnight and change their minds. How everything was working out, finally, for them both.

"You have to look at the comps," he'd told Mister and Missus Finley-Thompson after all the barbecue had been eaten, at least by the three of them; the first bit of pork had made Melissa gag. Gil pulled out his three-ring binder stuffed full of printouts of MLS listings he'd made at work, on the company printers. "The houses that have sold up the road are actually going *down* in value. Prices are flat at best. Thanks to the economy and all the development in Chapel Hill and Pittsboro, this area's being left in the dust. Too far out, not enough amenities. And I know that twenty-five acres can be a lot to manage." He'd laughed then, light and easy. "Just my opinion," he'd added. "I could be full of shit for all I know."

The twin looks of desperation on the older couple's faces made Melissa want to pull Gil away from there, but he just wriggled free of her grasp, still talking.

"That's not to say that you'd lose money selling the place," Gil continued, flipping through his pages of printouts and fiddling with the map of the area he'd brought along. "You'd probably do all *right*, selling to a developer."

The name "Smoot" hung over everyone at the table like a storm cloud trapped indoors. Melissa knew the good ol' boy from up the road had been keeping his eye on this place ever since she and Gil had seen Smoot's big white Chevy pickup in the driveway on their first visit to the farm. Everyone in the area knew who Smoot was.

"I just don't want to deal with that fellow," Missus F-T said, running a hand through her short, spiky hair. She'd just finished up a year of chemo for her breast cancer, and her face was flushed with her third glass of Cabernet. A petite and handsome woman in her late sixties, she was gazing intently at her husband, an odd look on her face. Mister F-T was silent but nodding as he fingered his grizzled gray beard.

"And then," Gil said, pausing to stare into his empty wine glass for effect, "there is the fact of what *he'd* do to your land if he got hold of it."

"Build houses," Mister F-T grumbled. "Shitty houses like the ones they're building up the road. All on tiny little lots. Ray warned me about him ten years ago."

"All house, no lot, you'd better believe it," Gil said. "Close to a hundred of 'em, I'd guess, if he did some postage-stamp-sized lots, which he would, maybe even drain your pond. Totally hose up the watershed for the area. And all the buildings would have to go, too, I'm sure."

"Tiny little lots," Mister F-T added, brows furrowed.

Everyone sat back in their chairs to ponder that a while. Melissa nibbled on a hush puppy left over from dinner, hoping it would soak up the acid in her stomach. Everyone said the first trimester was the worst. They'd better be right.

As she chewed, she looked around the spacious kitchen, admiring the oval island, currently coated in cookbooks and the remains of their barbecue dinner. Glinting pans of all sizes hung down from above the island, with two big black skillets sitting on the six-eyed stove against the far wall. In every nook and cranny were small carved figures made from wood, including a couple that looked like tigers or lions and one that had to be a dragon, along with colored marbles and a couple black spheres the size of softballs. Melissa had wanted to pick up one of those black balls striped with gray, or at least ask about them, but Gil hadn't let her get a word in edgewise.

Until now, that was. A strange tension filled the air, and she realized Gil and the F-Ts were having a sort of non-staredown, avoiding each other's gazes as best they could, not wanting to be the first to crack.

"Gil would farm the land," she said, unable to bear the silence or the averted eyes any longer. "Organically. No pesticides or other contaminants to ruin the water. And we'd like to start up a therapy service to help people recovering from strokes or other disabilities. People of all ages, working on the farm as part of their recovery. Occupational therapy," she added, feeling foolish with everyone's eyes on her.

"We'd have goats!" Gil blurted, and grabbed the bottle of wine. He shot Melissa a goofy wink for the F-Ts' benefit. "And a pile of kids, too." He paused, a bit too long for Melissa's taste, before adding, "It's our *dream*."

Mister F-T looked over at his wife for a long moment, and then he cleared his throat and let Gil pour him another glassful. A smile poked through the wild gray hairs of his mustache and beard.

"Let's take one more look at those comps of yours, why don't we?"

༺◦༻

Usually the kitchen was Melissa's sanctuary, the one place where she felt like she could still control everything, but today she could only chop so many vegetables and give so many orders before she had to get out of there.

When she'd started, the kitchen had been full, with Julio, Dun, and Herschel, along with Mariana, Anna, and their son Cris crowded around the big table, working in an awkward silence on the four deliveries that needed to be made to restaurants in Chapel Hill and Durham.

Slowly, people began slipping away. They'd avoid her gaze as they headed outside, sometimes mentioning her son's name as if remembering that one place they'd forgotten to look earlier. Soon, she was there all alone, the kitchen table and island cleared off and empty.

"I give up," she whispered, dropping her knife. She left it where it fell and pushed open the back door. She kept trying to envision Noah all by himself: on the road, in the hay loft, in the lake, one second away from tragedy.

Did I look everywhere? Was he still on the farm?

Outside, she walked into a humid wall of heat that pressed against her for her first few steps out the door, then melted as her body adjusted to it. Typical July weather in North Carolina.

Nodding at Julio and Dun farther up the road, close to the store, Melissa hurried across the gravel drive and walked down the incline to the machine shed. She felt pulled there as if by some magnet. She could smell the oil and rust of the machines inside, even though the dented metal door was closed tight.

She had her hand on the knob, about to turn it—the knob was surprisingly cold—when her cell phone began to buzz in the pocket of her shorts.

Gil, she thought, exhaling. Finally.

"Hello?"

"Heard there's trouble up at the farm," a gravelly voice drawled, making her want to drop the phone into the weeds next to the shed.

Before answering, she let go of the doorknob and glanced off to her right. A big blue pickup sat in the parking lot in front of Gil's store. She hadn't even heard the truck drive up, but there it was, idling and puffing out black wreaths of smoke from its low-hanging muffler.

"No trouble," Melissa said, turning to glare at the truck. She'd seen this one, or a truck like it, driving around quite a bit the past few weeks. Sometimes more than one, like the matching trucks for a landscaping company, yet there were never any logos painted on the doors. "But thanks for checking. Now I've got to go—"

"Maybe it's that trouble on your place that's got you avoidin' my calls. Not returnin' 'em like a good businesswoman should. Can't say I appreciate that. Especially when I know how hard it is to run a farm these days. All the problems you've been having with the water and such. My daddy did it for fifty years before it killed him and left my mama flat broke. Y'see, I'm just tryin' to *help*, Miz Anderson."

Smoot had a way of saying her name that set her teeth on edge, like it was all a big joke for him to be so formal to her.

"Tell me, Mr. Smoot. Did you get a new truck?"

Before she even finished her sentence, the blue truck a hundred yards—one football field—away from her lurched forward and rumbled toward Jones Ferry. All Melissa saw was the hint of a narrow head and long neck in the pickup's back window. Surely not Smoot, who had a head as round as a white beach ball and the neck of a bull.

"Let's stop kiddin' around for a second," Smoot said, raising his voice the tiniest bit in her ear. "I think we can come to an agreement that's beneficial to us all. A farm is no place for little kids. At least not that place. Plus you and I both know that land there just wasn't cut out for raisin' crops. I heard the complaints lately about the food coming from there. I don't like to hear it. Makes us all look bad."

Melissa's migraine stormed back into her skull, entering through her temples this time. In the past month, each restaurant owner that she'd been providing fresh fruits and vegetables for had complained about the food tasting bad and going rotten too fast.

"And you know, people have been talking about that pond of yours. After what happened to your neighbor's dogs and now all that food you've been selling there, why, could be the property values are already startin' to dip. I'm just saying—"

"Are you *spying* on us, Mr. Smoot?" The hand holding the phone had started shaking now, and Melissa made herself talk slowly so her voice wouldn't do the same. She had no idea what Smoot was talking about with the dogs. Did he mean Ray's crazy menagerie?

With her free hand, she reached down to turn the too-cool knob of the machine shed door, and she pushed her way inside. The place was a few degrees cooler.

"Look. I got an offer set up for your land," Smoot said, ignoring as usual her comments. His drawl was starting to get eaten up by static. "Two offers, actually. The best deal's for the whole thing. But there's another option, if you wanna just sell off some of your acreage. For now. Five-acre chunks if you want. While it's still holdin' its value. Hey, I'm nothin' if not flexible."

Smoot's voice and the dusty stink of old machinery and oil was all making Melissa want to gag. She slid down to the ground, her back against the closed door of the shed, and rubbed her temples. The dirt floor was a cool relief underneath her.

"This is *not* a good day to talk about this," she said.

"It never is," Smoot said, his voice softening. Melissa felt even more disgusted at that. The static grew louder. "But at some point, you and that husband of yours are gonna have to face reality. And when you do, you know my number."

After one last surge of white noise, the cell phone went dead.

"You are such a pompous good ol' boy pain in the *ass*," Melissa said into the silent phone before snapping it shut. She slid the cell into her pocket and wrapped her arms around her knees until she stopped shaking. Not a good day at all for this.

"Noah," she whispered, her words falling flat in the cramped space of the shed. "Where the hell are you?"

She sat there in the windowless shed, thinking of the sharp retorts and biting comebacks she should've used in her call with Smoot. How dare he call today? And how had he found out about Noah being lost? Or the food and their lake, for that matter?

She wished she'd told Smoot where to stick his offer. Either words would completely fail her when her emotions took over, or she'd snap off the harshest response, like the way she'd snapped at Anna earlier.

Or with Gil that morning after he told her about Noah. She couldn't forget the way he'd looked at her, the circles under his eyes so dark they looked like bruises. She'd had a million things to say to him when he'd followed her out of the house. But he just took off, and she'd been too angry—and too proud—to call out for him to come back.

From the floor of the shed, Melissa gazed at the pair of lawnmowers on her left, the rotting bags of mulch and fertilizer in a sloppy pile on her right, and the hodgepodge of old tools and small, torn-apart engines lining the far wall. Gil needed to get in here and straighten this place out.

So much work that needed to be done. The farm waited for no one.

Though what did all that work matter if we lose Noah, too?

That thought propelled Melissa to her feet. She refused to give in like that. She dusted off the bottom of her shorts and wiped non-existent bugs from her legs, and she was about to turn around and head back into the sun and the heat when something on the dirt floor by the far wall caught her eye.

"What the hell?" she whispered, creeping closer to the rotting piece of plywood underneath the bits of engines. A small metal ring, blackened with age and grime, stuck up from under the wood.

Casting a quick look behind her, Melissa bent down. A black chain was attached to the ring, and it came loose as she pulled. After about two feet, the chain went tight.

"Holy shit," she whispered, and then she began pulling and pushing the ruined engines off to the side, sending blackened screws and rusted metal flying, so she could get under the plywood and uncover whatever it was that was attached to the other end of that dirty black chain.

Maybe, she thought, Noah *had* come back in here this morning, after all.

CHAPTER FOUR:
A HANDY DRAGON

Whenever Noah felt scared, he would always try one of the tricks Mom taught him, even if most of the time they didn't really work all that well. He had more than a few to choose from, but sitting there in the dark, smelly cave with what felt like ten pounds of dirt on his head, the best he could come up with was whistling. He didn't dare move or try anything else.

At first, the only sound that came out of his lips was a single, repeated note, barely loud enough to reach his own ears, but it did the trick. A tiny peeping sound. Enough to help him unclench his fists, causing tiny trickles of dirt to roll down his arms and off his hands.

Dad was actually the one who'd taught him how to whistle, he realized. Noah had wanted to be able to do it for forever, listening to Dad birding away in the store or on one of their walks, but he didn't figure it out until recently, at the start of the summer. When he thought of Dad showing him how to breathe though his nose and blow out through his pursed lips, Noah felt tears filling up his eyes. He whistled harder to keep them away.

Tweet-tweet. You're Prince One-Eye, tweet-tweet. You're brave, not scared. You're exploring a dungeon. Tweet-tweet-tweet. You're a hero.

He kept whistling in spite of the stink all around him in the cave, which smelled like a bad mix of old socks and wet mud and dog poop. Rotting stuff. Feeling braver now, Noah shook dirt out of his hair and began looking around. Now that his eyes had adjusted to the gray-black dimness, he stood up. He saw that he'd almost be able to touch the dirt ceiling if he got on his tiptoes and put his hands up (which he wasn't quite ready to do just yet, not if the ground under him was going to give way again and drop him deeper into the earth).

He couldn't yet make out the walls around him, but above him, roots crisscrossed the roof of the cave like the old brown net Julio sometimes used for catching fish on the lake. In the middle of those roots, Noah could see a tiny circle of blue and white sky. That was the hole he'd just fallen through. Through the circle, tiny tree limbs waved at him, from very far away.

How'd I fit through that hole? he wondered, his whistle dying on his lips. And how do I get back *out*?

After almost a minute of just standing there, making no sudden movements, Noah took a shaky step, feeling the same way he did earlier, when he was about to jump off the swing. Excited, but scared he was about to do something stupid.

The floor cooperated, though, and Noah didn't fall.

He exhaled with a shuddering sound in the gray, smelly darkness. Just the simple act of moving calmed him the tiniest bit more, and he was able to look around the strange cave for something he could maybe stand on to reach the far-off hole.

On either side of him, as his eyes grew used to the dimness, he could see more tree roots dangling down the walls like electrical cords or super-long fingers. Hundreds of black beetles crawled over the roots, making them shimmer in the gray light.

Very gross, Noah thought, then he saw where those walls of roots ended, revealing a small opening. This *was* the entrance to a dungeon! Just like in one of Dad's Prince One-Eye stories!

He took another careful step, this time toward the entrance. A cool breeze traveled up to him from the opening, stirring up the stinky air and making him want to spit out the bad smells. The sweat covering his body turned cold, and he let out a small, helpless sound.

"I'm not scared," he tried to whisper. But just like those nights when he'd wake from a nightmare, his voice didn't work.

Figure out where you are, Dad's voice whispered inside his head. Get your bearings. Put your head on straight, kiddo.

Rubbing his arms, Noah looked around the cave once more. The place seemed bigger than Mom's art shack, maybe as big as the old machine shed. He could now see that the opening was made up of dark boards covered in strange symbols that had been pounded into the dirt. Not letters, though. Mom had taught him the ABCs long ago, and these weren't even the fancy letters she called *curses* letters. These letters were all wrong, and they made Noah's eyes want to cross.

Next to the doorway, the viney, beetle-covered roots hanging down from the trees above had all been tied into knots, and some of them had even been braided, just like Julio and Mariana's daughter Anna liked to do to her mother's hair. Anna had once tried to do that to Dad's hair, but all they ended up with were knots that stood straight up on the top of Dad's head.

Noah almost laughed at that, remembering the fast Mexican music playing on the boombox outside the trailer, and Dad's crazy dance on the back porch with his hair sticking up. But he wasn't able to laugh right now, not even at Dad's silly stuff. He probably would've gotten going on the tears if he hadn't seen something familiar climbing down a root on the wall next to him. Its head was aimed at the dirt floor, and it looked like a miniature dragon that had forgotten to grow wings and a tail.

Noah reached out a hand and, at last, caught his salamander. The cave became a tiny bit brighter when his fingers wrapped around the slick skin of the little critter, and as soon as he touched the salamander, his voice worked again.

"I *got* you," Noah whispered, cupping both hands around the subject of his kest. He could feel the salamander's tiny toes poking his fingers as it squirmed. He wished for a second that this pint-sized critter really was a dragon, and instead of toes they were sharp claws. A real dragon would come in handy, instead of a fake dragon he could fit in his hand.

"Now where's your tail?" he whispered, wishing he could reach one hand into his shorts pockets. "I just had it . . . "

Noah was so busy keeping hold of the salamander—which was currently running circles in his cupped hands—that he didn't hear the soft footsteps right away. The salamander did, though. It stopped circling and froze.

Noah looked up to see a thin man standing in the entrance to the tunnel, both hands resting on the dark, carved wood of the doorway. The man was staring right at Noah.

That morning at breakfast, Noah had gotten into trouble with Mom again. She caught him reaching down and feeding the dog the last half of his milk-soaked granola from Dad's store. She was grumpy all the time now, talking about the problems on the farm to either Julio or one of her old folks, thinking Noah couldn't hear her. If she only knew that her whispers made his ears perk up all the more.

Noah remembered her standing in the kitchen doorway that morning, both hands on either side of the doorframe, like she was holding it up. She barked out his name, and Noah almost knocked his head on the table, he sat up so fast.

The thin man Noah had just seen in the cave doorway had—for a second or two, at least—stood there the same way that Mom had back home. Noah felt like he'd gotten caught being bad again.

But when he looked back at the man between blinks, he couldn't see him anymore. The man had moved just the tiniest bit—or maybe Noah's head had flinched just an inch—and the man disappeared. Noah felt like his skin was shrinking up on him, like it was a shirt he used to wear last summer that was too tight this summer. He moved his head to the left and blinked.

There, in the door, right there. He could see him there again. Mostly.

If I could just whistle, he thought, I would.

The thin man in the doorway shifted, and Noah could see him more clearly. The sight made his entire body go straight and stiff. The man standing in the doorway was missing half of his face, as if the mask he'd been wearing had fallen off.

Last year, on the day after Halloween, Julio and Mariana's kids had made a mask for Noah. It was for a holiday from Mexico they still celebrated, even though they now lived here in America. The mask was too big to fit on his head right, but Mariana just laughed and said he could grow into it. Noah was already almost as tall as eight-year-old Cristobal.

They called the holiday that Noah and his family never celebrated the Day of the Dead.

The mask that was too big for him was painted all the colors of the rainbow, mostly yellows and oranges and blues, and it was longer than his whole arm. Narrow and spooky-looking, it was shaped like a half-moon. And the mask seemed to change shape when Noah glanced at it on his desk next to his Hot Wheels and action figures and comics.

The thin, silent man standing in the cave doorway had a face like that Day of the Dead mask—he never stopped shifting.

All of this remembering passed through Noah's head in less than five seconds. He could tell that the man wore old gray jeans and a stained white T-shirt, with shiny black boots. He worried that if he blinked again, the man would up and disappear on him for good. He didn't want to be left alone, but he also wanted to know where this other person went, so the guy didn't try sneaking up on him when he wasn't looking.

Noah squeezed his hands flat until he felt the salamander stuck between them wriggle again. That tiny movement gave him enough confidence to use his voice again.

"Mister?" With his hands full of salamander, Noah tried to point with his chin at the blue and white circle in the cave ceiling. "Can you help me get out of here? Please?"

After a long wait, while Noah listened to his own heart thudding, a clicking sound came from the doorway. It sounded like someone cracking their knuckles. Or licking their lips.

"Nope," the man whispered in a soft, crackly voice. "Can't get out that way. No deal."

Noah shook his head in the dark cave. "But that's where I have to *go*, Mister."

"Nope," the voice said again, and this time it was a little bit closer, still crinkly like newspaper. Noah thought he'd heard that voice before. "Won't fit. Only way out is—" Noah felt the rush of air as the man's hand lifted up and did some pointing of its own "—down thataway. That's the ticket. Yup."

The man was pointing at the doorway next to him, which probably led to a tunnel that led down into a dungeon. The doorway with that cold, crawly wind coming from it.

Prince One-Eye would've jumped past this skinny man and started striding down into the dungeon. The Prince did lots of striding in Dad's stories, even when he didn't have his Black Hoods with him. Noah figured striding was just being brave while you were walking. Walking fast, that is.

I'm on my own, but Prince One-Eye did just fine on his own, in those stories. And I *do* have this salamander with me. Can't forget that. He remembered hiding out under the porch with the black and green salamander a week ago, trying to feed it some crackers, chasing it across the cardboard box under them with his buddy Timmy's borrowed Gimli and Legolas action figures. He'd had a ball until he'd pulled the poor guy's tail off.

"How-how 'bout you just lift me up," Noah said to the thin man, who felt way too close to him, like he'd taken three steps closer without Noah seeing him do it. He could feel the man breathing at him. He swallowed hard. "Just push me up out of that hole, and-and I'll leave you all alone down here."

"Like I said. Can't get out thataway. Nope-nope."

Noah felt something in the man shift, even though he couldn't see him, and he remembered what Dad had showed him on the playground last summer, after the first time the mean boy Eric from up the road had come to play there.

The fake-out, Dad called it. He said that it was best to avoid a fight whenever possible, and you could fake-out the guy trying to hit you if you moved fast enough.

Time to try that one out, Noah decided.

He took a sudden step to his left, leaning so hard that he almost toppled over in that direction. Then he threw himself to the right and stepped as far as he could around the spot where he thought the thin man was standing. Hands gripping his salamander tight, he kept his head low and motored toward the doorway.

He would've made it if one of the roots on the cave floor hadn't reached up to trip him. Just a few feet from the black wood of the doorframe, Noah fell. His salamander popped out of his hands and narrowly avoided being crushed in the process. As the critter scampered off down through the doorway and into the dungeon beyond it, a hand grabbed the back of Noah's shirt and lifted him up.

Too scared to scream, Noah turned and saw the thin man again, this time from inches away. The man's weird shifting face now seemed to be missing an eye and half a mouth. The man's face came even closer, his breath sour as rotten apples and Dad's beer. He was making that clicking sound over and over somewhere deep in his throat, and then the clicking became words.

"You're not going *nowhere*," the man chittered. "We got some talking to do, you and me. Yep-yep."

Just like that, Noah remembered where he'd heard that voice before. Here in the woods, not so long ago. The trees rustling and bending low to try and grab him. Dad using the f-word, and this guy answering with his teasing, clacking voice.

At the same instant he recognized the voice, Noah heard a low growling purr from the tunnel behind him, just like the sound he'd heard before the hole had collapsed on him.

The man loosened his grip the tiniest bit at the sound, and as soon as he sensed the opening, Noah wriggled and kicked as hard as he could. He slipped free and fell to the hard, cold ground and rolled, his breath squeaking like a mouse from fear.

A heartbeat later, something big moved past him, fast, cutting through the air. The big thing slammed into the thin man, and wordless screams of frustration filled the air. Then the screaming stopped and the clicking sounds began again, like a dozen beetles talking all at once. If beetles could talk.

Noah rolled forward and crawled as fast as he could down through the wooden doorway into the tunnel of the dungeon. He made it ten crawl-steps in the smelly darkness before he had to stop to catch his breath—he was breathing as bad as Ray did after walking over to their house with one of his greyhounds.

When Noah looked back at the opening to the cave, the clicking sounds had stopped, and he saw a wide, low-to-the-ground shape walking on four legs in the gray light. The big creature seemed to be limping, and that lit a another spark of recognition inside Noah's brain.

The thin man was nowhere to be seen. The wide creature stepped under the weak circle of light coming down from up above the cave, and Noah saw spots on the big animal's coat.

His eyes widened, and he found himself grinning. In fact, he wanted to get to his feet and shout. Or at least, try and whistle one more time. Instead Noah sucked in air from where he sat on the tunnel floor, hugging his knees close to his chest as he remembered the name of the big cat he'd met not so long ago.

"Elwood?" he said. He let go of one knee, arms shaking too hard to hold tight anymore. "How did you get here?"

The growling purring sound grew louder, and a fishy smell filled the air that reminded Noah of Mom's tuna casserole. The pad-pad-pad of heavy footsteps paused right outside the tunnel where Noah sat, now holding his breath, both hands clamped over his mouth after the awful, bad, very terrible thought he'd just had: *Maybe this wasn't Elwood after all.*

CHAPTER FIVE:
BACK IN MY UNDERCITY DREAMS AGAIN

The instant he passed under the arch made by the two fused-together oaks, Gil felt a cold, heavy blanket of dread drop over his shoulders. His skin went from hot and sweat-slick to chilly and clammy, and the musky scent of moss covering the trees of the forest immediately made his nose itch.

Surely Noah wasn't in here, he thought. The kiddo would've turned and run the instant he smelled this bad air, right? *Right?*

And if he had come here, Gil reminded himself, he may not have been alone. Someone could have led him here, chased him here, or—*do not think about it*—taken him here, against his will. In any case, Noah may not have been afraid at first, but he was surely scared now. That put a new spring in Gil's steps as he moved through the trees, with Ray and his dog following.

He scanned every inch of the rapidly dwindling trail, sharp-bladed grass and vines pushing their way over the dirt, the trees crowding in on every side, and he started up a mental list of all the changes he'd seen on his dream-like walk here. For some reason, focusing his mind like this, on the here-and-now, took more effort than he'd expected. He blamed it on his months, almost years, of riding out easy days at the store, all out of fresh schemes and plots to get rich quick, not even interested in such things, going soft in the store's AC while Melissa sweated it out on the farm with her small posse of stroke victims and illegal aliens, picking up Gil's slack.

Ray and Bullitt walked a good ten feet behind him as they kicked and scuffled their way through the clingy, brazen undergrowth. Breaking through vines with his ankles and dodging cobwebs and tree limbs with his head, Gil remembered the three different times when he and Ray had taken wrong turns on the cracked, baked-clay trail leading here. Each time he could've sworn they'd been going the right way, only to end up at a dead end, or circling back to where they'd started.

And, most of all, he kept seeing in his mind that dark trickle of a stream he'd passed, the water inching its way past him as if hoping he wouldn't notice. He had never seen running water up there, not even after the rains that came with the hurricane late last summer.

Either he'd not been paying attention, or the land itself was shifting. Rearranging its topography.

And while Gil was starting to pant from inhaling the heavy air of the forest, Ray didn't even appear to have lost his breath, though he wasn't hooked up to his oxygen tank anymore. Everything today was as shifty as a fever dream.

Next thing you know, Gil thought, I'd learn that Ray's dog wasn't really a living, breathing greyhound, either, but just a figment of Ray's imagination.

"So," Gil said, glancing at his neighbor. "What do you see?"

"Same thing you do. Trees, bushes, cobwebs. Except . . . "

As Ray trailed off, Gil realized he'd completely lost the path now. Usually the deer had their own narrow little routes through the trees, their delicate hooves digging up the scant grass and trampling the bushes and weeds and saplings to expose the ground below. But maybe the deer didn't like the forest anymore. Gil couldn't say he blamed them.

"Except," he finished for Ray, "it looks *different* this time, doesn't it?"

Ray snorted and spat. "Yeah. Look, Gil, I think we'd better stop for a second. Get our bearings."

That suggestion, of course, made Gil want to keep plowing forward, even though the bushes were tearing the hell out of his jeans. Not long ago, Noah had come through here—*may* have come through here, that is—and he was wearing shorts. And sandals.

Then he thought of the way Ray had chased him down after he'd sucker-punched him, and Gil slowed. When he turned his head to look at Ray, he couldn't even tell where they'd walked after entering the forest.

Feel like I'm back in my Undercity dreams again, he thought. Wandering down endless curving streets and making wrong turns in a land I could never fully map or comprehend.

The Undercity. Gil knew he really didn't need to be thinking about that nightmare place right now. Not here, not while he and Ray were pretty much lost already, after barely ten minutes inside the forest.

Oddly enough, with his brain and body working overtime like this, Gil felt more alive right now, on his quest to get his son back, than he'd felt in years. In two years, to be exact. Going back to before he and Melissa lost Sophie.

Oh, shit, he thought. Shit shit shit.

He went down to one knee on the forest floor strewn with pine needles, dead oak leaves, rotting tree branches, and tufts of grass. Heavy forest air filled his lungs like lukewarm water.

I haven't thought about her in months, Gil thought. Years, almost. It hurt too bad.

"So tell me more about this Undercity of yours," Ray began, leaning on a peeling sycamore next to him.

Gil rubbed his arms from his sudden chill, doing his best to survey the ground for clues of Noah's passage, trying not to think about anything—or anyone—else but Noah.

What would possess a five-year-old to enter a gloomy, cool place like this? Was he looking for refuge from the heat, or maybe just looking for adventure? Or did something chase him in here? And would we lose him now, like we lost Sophie then?

God, Gil thought. We have to get moving.

Instead of jumping up and running off, though, he forced himself to calm down. Letting his eyes unfocus the tiniest bit, he looked at the forest again from his lowered perspective, trying to see the bigger picture. He could just make out a break in the trees ahead of him to the southwest, a less-thick patch of low bushes and dead grass that would make for a good way to get through the otherwise dense foliage.

If I were a kid, he figured, that's the way I'd go.

Feeling Ray waiting for him to respond, Gil pushed his way up to his feet, using the shovel as a crutch, his bad hip pinching out a warning in his nerve endings. Ray put up his arms as if to block another punch, but Gil could tell by the glint in the older man's eyes he wasn't worried one bit.

What do *you* know, Ray? Gil wanted to ask, giving the older, silent man a long look. And why do you care?

"Let's keep going," he said instead, "and I'll tell you what I know. For whatever that's worth. I mean, we're talking about a place that doesn't even exist."

"But maybe, somehow it's all connected? You were talking about it earlier like it was important."

"I don't know, Ray," Gil said. "I'll talk, but you got to promise me to keep on walking. Unless you lose your breath."

After Ray nodded and they started walking again, Gil inhaled deeply and began: "This all began a while back, when Noah was just out of diapers, and—" he almost said more, then stopped, gathered his thoughts, swallowed hard, and continued. "And I started having these fucked-up dreams . . . "

∽∘∾

As Gil described the Undercity to Ray, he tried not to mention it again by name. The tag his dreaming self had given the place felt small and foolish in the daylight, away from his disheveled sheets on his side of the bed, even here in the shaded forest. It was a label somehow connected to the land, though; Gil had never had such dreams before moving to the farm.

So he told Ray as much as he could bear, sure that Ray could fill in the blanks as needed. The hidden parks, his shitty old green car, the gray motorcycles and blue pickups on the twisting roads, the lack of maps. Gil knew that Ray had been close with the Finley-Thompsons, the previous owners, and Ray probably had a good idea of what they had cultivated and encouraged here on their land. Maybe they'd had dreams about the Undercity too.

Because the hippy couple that Gil always thought of as the F-Ts had left more than just a twenty-five-acre chunk of environmentally sound land covered in kudzu and ditchweed. *Much* more. The hay barn full of rats the size of small dogs. The lake bright green with algae. The ruined equipment in the machine shed. And, of course, the small stand of trees south of the farm that opened up onto the forest.

The F-Ts had left some sort of doorway open when they left, Gil had always thought. Like leaving the fridge open and letting the food spoil and start to stink. Melissa had just laughed when he'd told her this, back when she was in her last few days with Noah, belly round as if she'd swallowed a dragon's egg whole. He never talked about it to anyone else, and he sure as shit wasn't telling Ray about it today.

Ray listened to Gil's speech without saying a word as they walked. Meanwhile, Bullitt kept trying to stick his nose in Gil's crotch or lean against his leg, as if trying to trip him, making his hip act up again. In spite of the dog's treachery, Gil ran his hand down Bullitt's washerboard ribs, comforted by his presence somehow. He hoped the dog forgave him for trying to chase him off earlier. Not to mention sucker-punching his master.

"This way—" Gil began to say, lifting a hand to point at the hint of a trail he'd seen in front of him to the southwest. But at that moment Bullitt decided to take off. Ray must not have been holding tight to the leash, because Bullitt hit Gil one last time with his tail, then he was bounding over the ground, almost seeming to charge through the hanging tree limbs and reaching branches. He disappeared within seconds.

"*Shit*," Ray said. "He's got what all the others got now."

The damn dog, Gil realized, had run off in exactly the opposite direction as the trail he had picked out.

"Come on," Ray huffed, already slogging through the trees and undergrowth after his dog. "We can't catch him when he's on the run like this, but he tires out fast. Just hope he doesn't hurt himself before that happens."

"But it's the wrong way," Gil said, not budging, watching Ray bull his way through the trees.

"Come on, damn it," Ray called. "How do you know which way's right or wrong? What are you, an Eagle Scout now?"

Gil pointed, feeling petulant as a child. "Don't you see the trail?" I will not stamp my feet, I will not stamp my feet.

"You want to stop and argue about this now?" Ray was over thirty yards away now. The old fucker could *move*, Gil thought.

Gil had precious few options, standing there by himself. He could catch up to Ray and try to find the man's dog, then convince him to come back and try their luck on his trail. Or he could go off on his own down this trail and hope for the best.

What he could not do was stand here any longer, while Noah wandered around in this forest, alone and lost. He had to move.

"Damn it," Gil spat, turning after Ray. He left the clearing and took a tree branch to the face. He ripped the thin branch from the tree in a downward, angry movement.

Take a bite of me, will you? he thought. I'll bite you back.

Every ten yards or so, Gil tore another branch from a tree or uprooted a bush. Not only was it therapeutic, but the damage was giving him a clear path to follow back to the clearing and the trail he'd found leading southwest.

But first, he and his lung-less neighbor had to catch a former racing dog with a top speed of forty-five miles an hour.

⌒◦⌒

They'd been chasing Bullitt for a good ten minutes, and each step had dragged them farther in what Gil was now convinced was the wrong direction. He kept thinking they were almost at the edge of the trees now, about to break out onto his land again, or maybe even Ray's property, but the forest just kept going.

Gil gave Ray five more minutes before he turned around and went off on his own. He glared at the other man's back, expecting to see his little backpack holding his oxygen tank there, but all he saw was the swirling red and black logo from his sweaty Carolina Hurricanes T-shirt. The tank must still be where Gil had dropped it, outside the forest.

Once more, Gil wondered how well Ray had known the F-Ts. And now, conveniently, his dog had bolted. In the wrong direction.

What were the odds I'm being set up here? Gil wondered, skin prickling with paranoia. With my luck today, pretty damn good.

He checked his watch. Twelve o'clock. He took a shallow, painful breath. They'd been in the forest exactly an hour now. It felt more like an entire day.

Screw this, he thought.

"Ray," he said, "I'm turning—"

Gil stopped when he heard a sudden Little-Engine-That-Could chuffing of air ahead of them. Bullitt. The dog had collapsed onto his side next to a small mound of dirt in the middle of a clearing. The dog was huffing like mad. As he tried to get his breath back, the scant flesh over his poking ribs shimmered like a heat mirage on a hot highway.

"Is he okay?" Gil said, looking at the fresh cuts on the dog's slender forelegs, bright red slashes of blood, caused most likely by his wild dash through the undergrowth. He must have reached this point and then just collapsed.

"No," Ray spat, "he's *not*. None of my dogs are okay." He bent over Bullitt, swabbing at the dog's blood with his hanky. "What did you do to cause all this? What've you been messing in? My dogs've been beating themselves up all day now. Whatever you did, boy, you need to *fix* it!"

"Nothing," Gil said, stepping back from the force of Ray's sudden anger. "Jesus, Ray. I didn't do anything."

He looked around, first into the shadows made by the trees and then at that mound of dirt below them, as if looking for some sort of vindication. This was not *all* my fault, damn it, he thought. I can't take responsibility for the whole world.

That was when he caught sight of some movement inside the strange mound of dirt in the middle of the clearing. Ray was bent over Bullitt, his back to the dirt and to Gil, so he never saw the impossible approach of their visitor.

The man seemed to pull himself up out of the ground, right from the middle of the molehill, long fingers tugging his angular head and neck free, then his narrow chest and torso. His legs kicked free of the tiny hole in the ground, and he rolled to his feet without making a noise. Gil's eyes hurt just watching it happen. Freakin' impossible.

The man stood, grinning, his bony profile blending into the giant sycamores covered in a mix of kudzu and poison ivy behind him. Gil's breath stuck in his lungs, and his vision went gray.

Fuck, he thought, this *is* all my fault.

And then, just like the cool blanket of forest air that had dropped over him as soon as he stepped into this thicket of trees, Gil felt a calm sense of assurance fall onto him.

Compensate and adjust, he told himself. Roll with it, man.

"What *are* the odds of this happening?" he muttered, forcing out the air lodged in his lungs, just as Bullitt began whimpering, and Ray wheezed for the first time in an hour.

"Welcome back," the thin half-man said in his tittering voice, and all movement, all sound, all air in the forest came to a complete stop.

Here we go, Gil thought with a grin. About freaking time.

CHAPTER SIX:
NICE TO ANIMALS

Sitting there in the chilly darkness, curled up with his chest against his knees, Noah waited for the big animal to come for him. But now, only silence filled the tunnel where he sat. He'd figured that the creature that had saved him from the skinny man with the mask head was the big cat named Elwood because of the way the creature had limped.

He'd first met Elwood on a special farm outside Pittsboro, the town closest to their own farm. The big critter walked the way he did because he was so old, Dad had said. He's a jaguar, Dad had also said, though the big yellow-orange cat, covered in black spots, with paws bigger than Noah's own head, looked a lot like what Noah had always thought of as a leopard.

"Carnivore," he whispered in the darkness, remembering with pride the big word Dad had taught him. Though right at that moment he couldn't remember what the word meant. He was too distracted by the loud purr now filling the tunnel around him.

He *hoped* it was purring he was hearing. Elwood's purring, if possible.

The light coming from the cave had faded from gray to almost black now, but Noah knew it couldn't be night already. Please let it not be night already, he thought in a sudden panic.

He relaxed slightly when he realized that something must be blocking the hole. He squinted as best he could, wishing he still had his salamander with him. Somewhere, maybe from high above, he could hear the sound of voices, but they were hard to hear over the rumbling coming from just a few feet away.

He wanted to at least say out loud the name of the big, limping jaguar he'd met at the farm. That would be the brave thing to do. But he couldn't say anything because he'd just remembered something that he wished he hadn't: back at the farm they'd visited, a tall chain-link fence had separated him and Dad from the big cat, and there was no fence down here. Just the creeping, braided vines on the walls and roof of the cave, and the strange thin man somewhere on the other side of the doorway.

"Jaguars have the strongest jaws of all the big cats," Dad had read from the small metal plate attached to Elwood's cage, "which allows them to eat smaller animals like turtles easily."

"Poor turtles," Noah had said at the time.

Now he knew how one of those turtles felt, right before the big bite. He wished he could get to his feet and run down the tunnel, away from the creature waiting in the dark. But just like his voice, his legs wouldn't work either. For the first time that day, as he felt the creature creep closer, Noah began to wonder if all of this wasn't just one big, bad dream.

Which was why he almost wet his pants when the big cat began licking his cheek and rubbing against his shoulder hard enough to bowl him over.

"Elwood?" Noah managed to squeak out, and he could've sworn he felt the jaguar nod, his furry head rocking up and down so hard that he lifted Noah off the ground and back to his feet.

Noah hugged the big cat, barely getting his arms around Elwood's thick, scratchy neck. He was tempted to bury his face in Elwood's fur, but he thought better of it; he didn't know the big cat *that* well. It just felt so good to not be alone anymore down here. Elwood would protect him and show him the way out of this smelly hole. Noah was sure of that.

༺✦༻

Mom had always said to treat animals just as nicely as you'd treat people. "Maybe even more nicely," she'd usually add, giving Daisy another scratch behind the ears, "because they depend on us to take care of them."

"Even if they're not our pets?" Noah asked. That seemed like an awful lot of animals to look out for.

"Animals," Dad had said, "are our 'sponsibility. All of them. Even the ones that'll eat you for supper."

That made sense. Noah had a 'sponsibility to take care of the salamander he'd hurt. And someone would have to help Ray's greyhounds, who'd been running so hard in the field this morning they'd hurt themselves. Noah had seen them that morning, but he now realized that he hadn't *heard* them—usually they were barking and yelping, especially when they ran into each other. For a moment, he'd been tempted to stop chasing the salamander to go help them. Then he thought of meeting Ray with his oxygen tank and hissing breathing and squinty eyes, and he kept going, forgetting about the silent, sprinting dogs.

Now, with the big jaguar walking beside him down into the cool darkness, Noah remembered another time he'd not been nice to an animal. Not that long ago, before summer got so hot. He'd been outside on the far side of the house, trying to teach Daisy how to fetch, and he'd thrown the slobbery stick for her one last time. The stick spun its way right over the compost pile behind the house and landed in the brush, and Daisy had gotten distracted by something buried in the ground back there.

Daisy was the fattest chocolate lab Noah had ever seen. It made sense, of course, since the dog was probably half made up of chocolate, according to her name. Noah didn't know which half of Daisy was the lab part—whatever a "lab" was—but it was probably the not-chocolate part of her that led Daisy to the nasty little object that someone had buried in the ground in a slick black garbage bag.

She'd dug up the bag about twenty steps from the start of the trails that led to the forest, behind some sick trees that Dad had cut down a while ago with his chain saw, something Mom called his "noisy grownup toy." Noah didn't see what was so fun about the loud machine Dad used to cut up rotting trees into piles of sawdust and little chunks of barky wood. And there had been more rotting trees since that day, but Dad hadn't cut those down, for some reason.

Daisy kept dragging the thing around in its smelly bag. She tried to shake it back and forth, but it was too heavy for her. Her head just went back and forth like a bobble-head. Pretty soon she was yelping.

Noah, meanwhile, had crept closer to her and the bag. A prickling heeby-jeeby feeling swirled around in his belly, and he thought he saw something round and black, with gray lines carved into it, inside the bag. Something heavy.

He really needed to see what was in that bag, so he retrieved Daisy's fetching stick himself. When he came up to her as she whimpered and fussed with the bag, not listening to him telling her to drop it, he hit her on the nose with the stick.

The stick bounced off her nose with a thunk. He hadn't even thought about what he was doing. He just did what seemed like the right thing to do to get to that buried treasure.

Daisy's response wasn't to let go of the bag, but to growl at Noah with her eyes going all wide and white. He dropped the stick, his spooked feeling turning immediately into sickness at what he'd done.

I hit Daisy. If she bit me now, I'd deserve it.

Before he could even think about a different way to get the bag from Daisy, Dad had showed up. He grabbed Daisy by the top of her snout, making her mouth open up, and he pulled the bag free before she could bite him.

Once Dad pulled it away from her, Noah got one last look at the shape of the thing in the bag. It didn't look much bigger than a softball or a small pumpkin from the garden.

That shape, of course, ignited his imagination, and for the next week or two all of the adventures of Prince One-Eye he told himself dealt with enchanted crystal balls or poisoned fruit delivered in old black bags.

He also wanted, badly, to find out where Dad had hidden the thing in the bag. That was what he'd wandered off to find the second time he'd scared Mom and Dad that summer (the first time he'd just been hungry for apples, and so he'd taken a walk over to the crabapple trees close to Julio's trailer). Drawn like a magnet to the machine shed, he'd gotten trapped in there after the door closed and locked behind him.

He about screamed his voice into a horse, Mom told him once he was out of that place.

In the same way that he couldn't forget about the mysterious object Daisy had found that day, he'd also never forgotten how it had felt to hit his pet dog.

Part of him felt a weird, almost good feeling about the way the stick had bounced in his hand after hitting her nose. He felt like he'd grew-up, somehow. But then, every time he'd remember that almost-good feeling, he felt like he'd throw-up.

Daisy was his 'sponsibility, and he'd blown it.

⚬⚬⚬

The stink of dead animals and dog droppings from the cavern and the tunnel leading out of it had now been replaced by the happy smell of green plants and the clean odor of fresh water. Noah sat on the smooth, cool ground with his left hand on Elwood's furry head, his right hand wet from the bubbling pool that Elwood had found for them.

It felt good to rest, after so much walking today. The big cat was sprawled out on his belly next to him, his black nose buried in a tall green plant that grew next to the pool. The tiny leaves Elwood was eating like potato chips smelled like Mom after she'd soaked in a bath for a while.

Remembering Mom made Noah think of home, somewhere above them, far away. It suddenly hurt to swallow, and he wished he could see Mom and Dad again, out on the other side the forest where he'd chased the salamander. He had no idea how he was going to get back there.

Instead of continuing down that path, though, he drank more water from his cupped hand and felt the shakiness leave his legs and arms and belly. His throat cooperated and let him swallow.

This water didn't smell at all like the nasty lake water he'd sniffed that morning, or that tiny black river he'd come across on the way here. He thought of the stories the kids from up the road had told him about their neighborhood pool, and how it had been closed all summer, and how their moms made them drink bottled water all the time, like babies. Noah drank his water right from the faucet, even if it did taste like rocks some of the time.

Elwood had led him to this place after a long walk down the tunnel, which surprisingly had smooth walls and luckily no cobwebs or other invisible things hanging off it or sticking up for Noah to run into or trip over. He even got to hang onto Elwood's tail as they walked in the darkness. This adventure was going to make an awesome story to tell Dad later.

The jaguar didn't go very fast because of his limp, so Noah had no problem keeping up with him as they walked. And walked. And walked. It must have been for miles.

Finally, he saw a gray light in front of them, just a tiny circle at first, the size of the tip of his pinkie. Then it grew as big as his fist.

He could smell something good in the air for a change. Next to him, Elwood limped a little faster, and pretty soon they were both jogging toward the light and the sound of bubbling water.

They came upon another doorway made up bits of old, black wood pounded into the dirt wall. The wood was covered with faded gray words mixed in with curly vines, just like the other doorway back where the man had grabbed him. Noah wished he knew how to read better, but these words looked fancy, like curses writing. Yuck.

Lowering his gaze from the wooden gray words, he stepped through the doorway out into bright sunlight, and everything felt good again. Warm light came streaming down on him from a series of holes in the ground high above him. His chill vanished, and Elwood slipped ahead of him to roll in the patch of tall bushes with tiny little leaves that smelled like baths.

Noah saw the bubbly pool, and the water looked so good he almost jumped into it. At the very least, he could use a drink. His mouth was so dry it was almost stuck shut. Then he heard Dad's warning voice again, and he shot a look at Elwood.

"Is it okay to drink, do you think?"

Elwood cocked his big head to the side and pulled away from his sweet plants for a moment. He went to the pool and took long, tongue-filling drinks from it. After waiting a few seconds to make sure the big cat didn't keel over, Noah cupped his hands and took a sip as well.

Plain old water had never tasted so good. Noah drank and drank, and only let up when his belly started to hurt, and then he let out a long belch. With a giggle, he rested next to Elwood, who'd returned to nibbling on his plants.

Noah wished now that he could *talk* to the big cat, the jaguar, but he didn't know how. Maybe just simple questions, because he was pretty sure Elwood knew how to nod his head for yes. So maybe he could shake his head for no, too.

"Elwood," Noah said, his voice soft so it wouldn't echo so much in the big cave. "Did you run away from your farm?"

Elwood cocked his head again, like he was thinking about it, and then his head went up and down. Chewed-up green leaves fell from his mouth as he did so, then he stopped, turned his head again, and shook his head from side to side.

Yes and no?

Noah sighed. This wasn't going to be easy.

"Why did you come here?"

Elwood gave Noah a blank stare, all wide dark brown eyes and quivering whiskers.

Too hard, Noah thought. Try easier questions.

"Were you running from something? Is that why you ended up here?"

Elwood gave just one quick nod, and then his head stopped moving. He gave a little growl. Yes, he was running, for sure.

Who was chasing you? Noah almost asked, but caught himself.

"Did that man in the cave back there chase you?"

Elwood shook his head and gave a low, growl. Noah got goosebumps from the angry look Elwood shot back up the tunnel at the cave.

"Have you been here before?" Noah was getting the hang of this.

Yes.

"Can you show me the way out?"

Yes.

"Is it far?"

Yes. And no.

"Crap."

Elwood gave Noah a quizzical look, then began purring again.

"Is it safe to rest here a little bit?"

Noah felt something funny in his stomach at the thought of leaving this weird underground place, going back home to where everything was safe and normal. This was still his *kest*, even though he'd lost track of the salamander again. If he left now, he'd be safe, but the story he was making inside his head to tell Dad wouldn't have a very exciting ending.

Elwood nodded in answer to Noah's question, and then, when Noah hadn't asked any more, went back to nibbling his plants.

Noah scooped out and drank one more handful of water and patted Elwood's head, enjoying the spiky, warm feel of the jaguar's thick fur. He relaxed and inhaled the healthy, clean smells around him—even the jaguar smelled good, as if he'd just had a bath before traveling across the countryside to find him. Noah felt an urge to count all the spots on the big cat's coat, but it would have been easier trying to count the stars. The sunlight in the room warmed him, and he leaned back against Elwood and let his gaze wander around the bright room.

Off to his left, to his surprise, he saw a door made of rusty metal. It was almost the same color as the walls, which must have been why he'd missed it at first. The red color of the rust jumped out at him now, when he was looking at it head-on.

Just like the shifting thin man, he thought, and shivered.

Next to the door was a trickle of sludgy water that came up from the ground somewhere close to the door. The water seemed to flow *up* instead of down, somehow. Luckily, the nasty stream didn't touch the bubbling pool next to Noah and Elwood. The thin, dark brown stream crept away from them like a wounded snake, until it disappeared in the opposite direction, into an opening in the wall.

The tunnel continued through there, Noah noticed, blinking. He craned his neck and saw the hint of sunlight lighting up that tunnel, much farther away. He'd missed that earlier, too.

"Elwood!" he said, his voice echoing around the high room as he pointed at the backward water worming its way out of the tunnel. "Where does that go?"

Elwood followed his hand, lifting his big head. He didn't answer, of course, because Noah realized he'd asked too hard a question again. But he did imagine a tiny change in the jaguar's spots, as if they were moving together while Elwood straightened up. Noah blinked, and in the time it took his eyes to close and open again, the spots had indeed shifted together.

Five blinks later, and Elwood's spots had formed a shape that looked like the outline of Noah's house—front porch and all. Just for a second.

"Home?" Noah asked, blinking one more time. Elwood's spots had returned to their original location. The farmhouse was gone.

Yes, Elwood nodded.

Noah had gotten up and taken three steps toward the tunnel before he realized what he was doing.

Home! Mom and Dad! Lunch!

Something smelly tickled his nose again, this time coming from the door, and he looked down. It was the water—the nasty water that led out the tunnel. He saw now that it flowed out of a big grate set next to the rusty door like a Welcome mat kicked off to the side. Noah had smelled that same odor before.

He didn't want to touch that sick-looking water, and the door itself was still creeping him out too. Now he realized why. The door had no handle.

"So if that tunnel leads home," he said, turning on his heel and peering first at Elwood's deep black eyes, and then at his swirling black spots, trying to find the shape of his house again, "where does this door go?"

This time the black spots on Elwood's back jumped into motion, without hesitating. Noah blinked and saw first the shapes of tall mountains, then crooked streets with skinny houses leaning the wrong way on either side of them. More shapes formed on the jaguar's back that Noah couldn't figure out, but the sight of them spreading and taking shape like inkstains across Elwood's coat made Noah's mouth go dry again.

Undercity, a clicking, high-pitched voice whispered inside his head. A bad-dream voice.

"I don't want to go there, do I?"

Nope, Elwood shook his head.

"Okay. Then I'm going home. Come with me?"

Instead of answering, Elwood lowered his head with a mewling sound. Noah inched closer to the tunnel and pretended he hadn't heard that.

This big cat wasn't my 'sponsibility, he thought, rubbing his growling stomach. Right?

The smell coming from the water and maybe from something on the other side of the door reminded Noah of someplace else, too. The machine shed back on the farm—oil, dirt, and metal, mixed in with something sweet, too sweet to be a nice smell. It made him feel small and afraid. He glanced at the tunnel leading out of here, and then turned to Elwood.

"Are you going to be okay here by yourself if I go home? Will *he*—" Noah shivered, "—will he bother you? Or did you eat him?"

Elwood growled in a way that sounded like he was laughing and shook his head, no.

"What do you want? Do you want me to open this door for you before I go? I mean, you don't want to go in *there*, do you?"

Elwood cocked his head at Noah and waited. Too many questions, Noah realized. He paused, unable to walk away and follow the stream up the tunnel out of here just yet.

That water, he thought, would probably lead me back to the forest and all the creepy trees with their dark roots and dead leaves. I'd be alone again.

That thought didn't thrill him. But something else bothered him about this smelly brown stream that flowed the wrong way.

"Why *did* you come here, Elwood?" Noah looked down. The jaguar's spots weren't moving. "Did you come to help me?"

Yes, Elwood nodded. Then he shook his head, his shoulders lifting up as if he was getting frustrated. Yes and no, both.

"Was there something else you have to do?" Noah swallowed. "You're on a kest, too, ain't you?"

Yes, Elwood nodded, claws digging into the dirt floor as he rocked back and forth. Yes yes yes! Noah hadn't seen the jaguar so enthusiastic before, even when they were feeding him raw meat back on the cat farm. As Elwood nodded, the jaguar's spots moved again, forming a cluster of different shapes.

"Elwood," Noah whispered, inching closer. He wanted to touch the spots to see if that helped him understand what he was seeing. "What is this?"

Elwood stopped moving, and the spots came into focus a bit more. Noah sucked in his breath, afraid to blink and lose the picture on the jaguar's pelt. He saw his house again, with the hint of a person sitting on the porch, in a rocking chair. He moved his head back to try to see the bigger picture being put together on the jaguar's wide back.

It's a map, he realized. This was our farm. The store, the pasture, the orchard, the pond, even the machine shed.

And right through the middle of the map was an ugly black line. The line cut through the farm and then continued spreading, until it ran out of jaguar.

Noah figured it out—this bad stream was going to reach *us* soon. On Mom and Dad's farm. And when it came to our house, nobody would be able to live on Dad's farm anymore, or eat the food we were growing. And it would keep on spreading. Maybe it had already reached Ray's trailer.

"We need to go through there, right?" Noah pointed at the door, almost touching it. "Not go home yet? Even if we don't really want to?"

Yes.

With Elwood now at his side, Noah took a deep breath and stepped closer to the door. As soon as he set his sandaled foot down on the ground, three feet away, something in his pocket began to wiggle like a trapped salamander.

He reached in and dug through all the junk in his pocket until he could grab hold of the fat black magnet he'd taken from the fridge that morning. The magnet nearly jumped out of his hand. Noah stared at the twitching magnet for a long moment, fascinated, wishing he understood how it worked.

Just for the heck of it, he held the magnet up to the door, in the place where a knob should've been. When it was a foot away from the door, the magnet shot from his hand and stuck to the door with a clacking sound.

Immediately, something clicked into life on the other side of the door, once, twice, then a bunch of clicks, all at once. Clack-clack-clack-clack-clack. Something popped, followed by a strange rattling sound far away on the other side of the door. Then the door opened inwards, swinging away from Noah without another sound.

Staring at the darkness on the other side of the door, Noah pulled three wrapped mints from his pocket as well, feeling a sudden pang of hunger. He also wanted to put off going into that dark area that smelled so much like the machine shed back home. He unwrapped one, offered it to Elwood, who gave it a sniff before shaking his head no. Noah put it in his mouth with a shaking hand and shoved the other two back into his pocket.

Next to him, Elwood hadn't moved. The jaguar just stared into the blackness on the other side of the door.

"Are 'ou comin' wiff me?" Noah said around the mint, trying to keep it from slipping out of his mouth. "P'ease?"

Yes, Elwood nodded. Of course. Do you think I'd let you go in there alone?

Noah almost swallowed his mint. Had Elwood said all that out *loud*? No. His cat mouth never moved.

Before he could think about it anymore, Noah put his hand on the scruff of Elwood's neck, and together they walked through the doorway.

A cold, dirty wind filled with the smell of garbage and broken-down machines washed over him as they passed through, wiping away the fresh-scrubbed smells of the cave behind them. He shuddered as he went from sunlight to darkness again, and the stink made him want to hold his breath. Being in here was like taking a bath in someone else's dirty water.

The door slammed shut behind them the second he and Elwood walked through it, almost catching Elwood's tail. The room they were in now was black as a nightmare, and Noah took a sudden gasping breath of foul air.

I'm in a whole 'nother world down here, he realized, biting down on his mint. The crunching sounds felt way too loud inside his head, and he had a hard time swallowing the pieces.

He reached for Elwood, but the jaguar had slipped out of his grasp and moved on ahead of him, his claws clicking on the floor under them, which was hard as concrete. He took a few steps after the big cat, but he lost his courage quickly when he couldn't hear his footsteps anymore. Just like that, Elwood was gone, and Noah felt utterly alone in darkness so thick he could feel it on his head and chest and arms.

I made a big mistake coming here, he thought, creeping backward until he reached the rough metal of the door. Of course there was no handle or doorknob to try and open it once it closed. And Noah was out of magnets.

I'm all by myself. Again.

He sank down to the cold, smooth concrete that made up the floor of this place, thinking of Dad and Mom and the safety of his step on the front porch, and he squeezed his eyes shut, but that did nothing to stop the tears, followed by terrified, hiccuping sobs, that rippled like storm-tossed waves from his five-year-old frame.

CHAPTER SEVEN:
THE FOREST FLEXING ITS MUSCLES

Gil's rocky relationship with the forest next to his land started on the first day he and his family moved to the farm. Late in the afternoon of their moving-in day, tired and irritable, he'd left Melissa in the kitchen unpacking boxes of plates and bundles of silverware, and took a hike, claiming a need for some fresh air. In hindsight, he knew he was just reeling from the move and the abrupt realization that all this land and the hefty mortgage that accompanied it—even with the amazing deal they got from the F-Ts and the fat down payment they plopped down on the table from years of saving and a large gift of cash from Melissa's parents—were now his.

We're *this* close to living out our dreams, Gil thought as he left the house through the kitchen door and began walking. And just as close to seeing them crash to the ground around us.

He detoured around the rat-infested barn and the rank smells in the machine shed and hiked around the lake first, inhaling the green stink of the algae on the water. He kept going north, toward the overgrown shaggy fruit trees (apples, pears, peaches) and the fields of wild grass neglected by the F-Ts that would one day become a well-pruned orchard and rows of organic corn, soybeans, sweet potatoes, cukes, and anything else he could squeeze in there.

Off to his right was a falling-down fence protecting an empty patch of dirt. Kudzu, the vine that would become his sworn enemy in the coming months, covered the nearly petrified gray wood of the fence. In less than a year the fence would be repaired, the dirt transformed into a half-acre goat pasture.

At the northern reaches of his new property, he came across an electric fence so old he could almost hear the humming of its two horizontal wires. Probably would've electrocuted him if he'd been stupid enough to touch one of them; blackened leaves dangled from the wires and crisped fronds from bushes lay on the ground under the fence. Gil made a note to himself to find out where the power came from for this lethal-looking fence so he could cut the juice as soon as he could.

Keeping a healthy five-foot distance from the fence, he turned and walked parallel to it, heading west now as the sun began to drop in front of him.

"Check out this air," he muttered, inhaling deeply and holding it in as long as he could. Which wasn't long, thanks to the slow damage done by years of working at a desk: he was thirty pounds overweight, with aching arms and wrists and eyes from too much mind-melding with his computer at his cube.

As he exhaled, he felt some of the toxicity of his old life begin to drain away, replaced by pure oxygen and the slightest hints of sage and manure. He felt like a wine-taster, savoring the flavors of the air instead of some fancy cabernet.

Grinning at the image that created in his mind—a snooty version of himself in a suede smoking jacket, looking skyward as he swished the air around in his mouth to get all the nuances of the scents and flavors of the oxygen—Gil hit the northwestern corner of their land. Here the murderous, humming fence was replaced by barbed wire, three rust-flecked strands of metal held up by rotting wooden posts bleached gray by the elements.

He turned south and continued walking. By the time he could once more smell the uncared-for lake off to his left, the trees had sprung up on the other side of the fence on his right. Most of them were pale, fat sycamores, with pines and oaks crowding in next to them. He kept walking, telling himself he'd go back and help Melissa unpack as soon as he made it to the southern boundary of their land.

Soon he drew even with where his new house sat, looking huge as a hotel as it peeked out of the oaks and magnolias surrounding it (Julio's trailer would get wedged inside those magnolias three and a half years later, first inhabited just by him, then his wife and two kids, once Gil helped get them over the border and up to North Carolina). Next to the fence, the trees had grown so thick he couldn't see through them, and the barbed wire had gone slack, in some places drooping down to kiss the ground.

Within twenty more steps he came across the first downed fencepost. The three strands of barbed wire disappeared into a mess of tree limbs, shrubs, and bits of litter. Apparently, the previous owners, and most likely the owners before them, had used this area as their personal dumping ground. Broken bottles, old shoes, rotting wood, bulky appliances, rusting tools, even the strewn bits of an ancient car engine spread out over an area as big as the first floor of their new house. A low reek of decay and motor oil hung over this chunk of forest.

Gil wanted to go over the fence right then and there and start piling up shit to haul away in his new pickup, but something stopped him. He told himself he needed to get back to the house and finish the work waiting for him there.

But now, looking back, he could see that it was really the forest itself that had kept him away, flexing its muscles. As if it were saying, *Don't think you can just waltz in here, office boy, and think you can clear away years of accumulation and history.*

The trees beckoned with their long limbs, taunting him as they jutted out their fat trunks like bare-knuckled drunks in a bar parking lot. Something moved deeper inside the trees, a brief moment of crunching leaves and slapping tree limbs, then the forest went silent again.

"Yeah, better get back and help Melissa," he muttered. The trees laughed in the wind in response, and as he walked away in the graying light, he couldn't help but glance behind him every few yards, just to make sure the forest stayed put.

Gil was panting for breath when he finally made it back home. On any other day, he'd be dying to tell Melissa about what just happened, but one look at her angry, tired face silenced him. She'd unpacked the whole kitchen all herself. Gil had never told her the story about his first run-in with the forest.

✷

Trying not to put too much weight on his bad hip, Gil dug the blade of his shovel into the ground for balance and stared at their new arrival. It was like a bad joke.

This homeless bum. The half-man. Seeing him again in this clearing under the hot noon-day sun, caved-in face and all, made Gil wonder if *this* world was the imagined world, and places like his dreamed-up Undercity were reality. In some ways, on days like today, that concept made so much more sense. Because what he was seeing here now was worse than a bad joke.

Below him, just a few feet away from Gil's wet boots, his neighbor Ray was on his hands and knees, choking on his own breath. Ray's dog was next to him on the ground, convulsing, long legs kicking like eggbeaters. The sky was purple with green-tinted clouds, the air thick enough to clog your lungs.

I can wake up whenever I want to, Gil thought. He raised his shovel from the rich, black dirt and took a step closer to the thin man.

"I thought I told you to leave," he said, matching the distorted grin on the tittering man in front of him. Now he could smell the man's too-sweet smell of sweat and rot. He had to bite back a moan from the flare of pain in his hip.

"*Told me?*" the man said, clicking his tongue five or six times, the sound like bugs crawling inside Gil's ears. "You *told me* to leave by caving in my skull. Not very neighborly, I'd say."

A few feet away, Gil heard Ray drop onto his belly with a thump. He sounded like he was retching. Bullitt, meanwhile, had gone quiet next to his master.

"Might want to get your friends out of this forest," the man said. "I think their time's about up."

They didn't have any problems 'til you showed up, Gil wanted to say, but he managed to keep his lips shut tight. Anything he said or did was going to be used against him, he could tell. After that day in March, he was as guilty as a pickpocket with a coat full of wallets.

"Ray," he muttered, "hang in there, man." That was all Gil could say or do for him, right now.

More clicking from the newcomer. Laughing at them. This wasn't Gil's turf anymore. He'd lost touch with the forest, ever since he started avoiding it on his early-morning walks after March.

Hell, he thought, remembering his freakout on his walk on move-in day. Had I ever *been* in touch with it?

That mocking laughter did the trick for him. He dropped his shovel and bent down to drag Ray up into a sitting position. As Gil smacked Ray's back, great gobs of phlegm shot out of him, almost landing on Bullitt. Even as he was struggling for life, Ray was still reaching out for his dog, his thick fingers massaging the animal's side. Bullitt had stopped kicking.

Finally, after one last back blow, Ray sucked in a long, screeching breath. All the tight, rock-hard muscles in his back relaxed as he let it out, slow and long, and inhaled another.

"Why the *hell* did you leave your oxygen outside?" Gil hissed.

Ray rolled toward his dog, ignoring Gil as he put his face up to Bullitt's half-open muzzle. The dog's pink tongue lolled onto the black ground, touching a flat white rock as if he were trying to lick a treat.

Gil knew what was coming next. He didn't want to watch, but looking away was impossible right now. So he got to watch Ray perform mouth-to-snout on his dog. Think of a bellows filled with water, being blown into two holes the size of pencil erasers. It wasn't as disgusting as Gil had feared it would be. Though it wasn't anything he'd like to experience again.

Ten rescue breaths later, Bullitt kicked himself into gear and popped to his feet, sneezing. The dog was alive, again.

"Nicely done," the thin man said, behind them.

Gil jumped, cursing his distraction. This was the same homeless bum who'd been scavenging out of the garbage from his farm as well as Ray's trailer this past winter and most of the spring. What else had he been up to out here since winter? Looking for a chance to get revenge, possibly?

A creeping sensation filled him when he realized, out of the corner of his eye, he could barely see the other man from this angle. He had to turn his head to look at him directly.

Still wearing the ragged white T-shirt and acid-washed gray jeans coated in grime he'd worn back in March, the half-man stood there, skinny arms crossed, leaning back impossibly far. His black boots, clean and shining as always, glittered in the sun. Gil's own wet, raggedy boots looked pathetic in comparison.

In the yellowed fingers of his right hand, the half-man held a three-inch-long spike, green and black. It wasn't metal like a nail, but Gil couldn't make out what it was. It reminded him of something organic, something that had once been alive. A tail, maybe.

A fresh chill blossomed out from the center of Gil's heart, unraveling the blanket of dread he'd been wrapping himself in for the past hour. He remembered the salamander Noah had been chattering about non-stop earlier this week. Worrying that he'd killed the little critter when its tail popped off in his fingers. Noah had showed Gil the tail—he wanted to give it back to the salamander until its new one grew in. He'd mentioned something about glue as well.

And here it was again, held pinched in this sneering man's hand, the stiff salamander tail quivering slightly as it pointed straight down at the small mound of dirt on the ground.

"Let's make a deal," the half-man said.

∽o∽

I asked him to leave nicely, the first three times.

I didn't buy his argument that the F-Ts had always let him camp out there during their tenure on this land. The man was empty-handed, and I saw no trace of a tent or any other shelter nearby. Maybe he'd found a cave deeper inside the forest. Even so, nobody could survive a winter in these woods without stealing some of the necessities from the neighbors, which in this case would undoubtedly be me or Ray.

I'd argued with him each time, my anger surging up out of me like bile, making me swear like a sailor in a voice that hardly felt like my own. I told him to get the fuck out before I had to call the cops to remove him. Or I removed him myself.

The homeless man, who probably weighed all of one hundred pounds, soaking wet, had laughed his clucking laugh at me, and then promised he'd be gone by sundown. Soon as he finished some business there in the trees. He made me see red, every time.

I figured the flathead shovel I'd started carrying along with me on my walks—hey, it made a good walking stick, honest—had made his conversion to my way of thinking much easier. I kept my eye on him on his way out of there as I left the forest, checking every now and then to make sure he was suitably cowed. Another piece of garbage removed from my land, I thought, leaving the trees and heading home with a spring in my step and no pain in my hip.

So imagine my surprise and frustration when I saw this man again just a week later in early March, at the crack of dawn—though by that point I'd started detouring around the woods, sticking to the outer edges of the trees on my daily wanderings. Fifty yards inside the trees, he sat with half his bony butt hanging out of his pants, hunched over a smokeless fire, cooking what looked suspiciously like the remains of a dozen Stayman apples. Just like those I had stored in my back pantry from our now-leafless apple trees.

"I don't fucking believe it," I said the moment I saw him, my anger switch already thrown for the day. It was his bad luck, I thought at the time, that Melissa and I had just had one of our knock-down, drag-out "discussions" about the future of the farm the night before, and we'd both gone to bed mad. She'd brought up the idea of selling off a few acres to pay some debts down, and I'd hinted strongly that she was being a quitter. Not one of our better nights.

"Hey!" I yelled at the half-man, showing him my shovel. "I thought you and me had an understanding, man."

He didn't even jump. Just kept on roasting his—my—apples.

"You own this forest?" he said, clicking his tongue once more at me. The sound grated on my nerves, made my jaw clench.

"Yes," I said. "As a matter of fact I do."

Technically, that was true, but my sliver of the trees was thin and narrow. I was probably well over the border of my own property, but he didn't need to know that.

"Am I hurting anyone, staying here?" The thin man pushed himself up, his narrow body gaunt as a skeleton. His fire went out with a tiny popping sound. I felt a pang of regret, thinking that this was a fellow human in front of me, out in the cold. I probably would've relented if he'd simply stopped talking and kept his hands where I could see them. Probably.

"Am I bothering that pretty little wife of yours? Giving that handsome young fella of yours some bad dreams?"

The redness growing inside my eyes welled up, a gusher of sudden rage. He should've never mentioned Melissa and Noah. Now I knew that he'd been spying on us. We were not safe.

"You stay away from my house, and stay the fuck away from my family, you sick bastard." I was gripping my shovel tight enough to give me splinters.

"Living the American dream, aren't you? Your store, your farm, your family. While other people like me are starving to death."

"That's your choice," I said, thinking of him outside our kitchen door, digging through our garbage. Peering into our bedroom. Following Noah as the boy played outside. I hefted the shovel, bringing it to my shoulder like a batter on-deck.

"I swear to God," I said, my voice unsteady, "if you don't leave now, I'll . . . "

"You'll what?" the man said, aiming his misshapen head at me and my shovel. I was having trouble focusing on him—he was so thin it looked like something had already taken a bite out of him. "Hit me? What would Melissa think? Or little Noah?"

He shifted a bit, bringing his other arm into view. The hand of that arm was stuffed down the front of his filthy jeans, and he was busy rubbing himself. And laughing.

My vision clouded over, and I could only act: I swung the shovel at him as hard as I could.

Some still-rational part of my brain made sure the flat blade of the shovel remained perpendicular to the ground so I didn't decapitate the half-man in front me. But still. The impact of metal and bone reverberated in my arms and ears.

He dropped to the ground, and his head bounced a couple inches off the dirt before coming to rest. He'd fallen face-first like a bag of sticks, arms and legs askew, his ass poking straight up at me in a final act of defiance.

Melissa and little Noah?

"They don't need to know," I spat.

I'd killed him. Lifeless, the man was much heavier than I'd expected, and when I tried to lift his dead weight over my shoulder in a fireman's carry, I heard something pop in my right hip. I heard it, I swear to you. Like a tiny pistol, louder than a cap gun. If I'd had any air in my lungs, I would've screamed.

I managed to carry him about ten feet off the path before finding a rock suitable for hiding his body. After five more steps, the hot, almost liquid agony running up my side and down my leg from my injured hip was making me whine like a dog.

I asked him nicely to leave. Three times.

I shuffled the man off my shoulder and let him lay where he fell. I didn't even bother covering him. I was a mass of instinct and anger, not thinking straight, not thinking at all.

I picked up the shovel sitting on its side next to the trail, blood slicking the concave side of the blade, and used it as a crutch to get me out of the forest. More than once the tree roots and vines tried to trip me on my way out.

He never should've said their names to me. Never should've.

Back out under the open air, I threw the stained shovel behind one of the rocks on the trail leading back to the farm, and I refused to ever enter the forest again. A promise I'd kept to myself, successfully. Until today.

∽o∾

Staring at that salamander tail held by the half-man like a damning piece of evidence in a murder trial, Gil felt the same impotent rage he'd felt that morning in the woods earlier this year. Anger and fear and desperation conspired to shut his throat and cut off the air from his lungs, like Ray and one of his fits. Gil always felt panicked when he wasn't able to talk.

This time, he knew he had to keep it under control.

At last he managed to say, "*Where* did you get that?"

The thin man did his clucking again, a mother hen scolding her chicks, and Gil knew this encounter would only end with his shovel upside the man's skull again. The clouds crept closer, turning as dark green as the algae that once covered his pond, and he could feel the air fill with the ozone-rich scent of a summer storm approaching.

"You're in no position to ask questions," the man said, tittering and clicking. "Or make any more demands of me."

Gil looked over at Ray, but he remained on his side, turned away from them. Every few seconds he'd remember to take a breath.

"Tell me where my boy is," Gil said, only to be answered by more clicking laughter. The shovel in his hand lifted, as if of its own accord. The air around him turned heavy and hot, and he could now smell his own sweat—a desperate, bitter odor.

"I've seen him . . . around," the thin man said, shrugging his narrow shoulders in a way that seemed to dislocate them both. From this angle, he looked like he only had one arm.

If your other hand is stuffed in your pants, Gil thought, you are a dead man. Again.

"Give me the shovel and we'll talk," the man added.

Gil noticed the man was standing over the mound of dirt that Bullitt had found, before the dog collapsed. He saw a small hole in the ground next to those shiny black boots.

Screw him—Gil didn't need the man's advice or his blame. Noah was down *there*. He knew it.

"I'll ask you again," he said, sizing up the man who kept shifting in and out of his vision, "to get the fuck out of here. That's as nice as I can get right now."

Standing there in profile, the thin man truly looked like half a man—just one arm, two legs fused into one, one eye, a split, too-short mouth.

I surely hadn't caused *all* that damage, Gil thought, even if I did try to kill him.

"Get a good look," the man said, clicking once more. "I'm the last thing your boy ever saw."

Gil had been expecting a cheap shot like that, so he managed to keep his rage in check. He had to get at that hole in the ground the half man was guarding. He could make that hole bigger with the shovel in no time.

"Kid was down in the dark, scared," the thin man continued, and Gil felt a surge of hope. He tried not to let any emotion show on his face except for rage. Simple enough task, there.

"I just tried to console him, that's all. I'm a softie at heart, I guess."

The wind picked up, hot and harsh in the forest's unearthly coolness. It blew dead leaves against Gil's jeans and peppered his face and arms with dirt. And the wind made part of the thin man's face peel loose like a torn mask. A strip of yellow-tinted flesh flapped down his cheek as if he were a snake shedding its skin. Underneath that flap was just gray meat, no blood.

Gil was having trouble keeping his poker face. Precise as a surgeon, the half man was cutting him in all the sensitive places.

"You should be thanking me, really, for taking care of Noah," the man continued. His greasy gray hair slid forward like a wig, until the wind caught it and pulled it back. His scalp was a map of white scars.

"You should see the beasts down there, hungry things. And the people living down there, well . . . if you can call them *people*. Monsters, every one of 'em. A kid could have a rough time, all I'm saying. I gave him what comfort I could, of course."

Keep talking, freak, Gil thought. I'll let you incriminate yourself. And I'll take care of the sentencing and punishment myself, thanks.

As the half-man's good arm began to dangle, threatening to pull free of his soiled T-shirt and drop to the ground, Gil heard a scream of pure rage welling up next to him.

He'd never seen Ray move so fast. He entered Gil's vision from the right, a blur of short white hair and thick arms and legs as he rolled on the ground like a cut tree breaking free of a logging truck. He took out the rotting half-man at the knees. The thin man crumpled just like he had after Gil had shoveled him upside the head months ago.

"Wait!" Gil yelled at Ray. The salamander tail went flying into the air as Ray barreled over the half man. Gil could hear the breaking of bones like dead sticks splitting in half. Bullitt followed Ray, trampling the half-man with all four paws on his way past. Ray had knocked the half-man out of his shiny black boots.

Even under Ray and Bullitt's assault, the half-man never took his eyes off Gil as he rolled back to the hole he'd been protecting. His body was already bent and fractured, so when he hooked all ten of his impossibly long, gray toes inside the hole, Gil was hardly surprised at his contortions.

He just stared as the broken man inserted the rest of himself into the too-small hole—feet, legs, torso, arms, then damaged head, mouthing the word "Bye-bye" to Gil on his way down, pulling his boots after him with a stick-like arm.

The hole couldn't have been any wider than Gil's fist.

"Got my second wind," Ray said as he crawled back toward Gil with a grin. Sure enough, his helpless gasping was gone.

Gil could've suffocated his neighbor himself at that instant. Instead, he pointed at the hole where the thin man had been standing.

"Did you see that? Tell me you saw what he just did."

"See what?" Ray said. "Hey. Where'd that annoying bastard go?"

Gil tore his gaze from Ray's wide, pop-eyed face and looked down again at the hole. Something shifted down there. He squinted, trying to make sense of what he was seeing, and when he did, the hole formed a tiny whirlpool of dirt and clay as it disappeared with a burping sound.

"Damn it, Ray! Why couldn't you have waited thirty more seconds? I had this under control. Now we've lost everything."

Ray blinked at Gil, speechless for a change. Gil couldn't read his expression any more, and he didn't like that one bit.

Brushing past him, Gil used his shovel to stab at the ground where the hole had been, but the only give he encountered came from the blade, not the ground below. His arms took most of the impact as the blade bent against the unforgiving ground. He struck the unforgiving ground five more times, until the head of the shovel broke free of the wooden handle.

He would've continued beating on the sealed ground with the wooden cylinder of the shovel until all he had were toothpicks, but Ray grabbed his arm. Gil lowered the shovel when he saw that Ray was pinching something tiny and fragile-looking between his thick thumb and forefinger. The salamander's tail.

The tiny spike had been pointing straight down at the hole, but slowly it began to rise until it was pointing slightly downwards, and to the southwest. Back the way they'd came, chasing Bullitt.

"It's like a divining rod," Ray murmured. "It's another way to get to your boy."

Arms numb, mind blank, Gil left the metal head of the shovel behind and trudged after Ray and the tail. Gil followed him without a word, head spinning, and the tail led them back to the smaller clearing where they'd rested and carried them down the trail that he'd imagined seeing earlier. He could still make out the hint of path through the leaning trees and the grasping undergrowth. This was the way Gil had wanted to go in the first damn place.

"Hope he's still got that salamander with him," Ray said, holding Bullitt's collar with one hand, the tail with his other. "Otherwise I'm not sure this'll be much good. You never know how these thing work," he added with a nervous chuckle.

We're being toyed with, Gil thought. We'd been so *close*, back at that hole in the ground.

"Look at that," Ray said, pointing with the tail, which was wagging slightly, as if it were still attached to a tiny amphibian instead of an old man's hand.

They stood in front of an embankment covered in brush and kudzu. The wild growth almost completely hid the black opening to what looked to be a natural tunnel. Dank water smelling of sulfur flowed down the middle of it, punctuated occasionally by a dead beetle, spider, or mouse. The water was flowing *up* the slight incline leading down into the tunnel. Impossible. Gil knew that this polluted water formed the newly made, sickly stream they'd passed earlier today.

How long had this water been flowing out of here, he thought, infecting my farm?

Looking down at the water, Gil noticed a hole over the big toe of each of his boots, as if the leather was breaking down and letting loose. And then he looked back at the tunnel, knowing the answer to the question he was about to ask:

"Noah's in *there*?"

"I think so," Ray said, breathing shallowly, as if scared that he'd have to make his lungs work too hard again.

"Then let's get to it, damn it anyway."

The arch at the opening to the tunnel was framed with large, irregular stones and dotted with bits of glass that must have been inserted before the concrete had set.

Concrete? Gil stopped, looked up. This shit was man-made?

He looked closer and could see tiny, lacy designs cut into the concrete, working their way around the embedded bits of glass. Vines and leaves, curling around the entrance arch like an unending snake with wings. Faded letters had been carved under the vines, but they were too faint to make out. Gil felt something tighten in his throat, as if the vines had taken root there and started to grow inside of him as well.

He swallowed hard and looked away, not mentioning any of this to Ray. The arch with its evil-looking carvings and glass decorations, the downward-sloping tunnel, and even the trickle of water flowing uphill through the middle of it and out into the forest—all of it felt familiar. Familiar as a dream.

I should call Melissa and let her know how close we are. That would be the right thing to do. He pulled his cell phone out of his jeans pocket and opened it.

Then he thought of her dismissal of him today, how crazy-mad she'd made him with just one simple sentence. The contempt on her face bright and hot as a sunburn. Gil shoved his phone into his pocket again. Melissa was on her own.

Hefting the battered remains of his shovel, his wet socks squishing inside his ruined boots, with Ray and Bullitt once again at his side, Gil entered the outer boundaries of his Undercity nightmares in search of his son.

CHAPTER EIGHT:
DIGGING FOR A DOOR

Dazed and dirty, holding a tiny wooden carving of a tree in her left hand, Melissa slammed shut the door to the machine shed and nearly toppled over backward from the wave of heat that hit her. Outside, in the late-morning humidity, her farm was now crawling with neighbors. She stood in the meager shade of the shed's jutting tin roof and waited to catch her breath, hands trembling at her sides. As she inhaled deeply, she noticed that the punky smell of decay and fishy algae that had coated the farm in the days after they'd first moved here was back again.

Unaware of her standing there, the band of neighbors approached the house—two women from up the road, still in their workout clothes, followed by Mary Jane and Billie, the retired lesbian couple from the other side of Jones Ferry. A half-dozen of her therapy patients had already gathered on the porch. Next thing you knew, Mom and Dad would drive up and try to run the show and get their baby Noah back.

No one else goes in the machine shed today, she decided, with one last glance at the red marks on the inside of her fingers. Not with that rectangular metal door she found wedged into the ground in there, attached to its chain. The door she'd spent half an hour trying to open, pulling on the chain and digging in the cold, hard dirt around it until she thought her fingers would break. The door wouldn't budge, and she'd be damned if she'd ask anyone here to take a look at it. Not this motley crew.

She pushed away from the shed at last, sliding the carved tree into the pocket of her shorts. She'd unearthed the miniature oak while she was digging around the concrete base of the horizontal door. After finding the carving, she'd sat on the floor and spent—wasted—a good ten minutes just running her sore fingers over the four-inch-tall tree, staring at it, admiring its intricacies. Mister F-T's handiwork, she guessed. The sprawling, curved limbs of the oak seemed to be talking to her, filling her with trepidation about Noah and his fate.

Why Mister F-T had buried it in the machine shed, next to that cement door in the ground, she had no idea. Maybe early-onset dementia for all she knew.

Out in the hot sun, Melissa paused in the middle of the driveway, standing exactly halfway between the machine shed and her house. Up on the crowded porch, Dun and Herschel noticed her and began groaning down the steps toward her. Melissa waved them off, face hot, and then she reached down to touch the carving in her shorts pocket, making sure it was still there.

Too many people, milling around. This situation had to be contained, she knew, and no one else was going to do it but her.

"I've already searched all the buildings," she told the crowd once she'd made it to the porch, feeling like a drill sergeant addressing her ragtag bunch of recruits. "But if you can just keep walking the property and calling his name into the buildings, that would help us out immensely. Noah will recognize your voices. He's probably just playing some game or acting out something he heard in one of his dad's stories. Just stay out of the machine shed. The roof is about to collapse in there."

As everyone dispersed, Melissa ignored the alternating, distracting thoughts spilling over in her head. He'll show up. He'll never show up again. He's here on our land. He's gone.

She found a seat on the top step of the front porch, rubbing her temples with dirty fingers, her hands aching from her crazed digging in the shed. The accumulated weight of all her projects here on the farm kept her back bent low enough as it was, without having to worry like this about her two boys, Gil and Noah.

Gil. I should call his cell. Ask him what he's found. Noah's been gone for almost three hours now. Maybe longer, since there's no telling how much time passed before Gil even *noticed* the boy was gone.

She pulled out her phone and opened it. There was the tiny digital picture of Noah she'd taken last year after a freak snowstorm. He stood beaming with pride next a misshapen, one-armed snowman covered in dirt and dead leaves. The snow looked gray, almost ashy, in the weak winter light. Off to the left, just barely in the frame, was Gil's muddy boot. He'd been standing right there, hovering, not wanting to miss a second of the fun. As always.

Call Gil? I don't think so. Not yet.

She shook her head with a bitter smile, closed the phone, and slid it back into the pocket of her shorts. The phone touched the tree in her pocket with a tiny clicking sound, making her jump.

She walked over to the first of the two men still left on the porch, sitting in rocking chairs. They'd been watching her with protective, fatherly eyes, knowing better than to try to talk to her right now.

"Herschel, what do you think?" she asked the elderly black man scribbling on a stack of papers wedged into a clipboard. He cleared his throat and gave her one of his patented professorial looks: mouth a straight line, eyes questioning from above the tops of his bifocals, bushy eyebrows forming two overturned Cs. "Do you want to know the odds?"

"No!" Leaning over him in his rocking chair, Melissa realized she'd grabbed him by the arm, and she pried her fingers loose. The old guy had some serious muscle there, in spite of the damage to his right side from his stroke. "Sorry. But this isn't some sort of game or hypothetical situation, you know. Just tell me what you *think*."

"Yes," Herschel said with a knowing tone. He'd taught statistics for over forty years in the UNC Mathematics department, and Melissa had learned the hard way that he could be completely emotionless at times, focusing on the equations of his work. But he also understood people and how they worked.

"I've got the numbers crunched here—Noah's average foot speed, the size of the farm, the time elapsed. I've factored in all you—and Gil," he added, a heartbeat later—"have no doubt taught him about staying away from the road and not leaving with strangers."

Melissa's heart took a sudden downward turn at those last words. So used to Noah wandering off, she'd never allowed herself to think about Noah getting in some stranger's car. Being kidnapped. Oh God.

She risked a look at Mr. Dunleavy, a white retired Durham cop who lived to punch holes in Herschel's theories, pulling from his years of walking a beat in the worst part of his city. He claimed Herschel lived in a made-up world of numbers and mid-terms. "Show your work," Dun liked to say to Herschel. But Dun wasn't talking right now, his face flushing red under his carefully trimmed white beard and mustache as he gazed off toward the gravel road and the machine shed beyond it.

Don't even think about it, buddy, Melissa thought.

"So," Herschel continued, holding her hand now. "This is what we've got."

He held up his clipboard, a mess of numbers surrounding an uncannily detailed map of their land. The scribbled-out areas looked like tiny black lakes cropping up at random across their property. None of the words or numbers looked recognizable to Melissa. In blue pen were various trails snaking out from the house, accompanied by more numbers and labels in Herschel's spidery handwriting.

"What's it all mean?"

"Nothin'," Dun snapped, leaving Herschel with his mouth pursed, about to begin lecturing. "Herschel here's never had kids. I got four grown and seven grandbabies. They come *back*, Missy. They go just so far, then they panic and come running back home." Dun rubbed his beard and gazed once more at the machine shed. "You just gotta trust in their judgment."

"I hope you are right," Julio whispered from behind them.

Melissa jumped. She hadn't heard him approach; usually he was whistling or singing softly under his breath. He must have come up from the other side of the wraparound porch, avoiding all the squeaky boards.

"Damn, Julio," Dun muttered. "'Bout scared the crap out of all of us, *hombre*."

"*Lo siento*." Julio lowered the brim of his faded Durham Bulls cap, as if trying to hide his eyes. "I just . . . I don' feel so good, having Noah gone so long."

Melissa wanted to glare at the stocky man standing above her on the porch, but this was *Julio*. They'd known each other for years now. She nodded and gave him a smile that she hoped looked somewhat authentic.

"He'll show up," she said, refusing to blink. "Have faith."

"Oh, I do," he said, gazing at the farm spread out around them. "Mariana an' me an' the kids, we been praying all morning for him. Even while we been out looking."

The hint of condemnation in Julio's voice—real or imagined—was too much for Melissa. She nodded and walked away from the porch, listening to Herschel defend himself as Dun worried at him for showing her his diagrams and figures.

"The numbers don't lie," Herschel insisted as Dun gave another snort of derision. "I'm just explaining the odds . . . "

When she looked back at the porch, only Dun and Herschel sat there. Julio had disappeared.

She stepped away and entered the kitchen through the back door, grabbing a clean glass from the cupboard. She began filling it at the sink, glad to see her hands had stopped shaking, though the tips of all her fingers were coated with caps of black dirt. As the water dropped into her glass, she thought of the tiny figures and striped black spheres covering the counters and shelves of this same kitchen, almost six years ago. Strange treasures from the F-Ts. Just like her new carving, uncovered in the machine shed. Had to be Mister F-T's handiwork.

Water poured over the rim of her glass in a tiny gusher. She snapped off the faucet and smelled once more the fishy scent of algae. Setting the full glass next the sink, she watched as the caked dirt on her fingertips turned to mud, running down her fingers in black rivers.

She lifted her left hand and touched her muddy index finger to her tongue.

Before she could draw another breath, with the salty, muddy taste of earth in her mouth, Melissa found herself in the middle of a dark forest. Leafless branches and black roots reached for her as she trudged through mud that sucked at her bare feet. Cold seeped from the pines surrounding her, while an army of unseen owls hooted out distress calls. Tiny bugs dropped onto her bare arms and into her hair. And a tiny voice cried out from somewhere in front of her.

When she heard that voice, she knew she was lost. She turned in a circle once, twice, three times, and stopped spinning when she saw, flaring to life miles from her inside this hellish forest, a giant oak burst into flame amid the dark green mass of pines all around it, lighting them up and turning the forest yellow-orange. She had to close her eyes against the nightmare image.

When she opened them again, she was back home in her kitchen, and the house around her was silent.

"What the hell was *that* all about?" she whispered, looking around, dazed.

When nobody answered, she flicked on the water again, just the hot, and scrubbed at her dirty fingers and hands until they were as clean as she could get them. Even after half a minute, though, she couldn't get the deepest stains of mud off the inside of her hands and fingers. Battle scars.

Drying her hands on an old towel, feeling something crawling up her neck that she knew wasn't really there, Melissa looked down at the red, sore fingers of her right hand. Back in the shed, this was the hand she'd used to tug on that ring attached to the chain. She pulled out the tiny oak tree, leaned against the counter, and stared at it.

Don't tell me Noah's lost in the forest. He wouldn't go there by himself. Not after all the times we told him not to.

As she stared and argued silently with the tree, she reached for her untouched glass of water and took a quick swallow. She nearly gagged at the gritty taste. The water from the tap had tasted this way for a few weeks now, but today it seemed even worse. Just great.

Palming the tree, her glass of water still in her other hand, she walked out through the screen door, feeling like she was stuck all alone in that black forest again, looking for someone without any luck. The front porch was empty, so she crunched across the gravel lot to the machine shed and poured the remainder of her glass of water on the entryway, splashing some of it on her shoes. It felt important, like part of some ritual.

Then she set down the empty glass, and with the carved tree tight in her left hand, tiny branches poking into the sore spots inside her fingers, she walked into the unnaturally cool air of the machine shed and reached for the chain set into the floor of the far wall once more. She had to give it one more try.

෯෯෯

Digging.

The dirt around the frame of the horizontal door had hardened to a cement-like texture that Melissa had to hit with the handle of her hand shovel before she could dig the blade into it. Since the door on the end of its chain refused to budge, her plan was to get under the door frame and dislodge the whole works.

Digging led to thinking, and thinking to remembering. Noah and Gil. The farm and her therapy practice. The way time had gotten so distorted, moving way too quickly at times, too slowly at other. Today felt two weeks long, and it was barely noon.

And the day had started long before daylight. She'd been roused from her sleep, as usual, by Gil's restless stirring and grunts. It never failed: whenever she had a big day ahead, he'd wake her at two or three a.m. with his nonsense words or his violent tossing and turning.

Today was supposed to be the day she got her shit straight, a jam-packed day of planning, phone calls, and just plain, flat-out hard labor. Her first order of the day, after a quick breakfast of coffee and more coffee, was recovering the farm's failing relationship with two restaurants in Chapel Hill. The restaurants were both owned by the same woman, who had been complaining about the quality of the organic vegetables.

The woman was either deluded, or she'd found someplace cheaper, because the vegetables here were some of the best Melissa had ever seen, even if they weren't as plump and defect-free as the frankenfood grown up the road might have been. The owner had claimed that all their food had been tasting like dust, and her customers had been complaining for a while now.

She sighed in frustration, thinking of that arduous phone call. She felt like she'd been making and taking calls all morning. This was supposed to be Gil's area—customer service—but he'd handed that off to her at the start of the year as well, claiming he had to focus more on the store and Noah. Luckily for Melissa, Dun and Herschel had long since foregone any semblance of occupational therapy—the former cop for early-stage dementia, the former professor for his stroke recovery—so they could work here more or less full-time. It wasn't their fault they were about to lose the business of Piewacket and La Residence.

Melissa had been planning on telling Gil all about it that morning. In fact, though she would never admit it, she'd been sort of looking forward to letting him have it.

And then Gil lost Noah.

For a moment, sitting there in front of the cut-up dirt and the concrete-encased metal door set in the ground, Melissa felt an ache, down low, below her belly. An emptiness that she'd tried to fill with more and more work.

Noah, she thought. *Baby, we'll find you. Soon. This will all just be a tiny blip in your memory, a bad dream you won't be able to recall. Just like your father and his dreams.*

Sometimes, in the middle of the night, when Gil had woken her with his dreams of places that he could never fully describe to her upon waking, she would lie in bed, mind too uneasy to return to sleep, worrying about the finances and farm. Gil always thought she was sleeping, so he never reached for her.

Take last night. After Gil nearly rolled himself out of bed, muttering about getting lost in his old car in some city, she lay staring at the shades of gray and black criss-crossing the ceiling. She ran a finger across the thin indentation that ran from one side of her lower abdomen to the other, feeling the tiny horizontal trough of the healed incision from Noah's birth, like a borderline between her top and bottom halves.

In the far corner of the cool shed, dirt on her tongue and under her fingernails, Melissa went back to digging, thinking for the first time in ages about childbirth.

Noah's had been a textbook-perfect birth, from the water breaking at ten p.m. the day before his due date to the gradual, insistent contractions over the next six hours, to the two hours of hard pushing—she'd decided early on for no epidural, and she remained surprised to this day that she'd felt none of the wrenching agony described by so many other mothers, who always seemed to enjoy telling their horror stories to her every chance they got during the pregnancy.

And then Noah had gotten stuck, mere centimeters from the open air. He was supposed to turn and work his way through the tunnel of her pelvic bones, but his infant shoulders were too wide, his head too big. Melissa had pushed and pushed, until she was screaming at Gil to help her, somebody just come *help* her, and then the doctor fired up the awful vacuum.

When that failed to dislodge Noah, Melissa knew she'd lost him. Even with everyone telling her everything was going to be fine, that the emergency caesarian would be no problem, happens all the time, a part of her soul knew she'd failed.

It was *my* fault Noah was lost, she'd thought, over and over, until the drugs knocked her out and the surgery began.

She'd been digging so hard she bent the little shovel in her hand. Now that she'd gotten the frame of the metal door uncovered, she sat back to get a better look at the big picture.

The frame was set in concrete, and the concrete was decorated with vines the like of which she'd never seen before. Curling into figure-eights and snaking back in on itself, with leaves jutting out like spines, the vines came into sharp focus now that she'd stopped laboring so hard on the door and its frame. The delicate designs should've been benign-looking, but the harsh curlicues filled her with a sense of trepidation.

What did we get into, she wondered, buying this place?

As if in response to the dark feelings creeping into her at the sight of this horizontal door, her cell phone began to vibrate in her shorts pocket.

Melissa jumped, thinking something had crawled up onto her thigh. Then she groaned. Better not be Smoot. If it was Gil, it had better be good news.

But when she saw the caller ID pop up, she closed her eyes on the labyrinth of vines and leaves covering the door on the floor of her machine shed, still seeing the after-images of the crawling plants on the inside of her eyelids. She hit the TALK button.

"Hello, Mother," Melissa said.

CHAPTER NINE:
ESCAPE STRATEGIES

Gil felt an itch for the first time after he and Ray entered the narrow tunnel that housed the rotten, backward-flowing stream. He thought it was just a mosquito bite at first, or maybe a thorn embedded in his skin from one the countless bushes he'd brushed past on his way here. He scratched his right ankle near the top of his old, wet workboot, but that only gave a moment's relief. To really do this itch justice, he'd need to sit down and go at it with the fingers of both hands.

Instead he straightened up and did his best to keep up with Ray, who'd passed Gil while he was bent over, inhaling the noxious fumes from the stream next to him and scratching. When Gil looked up at where Ray was heading, he forgot all about the tiny, spreading dots of irritation on his ankles and his falling-apart boots.

The tunnel opened up onto a cavern bigger than the entire first floor of his farm house. The oval-shaped space was filled with creamy yellow sunlight streaming down from high above. Gil stumbled into the bright cavern and nearly splashed once more into the rancid stream they were following before he came to its source: a wide grate set in the floor in front of a reddish-brown smudge on the cave wall. Just a few feet away was a bubbling pool full of clear water, untouched by the foul trickle they'd followed in here.

Between the grate and the pool stood a tumbled clump of what looked like rosemary bushes. Something had been here recently, grazing on those leaves, and whatever-it-was had left a few wet fronds on the ground, but not many. And in the smooth dirt next to the pool were easily a dozen oval footprints. Child's size twelve sandals, Gil was sure.

Noah.

A triumphant grin plastered on his face, Gil looked over at Ray and Bullitt. The tail in the old man's hand was pointing right at the smudge on the wall, which—Gil could tell now, squinting through the bright sunlight—was actually a slab of rusted metal embedded in the black rock. On suddenly shaky legs, with the scents of sulfur and rosemary in his nose, he walked up to the metal. This had to be a door. *The* door, to the Undercity.

The light shining down from high above them was warm as an oven full of fresh bread, and Gil looked up to see a pair of windows there in the ceiling of the cave. The light dimmed as clouds moved in front of the sun, and in the sudden gray murkiness, he looked down and saw a tiny black square attached two feet from the bottom of the rusted door.

That, Gil knew, was the magnet from his fridge back in the store. Noah had really been here. And not that long ago.

Then the itching overtook him. He felt like he was covered in tiny bugs, biting him. Not caring a bit about his pride, Gil dropped his hands to his ankles and scraped and rubbed his fingertips over his socks, but still the itching continued. It felt bone-deep.

After a wondrous half-minute of itching, Gil could stand up straight again. Exhaling deeply, he put the burning in his ankles out of his mind and began running his hands over the door. His elation was quickly fading into a sense of dread. What the hell was the kid doing down here, all by himself?

And how was I going to get this damn door open?

"Gil."

Gil slid his fingers up and down the edge of the door, but it was flush against the smooth rock wall. This was damn near impossible.

He bent down and reached up high, looking for a way in. He alternated between wiping dust and rust on his pants and raking his fingernails over the burning itches on both his ankles.

"Gil."

He looked down at the water trickling up through the grate below him and out through the tunnel. He stood on top of the grate, the thick, almost warm water coating his ruined boots. His big toe had pushed through the rotten leather of his left boot. He dropped to his knees and began pulling at the metal grate embedded into the ground, and the water rolled hot now over his hands. He was panting like a dog, slobber dripping out his mouth. Didn't care.

"Gil!"

He felt something give on that last pull. Slapping at his ankles on more time, he was getting ready for one last heave on the grate when a pair of hands gripped his shoulders from behind. Here we go again.

Gil saw red. Red, red, red. Noah had been here. He had to find him.

"Stop for a second," Ray murmured in his ears, his voice surprisingly calm. "You're tearing yourself apart, man."

At first, Gil couldn't let go of the grate. Finally his hands and arms relaxed, and he sat back and pulled his wet, ruined boots out of the rancid water. His shoulders ached, and he felt like he'd broken all his fingernails on the door and dislocated both shoulders pulling on the grate. His jeans were red with rust and his socks were crimson with his own blood.

Some rescue this was.

He wanted to go soak his head in the clear, untainted water of that pool for a minute until he got his strength back and could attack this door again. But before he could make a move, Ray stepped away from him, and Bullitt flopped onto the ground. That allowed Gil to see the *other* tunnel, on the far side of the cave.

Maybe there was another way in, Gil thought.

But he didn't trust that tunnel. He knew he hadn't seen that tunnel when he walked in. If this was really an entrance to the Undercity, then he couldn't trust his senses anymore. Everything was shifty there. All he had to rely on now was the unnatural logic of his dreams of the Undercity. In his dreams, he'd been on the receiving end of one too many unfortunate switches and shiftings in the Undercity. He didn't need to live through one of them while he was awake.

∽o∾

This was how most of my dreams of the Undercity went:

I'd be deep asleep for the first time all night, my brain finally relaxing enough to recharge itself instead of turning over the events of the day, fretting about the details and debt and stresses of tomorrow. Once I hit the necessary REM sleep and ratchet myself down into a dream, almost with a sudden clicking sensation—something my sleeping self couldn't hear or feel so much as taste and smell—I would enter the Undercity.

On most of my visits, there'd be this voice I'd hear in it, an overly enthusiastic bass rumble belonging to a bodiless person I called the Tour Guide. Just a voice, not an actual person. He'd give me a history of the city as I made wrong turns and shot down steep curves or groaned up sudden hills, narrowly missing a bent rider on a crotch rocket or avoiding a voluptuous, dark-eyed mother pushing a pair of twins in her stroller.

Each time the history of the tour changed.

"The restored carriage house on the right once hosted such dignitaries as the wife and mistress of the vice president during Andrew Jackson's presidency. The old general buried in the main Undercity cemetery coming up on our left once drove a tank over a dozen enemy soldiers before dying of a stroke right there inside the infernal machine; they entombed him in his tank, there on the far side

of his crypt. At the heart of the park across the street is a time capsule containing, among other things, five strands of that dead actress' original hair and a pair of batting gloves worn by that baseball star before he took a fastball to the neck."

Each bit of trivia was connected to a distorted, eye-straining monument or a leaning, unkempt building. I could still remember all the myriad, ridiculous details. I just couldn't recall how to get back to these sites the next time I visited.

No consistency at all in that place. Hell, after I'd been there no more than a few blinks of my sleeping eyes, the place would start to shift on me.

Like an old tale-teller spinning out the same yarn night after night around a camp fire, but improvising twists in the plot and tweaking the names and locales just enough to leave a strong taste of familiarity in your mouth. Eventually, that other flavor overpowers the rest of the story stewing over the fire, and you wake up in a new restaurant altogether.

Like the Undercity dream in which I was driving my old puke-green Escort—except it was new in my dream, with all the lights in the dash still working and the clutch tight and responsive—and I was young and full of sleepless energy. I drove past fenced-in factory blocks in a lifeless industrial sector, watching the warped asphalt of empty parking lots blur into five-story factories spewing green or brown smoke.

Each block a new factory. What they built or broke down or packaged inside those buildings, I didn't want to know, but that bile-colored smoke made me furious. Had we learned nothing since the goddamn industrial revolution?

I drove faster, breathing through my mouth in spite of the fact that the ever-present pollution gave off no odor, and then my dream did its unexpected (though not surprising) shift on me.

New roads were always opening up in the Undercity. I found it best to try to keep control of the dream by simply going straight, no turning off side streets. As far as I could tell, no short cuts existed in the Undercity.

I didn't even have to make a turn to experience that shifting. As my old reliable car rolled past yet another block-long factory, the darkened underpass ahead of me disappeared. Instead of driving onto a ramp that would throw me up onto one of the many spiraling highways crisscrossing this city, I found myself shuddering over a set of railroad tracks that seemed sure to bend my tire rims, and I then entered the low-rent district.

Factories and warehouses and empty parking lots were replaced by high-rise apartment complexes made of brown concrete and rusting steel. Sparse windows, barely a dozen per floor, peppered the side of each artless box of a building like holes from a shotgun blast. Gray laundry hung limp on lines strung high above the street, connecting the apartments like webs.

Now I could smell the pollution from the factories, as if it all collected here and stuck fast. Wood smoke, burnt plastic, charcoal, and worse, deeper odors that I couldn't recognize.

The apartments were dark as closed, bruised eyes, but every now and then I could see movement behind the black-shaded windows. These buildings should never have been built here. Not in this sector, so close to the factories and bad air. How many sick kids lived here? Dying grandparents? Asthmatic parents?

My dream-temper flared and I drove faster, needing to get out of there or at least find some other living soul here to demand an explanation. These people needed an escape strategy.

I thought the apartments—"factories for the production of more families" my old friend the Tour Guide announced inside my dreaming head—would go on forever, but at last the road ended at a T intersection and a stop light. The light was red.

I slowed to a stop, wondering why I even bothered. I hadn't seen another functioning car on this entire excursion.

As soon as my Escort came to a rest, I heard the hollow scrape of metal on concrete. Bursting free of the shadows of the apartments were garbage cans, rolling and crashing on their sides. They thundered toward me, spitting out dirty diapers, molding fruits and vegetables, and the occasional black ball the size of a cantaloupe, all of the refuse strung together with yellowing vines. The cans were followed by Dumpsters, all careening my way.

I hit the gas and lurched forward, knowing intuitively that the Undercity would compensate and shift. I'd probably end up on a road leading to the ritzy part of town, or down to the lower reaches I'd barely even started to explore. I knew the last apartment block in front of me would shift and go away. I was banking on it. That's what the Undercity did.

I woke up right before my old car plowed into the metal double doors of the main entrance to the last high-rise apartment in that sector.

Thank you, Undercity, for once again proving me wrong.

⧼∞⧽

The abrupt appearance of that other tunnel was like a gritty finger in the eye. If he had more energy, Gil would've been up banging on the door and yanking on that grate again. But his legs weren't cooperating yet. He just glared at that new tunnel, yet another affront to his sensibilities.

He knew he had scoped out the entire cavern at least twice before coming to the door with Noah's magnet stuck to it. He'd taken inventory of this impossibly bright cavern and counted the stream in the tunnel leading outside: the rusted door, the bubbling pool, the overhead windows, even the rosemary bushes. There had been no other tunnel. The place had shifted on him.

The second and larger element of Gil's disquiet was this place altogether. He realized that he shouldn't even be looking at the bigger picture right now, not with Noah just on the other side of this door. But that was a tendency he couldn't help, one that had led to him picking up organic farming in the first place. That he needed to feel like he was doing good, saving the world one toxin-free apple at a time. That what he was doing had a purpose.

The fact that they may have uncovered a place akin to the Undercity hit him now, like the sudden inspiration one finds after beating one's head against the wall for a couple of minutes.

Actually, Gil corrected himself, my *son* had uncovered it, and he was very likely living out the worst of my nightmares while I stood here wasting time in this cave.

The clouds had gathered on the other side of those high windows, blocking the sun even more, and Gil felt a cool breeze blow over him from that new tunnel, carrying with it a vaguely familiar odor of decay. He bent down, a little unsteadily, to rub a hand up and down his itching ankles.

"Time to go, Ray," he muttered.

"Easy now," Ray wheezed, standing with his hands on his knees. Bullitt still lay on his side next to him. Gil went to one knee and scratched himself for a few blissful seconds more.

"Chiggers," Ray said, gasping.

Gil could hear the phlegm rattling in the older man's chest as Ray exhaled. He was having another one of his spells.

"That's," Ray gasped, rocking forward, "what you got," he cleared his throat loudly. "Into."

And then the mad coughing began. At that moment, Gil was hard-pressed to think of anything worse than listening to another man cough so hard that he could *feel* each explosion of the other man's lungs. The sympathetic pain was even sharper with the knowledge that Ray had been fine just a minute ago. As Ray doubled up and coughed, the tail slipped from his twitching fingers, and it rolled down to Gil as if he were at the bottom of a hill, waiting for Jack and Jill to come tumbling down.

Gil grabbed the tail and slipped it into his pocket without thinking about it, too distracted by Ray's coughing and his fervent wish for the sun to break free of the clouds and warm them before Ray's spell ended. The sweat Gil had worked up from pounding on the rusty door still coated him like a bad second skin, turning cold thanks to the breeze from the new tunnel.

Ray pointed at Gil's ankles between coughs. "Chiggers," he said, then held up a hand as if to say, "Gimme a minute here."

Gil realized what Ray was trying to tell him. Glad to be able to look away from Ray and his coughing fit, he peeled away the sock coated in blood and dirt on his right foot. Easily a hundred tiny brown spots, no bigger than pinpricks, covered his ankle, in a good six-inch area that ran all the way around his leg.

Chiggers. Redbugs. Tiny little mites—larvae, actually—that get under your skin and take a good suck on you. Next thing you know, their microscopic saliva is causing the most ungodly itching. He'd been tagged. The next few days were going to be torture; he wouldn't be able to keep from scratching them, which only irritated the bites and made them itch more.

A minute passed as Gil counted chigger bites on both ankles, accompanied by Ray's wet, barking cough. The toes and sides of both his boots had peeled back, leaving him with sodden leather sandals. Gil blamed it on the water he'd stepped into earlier. His bites already starting to swell into tiny red mounds, he counted a total of 162 of them.

By the time he was done counting, the cave was filled with just the soft burbling of the pool, the tiny hiss of his fingernails running up and down his ankles, and the fading rasp of Ray's breathing.

Gil looked around and couldn't see the new tunnel anymore.

He was ready to go back and give that door another go, and maybe take a closer look at that pool, when Ray clapped his hands next to him and popped up into a standing position.

"Enough of that shit," he muttered, glancing at his watch.

Even when Gil stopped scratching, he couldn't hear him wheezing any more. Not even out of breath.

"What the hell, Ray?" Gil shivered as another cool breeze blew up on him from nowhere, like cold exhaust from the belly of the Undercity. "Can you maybe explain this condition of yours?" Ray looked down at him with a sheepish look, as if he had forgotten himself, or at least had forgotten he was there.

"You know my condition," he said, rubbing his barrel chest. "COPD. Chronic Obstructive blah blah blah. Lungs're failing."

"They *were*. Just a minute ago. You were dying for air then, but now? What the hell was *that*?"

Gil looked from Ray to the cavern around them and sucked in his own attempt at breathing when he saw not just the other tunnel shifting back into reality, but a thin man standing inside of it, leaning against the doorframe as if he were bored of all this. The son of a bitch was back.

Then Ray stepped closer to Gil, and the man and the tunnel blinked back out of existence. Just another trick of the light.

"That little spell," Ray said, "was my reminder."

He lifted up a burly arm and showed Gil the face of his watch. Gil never would've guessed his neighbor would've worn, much less ever afforded, a Rolex. The time according to his pricey watch was one fifteen. Had to be a fake, a replica.

"Every hour, on the hour."

"Every hour what?" Gil suddenly felt all twitchy around Ray. In spite of their six years of being neighbors, he didn't really know the man. He'd only been to Ray's trailer a handful of times, and it hadn't been the most pleasant visit—aging bachelors who collect dozens of dogs tend not to have the sharpest housekeeping skills. Not to mention all the weeds in his yard and so-called garden.

All those years, Ray had always been armed with an oxygen tank on his back, a tube up his nose. Now he didn't need them?

"Every hour, I get a reminder of who's in charge."

Gil put his hands on his knees and felt the burning bites coating his ankles, calling out to be itched some more. He didn't give in to them. Instead, he sat back and waited for Ray to continue. He thought he could hear the tick of Ray's pricey watch as he sat there, growing more impatient by the second. Finally, when the silence became overpowering, he had to ask.

"Who *is* in charge, Ray? Tell me."

Ray let out his breath in an exhale that seemed to take half a day to finish, and then he began to talk.

"We only have so much time, you see. And so, when push comes to shove, we make deals. You're still young. I remember being your age, full of piss and vinegar. You don't really know what it's like to face the end, but when you do, your whole point of view will change. You haven't faced death, Gil. Just wait."

Gil bit his lip instead of saying what he wanted to say—that after a dozen plus years in the corporate mines, he knew all too well what being dead was like. He didn't recommend it.

And he'd faced death as well, with Sophie. They hadn't told many people about all that, but surely the neighbors had figured it out. They'd seen how big Melissa had gotten, before Sophie had stopped growing, then stopped moving inside her.

"I got tired of dealing with doctors and specialists. I needed other options. So I started meeting with the F-Ts and discussing what they were growing over on their farm, and sharing with them what I had in my own garden. This was years ago, back when Francine first fell ill. Harold was desperate to find something to make her condition clear up, to at least ease her pain. He thought he could put something together himself. Now, they had plenty of pot growing on their land for her to smoke, and this was way before anyone ever called it medical marijuana, but the cancer had spread too fast. Got into her lungs. That's where I came into the picture."

"Wait," Gil said, calculating years and recalling the perky little lady with the white Annie Lennox haircut who'd sold the farm to him and Melissa. "Are you telling me Missus F-T made a complete recovery from breast and lung cancer? To make a long story short, that is—we *do* have a job to do today, Ray."

"Herb-ology, I always called it, back before the hippies at Whole Foods grabbed hold of the word." Gil could *hear* the hyphen in the word, from the way Ray said it. "After my parents passed and left me the house—this was years and years ago—I started gathering different herbs and plants from around the world, through mail order and my trips to pick up a new dog. I'd get the cuttings or the seeds and plant 'em in my side garden. Had stuff from Eastern Europe and Russia that just went nuts in this soil, but the African roots and seeds barely made it. Then I got into it a bit deeper—there's a whole black market for the rare stuff. You should see the stuff you can find on the Internet. And you probably thought those were just *weeds* growing wild at my place."

Gil shrugged and held out his hands, as if conceding the point, needing him to hurry up. But Ray digresses, Gil thought.

"That mix of rare herbs from around the world, my friend, was what cured Francine of her cancer. Well," he said, glancing at the rusty door, "those herbs from my garden as well as some other plants I'd found here in the forest."

Gil couldn't sit still any more, thanks to his chiggers. He inched across the dirt floor away from Ray and tried to kick off his boots on the way, but they simply fell apart, the sole breaking in half like soft cheddar. Just great. He peeled off his ruined socks and set his feet in the bubbling pool, hating to pollute the clear, cold water with his filthy feet, but the itching was about to drive him mad. As soon as his ankles were submerged, the chiggers stopped stinging immediately.

Ray and his dog Bullitt watched him with identical expressions of curiosity on their faces.

"So anyway," Ray said, "when my lungs started crapping out on me thanks to all that asbestos in the mill where I worked, I tried to do the same for myself, using my plants to heal myself. But I never could find the right combination, even after I asked all my contacts in the herb-ology world, the legit ones and the not-so-legit ones. Not even Harold's pot helped—just made my breathing worse. So I went deeper into the forest and found this place."

Gil had been gazing at the tiny bubbles in the pool below him as they rose up from some hidden depth, tickling his toes and ankles as they popped against his skin. He turned back to Ray as his words finally sunk in.

"You've been down here before?"

Ray nodded, and Bullitt shook himself until he was standing on his skinny legs. The dog hunched down long enough to scratch at his floppy ears with a front paw for a few seconds, watching him the whole time, and then he wandered off.

"How do we open this door, then?"

Ray ignored his question. "I never did find the herbs I was looking for down here. But it was the damnedest thing. Every time I came down here, there was a different plant growing next to this little pool. Rosemary today, but a couple years back it was mandrake, and before that it was some sort of rare coriander. At least that's what I think it was. In any case, whatever was growing down here was always what I needed."

Gil pulled his feet out of the water, feeling suddenly vulnerable and exposed. In spite of the ridiculous aspects of Ray's story, he was worried some hands would reach up from under the water to grab him and pull him down. He glanced around to see if the half-man and his hallway had reappeared. Nothing.

"But you should've seen the look on the F-Ts' faces when I brought back those clippings from that mutated bush I found here on my last trip down here before they moved away. Apparently, according to Missus F-T, whoever plants their stuff down here doesn't like it when someone else borrows from their garden. Harold and Francine called that person the Gardener. Somehow they knew about this place too."

Gil let his ankles air-dry and ran a hand over the surface of the pool. A couple bubbles burst and sprinkled his hand with a tiny, fine mist.

"I remember going home from the F-T's place, convinced they were crazy, and pulling apart the dozen or so odorless leaves the F-Ts refused to take from me. I dried 'em in the toaster oven and turned those leaves into a tea. I thought I'd opened up my lungs again, after I'd been drinking that tea for a week, reusing the leaves until they were bleached and tasteless as well. But all I'd really done was make a deal with the devil."

"The devil's a gardener?" Gil tried to keep his voice light, but Ray's words chilled him.

"Don't scoff, boy. The Gardener left a mark on me as payment, something you can't see. Every hour, the cure from the Gardener's leaves goes away, and for about five minutes, I go back to the way I was before, when I was still sick with the COPD. Every hour at fifteen minutes past. So I get twenty-two good hours versus two cumulative bad hours every day. It's worth it, I tell myself. Even with the broken sleep. Ever had a time when you couldn't get any air in you? It was like that all the time for me. At least I can *breathe*, man."

Gil put both bare feet on the floor of the cave, creating a small layer of slick mud on the packed dirt. The itching in his ankles had subsided for now. Above them, the sun had gone into remission, and Ray's face was unreadable in the gloom. Gil couldn't find Bullitt anywhere. He shivered from another chill.

My neighbor, he thought, has totally lost it.

"But I don't want you to suffer my fate, Gil. You're my friend, and your boy is one of the best youngsters I know. Which is why we're going to have to leave now and forget ever coming here. Never thought we'd make our way here anyway—the route changes each time, thanks to the forest. So we'll all be safe from the Undercity. That's the Gardener's world, and it's not for us. Trust me on this."

Gil stood up, almost slipping on the mud he'd made.

"Aren't you forgetting that my boy is in there?"

Ray shook his head, gazing at him sadly as if he was touched. "He's not in there, Gil. That door doesn't open. I've tried. Believe me, I've tried."

Gil took a step toward Ray, needing to wipe that smug look of certainty off his face. He made it three steps on the cold dirt floor before Bullitt ran up from the shadows and parked himself between them, growling. Gil's bare feet felt suddenly numb when he saw, behind Ray, a shifty shadow take shape inside the tunnel that should not have been there. One second the shape was there, the next, gone.

"It *is* time for us to go," Ray said, flexing his big hands. Gil could hear the pop of his knuckles as his biceps flexed under his shirt. "Back home. This is a dead end, Gil. I've let you wander around in the dark for too long. Let's get back to your farm and find your boy."

Gil stood there for a long moment, outnumbered, gazing at the neighbor he thought he knew, the old man he'd tried to knock out with one good punch, and his growling dog inching toward him with drool forming around his yellow teeth, and he took in as deep a breath as he could hold. He touched his jeans pocket to make sure his cell phone was still there, along with the salamander tail that had started all of this.

Then, before Ray and his damn dog and his friend the half-man could even dare to try and take him away from here and his son, Gil spun on his bare heel in the mud that his wet, itching feet had made and dove head-first into the deep pool of bubbling water.

CHAPTER TEN:
THE START OR THE END OF THE ROAD

Alone once again, in the dark, Noah waited for his sniffles to stop and his eyes to adjust to the dark. Time to straighten up, he thought. Soon, he could see the gray, fuzzy features of the place: he was at the start of a long road made of smooth concrete, with curbs almost as tall as he was. Or maybe this was the *end* of the road, not the start. How were you supposed to tell? In any case, the road ran between two rows of houses sitting back so far they seemed to be allergic to the road.

Every house was gray and murky-looking, but they were gaining more details as Noah walked down the road, one careful step at a time. He could just barely make out distant spotlights set high above, aimed down at the front porch of each house.

Noah wondered who in the world would do that. He thought of something Dad had said, usually when they drove by a new group of houses where there used to be just trees: Just because you *can* do something doesn't mean you *should* do it.

Noah looked for more of the dangling vines he'd seen in the first cave, but the light didn't reach that high. Or maybe somebody had cut all the roots and vines, so the trees up above were just barely standing up on their own. A stiff breeze would knock them over like stacked dominoes.

When Noah lowered his gaze from the lights high above him, he felt the rustle of whiskers on his bare legs, and just like that, Elwood was back at his side. Noah had never heard the big cat's paws on the concrete, until now.

"Why'd you leave me?" Noah hissed, afraid to speak too loudly in this place. He thought about asking him where he'd gone, but doubted the cat would be able to answer. Maybe he just scouted ahead to make sure it was safe ahead of them.

As they walked down the middle of the street, the curbs reaching up around them like walls, Noah kept his eyes and ears open for any sign of the nasty stream of water. In here, he couldn't even smell it any more. All he could smell was dust, and something else, a stink he didn't want to smell too closely.

With each step they took, the houses seemed to lean farther away from them, all the windows crooked and uneven and dark. Noah tried to distract himself from their weird appearance by trying to remember the name of this place. He'd heard it in his head, outside.

Underground? No, too simple. But close. Town Under? Belowground? Downbelow?

Undercity, Elwood murmured inside Noah's head, baring his teeth in a jaguar grin as they turned and approached the right-hand curb. Noah followed, and up and over the curb was the strangest house Noah had ever seen. It was wider and taller than all the others, with more crazy, crooked windows scattered around a trio of porches, and he knew Elwood was going to want to go into it. Noah was mostly glad about that, just to go somewhere new beside this long, empty street. Mostly.

"Did you see anybody?" he asked Elwood, startling himself with the too-loud way his voice sounded. "When you left me?"

No, Elwood shook his head. *Not people, that is,* he added in his strange voice that Noah couldn't hear with his ears. Elwood's voice inside Noah's head felt all growly and shivery.

Must be my 'magination, Noah thought. Still, it was nice having someone to talk to, even if it was impossible.

The streets and the lawns in front of the gray, leaning houses were completely dry, not a trickle of dirty water to be seen. Noah tried to sniff the rotten-eggs odor again, but all he could smell right now was the smell of Elwood's tuna breath. And, underneath that, old dust, if there was such a smell.

"Boost me up?" Noah said to Elwood when they got to the curb, easily four feet high.

Elwood put his head under Noah's rear and scooted him up the smooth concrete wall until he was almost touching the grassless lawn in front of the house. Before Noah could turn back to try to somehow help Elwood up the wall, he heard the fast clicking of Elwood's paws, heading away from him. Again.

"Elwood?" Noah whispered as loud as he dared. "*Elwood?*"

Noah crouched on top of the curb, not wanting to step off the concrete onto the dusty ground that pretended to be a front lawn, but at the same time not wanting to leave his perch.

Drawing and letting out a shuddery breath, Noah kept his back to the house as he looked up and down the street. The spotless white road below him seemed to have stretched while he wasn't looking, because he couldn't see the door they'd walked through anymore, even though it couldn't have been more than thirty steps to his left.

Now, all he could see were houses and dead lawns and big curbs all connected by that concrete road. No sidewalks, no streetlights. Just houses and concrete. Maybe the road went on forever, stretching like a giant stick of white taffy underneath the forest and everything else up above him.

Who would want to live on a street like this? Noah wondered as he balanced himself on slightly shaky legs. No cars sat on either side of the road, and none sat in the dirt-black driveways next to the houses. How can anyone live here?

He remembered Mom and Dad saying the same thing whenever they drove over to visit their friends Stan and Jan in their town so that Dad and Stan could drink their beer together. Noah figured the people in that town were normal just like him, but his parents' comments had made him curious. Maybe they were people who didn't like to farm or help people get better, or maybe they just liked spending their time inside their small houses, behind their fences. All the houses had fences in Stan and Jan's neighborhood, but not many had porches. None of them had a front porch big as a boat like Noah's. He felt sorry for Stan and Jan's kids. They were missing out.

The houses down here looked like the cardboard houses girls folded out for their Barbies. Noah turned slowly to look at the big, wrong-looking house in front of him now, *really* looking at it, and the more he inspected it, the more he thought about a house of cards, stacked by some giant in a hurry.

This house had three sets of steps leading up from the lawn into three tall, narrow doors. Two dozen windows popped up between and above the doors, as if the builder (the giant) had just closed his eyes and slapped them into place wherever they stuck. At one point on the second story, three windows sat next to each other, each a different size, each sitting at a different height.

The gray-shingled roof was almost flat on every side that Noah could see. Strangest of all—best of all—there was a tall middle section that leaned to the right, and it had no windows. Noah sucked in a dust-filled breath, excited. A *tower*.

Inside one of the three uneven windows, a yellow-gray shade sprang up, opening onto a room of flickering gray light that blinked once more, then went out as soon as he squinted at it.

Elwood had better get back soon. Noah was starting to feel bad, mostly because of the lack of color.

Everywhere he looked, he saw only grayness—gray dust, gray concrete, gray siding on the houses, gray light trickling down from above. Not a single tree or bush lined the false lawns, and Noah wanted to cough the unhealthy air out of his chest. He looked down at his hand and was glad to see the hint of pink in his skin. He was afraid he was turning gray too.

"Elwood?"

When only silence answered him, Noah decided to shimmy down the curb and follow the jaguar. He was pretty sure the big cat went farther ahead down the street instead of backtracking back to the door without a knob and the world outside. Hadn't he?

Noah was about to slide down and take his chances alone, determined to continue his kest, when he heard a familiar voice singing his name from the house behind him.

"Noah, Noah," the high-pitched, taunting voice sang out, "who eats yellow snow-ah. Banana-bana-foah, Nooooooo-aaaah!"

Still on the top of the curb, Noah turned with a heavy feeling in his arms and legs. The boy from the playground earlier today sat on the middle set of steps leading into the house. He held something tiny and black trapped in his chubby hands, something very wriggly. Something that looked quite a bit like a salamander that had lost its tail.

࿊

Some of the best Prince One-Eye stories took place in what Dad called dungeons. Noah could never really understand why, but most castles and towers in the Prince's land had deep tunnels built under them, full of strange monsters and sort-of-crazy wanderers and tons of twists and turns and secret passages.

Of course, Noah had right away wanted to search under their house and the store for the entrance to a dungeon. But both of the cramped crawlspaces he found were disappointing—just uneven dirt floors, cobwebs, and piles of junk and old equipment. No secret doors leading downward into more adventures. Nobody around here seemed interested in dungeons.

In a way, Noah had been relieved. The dungeons in Dad's stories were filled with so many creatures for the Prince to fight that Noah didn't really like the idea of one of them underneath their house. What would keep the monsters in the dungeon from breaking loose?

There was a small voice in Noah's head different from Dad's voice or that of anyone else's, and that voice would remind him, very quickly and quietly, of the fact that Dad was just making these stories up. The Prince and his friends were just a part of Dad's 'magination.

Mom and Dad would sometimes whisper about Noah's 'magination. Mom didn't think Noah had much of one, he guessed, because she'd ask him about the stories Dad told him, but Noah never told her much—it didn't feel right. The stories were just for him and Dad.

Noah paused, still crouched on the tall curb in the underground city (*Undercity*, that small, know-it-all voice whispered), and he tried to remember when he'd first stopped believing every single word of Dad's adventures. Trying to focus on that memory was hard to do with that singing going on, coming from the boy on the porch in front of him, but finally he remembered.

He'd stopped believing about the same time he first heard the know-it-all voice, with Mom and Dad sitting behind him on the porch one day a long, long time ago—a year, maybe even two years ago—when the days had been hot and seemed to last forever. Days just like today. The frogs and crickets had woken up around them as the sun went down, their singing and creaking filling the still-hot air, and Mom and Dad had been talking about Noah's little sister.

Noah had heard tears in Mom's eyes as he sat there on the front steps, building a twisty house made of Legos that stretched from the top of the porch down three steps, all one big piece. He was almost out of pieces, and he was gearing up to go inside to look for more— knowing without really admitting it that his time was almost up on the porch for the day, due to the growing darkness—when he heard the change in Mom's voice.

Noah had looked up at Mom, sitting in the rocker next to Dad. She smiled and gave him a little wave of her hand, but her eyes were sad. He wanted to get up and go to her, work his way onto her lap now that her belly wasn't so big anymore. He also wanted to hear her groan at how big he'd gotten and help her get rid of that sadness, but something held him back.

"It's okay, honey," Mom said. "We're just talking. Mommy's tired, that's all. Finish up your house, 'kay? Then we'll go inside and read a book."

"It's all right, kiddo," Dad said, winking at him.

Then Dad had looked at Mom in a strange way, a way that made Noah turn back to his long, impossible house. Dad had been holding Mom's hand, like he usually did, but he wasn't smiling at her. Dad had looked mad, but Noah could've sworn he'd seen the glitter of tears in Dad's eyes, too.

They're not just talking, that voice had said, and Noah had jumped. *Something is wrong. Really wrong.*

Like a zombie from the King's dungeon, Noah moved his heavy arms and numb fingers, clicking together piece after piece, not paying attention to the shape of his house any longer. He felt warm in spite of the breeze running through his hair and up into his T-shirt.

That night in bed, he came up with his own ending to the story that Dad had started that morning in the store. One-Eye and three of his Black Hoods were stuck in a mine shaft, riding on one of those little train cars, chasing a gang of troll thieves who claimed to have the Prince's eye he'd lost as a child. The Black Hoods were trying to convince the trolls to give the eye back so the royal wizard could use his magic glue to put it back into the Prince's empty eyehole, so the Prince could remove his leather patch for good.

In Noah's story, the heroes caught up to the trolls when the creatures' little coal car ran out of track and wrecked. Most of the half-dozen trolls had been knocked silly, and the Prince's eyeball had slipped out of its magical tube of water and got squished. The Prince would never get his eye back now, though when he wasn't looking, silent Archibald of the Black Hoods had slipped the squished eye into a container on his belt.

For now, though, the young man would remain Prince One-Eye.

Which made sense, because Noah didn't know what other name he'd have if he had two eyes again. The Prince wasn't himself without his missing part—his lost eye made him who he was. Just like the salamander across the long lawn of dust in front of him, missing its tail. If he had his tail reattached, Noah never would have recognized him, especially not at this distance.

∽◌∾

"What are you doing here?" Noah said at last, the memories of his parents and the Prince flickering through his head like a movie on fast forward. The older boy had finally stopped singing his annoying song. "Does your mom know where you are?"

"My *mom*? Right."

The older boy poked the narrow head of the salamander halfway up his nose, very carefully, a fat grin on his face. He pulled the poor salamander out, wiped any boogers it had picked up on his shorts, then stuck it up the other nosehole.

He looked over at Noah long enough to share one word of wisdom: "Duh!"

Noah stood up straight again. As much as he didn't want to cross that long lawn, he couldn't let that boy keep hurting the salamander. He didn't really care about how the other boy had gotten here, not anymore. He was tired, sweaty, and frustrated. And he felt 'sponsible again for the salamander, and the gray light and thick air down here made him angry for some reason. Like the way Dad got when he saw someone not recycling a soda bottle or throwing a cigarette butt onto Jones Ferry. Or when Dad looked at Mom sometimes when he didn't think Mom—or anyone else—was looking.

Giving up on waiting for Elwood to come back, Noah borrowed a trick from Prince One-Eye: he leaned back as far as he dared on the curb, sucked in a quick breath, and yelled "Charge!" at the top of his lungs. Then he leaped onto the gray lawn.

He didn't feel brave. He just felt like he was doing what needed to be done.

Immediately, his foot sank six inches into the dust. His initial impulse was to pull back and find the concrete curb again, but he forced himself to go forward. Each step went deeper than the last, kicking up a cloud until he was coated in the chunky, dusty gunk. Soon he was up to his lower thighs and still sinking. He threw his arms out for balance. If he fell over into this stuff, he'd be in big trouble.

The other boy burst into laughter when he saw what Noah was doing. His teasing voice echoed in Noah's ears, changing with each churning step Noah took, becoming higher and higher and more ear-piercing. Like a wild animal, screaming on the Discovery Channel shows Mom liked to watch after a busy day.

Noah pushed forward, not even halfway across the lawn, scared now because he was in dust up to his hips, and the dust was heavy, and there were things *moving* in it along with him. Every now and then he'd feel something that felt like a bony finger poking into him, and once something pinched him.

"Go back," the other boy shouted. "It's too deep for you, Noah-Noah-Noah!"

The slogging of one footstep after another suddenly became a tiny bit easier at the sound of those words. Noah looked up from the loose, shifting dust he was wading through and glared at the other boy on the steps.

You shouldn't have said anything, Noah thought, in a voice that sounded more like Prince One-Eye than anyone else. But now I know something about you. You're *scared*. You don't want me getting too close.

He was halfway across the not-really-a-lawn, the dust in his mouth and nose making him want to either spit or sneeze or both, and the other kid went quiet on him. Even as he crept forward one more heavy step, something pinched Noah's big toe through his sandal. Just a pinch. Definitely not a bite.

We're wading through the Sad Black River, he told himself, imagining the he was the Prince. He closed his left eye and focused his right on the tiny creature wriggling in the other boy's trembling hand. These are just fish in the river, bumping into us. And we're not afraid of some big-mouth who likes to punch littler kids and sing dumb songs.

Noah was fifteen yards away from the house now. The narrow trail he left in the dust was slowly closing up after him.

"I'll step on him if you don't stop!" the other boy called out from the top step of the crooked porch. "So . . . stop!"

All the steps were uneven, Noah noticed, with nails sticking up out of them like tiny metal mushrooms. The boards under the boy bent from his weight, and the boy almost fell off the porch altogether. He caught himself with a panicky, squeaky-sounding shout, making Noah smile in spite of his efforts.

"Don't laugh at me! And and and, you better stop!"

Ten yards away now, Noah rubbed the stitch in his side, bit down a sneeze, and pressed forward again. His legs were tired, and the dust was up to his belly button now. But as long as he kept moving forward, he felt like he could reach the porch and the boy and the salamander. He'd *swim* through the dust if he had to. Dad had taught him how to use his arms and kick his legs.

"I'm squishing him!" Swaying on the bouncy porch, the boy almost lost the wriggling salamander.

"Go ahead," Noah said, out of breath, though he wasn't talking to the boy. "Go."

Noah knew first-hand how quick the salamander was—he needs a name, he thought, out of the blue—and he knew the other boy didn't have a chance of keeping up with the critter if the salamander got loose. No way would the boy be fast enough.

Noah was ten giant steps away from the porch. The dust was up to his chest now, and his lungs were burning, and his left leg was throbbing from where something had pinched him, hard. He didn't want to admit to it, didn't even want to think about it, but he was pretty sure that it was a hand that kept reaching through the dust to grab at him and harass him. But he didn't want to imagine who or what the owner of such a hand might be.

The dust was up to Noah's chin now.

When he was seven feet away and gasping for air and inhaling nothing but dust, the other boy went down on one knee. He reached both hands down to porch floor, squeezing the salamander tight in the fingers of both hands.

"This is all your fault," the other boy whispered. He set the toe of his tennis shoe—his dust-free tennis shoe—above his fingers and the salamander.

Noah took another heavy step forward, forcing his arms through the dry muck. He kept spitting dust from his mouth.

"Stay back!" the other boy screamed. "I'll kill him!"

"No," Noah panted, four feet away, dust puffing up in front of his face. "You," he said, pushing his head above the dust. "Won't."

Noah kicked with his feet and pushed himself forward through the last few inches of dust as the other boy raised his foot and let go of the salamander for a split second. The sound of his shoe coming down hard on the flimsy wood of the porch filled Noah's ears like a gunshot. At the same time, his hand touched the first step of the porch.

Too late, he thought.

He looked up at the boy grinning and crying above him. Noah held his breath and stopped moving until he was rewarded by the sound he needed to hear: tiny skittering sounds as little feet scurried away from the boy and into the house behind them. The tail-less salamander had once again gotten away.

Noah's arms were shaky and weak as he tried to pull himself up out of the dust. After three tries he was able to get up onto the front step.

He was worried the other boy would try to keep him off the

porch, but the bigger boy had moved back away from the steps, and he was now huddled up in a ball in the corner of the small porch, head on his knees, sucking his thumb and crying.

"Wanna go home," the boy kept repeating around his thumb.

Noah rested for a second on the bottom steps, and then he crawled up to the unsteady porch, keeping his distance from the bawling boy. He shook dust off his clothes and wiped it from his sweaty arms as best he could, but it just smeared and turned to mud. He gave up and shook the dust out of his hair.

He had a house to explore—especially that tower—and a salamander to find once again, but all of that could wait a bit. Noah had to get his breath back first. And maybe this other kid would help, once he stopped crying for his mother.

Noah felt strange, being this close to someone else who was so upset like that, someone he didn't really like. He felt like he should do or say something, but he had no idea what that was.

As he rested, Noah thought about the story of Prince One-Eye's lost-and-found eye, and he remembered bits and pieces of Dad's original story. In Dad's version, the trolls had gotten away, and the Prince's lost eye was never seen again.

"Or *was* it?" Dad had added at the end. He always liked doing that, after waiting a couple of seconds. Maybe he'd seen the disappointment on Noah's face. Dad had trouble with the endings to his stories. That's why they never really ended, but just kept right on going into the next adventure.

"Alexander," he said, making the other boy jump. "That's a good name for a salamander, isn't it?"

The other boy didn't answer. Noah wiped his dirty hand on his dusty pants and dug the last two mints out of his pocket.

"Here," he told the boy, reaching his hand out with the wrapped mint in his hand like a white and red coin. The other boy grunted and pulled away from him. "Take it. It's okay."

The other boy shook his head and hugged himself harder.

"It's okay," Noah said again, popping his mint into his own dry mouth. It stuck to his tongue for a few painful seconds, until he got some spit going in there again. "I'm not going anywhere." He looked out over the impossibly long gray lawn he'd just crossed and tried to get a good view of the concrete road beyond it, to no avail.

"'Least not right *now*, not 'til my friend gets back."

CHAPTER ELEVEN:
THE NOAH SITUATION

Elbows resting on the dark wood of the kitchen table, fighting the temptation to cup her face in her hands until her pounding headache receded, Melissa looked up at the three other people surrounding her, examining them with a clinician's eye. The two men seemed like exact opposites—one lean and dark-haired, skin pale and fingers lightly drumming on the tabletop (anemic, borderline OCD?), avoiding her gaze. The big man seated to her right, with his shock of white hair and rosy cheeks (adult-onset diabetic? cirrhotic?), was all bluster and watchful blue eyes. The unsmiling woman across from her wore her gray-black hair long and loose on her thin, slightly slumped shoulders (early stage osteoporosis, possibly anorexic?). The woman smiled at her in a cold way that made Melissa think of her mirror the morning after a sleepless, agitated night.

Who are you people, she wanted to ask, and what are you doing in my kitchen?

"Mel," the dark-haired man said, his voice blunt as a rock. He still wouldn't look at her. "You have to get a grip. Mel?"

"That's enough," the woman added. Did she ever smile?

The big man on her right said nothing, but he sighed and flicked his arm up so he could gaze at an expensive silver watch. He grunted and looked at the kitchen as if calculating the cost of the various appliances, cutlery, and dishes, or more likely, the expense of removing it all from his sight.

MICHAEL JASPER

Melissa snapped back to reality with one word. Smoot.

And he was in her kitchen. With her parents.

"Just a second, everybody," she began, but her voice was cracking, and she couldn't make it work. Talking to Mother on the phone while she was digging in the shed had opened up a gusher of emotion inside, something that hadn't happened to her since she was a kid. She'd let her have the whole story—the troubles on the farm and the problems she and Gil had been having, and last of all, almost afraid to even bring it up by that point, Noah's most recent disappearing act.

Mother had told her to stay right where she was while she ran to her father's office in downtown Chapel Hill. They made the drive in barely half an hour, record time for the twisty roads leading to the farm. They'd been sitting here in the kitchen ever since. With Smoot, of all people. He'd walked in the door right after them.

"Mel, we need to deal with the Noah situation," Daddy said from across the dark expanse of the table. Distant as always, but there when she needed him, ready to dole out his support —and part of her inheritance—as needed, tabulating each emergency withdrawal and noting the interest.

"Noah," Melissa said. He'd been gone too long.

"We know," Mother answered with a cool smile. "They'll find him. I mean, this isn't the first time, is it?" Her smile melted a few degrees as she turned her sharp face on the white-haired man next to her. "Mr. Smoot has his people combing the neighborhood right now, doesn't he? They could've been out looking for the baby hours ago, but you didn't *ask*. You've got all those boys in their blue trucks looking for him, don't you, Mr. Smoot?"

Smoot just nodded, the hint of a smile of his own on his red face. He touched the band of his watch, but didn't look down at the face of it.

If she keeps ending her sentences as questions, Melissa thought, I'm going to stab her with this little wooden tree I dug up this morning.

"Anyway," Mother continued. "This isn't about Noah right now, is it? This is about the farm. We've come to an agreement of sorts, haven't we, gentlemen?"

"Always thought this farm was a bad idea," Daddy muttered.

Melissa could hear Smoot's mouth-breathing next to her, and she knew it had to be killing the good ol' boy to have to keep his trap shut like this for so long. But she also knew that *he* knew that he was walking through a minefield here in the house that sat on the land he'd wanted for so long.

"Now," Mother said in her best hostess voice, "why don't we show Melissa the pieces of the farm Mr. Smoot would like to buy to help pay off one of your mortgages, okay? Those sections to the south looked promising, didn't they?"

"Wait a minute!" Melissa shouted. "What the hell? This is about Noah, not selling off our land—"

"Oh really?" Mother cocked her head a tiny bit to the side, wrinkles forming around her mouth as she pursed her lips. "Then why did you tell us to come over today when I called?"

"I just," Melissa began, reaching into her pocket to touch the small oak figurine. Trees burst into flame when she blinked, and she tasted mud and algae on her tongue. She pushed back on her chair. A setup. This was all a setup. She squeezed down on the little tree, wanting to break it in two now at the thought of this most recent betrayal by her parents.

"You three have been talking, haven't you?" She took in her father's downturned nose, her mother's fading smile, and Smoot's wordless smirk, and knew the answer. "Were you just waiting for the right opportunity to pounce? Damn, Mother. I expect this from him," she pointed a dirty finger at Daddy, who just stared at the table, a distracted look on his face. "But you too?"

"Look," Smoot said at last, suddenly holding an expensive fountain pen in the bear paw of his right hand. "We can handle all the details right now. Piece a' cake." Her parents leaned forward at the same time, trained seals smelling fresh fish.

Melissa pounded the table in triumph, the tiny tree in her hand scratching the wooden top. Smoot had cracked, too soon. The old bastard couldn't help himself.

"Everything's in *my* name, Mister Smoot. That money Daddy loaned me to get us off the ground was off the books. Just a gift, right, Daddy? They've got no stake in this, other than, well, other than blood ties. For whatever that's worth . . ."

Staring at the trio of blank faces surrounding her, hating the quaver she heard in her own voice—was it anger or love or fear, or all the above?—Melissa shut her mouth when she heard the familiar tinny sound of a cell phone outside the screen door, which she'd left cracked open. Tango music. The ringer to Julio's cell phone.

Gil was calling. And he didn't call *me*, but his hombre Julio.

"Now, Miz *Anderson*," Smoot began again, but his voice was just a southern-fried buzzing sound.

What was Julio saying out there? Melissa stood up when she heard him say her name, and the room spun slightly, flickering from daylight to night and back again. Burning leaves dropped from blackened tree limbs.

"Melissa!" her father said, his voice ringing off the pots and pans above the stove.

"Sit down," Mother said. "We're not through here."

Melissa pushed away from the table and gave the trio of dealmakers a distracted wave. "Be right back."

She did her best not to turn and look at Smoot before she rushed outside, but she couldn't stop herself. He was nodding and smiling with his pinkie finger in his ear, rooting around in there as if digging for gold. He shot her a wink as she closed the screen door behind her.

"I'll be right here waiting on you," that wink said.

Melissa let the heat outside clear her mind, which had felt befuddled in the cool, unmoving air of the kitchen, surrounded by sharks on all sides. They'll never get me to sign away any piece of this farm on their terms. Bad water or no bad water.

Julio was almost shouting into the cell phone Gil had bought for him a year ago, and when he saw Melissa come up to him, he tried to hold up a hand to ward her off. She heard him say something about Ray, then Smoot's name, and then her name. Her headache intensified, filling her vision with black spots. Mariana stepped up to Melissa, about to say something, but she shrank back when she saw the look on Melissa's face.

Before she knew what she was doing, not even thinking anymore, Melissa ripped the phone from her Mexican employee's hand. Her vision went perfectly clear the instant she held the phone up to her ear, and when she spoke, her voice was filled with a sudden calm. If she kept her emotions out of it and explained everything, Gil would understand and get his ass home.

"Gil. You've got to come back now and help us. We're just getting together people to search for him the right way. *Organized*, not just running off. Do you hear me?"

She could tell most of her words were eaten up by static. Gil was talking too, at the same time, and he sounded like he was miles away on the other end of the line. Like he was in another world. As usual.

Stay calm, and get him under control again. She turned on the speaker for the cell phone, and an ocean's wave of static burst from her hand. She held the cell up to her mouth and, amazed at the lack of emotion in her voice—her bitch voice—spoke again:

"Gil. You've *got* to come back now and help us."

All she heard in response was static. His battery was probably dying. He never kept a charge in his damn phone.

Frustrated, without waiting for any additional response from her husband, Melissa pressed the END button and tossed the phone back to a shocked, white-faced Julio. She knew what had to be done. She just hoped she hadn't waited too long.

Still thinking about the distant sound of her husband's voice swimming weakly through the waves of static, Melissa looked up and realized she was surrounded by patients, neighbors, and employees. Not a friend among them, really, she thought. Nobody close to me, just people who lived and worked near or for me.

"*Dondé?*" Julio asked, his voice a whisper.

"I don't know where he is. He had to go," she added, as if she needed to explain the call's sudden end. "And so do we."

"Melissa," Herschel said, "are you sure you don't want to stop for a bit, maybe go back inside out of this sun?"

"I've *been* out of the sun. And my boy is out there, somewhere," she said, watching Julio's dark eyebrows rise as he shared a look with his petite wife. "We've covered every inch of the farm twice now. So I say we go over to the neighbors on either side and see what we can find out there. For all we know, Gil and Noah are at Ray's, drinking root beers and playing fetch with those skinny damn dogs of his."

And if they're not there? she thought. Where to then?

Standing there, sweating all over again in the sun's unrelenting heat, Melissa watched Billie and Mary Jane from up the road passing out compasses, canteens, and sandwiches.

Don't forget the forest, she reminded herself. Noah used to love walking there with us, back before all this mess . . .

Melissa looked up and saw that one of the mothers from up the road was crying. Surely not about Noah being missing. She felt a surge of frustration as the situation spiraled further out of control, with Mother and Daddy and Smoot standing now at the back door, watching her.

But before she could say more, she heard a sound that could only have originated in one of Gil's nightmares: an old man screaming in pain and fear, coming from—of all places—the machine shed.

Melissa had never heard a man scream in that way before, not even in the movies. A mix of fear, agony, and something else. Insanity, probably. The screaming had stopped by the time she began running toward the shed, but the awful echoes of it continued in her ears with every step she took across the gravel driveway.

Inside the shed, Herschel was bent crookedly over the far side of the shed, his starched blue workshirt pulled out of his jeans, exposing a black band of skin and the top of his butt crack. "Herschel, don't touch it!" she shouted, filled with a rush of fear and greed: that was *my* door, and the old man was messing with it. She pushed past Billie and Mary Jane, who stood back with matching looks of disbelief on their pale faces.

Melissa was ready to knock Herschel off to the side, breaking his connection from the door as if it were an electrical outlet electrocuting him, when she realized he wasn't trapped by it all. He hadn't been the one screaming. That had been Mr. Dunleavy, who Herschel was now hauling up out of the ground. Through the *open* door in the floor.

"What the hell? How did you open that?"

Her question was lost as Dun and Herschel toppled backward and fell on top of her. They rolled to either side of her, Herschel awkwardly and grunting, falling on his good side and dragging his unmoving right arm with him, as Dun let out one more high-pitched scream.

Reaching out to each man, Melissa touched Herschel's sweaty upper arm with one hand and Dun's ice-cold neck with the other. Herschel pulled away from her, and in the process he kicked closed the door she'd been trying to open all morning. Melissa's ears popped from the sudden change of pressure in the shed.

Next to her, Dun lay face-down in the cool dirt, unconscious. She did a quick visual check: he had all his limbs, no blood from any wound, no visible trauma of any kind that she could see. His right hand was fisted tight, which made her think *stroke*. That was something real she could focus her energy on.

"Get some blankets from the barn," she barked at Mary Jane, glad to finally have something familiar she could attack. Dun was going into shock. "Close the door, Billie. We don't need *everyone* in here, for Christ's sake. Herschel, you okay?"

With the door shut, Herschel's voice sounded canned in the tight confines of the shed. "I'm fine. But what about him?"

"He's breathing," Melissa said. "But the way he was screaming, you'd think he took a bullet in the belly. What happened here?" Herschel tried to brush the dirt off his shirt and sleeves with his good hand. He cleared his throat, about to speechify.

"Hold on," a voice said, muffled by the floor. Dun rolled to one side and rocked himself to a sitting position. His white beard had flecks of mud embedded in it. He looked down at his closed hand as if not sure what might be trapped in there. "Let this guy try and tell the story, we'll be here all today."

"Come on now," Herschel said, his professorial tone gone. "Give me just an iota of credit for pulling your skinny white butt out of there." He gave the closed metal door a shuddering look. "Wherever *there* was. Didn't sound like you were in some sort of crawl space, Dun."

"Anyhoo," Dun said, glaring at Herschel. "Let me speak. See, I just thought I'd check out this shed, since Melissa's been in here half the day already. Had a feeling. Didn't know old Mr. Stats Prof was gonna follow me in here. Guess the door in the floor was a bit too narrow for you, eh, Hersch?"

"Get on with the story," Herschel said, rolling his eyes. Mary Jane burst through the door with two heavy, musky-smelling blankets, and Melissa wrapped Dun in one of them. She watched him closely, wondering if he was having a dementia relapse.

"So," Dun said to Melissa, wrinkling his nose as he sniffed the blanket like a dog, "you got yourself some sort of tunnel system going on here, huh?"

Without realizing it, Melissa had inched closer to the door set into the ground of the shed. She pulled up short.

"Tunnels?"

"I popped the lock in this sucker with my lock-picking tools from my truck in no time, and dropped down the ladder. The tunnels took me over to Ray's place. There's some bad shit happening over there right now, let me tell you. I've never seen so many dead animals in one place except for that time we had to stake out that pig rendering plant out east back in the seventies. Dead dogs, everywhere you stepped."

"At Ray's?" Billie hissed. "I'll kill that old asthmatic bastard if he's hurt any of those dogs."

"I don't know who did it," Dun said, opening his hand with a grimace. On the soiled palm sat a perfectly carved wooden greyhound at full stride, legs almost horizontal as it ran. The scale and style perfectly matched the tree in Melissa's shorts pocket. "Whoever it was, we need to stop them. I'm not sure they're gonna want to stop at dogs. If you know what I mean."

The echoes of Dun's screaming not five minutes earlier had finally stopped bouncing around in Melissa's head.

"Dun," she said in a low voice that she hoped only he could hear. "What else did you see? What scared you so badly?"

Dun flipped the wooden greyhound over and over in his veiny hand. He shook his head as his face colored with a mix of embarrassment and shame. "Other than all the dead dogs, buried all half-assed? And the wreck of a place that Ray calls home, all overgrown with weeds and kudzu? Don't know. I did find this dog, stuck in the ground next to the door over at Ray's, so I grabbed it. Couldn't help myself. Some crime scene inspector I am, huh?"

"Come on, Melissa said. "*Something* in there got to you." She lowered her voice. "I heard you screaming."

Dun took a sudden breath, and Melissa could see his eyes cloud slightly, just like they did whenever he had a bad day and the frayed mental wires in his head sent him the wrong messages.

"Doors," Dun breathed, loud enough for just her and maybe Herschel. "I saw so many goddamn doors down there, Missy. I got *lost*, and for a cop to ever admit to that, even once, is a bad mistake. I didn't know which one to hit to get back out of there, and then I swear I heard dogs coming up behind me. Lots of 'em. The ghosts of Ray's dogs, I figured. Dogs, and . . . something else. Right behind me. Something big. Had me screaming like a damn little kid. Then I saw Hersch's big ol' bear paw dangling down from this hole, and I grabbed it."

Dun closed his hand on the dog statue and leaned so close to Melissa she could smell what he had for lunch—Julio's chips and salsa. "Tell anyone about this, and we're through." He cut his eyes at Herschel as well, and just for an instant, he was forty years younger, a hardened cop at the scene of a crime, pocketing some crucial bit of evidence. Then he blinked and grimaced, and he was seventy-two again. "Now let's get your boy back before we do anything—"

"*Excuse* me," a sharp voice said. The door to the shed now stood open again, letting in both bright sunlight and a wave of heat. "I really need to get Melissa back now. We have some important material to discuss, thank you."

"Daddy," Melissa began, but her recovered patient overrode her.

"Who the living shit are you?" Dun shouted, on his feet in a flash, shoulders thrown back, blanket falling off his shoulders, his hackles up against some punk of a perp. "You want a piece of this action? Don't even get me started, buddy."

Daddy's mouth pursed so tight it looked like it was sealed shut. His face colored for an instant—the biggest burst of emotion Melissa had seen there in ages—and then he strode off for the front porch, dragging Mother and Smoot in his wake.

Melissa could only look at Dun and smile.

"Good to have you back," she said, "you old fart."

"Yeah, yeah. Now what's this about finding your boy, missy? Time's a-wasting, and your friend Ray's got some explaining to do, I'll bet. Let's get that search party together. Now."

∽o∾

Initially, there had only been Julio, ready to get out and search again after claiming to have covered most of the twenty-five acres of the farm at least twice today. His Durham Bulls baseball cap had a two-inch band of perspiration above the bill, and his normally pristine white T-shirt was sweat-damp, with three horizontal bars of mud on one side, like claw marks, where he must have run into something.

Julio had been recruiting, apparently, because he now had a small posse gathered next to him, including his wife Mariana and their two kids, chatting softly in a mixture of English and Spanish. Along with Herschel and Dun, who still looked shaken but angry enough to chew nails, and Bobbie and Mary Jane, Melissa recognized the two soccer moms from up the road, one of whom was crying and saying something about her own lost boy: "My Eric is missing too, what about *my* son?"

Something began to buzz just at the edge of her perception, like a plane high overhead that never dopplered out of hearing.

Squinting in the bright-white afternoon sun, Melissa passed Dun and Herschel arguing about something on Herschel's hand-drawn map, taking breaks now and then for one of them to cough or regain their balance with their canes (Dun called his a "walking stick," but Melissa wasn't buying it for a minute). Despite their arguing, the two old men never let her get too far away.

"I think everyone's got sandwiches and water," Mary Jane said, holding up a canvas bag with a faded logo for the Weaver Street Market on it. "And here's one for you, of course," she added, handing Melissa the surprisingly heavy bag. "You may want to eat something soon, sweetie. You look a bit puny."

Melissa nodded, and the buzzing grew loud as an army helicopter from Fort Bragg on a training mission. She looked once more at the circle of people surrounding her, and she realized they were all waiting for her to give them the word to start.

The buzzing wasn't inside her head. It came from somewhere inside the circle of people. She looked at the tattered bag on Julio's shoulder, and the buzzing became a band saw slicing into her ears.

"What's in there, Julio?" she said, nearly shouting to be heard over the sound.

Julio gave her a blank look that was quickly followed by a look of pure guilt. He opened the bag and something round and black dropped out, landing on the ground with a dull thunk. The buzzing receded to a dull hiss in the back on Melissa's brain.

Everyone else stepped back from the wad. Melissa could feel the sandwich packed inside her canvas bag reduce down to a ball of bread and cheese in her fist.

"How did you get that?" she whispered.

Julio opened his mouth to speak, but nothing came out. He reached down and grabbed the ball, and Melissa flinched, waiting for the light to wash over him.

But all that came out of the ball was a tiny green beam, almost too small and thin to be seen, like a trick played on the eye. The beam shot past their little cluster of searchers still waiting to start searching, and aimed south, toward the trees at the edge of their land. The forest, again.

That was part of the chunk of land Smoot wanted to buy, Melissa realized. What the hell was that old bastard up to, today?

"I think we must follow it," Julio whispered, sweat dripping off his nose. "Not go to Ray's. We must go to the forest, I think."

"Not after what I saw over there," Dun began. "We need to go to Ray's first. It's a crime scene over there, and we have to seal it off and close it down, all that shit. Ray's place," he said, speaking so slowly to Julio that Melissa wanted to smack him. "Not the forest. Nothing in there but chiggers and squirrels, *hombre*. I ain't going into no forest."

"You sure 'bout that?" Billie said. "I can see a kid going in the woods there and getting lost, fast."

Soon everyone was arguing, each person adding their opinions at top volume, even Anna and Cris, Julio's kids, arguing that the forest was haunted and spooky, that Noah liked talking about it to them, and that it had probably grabbed Noah earlier today. As the voices grew louder, the two soccer moms slipped away to their SUVs in the parking lot, as if afraid of all this raw emotion.

Meanwhile, poor Julio struggled to keep the ball balanced in his hands. Melissa remembered how it had felt to hold that thing, how heavy it was, and how sick it made her afterwards.

We can't waste any more time, she knew. For Julio's sake, and most of all, for Noah.

"Let's go to Ray's first, give it a quick once-over, then head to the forest if we have to," she said. Julio was already walking to the south, his family a step behind him. He stopped, but didn't turn to look at her. "Look. We can't just rule out Ray's place. Not after what Dun saw. All three of them could be there for all we know, trying to do something about those dogs."

She was about to go over to Julio and lead him to Ray's herself when a heavy hand fell onto her shoulder.

"Need a lil' help here, Miz Anderson?"

Melissa swallowed and turned hard, freeing herself from the big, callused hand. A shock of spiky white hair topped the red-faced man's head, and he stood a good six feet three inches tall, even with the slight hunch in his shoulders.

"Mr. Smoot," she began, "*why* are you still here?"

"Can't miss out on the fun, hun, now that your folks took off in a huff. Plus, I want to find your boy almost as much as you do. We all been lost ourselves, once or twice. You're not gonna turn down free help, are ya?"

She almost told him to go do something anatomically impossible to himself, but instead she bit off her angry retort. She could use his help.

"Suit yourself," she said at last. "Just do *not* try to talk business right now."

Without waiting for Smoot's response, Melissa began walking to the southeast, toward Ray's place. There was a path beat down in the brown grass connecting their property with Ray's from all the older man's trips over here, with at least one dog on a leash at his side. The rest of the party fell in behind her, including Julio and his family, bringing up the rear. Luckily, nobody suggested they use the portal in the shed to get there quicker.

As the land began to rise, Melissa stepped over a dark stream of water trickling toward the farm, like an oil leak from an aging car parked uphill from her. An acrid smell rose up from the water. She didn't remember Gil mentioning a stream up here.

"Now that," Smoot muttered, "has got to be bad for the property value. Got some erosion going on here, too, I see."

Melissa had to unclench her jaw to respond; she had to say *something*. What she managed was: "You're barking up the wrong tree, Smoot."

"Excuse me?" Smoot said as they approached the gate connecting Ray's land to theirs. The old fence on either side of the gate had been overrun with kudzu and wicked, thorny vines.

"Look. I do appreciate you coming over on such short notice and helping us search and all, but this is not your land yet, Mr. Smoot. And I have a strong feeling it never will be. Not anymore."

Melissa almost wished Gil had been here to see this. If anyone disliked Smoot more than her, it was Gil.

"Well, I . . . that's just . . . " Smoot stopped walking and shook his head like a condescending father scolding a wayward child. "Girl, you got a *lot* to learn. I tell you that right now."

Melissa waved a dismissive hand at Smoot and stretched out each stride of her long legs to their capacity. Seemed like everyone had something to say to her today, sharing their unsolicited words of half-baked advice.

Half a minute later, after pushing through a surprising amount of overgrown vines and weeds choking the path, Melissa and her band of unlikely searchers arrived at what was left of Ray's trailer and his dogs, and the devastation there was utterly complete.

CHAPTER TWELVE:
NOT SINKING, AFTER ALL

You never know how far down you've gone until you find yourself ten feet underwater and still sinking. Outmatched and overwhelmed, running again. But this time Gil wasn't running away so much as running *toward* someone.

Maybe I'm not sinking, after all, he thought. Maybe I'm finally making progress.

His lungs were just starting to hurt in that good way, stretching them a bit as he held them tight and full of air, when the dwindling light from high above illuminated two different metal doors cut into the concrete sides of the well in which he was currently sinking. Bubbles filled his vision, like the contents a hundred cans of shaken soda, but he could still make out the unrusted metal handle for each square door.

The first door was on the Ray side of the well, and the other was on what he was assuming—betting—would be the Undercity side of the well. Gil had no idea if he'd kept his bearings after diving into this puddle of bubbles, though, so he was going to have to continue trusting his instincts. Plus his lungs were starting to remind him that some oxygen would be nice about now.

He went for the door in front of him, the Undercity portal. The handle opened away from him, with hardly any resistance. Kicking forward, he squirted through the rectangular hole into darkness.

He knew he'd made the right choice immediately, because the water almost stopped his heart. It was cold, silty black. No bubbles here, just the taste of tar and mud and a current that sucked him up and away from the hole and its door connecting these two opposing streams.

The bends, he figured, or my lungs filling with water. One or the other would kill me. Or maybe I'd just plow into something like a metal grate embedded in more concrete, and that would end it for me. A nice impalement, probably.

But I'm *moving*, damn it. I call that progress.

Then Gil remembered the door, below him.

He'd done the typical thoughtless guy thing—he'd left the toilet seat up. Or, in this case, he'd left the door open. Now the polluted and cold water he was marinating in would seep into the clean water of the well and most likely spread beyond here and to the world above. No more nice, clean, chigger-easing 7Up bubbles.

The ache in his chest was becoming less friendly now, filling him with a panicky heaviness, but he still managed to turn against the upward-pressing current and kick himself back toward the door he'd left wide open below him. He couldn't just leave it that way for someone else to close. Nobody wanted to buy fruits and vegetables for their kids from a lazy farmer who didn't follow the rules and clean up his own messes.

Can money pay?

Kicking down against the current, Gil fought off another wave of exhaustion as a bit of song kept spinning round and round inside his head.

Can money pay for all the days?

Eyes stinging, arms aching, mouth threatening to open and ingest as much of this brackish ice water as possible, he finally made his way back to the open metal door. A red glow of panic began to glow inside his squinting eyes.

Can money pay for all the days I lived awake but half asleep?

The light shining down through the well on the other side of that little portal was tempting. He could have air within three seconds if he went back through and shot up to the surface in that shifty cave. Maybe Ray and his cohorts wouldn't be waiting there for him. Possible, but not likely.

Everything was turning red.

And who, Gil wondered, his lungs aching and heart racing—who would come through this portal to enter the Undercity and find my son for me?

I lived awake but half asleep . . .

He was having trouble feeling his face anymore. He needed air. All he could think about was air. Air and that damn song.

He pushed against the metal door until he felt it click shut, sealing off the bubbly well from this heinous water, and then he just closed his eyes and let go. The current, triumphant at last, threw him up, and he let it take him.

Awake but half asleep . . .

My epitaph. A zombie for years. If not all my life.

Lightheaded, Gil gave one last surging stroke with his leaden arms before his vision went gray. He was out of air. He'd stayed down here too long. He wanted to sleep, again. Out of air.

He cracked open one eye, and instead of the redness he was expecting, he saw the light high above him turn dark.

〜๑〜

There were never any working lights in my dreams of the Undercity.
Sometimes the light bulb itself—streetlight, porchlight, even headlight—was broken, burst like an egg from some thrown rock, or the socket was left empty as an old mother's arms. Usually, if there was an intact bulb, the damn thing was flickering. Shaky gray light filled every last one of my dreams. If it wasn't the bad lights flashing on my Escort's dusty dashboard, it was the distant streetlights going

bad, lights so high above me all I could see was a pinprick of blinking whiteness that strobed down onto the changing structures around me as I drove.

Maybe I just needed to get my dream vision checked, or get a prescription for some sub-conscious glasses. Or something. The bad light always cast the Undercity into gray ambiguity. I could never tell if that was a dump truck approaching me down the blind intersection, or if it was simply the twisted wreckage of a poorly designed house. No wonder I had no maps for this world—the place thrived on shadows and illusions seen only in the corner of a person's sleeping eyes.

Like the dream when I was driving next to a black lake filled with what looked like two hundred miniature metal battleships the size of Noah's clenched fist. Each boat came armed with cannons above the surface, and—I kid you not—torpedoes below. The lake was boiling with tiny explosions and echoing with the voices of small children. I could never tell if they were cheering the devastation or crying in fear and pain.

I tried to slow down to take in the sight of the miniature naval battles, but the faceless, helmeted motorcyclists I'd cut in front earlier of were now roaring their displeasure at me with their machines' engines. Dream logic had convinced me that at any moment, one of the cyclists would make a run at me and try to commandeer me vehicle.

But then I saw her. Viewed from my passenger-side window, at first just a flash of white in front of the embattled lake, I caught sight of a young girl, maybe two years old, in diapers and a pink dress, toddling her way down the pier leading out over the lake. Just before I could make a dream-logic connection in my sleeping brain to recognize who she really was, the light of the pier above her burst with a stray shot from one of the boats, casting her head full of blonde curls into shadow and turning her dress a dull flat gray. The light was failing her and me both. I just hoped the glass from the exploded light didn't fall and cut her bare feet to shreds.

None of the other children seemed to notice her—and where the hell were all the parents? I wondered as I touched the brakes—even as she tiptoed to the edge of the pier.

Just as I was about to rear-end the blue pickup in front of me, she fell. I never got to see what happened to her, because all the lights of the Undercity went out at that moment, a conspiracy of bad bulbs and tired dream currents. In the darkness, I lost her.

And I knew then who she was.

Sophie.

I lost her.

Sophie.

We lost her.

∽o∾

First thing in the morning, on a daily basis, the sun's light entered Gil's eyes like a series of pinpricks that punctured the darkness one tiny hole at a time. He felt every single poke. This was what waking up was for him—a series of assaults. It was bad enough, back in the real world, to make him want to stop getting up in the morning.

But *this* waking was much, much worse than any of that. Gil pulled himself out of a puddle of cold, heavy wetness and immediately started coughing until he'd cleared the worst of the tar-flavored crap from his mouth and nose. He still hadn't opened his eyes. He didn't want to deal with that tiny stabbing feeling, because he could tell through the red glow of his eyelids that the light was bright in here, wherever he was.

Maybe I'm not really in the Undercity, he thought with a glimmer of foolish, cowardly hope. At least not the one I'd been dreaming about. That place was all about bad lighting.

The *where* of this place he'd ended up didn't matter. What mattered was picking up Noah's trail again, as soon as he caught his breath. Which meant he had to open his eyes.

It hurt, but he was used to it. Just a tiny crack at first. Yellow light bright as noon-time flooded over him, and it was only his thoughts for Noah's rescue that kept him from screwing his eyes shut and going back to unconsciousness. He was close now, he could feel it.

He peeked around and saw that he was in a cave with smooth concrete walls; round, no openings. Just this tiny black disk of water at its center. Somehow he'd popped up out of that hole and gotten himself some oxygen after he'd blacked out. He sure as hell didn't remember it, but that didn't matter now.

High above was some sort of light, not the usual Undercity bare 60-watt bulb like he was expecting, but an actual light fixture. The frosted glass globe looked like a suspended boob with its black nipple pointing down at him. Flies or some other critters danced inside the half-globe, and Gil risked opening his eyes a bit wider to see that the light was attached to what looked like a dirt ceiling, tree roots and vines and all.

No doors. This place had no doors.

Tar, frustration, and other nastiness filled his mouth, and he leaned over and heaved. There goes my toast and coffee, he thought. His arms shook with weakness and fatigue as he rolled back over, filled with cold desperation now that the adrenaline had left him. He almost started scratching his ankles again.

I took the wrong turn, Gil decided. Guessed wrong. Again.

He had no idea who could've designed a place like this—a room without windows or doors, just a pool of waste with water flowing the wrong way. He thought about the vicious, viscous current that had carried him here and wondered why that black water wasn't gushing up out the hole next to him; the water sat still as an oil slick.

Gil moved away from his own mess and lay on his back, staring up at the boob light. Tried counting to ten, but kept getting stuck at six or so and panicking. He was wasting time not moving. He let his hands fall down to his side as he lay there, and his left hand hit something small and solid in his wet jeans pocket.

"No way," he said. He had to struggle like a fat man in undersized pants to get it out of his water-tightened jeans, but after a few seconds of struggling that made his head spin a few more times, he was able to dislodge his cell phone. The salamander tail tried to escape as well, but Gil poked it back in with his wet fingers. No time for that now, he figured. I have a phone call to make. He turned on the phone and waited for it to come to life. Surprise number one: it still worked.

Surprise number two: as soon as the phone was on, Gil hit the speed dial for Julio, his right-hand man, instead of punching in Melissa's number. As soon as he hit Send, the light above him began to dim.

"No way this is gonna work," he said, watching the small square screen of the phone blink like the bad lights of his Undercity dreams.

Connecting . . . the phone reported.

Blink. Blink. Blink.

Out of the corner of his eye, Gil saw something move in the fading, uncertain light. Something big, a shadow the size of a car. Which was, of course, impossible in this doorless room.

But when he pulled his gaze from the *Connecting . . .* phone in his hand and put the phone to his ear, he didn't see anything but an unbroken concrete wall.

"Hello?"

Gil jumped at the sound of the voice in his ear and dropped the cell phone onto the concrete floor. It was Julio.

"Oh *shit*."

He went to his knees, snatched up the phone, and commenced babbling.

"Julio! It's me! Gil. Where are you? What's going on up there?"

"Gil?" Julio always stretched his name into at least three syllables. "Ge-eee-eee-eel? You okay, hombre? You found Noah?"

"Not yet, man," Gil said, grimacing at a sudden curl of static in his ear. He realized that he was so sure the kiddo was down here, the thought of asking Julio if Noah had already been found had never entered his head. "I'm still looking. Any luck up there? *Donde está,* man? What the hell's happening up there?"

More static, followed by Julio calling out his name. No, no, no. The connection was giving up the ghost. Gil felt a series of tiny, staticky shocks on the hand holding his phone.

"Tell me what's happening," he shouted into it, turning on the speaker so he could hear any possible tidbit Julio could squeeze in through the static before Gil lost him. Julio was talking fast now, every couple of words eaten in a crash of interference.

"We look for you and Ray but couldn't . . . then Smoot stopped . . . Miz Melissa in machine shed all morn' . . . us waiting . . . outside, ready . . . look for Noah . . . "

"What?" Gil's ears rang from the roars of static, but he didn't dare pull the phone away from his ear. "The shed? Smoot's there?"

The phone filled with a sudden silence that hurt as much as the gushing static. Gil thought he'd lost the connection, and then he heard his wife's voice speaking loud and clear through the speaker of his cell.

"Gil. You've got to come back now and help us."

Melissa's voice had gone dead in that way that told Gil she was moving into the realm of actions she'd later regret as she tried to wrestle control away from the unthinking universe.

"What the hell do you think I'm trying to do, Mel? Would you rather I sit around and wait all day and *then* go out and hope for the fucking best?"

"Gil. You've got to come back now and help us."

"Is this a recording?" Gil shouted, but the phone was dead in his hand. The display was black, not even a *Call was lost!* message. Just . . . dead. Like his wife's voice.

He spun on his bare heel and threw the phone into the pool, relishing the dark splash of water and the sudden ache in his throwing arm. Making that call was a huge mistake.

What did she think I was doing, he thought, making a run for the border instead of going through hell and worse to find our boy while she sat on her ass back home? Gil took a sudden, shuddering breath, thinking of what Julio had said amid all the static. Was *Smoot* up there too? What the hell was that redneck bastard trying to accomplish? He glared up at the boob light, stifling a scream, and his equilibrium went kaflooey on him. He ended up sitting down, hard. Noah was down here somewhere, Gil knew. His breath caught in his chest. So why did Melissa want me back up there so badly? She hadn't needed me in months. Years.

Clenching his jaw so hard it made his whole face ache, he rolled over and crawled to the rounded wall, his clothes now cold and heavy on his back and legs. His bare feet slid across the smooth concrete floor, and when he looked back, he saw that he was leaving a black trail behind him. He couldn't believe that he'd actually been submerged in that polluted water. What the hell was I thinking?

When he turned his gaze forward again, expecting the smooth, round concrete wall in front of him in this cylinder of a room, he saw instead his old '93 Escort, engine idling, exhaust pipe spitting out a gray dribble of smoke. On this half of the room, the wall was gone, leaving just Gil in his soaked clothes and his black kiddie pool.

"I'm not even going to ask," he muttered, rolling to his feet with a now-familiar head rush. As if on cue, the boob light above him began to flicker, just enough to keep what lay beyond his waiting vehicle in unsteady shadow.

Gil staggered to his old car and nearly burst into tears when he fell into the driver's seat in a puff of dust, the seat already contoured to his ass, back, and shoulders from years of use. He happily inhaled the familiar old-car odor of dust, oil, and burning plastic.

From his new vantage point behind the wheel, Gil exhaled and allowed himself a smile. He was back home.

He clicked off the emergency brake, put the car in gear, and released the clutch while touching the gas pedal, moves programmed into his body after years of repetition. As if he'd slipped off to sleep and entered one of the dreams that had been haunting him for the past two years, Gil was once more driving in the Undercity.

God help me, he thought, unaware of the shit-eating grin on his face, I'm going back in.

CHAPTER THIRTEEN:
BAD DOORS IN THERE

Noah had always liked front porches. He loved just sitting on their front porch back home, listening to his parents talk, the living room and kitchen waiting patiently for all of them to return. But this porch was falling apart, all loose gray boards and rotten black nails, and it was just too small. Too small, that is, for him and this other kid. Eric. The other kid's name was Eric. Noah remembered it at about the same time he came up with a name for his tail-less salamander.

At first Eric was all whiny and afraid to take the candy Noah was offering him. He kept crying about how much trouble he was in now that Noah was here. But after a while Eric gave in and snatched the mint from Noah's hand. He tossed the wrapper onto the dusty ground, where it disappeared with a burp of air.

Noah was still catching his breath and sucking slowly on his own mint, enjoying the way the candy made the dust in his mouth slide away. He sat Indian-style on the creaky, splintered porch, listening for Elwood. Next to him, now that he'd already chomped up the last bit of his own mint, the other boy was up, walking in circles and bragging about the house and how he'd found Alexander the salamander.

One thing Eric *wasn't* doing was teasing Noah.

For a quick second, while Eric paused for breath between stories about the house and his new friends down here, Noah thought he heard the sound of tiny salamander feet from inside the house. He stood up, making the other boy jump back, almost falling off the small porch.

Noah still had to give the salamander his tail back. But when he checked his pocket, his lips came together to create an unconscious raspberry. The tail was gone. At some point he'd lost it, who knows where.

Noah made an attempt to rub off the black mud made by the dust on his sweaty skin, but it wasn't working. He just ended up smearing it around. Even the air down here felt bad, like all the freshness had been taken out, and all the smells and garbage from up above had sunk down through the ground and came down here to rest—Mom called that stuff germs and back-teer-ya, whatever those were.

Noah reminded himself not to breathe too deeply down here, or else he'd end up like their neighbor Ray with his cough. Noah had always been a little afraid of that tube in Ray's nose, and the hissing tank hidden in Ray's backpack. Even though Ray had shown him the tank and explained how it worked and why he had to wear it, Noah never really got over his fear of that contraption, or his uneasiness with the old man wearing it.

As the last bit of sweetness from the mint faded from his tongue, replaced once more with the nasty taste of dust, Noah spoke to the other boy, interrupting his jabbering.

"I need to go inside and get my salamander. Can't stop me."

Eric flinched back again and shut his mouth with a snap. His muddy brown eyes went wide, and he started rubbing his arms.

"Take me with you," he pleaded. Eric's fingers and hands were turning blue, Noah noticed, but he didn't feel very cold down here himself. "They just left me here on the porch and told me to wait for you. I was too scared to go in there by myself." His voice lowered to a whisper. "There's bad doors in there. They've been slamming all day long."

Noah had his hand on the cold metal handle of the front door— one of those fancy kinds, not a knob, but a curl of metal with a button on top you had to pull down with your thumb—and he let go if it suddenly, as if it were hot. He held his breath and listened for a few seconds before turning to Eric.

"I don't hear anything in there. And who's *they*?"

Noah looked from his dirty arms over at the other boy. As he waited for an answer, he felt a tinge of cold in the unhealthy air.

"You better tell me what's going on."

"Don't," the other boy said. He inched back to the uneven edge of the porch and tipped backward. Flailing his arms and squealing in complete fear, he managed to catch his balance right before falling.

"They told me about you. You're Noah. My mom—" he gave a quick, hitching sob as he said this word "—she said you and me ought to be friends, but your dad was too much of a crunchy granola bar. Whatever that means."

Strangers. Doors. Eric. Alexander the salamander. Elwood. This kest is getting really crowded, Noah thought. Dad's stories about Prince One-Eye were much easier to follow than this.

"Okay," he said. "Who brought you here, Eric?"

The other boy was suddenly distracted by the shape of the warped boards that made up the rickety porch under their feet. He bent down and ran his blue-tinted hand along the twisted gray board nearest him, then he began untying his shoe.

Dirty water. The disappearing man. Hitting Daisy when she wouldn't give up that black ball. Mom's mean face.

"Eric! Pay attention! I need you to answer me." Noah tried to talk in his best angry voice, and he was surprised to find that he didn't have much trouble using it once he remembered this kid was a puncher and a teaser. "Tell me, or I'll leave you here all by yourself."

"There were these guys in blue trucks," Eric said, the words spilling out of his mouth like he'd sucked down a too-big mouthful of water. "Pickemups. They drove up to my house this morning, right after we got back from your dad's store. My mom was inside, doing something. I was in the back, chasing the dog. These guys, they were . . . funny-looking." Eric's voice began to waver. "They were the *bendy* guys from my bad dreams."

Noah stared at Eric, totally confused. He could never remember his own dreams, not even the good ones. He just remembered waking up scared sometimes, almost able to see and feel what had made him feel so afraid. But it would always fade away, just out of reach inside his head. Bendy men?

Somewhere off in the distance, maybe farther down the road where Elwood had gone, came a banging sound, followed by a small explosion that could've been the angry roar of a big cat. Noah's mouth went dry at that sound, and he wished he hadn't given away that other mint.

"How come they were bendy?" he asked, remembering Eric's story again as he stared at the goosebumps rising up through the mucky dust on his forearms.

"I don't *know!*" Eric said, his sentence starting out as a whine and ending in something close to a scream.

A low rumbling now came from where the tall curbs and the long road were. When Noah looked in the direction of that noise, though, he couldn't see anything. Just the empty road and crooked gray houses.

"Okay," Noah said in a soft voice. He really wanted to get inside the house, now. "So they took you out of your own backyard?"

"They said they had something for me. A prize for being the strongest kid in the neighborhood. I knew I was, so it was nice to get a prize for it. Plus, I thought I heard video games in the back of their truck. Like the new Motocross Smashup game my stupid Mom—" another quick hiccup "—won't buy for me."

Noah thought that Eric looked a lot like a big pile of Jell-O right then, all flopped down on the porch but careful not to touch the house or the door leading into it. Usually he was pretty patient with other kids and their strange ways—as an only child, he preferred adults most of the time over kids, because old people weren't so spazzy—but Eric was being a baby about all this. It was his own fault for talking to strangers. Everyone knew not to do that, even the dumbest characters in one of Dad's stories.

"So what are you supposed to do down here?" he asked Eric the Jell-O boy.

Eric sniffed. "Scare you off so you don't go inside."

Noah laughed out loud at that idea. Then he stopped when a thought struck him like the flat hand of the strange man back in the cave, sending a fresh chill down his spine.

"Are you going to get in trouble if I go in there?"

Eric nodded from below him, crying again.

"Fine," Noah said. He grabbed Eric by the arm and pulled him to his feet. He was surprised at how cold the other boy's skin felt. "Then you're coming in with me. We'll only be in here long enough to get my buddy Alexander."

Ignoring the other's boys sudden screams, surprised he was able the drag the so-called strongest boy in the neighborhood across the porch like this, Noah once more gripped the handle to the front door.

He was immediately reward by a shock so big he could see it, all white electricity arcing between the door and his fingers, which were starting to look blue under their coating of muck. A heartbeat later, the rumbling sounded from behind him, louder and quite possibly closer this time.

"The bendy men's trucks," Eric mumbled, but Noah was forging ahead. It was the only thing he could do down here: just keep moving forward until he found out what he had to do next. It beat sitting around getting scared. Even if he did get another shock in the process.

Pulling down on the lever to the door handle with all the strength in his left thumb, Noah managed to open the door and keep hold of the now-struggling Eric. He was thinking about that tower that made the top floor of this house.

I could get a great view from up there, he thought. I'd bet I could find Elwood if he's not too far off, and maybe I can find out where that gross river comes from, too.

He somehow managed to close the door behind him without losing Eric or tripping and falling onto the uncarpeted floor of the house. When the exterior door swung shut with a click, a series of doors all over the house apparently had the same idea, except they chose to close with a slam instead. Noah counted about ten different slams, but it was hard to be sure when they all happened at pretty much the same time.

"Now you've done it," Eric breathed, and then he turned his head at a strange angle, repeating the angle with the rest of his body—looking very *bendy*, Noah realized—until the other boy simply disappeared.

∽o∾

Prince One-Eye and the Black Hoods were masters of exploring a new place. They used teamwork, Dad explained, and they counted on each other to look for booby traps (Noah always had to laugh at that) and sneak attacks and trap doors. They'd go from one room to the next, checking every inch of it before moving on. And they kept their swords drawn the whole time.

The Black Hood roster included the brave Prince, short Oligar the Giant, tall Mackenzie the Dwarf and his twin sister Kenziemac, the tattooed Druid, and the silent Archibald. All outlaws working for the King. Noah wished he had at least one of the Hoods with him right now, even smelly Oligar. But he was on his own, so he was going to have to be doubly careful about those booby traps.

He still hadn't figured out what had happened to Eric, but that was two rooms ago, and the slamming doors had made him mostly forget the teasing, whining kid. Mostly.

The house itself was empty except for dust, drapes, and doors. Doors of all kinds, and they were set on the floor of each room instead of in the walls where they should've been. Sometimes the doors were lined up on the floor so neatly that they created a nice straight path between them. Others weren't as orderly, some of them overlapping or crooked, and Noah wasn't sure how they opened, if they did at all.

So far, none of the doors had opened and then slammed shut on him, though he worried that would happen each time he passed one. The weak gray glow let in by the faded, tattered drapes gave him barely enough light to see by. In the rooms ahead of him, doors continued to slam.

And somewhere in the middle of all that racket was the skittering sound of Alexander the salamander.

Noah paused above a six-paned door below him—he'd hoped to peek through the glass in the door to see what was on the other side, but the panes were frosted with yellow dust mixed with what looked like ice—and stopped at a faded red barn door with a rusted chain in place of a doorknob. Standing there, he thought about just walking away, leaving through the only doors that made any sense, the normal ones leading out of here.

Was that salamander worth it? He didn't want anything to happen to Alexander, since he was 'sponsible for the little critter, but at the same time, this house wasn't right. Nothing down here was right. And he had a bigger kest to accomplish as well, to help save Mom and Dad's farm.

Flinching as a door slammed in the distance, Noah thought again of Elwood, and the memory of the big cat allowed him to move forward again. He figured he just needed to get to the tower in this house, and then he'd be able to take a look out the crooked windows and find Elwood.

Surely the big cat was looking for me, too, Noah thought. Elwood was like one of Black Hoods, and those guys never left someone behind. Not if they could help it.

That reminded Noah of the story Dad had started yesterday that took place inside the Forbidden Forest, as usual. One-Eye was chasing those pesky trolls again. The two dwarves, Mackenzie and Kenziemac, were huffing and puffing next to One-Eye, their big boots churning up the dirt in the forest and flinging it into the trees, where it hit a den of where-cats.

Dad had stopped, then, and propped Noah up on his knee and turned down the scratchy old-time music on his CD player (but he didn't put it on Pause, Noah noticed; he'd been watching closely). Dad explained what a where-cat was, how it was like a where-wolf, and how the full moon made them into cats or wolves. Noah had lots of questions about all that, including how they got their weird names (because maybe people always wondered where the people went when they turned into cats or wolves?).

But then some customers came in, like they always did, and that was the end of the story for that day.

What about the where-cats? Noah had wanted to ask Dad that night on the back porch, but Mom had been giving Dad mean eyes while she looked over a stack of papers in her clipboard. Noah had turned back to his Legos and tried not to think about where-cats roaming around the farm in the bright moonlight.

Where are they? he wanted to ask. Where would they attack next? Noah figured that was what really made them where-cats—you never knew where they'd be from one second to the next.

And this morning, Dad had barely gotten Mackenzie and Kenziemac past the den of grumpy where-cats in the middle of the night (Noah was the one who had to remind Dad that the moon had to be full for the where-cats to be cats) before those two too-pretty ladies from up the road popped into the store, asking about the stupid mangoes.

For all Noah knew, Prince One-Eye had run on ahead of the two dwarves, leaving them and the where-cats in the dust, and the Prince was all alone now, too.

Still thinking about full moons and cats the size of dogs, Noah continued tiptoeing through the house, accompanied by the imagined courage of his Black Hoods.

He entered a narrow hallway with a floor made up completely of doors, the top of one touching the bottom of the next. Two slams came from behind him, along with a tiny tinkle of broken glass and the rattle of a small chain.

Who else was looking for me? Noah wondered, stepping lightly across the treacherous, unreliable flooring.

Even though he could no longer see the sun, he could feel time passing inside his head, like one of those hourglasses the Wicked Witch had in "The Wizard of Oz." This hourglass was as tall as Noah was, and it had a good bit of sand at the top. But every second, more bits of sand were dropping through the little tube into the bottom. The top and bottom looked about equal now.

Whatever happened down here, he knew that it had to happen *today*. Something about today made it special. Important. Noah just had to figure out what that special thing was.

⌒○⌒

He stopped at the landing to the second-floor steps before the slamming doors caught up to him. For the past fifteen minutes, moving careful as an old man in the dark, Noah hadn't seen a single door shoot open and then slam itself shut. Always the slams were ahead of or behind him.

Now, close to the tower of this big gray house, he saw a door move. The instant he put his foot down on the last step, the white wooden door in the floor at the top of the steps swung open and up. Noah froze, and the door whished through the air toward him, the metal knob aimed right for his forehead.

He ducked out the way just in time, and he tried to crane his neck around the door's bulk to see what was on the other side.

169

But the door was already moving back down at high speed. Noah instinctively pulled his hands back and jammed them under his armpits, not wanting to get his fingers crushed as the door closed with a sharp, cracking sound.

A second later, the door next to it, a cheap screen door, slammed shut with a booming rattle. Followed by the next door down the hall, all the way down.

Like dominoes, Noah thought, holding his breath. He moved forward and tried to step only on the tiny strip of pale brown wood here on the third floor. Pretty soon he had no choice but to run from one door to the next, needing to get to the end of the hall.

At the end of the door-riddled corridor, he threw himself through an archway and stood panting in a small alcove that contained just three items: a rope ladder leading up, a crooked metal shelf built into the wall, and a tail-less salamander sitting on the shelf.

"Alexander!" he called out, grinning with relief, glad to see both the salamander as well as the absence of any doors on the dusty tile floor.

But Noah's smile began to fade from his face as fast as it arrived. Something was different about the salamander, now that they were able to look at one another eye to eye. The look on its triangular face seemed full of mischief and trouble.

"About bloody time," Alexander the salamander said in a chirpy voice from his perch on the shelf, winking at Noah.

And then the tail-less salamander began to *grow*.

CHAPTER FOURTEEN:
PORTAL OF THE DOG

Ray's trailer sat barely half a mile away from Melissa's own house, but she'd only visited it once. The seven acres surrounding his tumbledown double-wide were as nasty now as they had been on the one time Melissa had gone over there, with Gil carrying baby Noah on his shoulder, and she'd never gone back.

The place looked like it had been leveled by a hurricane a year ago and left untouched since that force of nature had hit. Everywhere she looked, vines and trees and weeds grew together in a mat-like web, creating a living, swaying series of random fences and walls, like a labyrinth leading up to his home. The three leaning, kudzu-covered outbuildings where Ray kenneled his dogs looked to be completely cut off, thanks to the wild, unrestrained foliage.

As Melissa approached the trailer, leading her loud, clumsy party of searchers, a foul set of odors hit her. Rot and fresh dirt. Something dead. The stink came from a gap in the overgrown vegetation on the west side of the trailer, next to the outbuildings. Passing by Ray's boxy metal home, she peered around the corner and saw the mounds.

About three dozen of them, each one four feet long. The older mounds on the left were smoother, more even with the ground than the newer ones on the right, which bulged out like tumors. A sad, muddy paw stuck out from one of those recent piles of dirt, as if trying to ward off the lines of kudzu reaching for it. The smell rising up from the mounds made Melissa's eyes water.

"What did he do to those dogs?" Billie hissed, bending over one of the recent burial mounds, but unable to touch the dead dog that had been ineffectively covered in it.

Anna pulled up short as soon as she came around the corner. "Are they all dead?" she whispered. "All his dogs?"

"Go wait by the trail," Julio said to his wife and kids, softly but urgently. He moved in front of them, blocking their view. "This is very bad here."

"I think this is *all* of them," Melissa said. "All Ray's dogs."

She moved away from Smoot, who was just standing there in the sun, swearing as he gazed at the two rows of devastation.

"I can't figure what happened to them," Herschel said, brushing dirt off a poorly buried brindle greyhound, uncovering the thin, streamlined corpse. "Nothing good. Maybe he poisoned them over the course of a few weeks. This one here shows no other trauma, and it wasn't starved to death. Or maybe the dogs all caught some sort of disease, or ate tainted kibble."

Ray. He'd been at Gil's side this morning, with his dog.

"No way," she said. "That makes no sense, Herschel . . . Ray loved those dogs."

Julio had been standing close to the house, breathing loudly from his mouth. He checked once more to make sure his kids were far enough away from this dog graveyard, and then he held up the ball he'd been carrying and examined it as if it were a melon. Melissa watched, waited for him to thump it and listen to the sound it made.

"The water," Herschel said, snapping his fingers. "That could've done it. Killed all of them. Let's get Dun to take a closer look. He's got a nose for these things."

"Where *is* Mr. Dun?" Julio asked.

"I thought he was right here," Melissa said. Her throat had gone tight again at the mention of tainted water. She thought of the foul-tasting, hallucinogenic sip of water she'd taken that morning. "You don't think he wandered off again, do you?"

"He probably wanted to go check out that portal he claims he found over here," Herschel said in a distracted voice as he limped his way over to the trough Ray had used to water his dogs. The way he moved made her think of Gil, suddenly, the way he favored his bad hip. Something stuck in her throat for a long moment, and she wondered where her husband was right now.

Find him, she thought with all of her mental energy. *Find Noah and get both of your butts back here.*

"I think you're onto something with the water, Herschel," Melissa said at last, glancing at Julio for a second—he seemed to have made something in the ball flash green again.

"We need to go take a look inside the house," she said, though "house" was actually too generous a term at this late stage in the life of the rusted, sagging trailer in front of her. Cardboard sat crookedly in the glassless front windows, the siding hung down in long flaps in several places, and the amateur attempt at a cement foundation had been chipped and broken in a number of places, as if someone had been trapped inside and tried to break out.

"I think we better make our way toward those three buildings," Herschel said. "Odds are that he's there, digging for doors."

"Meet you there in a sec," Melissa said. She reached up and knocked on the metal front door to Ray's trailer, banging on it hard enough to bruise her knuckles. *Surely, if Ray and Gil and Noah were in there, they would've heard us out here by now.* But with Ray, you never knew.

As the rest of her search party, including Mariana and the kids, trekked past her toward the sheds, Melissa went up the two rickety steps of Ray's so-called front porch and turned the knob of the door. It felt cold and greasy in her hand. The sun moved behind the clouds as she pulled the complaining door toward her and peeked inside.

The stench she was prepared for, but not the plants.

She counted three different kinds of ivy crisscrossing the shadowy interior of Ray's trailer, along with more kudzu and a slender yellow vine she couldn't recognize. All the various plants had grown together, blocking out the windows in their hunger for sunlight. Ray's bare living room was gloomy as a cave, but moist as a greenhouse.

Pushing vines out of her face, she took a few tentative steps deeper into the trailer to examine what looked like a map on the crooked end table next to Ray's recliner, the only piece of furniture in the vine-choked room. The trailer was filled with the stink of garbage mixed with the bittersweet scent of the rampant vines.

Melissa paused, and as soon as she stopped walking, something rustled above and next to her in the vines. She jumped back instinctively and headed for the open door behind her.

Screw this, she thought, as the rustling continued. She felt behind her for the step down out of the trailer.

Then she stopped, feeling silly. She looked up and around her at the hodge-podge of wild plants and couldn't see any animals, but when she took another step, more rustling sounds erupted all around her. The vines over the windows thickened even more somehow, eating the remaining light in the trailer. Melissa forced herself to move forward, trying to laugh at her trepidation. All that came out was a ragged exhale.

This is just Ray's place, she thought, reaching ever so slowly for the map on the end table. The vines waved and flapped above her as if they were being whipped by the wind.

Panting now, Melissa grabbed the map and the slim book that had been hidden underneath it. The walls and the ceiling exploded with vines reaching for her as she spun and ran for the door.

Slapping at the squirming bits of vegetation tugging at her hair and reaching for her legs and arms, trying to trip her up, Melissa dove through the door and slammed it shut behind her.

No way, she thought. No way did the vines in that room come alive like that. I was just hyped up from breaking and entering. Kudzu just didn't *do* that.

Wiping sweat from her forehead and rubbing imagined kudzu tendrils from her bare arms, she tucked the map and small book into her shorts pocket. She thought about going back in to make sure Noah wasn't somewhere inside, but she didn't believe he could be here. Ray wasn't a kidnapper.

Instead, she gave the trailer a wide berth on her way to the smallest of Ray's buildings. As she grew closer, trying to rub invisible plant fingers off her neck, she saw that the web of vines appeared to have been hacked through here, opening up a tunnel-like walkway from trailer to shed. The rest of the search party had gathered there, half of them in and half of them out of the small shed. Déjà vu.

Smoot stood in the doorway, blocking the view for Billie and Mary Jane along with that of Mariana and her two kids. Typical. Melissa pushed past the big man to fit into the shed, which was about half the size of their machine shed back home.

"Here it is," Dun told her in a giddy voice from where he sat on the dirt floor with Herschel, with Julio hunkered down next to him. He was pointing at—but not touching—another rectangular metal door set in concrete in the exact middle of the floor. A familiar black chain stretched from the middle of the door into Julio's slightly trembling hand.

"This is the doorway," Dun continued. He pointed at a shallow hole in the dirt at the bottom of the doorframe. "See where I dug up the little dog? His paw was sticking out like one of those buried dogs outside, just waiting for me to snag him."

"It's not a doorway," Melissa said, her voice sounding far away even to herself. She forced her hands to stop shaking, and demanded that her brain stop thinking about the moving vines inside of Ray's trailer. "It's a *portal*."

Dun and Herschel exchanged a quizzical look, while Julio rattled the chain. Melissa didn't really know why, at that moment, she had to differentiate between a doorway and a portal.

"So how's this here portal gonna help us find your boy?" Smoot said, leaning in, his voice way too loud for this small, enclosed space. His presence seemed to take all the air out of the shed. "Can your boy pick locks?"

Melissa turned on him, a challenge in these tight quarters.

"Smoot," she said. "Let us do what we need to do, without the running commentary and criticism, okay?"

Smoot's initial look of surprise faded into a familiar look of indignation. But for just a second, Melissa had seen a person there, not an adversary. She wondered how well Smoot had known the F-Ts and Ray before she and Gil came along.

"Missus Anderson," Anna said next to her softly. Her small hand reached up to pull something from Melissa's hair. "You got something stuck in there."

Face growing hot—Smoot had made her so crazy-mad she'd forgotten there were other people around—Melissa squelched a scream when her own fingers encountered something long and slithery in her loose, wild hair. At some point she'd lost the rubber band holding it all back. She tugged at the object snarled into her hair, not surprised at all once she realized what it was: about two feet of yellowish, wiry vine.

She knew where she'd seen this before. All she had to do was look down at the frame of the door in the floor to see the same vine, etched into the concrete.

"Oh, why not," she muttered, and used the bit of vine to tie her hair back. She pulled it into a nice strong knot, while Anna looked up at her with eyes wide.

"Thanks," Melissa said, feeling suddenly calmer after her outburst with Smoot, just as Dun grunted below them: *Got it.*

She stepped back in the crowded shed and watched Dun's pale white hands, with Herschel's chocolate brown hands and Julio's dark tan hands, lift the thick concrete door away from its vine-decorated frame in the floor. The three men swung it up and back on hidden, silently working hinges. The room filled with the oily smell of machinery and dust and something underneath, something more biting, like sulfur. Only darkness could be seen on the other side of that door.

"So," Herschel said, pushing up his glasses as he looked around the crowded shed with a crooked smile. "Who wants to go first?"

✧

It's a shame, really, Melissa thought, down on one knee and squinting through the open door in the dirt floor. The two people who would have enjoyed seeing this the most aren't here.

This portal reminded her of the stories that Gil and Noah shared, but only with each other, not with her. She hoped Gil hadn't at some point made Noah promise not to tell her about the Prince with one eye and his gang—some mix of Robin Hood and his merry band along with a generous helping of Tolkien and Dungeons and Dragons, she figured. Maybe they thought she wouldn't understand, or wasn't interested. That thought stung her.

"Where's it go?" a small voice whispered from next to her, and Melissa felt a sudden rush, thinking of Noah. It was Anna, with her brother Cristobal squeezing in next to her.

"Can we go down there, Missus Anderson?" Cris chimed in.

"Hold on one second," Melissa said, pulling out the crumpled map and the slim book she'd grabbed from Ray's trailer and promptly forgotten about, thanks to Smoot and this portal.

The book was a battered day planner, paper-clipped open to two pages halfway through the year: yesterday on the left and today on the right. Yesterday had thick black lines running across it, one for each hour of the day, while today only had black lines running up to ten a.m. Flipping backward, all the previous days were blacked out in the same way. Going forwards, the future was blank and white, no appointments or birthdays or anything else. She tossed it to Dun for his eagle-eyed inspection.

The wrinkled, smeared map was more enlightening. Scribbled on the backs of the taped-together wrappers from cans of tomato soup—apparently Ray couldn't afford regular paper—the map was composed of hash marks, scratch-outs, and wandering lines made in thick black Sharpie ink. Encircling the outer rim of the map was a thick black line that could've been a highway or a river, but nothing was labeled in the normal fashion. Instead, short little bits of nonsense marked each landmark.

Pointing to a sloppy drawing of a triangle-roofed, windowless tower: "The Dragon watches over them here, from her tower full of flat panels."

Next to a winding road ending in a question mark: "Only the men in blue pickups know all the routes."

And, most disturbing of all, the label for a black pit: "The Gardener plots revenge from the bottom up, kids and all."

"Who's this Gardener?" Dun said from the corner of the shed. Melissa figured he'd been looking at the map as well, but he was pointing to the first page of the day planner on the floor next to him. He held the small dog figurine (still flecked with dirt) in his other hand. "We got a phone number and an email address. *Gardener1 at gmail dot com*. What the hell?"

"Local number?" Melissa asked, inhaling a mix of tomato soup from the map and burning motor oil from the open portal at her feet. The portal was slowly polluting the air of the shed.

"Can't make out the area code," Dun said. He held the book up to his face, which now held an oversized pair of black-framed reading glasses. His brown eyes were big as a fish's. "He blacked it out, just like everything else. Think it's 919, but I'm not betting on it."

Melissa passed the map to Anna and Cris and pulled out her cell phone. The little oak tree came out with it, and she gripped it tight, face growing again hot as she flipped open the phone.

"Read the number to me, would you?"

With a quick glance at the others surrounding her—Billie and Mary Jane and Mariana had pushed their way into the shed as well, so all the members of the search party were here—Melissa punched in the numbers that Dun read from Ray's little blacked-out book and hit SEND.

As she waited for the connection to pick up, listening to a series of clicks and soft beeps, she heard Smoot suck in air for another of his patented sighs. He shut his mouth with an almost audible snap when Melissa turned on him. Everyone else settled back, in no hurry to go through that gaping hole in the floor, content to wait for her to make her call.

At last, the phone began to ring on the other end, a buzzing beacon inside a fog cloud of static. Melissa squeezed the tree in her other hand tight, thinking of her vision from earlier that day—or was it yesterday? Or a week ago now? Time was all distorted and stretched. The tiny voice, calling out for help. The oak bursting into flames that turned the forest orange. The sense of wrongness pervading everything like a stomach virus. Melissa caught herself reaching for her lower belly, where her caesarian scar had suddenly flared up with a burning itch.

How would that look, she thought as she counted the fifth and sixth buzz on the other end of the static-filled line, me making a call on my cell and scratching my belly with Mister F-T's carved tree?

Voicemail should've picked up by now, but Melissa made herself wait a few more rings. On the thirteenth buzz, someone answered with a burst of white noise.

"This better be a misdial, Ray," a hard voice said, more annoyed than angry. Melissa could barely make it out through the rolling waves of static.

I guess she doesn't have Caller ID, Melissa thought, a thrill of power filling her like a shock. They were finally getting somewhere!

"We're calling on behalf of Ray Unger from Chatham County," she said as she hit the tiny speaker button on her cell so everyone else could hear who she was talking to. "He sends his regards, but he can't make it to the phone right now."

"I'm hanging up," the irritated female voice said. Melissa was talking fast even as she saw Mary Jane and Billie exchange a shocked look.

"That would not be a good idea," Melissa said. She held up a hand for silence in the shed. "Not while your friend Ray is here, incapacitated. We found your number as his emergency contact. They just took him away in the ambulance. His lungs, I'm sorry to be so blunt, but—they failed."

"Impossible," the woman said.

Melissa was about to continue with her ad hoc story, but the woman's response tripped her up. She needed to keep the woman talking; Billie and Mary Jane seemed to recognize her. But static was eating up the line, along with a low buzzing that didn't come from the phone, but the black ball in Julio's hands.

"You tell Ray, that dog-lover and traitor, that I've still got my tendrils in him. A puppet like him makes no move without the puppeteer. Call this number again and I'll show you what I mean."

The static was cut off as the line went dead.

"That was . . . interesting," Dun said, rubbing his beard. Melissa imagined him going through a mental transcript of the brief conversation. "Nice story there, about Ray. Didn't seem too worried about him, did she?"

Melissa shook her head, thinking of Ray with vines poking through his legs and arms, forcing him to move this way and that, gasping and wheezing the whole time. He'd shown up awfully conveniently this morning, right after had Gil walked away from her.

"Thought the big C got her," Billie was whispering to Mary Jane behind her. "Couldn't have been her—"

"Who?" Melissa said. The shed allowed for no secrets. Despite the static and the woman on the phone's angry, almost imperial tone, she'd felt a twinge of familiarity as well. A voice from a while back, with a Southern accent softening the hard words.

"It just all went by so fast," Mary Jane said.

"Make an educated guess," Melissa said.

"Sounded like Francine," Billie said, inching closer to Mary Jane in a protective way. "You know, the lady who used to live on your place. The Finley-Thompsons."

Melissa almost dropped the tiny oak tree pressing against the inside of her fingers. "Really?" She tried to match the voice from the phone with the face of the woman she'd last seen over five years ago, eating barbecue. "You know, I think you're right. She was just so . . . soft-spoken when I met her. But that was a long time ago."

You tell Ray, that dog-lover and traitor—

Someone snapped their fingers behind her.

"It *was* her," Smoot said. "I heard her talking in that tone of voice pretty often, a couple years back. Don't remember her as much of a gardener, though. The place was pretty wild and overgrown back then. Wonder what the hell she's up to these days."

Melissa met the gaze of each of the other people surrounding her as they waited for her or someone else to try and answer Smoot's question. Their expressions ranged from shocked and shaken to exhilarated, while Dun and Herschel simply looked exhausted and beaten. Herschel kept rubbing his bad arm, while Dun didn't seem to be able to let go of the open door—portal—at his feet.

"I think it's safe to say that Ray can't be trusted," she began. "If we run into him down there, please let me talk to him first."

"Down *there*?" Mariana said, pulling on her braided hair unconsciously. "You are really going down there?"

"I think we have to. *I* have to. If anyone else wants to come along, they're welcome. But only if you want to. I won't hold it against anyone if they decide to walk away right now."

Mariana seemed quite interested in that option. She was already pulling Cris away from the door in the floor and out of the shed. Melissa caught the look shared between Mariana and Julio, and saw him nod and lift the black ball in his hands a tiny bit. The ball buzzed in response.

"I can wait here . . . " Mariana trailed off, glancing outside. "Maybe we should wait back at the farm. In case Noah shows up?"

"That's actually a great idea," Melissa said, just as Herschel and Dun crawled closer to the rim of the portal. These two old men were seriously going to do this.

"Mary Jane will stay with you too," Billie said. Mary Jane started to put up a fight, but then she simply smiled, not hiding her relief well, and stepped closer to Mariana and the kids.

"Anna," Mariana began. "Come with us, please."

"Just wait, guys," Melissa called out, but Dun had already slipped through the narrow door. She watched his white head disappear with a small popping sound. Herschel squeezed through the opening after him a moment later.

I should've gone first, Melissa thought, stepping toward the door while Julio blew his wife and kids a kiss and simply stepped into the opening and dropped. The sudden cessation of the buzzing from the black sphere distracted Melissa for a moment, just as Julio's daughter slipped past her and followed him through the portal.

"Anna!" Mariana cried, holding tight to her son Cris. "No no no!"

"We'll get her back up here," Billie said, jumping into action and filling Melissa with shame.

I could've caught her, she thought. Grabbed her on her way past me.

Billie elbowed Smoot out of the way so she could ease herself down through the portal. "Love you, MJ," she called as her lower half disappeared. "See you soon."

Then it was just the three remainders who had chosen to stay aboveground, staring at Melissa and Smoot.

"After you?" Smoot said. His wide face was red, and he was sweating and mouth-breathing again. "Ladies first?"

"You don't have to come along, Smoot."

"And miss out on seeing what sort of funhouse might be down there? If this is gonna be my land someday, I consider this time well spent."

Melissa ignored his jab and turned to Mariana.

"Take care of her," Mariana whispered, holding onto Cris with all her strength. Melissa could see the turmoil on her friend's face; she knew Mariana wanted to go after Anna, but she wasn't willing to also send her youngest into the portal—a doorway Mariana looked at like a den of copperheads.

Cris kept saying "I wanna go, I wanna *go*, Mama."

"Thank you for staying," Melissa said. "You be careful, too. Call me if they come back."

She waited and watched Smoot fit his bulk carefully into the open doorway. A second later, he disappeared with a popping sound. No way was she going to go before him and leave him at her back again. Not at this point in this little adventure. She could just see him slamming the door on her and striding back to their farm to try to commandeer it.

"Mariana, you may want to close this door behind us. Just to be safe."

With the small oak tree still tight in her left hand, armed only with a cell phone and her determination, Melissa gazed into the blackness of the doorway and nearly lost her courage. But the others were already down there, she reminded herself. Maybe this blackness was just like one-way mirrors, some optical illusion of depth and nothingness, and she'd end up in some cramped root cellar or something.

She sat down, the back of her thighs touching the cool concrete vines of the frame. She half-expected icy fingers to cover her bare legs as she let her feet drop into the void.

"Good luck," Billie whispered.

"Wanna *go*," Cris insisted.

Melissa turned and met Mariana's eyes for a moment. The look of fear and loss there was aging her, calling up wrinkles around her eyes and mouth.

"We'll get our kids back soon," she told Mariana. "Anna and Noah and—" she stopped herself with a sudden jerking sensation, as if the chain attached to her heart had been pulled tight.

I was about to say her name, she thought. Good Lord.

"We'll find them," she added, with as much confidence in herself as she could muster.

And then Melissa let herself drop through the opening and into the nothingness on the other side of this impossible portal.

CHAPTER FIFTEEN:
SOME STORIES JUST DO NOT HAVE HAPPY ENDINGS

The best stories always begin like this: our hero, tired, grimy, and all alone in a bizarre place—preferable a castle or a desert or a forest or a tower—in the middle of a strange, unfamiliar land, facing a person or a creature or some other challenge that's bigger and stronger than him; and our hero's courage never fades, not even for a tiny moment.

Prince One-Eye stared at the tail-less dragon perched in front of him at the bottom of this haunted, noisy tower and imagined for a moment that he was sitting around a fire, listening to the King belch his way through a story just like this after too many belts of his favorite black beer. The thought made him smile, even as a series of portals clanged shut in the hall behind him, one after the other, like stricken wooden soldiers falling to the floor.

"Why didn't you tell me you were a dragon, Alexander?"

The injured dragon made a scoffing sound that filled the tiny room with smoke darker than any cooking fire in the Black Hoods' forest encampments. The beast's long body now filled the alcove, its brilliant blue eyes wide as windows, staring down at the Prince.

"Never asked me, mate," the dragon said with another coughing scoff. "Too busy pulling off me tail, weren't you?"

"But that was when you were the size of my finger."

"So that makes it all right, now, does it?"

This conversation was going downhill already, the Prince thought. His empty eye socket ached, just like it always did when he was thinking fast. I could back up and try my luck leaping through one of those doors behind me, or I could shimmy up that ladder to get away from this beast that was once small enough to fit in my pocket. Alexander now was much too big to fit through the hole cut in the ceiling of this alcove.

Or, the Prince thought, I could take my chances talking to him right here. Maybe he'll remember how I saved him from that troll boy down at the entrance to this tower.

"Sorry about that tail incident, friend," he said, slipping his hands into his pockets, searching for that lost salamander body part, hoping maybe he'd just missed it earlier. No luck. "I fully intend to return that to you, as soon as I can."

Alexander puffed hot smoke in his face, and the green-gray smoke filled the alcove, making the Prince want to cough.

I guess I deserved that, he thought, pinching off as best he could the tickle in his throat from the dragon's breath. Can't show a hint of weakness to a dragon.

And then a thought hit him, something he knew was true.

"My father. He'll give you your tail back."

"Oh will he now? Do I have your word on that, Prince?"

"Yes." The Prince squinted shut his good eye, imagining the king, armed with sword and dragon tail, striding through the dungeon and into this tower. "He has it, I'm sure of it. I just . . . I didn't think it would just come off like that," the Prince added.

"Aye," said the black and green dragon, wrapping his gray wings around his chest. He leaned closer to the Prince, and One-Eye did his best not to flinch away. "Yer a quick fella. Nobody's snagged me tail in ages. Which is what brings us to this place." Alexander flicked his head up at the ceiling, nearly scraping his flared nostrils on it. "Want to go up and see her?"

"Who?"

"Go on, no more questions. I got an entrance to guard. You've been granted permission. So go, eh? Before she changes her mind."

The dragon moved his narrow, pointy green-and-black head in the Prince's direction, and this time One-Eye *did* flinch. He scooted away from the oncoming teeth and smoky nostrils and leaped up onto the ladder. The ropes cut into his hand, but he didn't stop climbing until he had squeezed through the round hole cut in the ceiling.

I'll get your tail back, he thought, not daring to speak his thoughts aloud. Father surely had the tail; of this fact in the narrative, the Prince had not a doubt.

Though he didn't like the idea of turning his back on a dragon that he owed something to, he continued climbing upwards.

After pulling himself up thirty rope rungs, he risked a look around him. He was in a vertical tube of rock, and high above him was a smoky, flickering orange light. This tower hadn't looked this tall from the outside. Nothing seemed to stay the same size down here in this gray underground world that he'd found himself in this morning.

He thought about the huge pine tree he'd climbed just yesterday—an eternity ago!—to escape that den of where-cats. That tree didn't seem as tall as this shaft. And the Prince knew that it wasn't a full moon waiting for him at the top as it had been in the pine. He could smell the sulfur already.

He didn't understand how or why—usually at the start of a new day—he would sometimes found himself in another place outside his father's kingdom. But he'd grown used to the abrupt movements from one land to another, sometimes in the same day. Occasionally he was alone, other times he was with his band of misfit heroes. He'd braced himself for the constant, but always unexpected shiftings of his life long ago.

Wish you were here, Black Hoods, he thought. You're going to miss all the fun. And what a story this will make.

Sweating freely now, his long-knife loose in its pocket hilt, Prince One-Eye popped up out of the hole at the top of the ladder tube and leapt into the impossibly large room at the top of the tower. As soon as he hit the floor he ducked and rolled away from the hole, dodging a white-hot blast of fire exploding next to him. He scrambled for cover behind a chest of overflowing gold doubloons, tripping over a bag of diamonds and a shiny suit of chain mail.

"Welcome to my humble abode," a soft voice whispered in his ears.

Prince One-Eye stopped trying to hide and looked up. A green-scaled dragon filled the entire far half of the cave, her gray, barbed wings tight against the slope of the peaked tower roof, but her size wasn't what had frozen him. It was her voice. She had a voice as sweet as the Queen, Prince One-Eye's mother.

༄

The Prince had some experience with dragons; they were actually his best adventures, and many young boys and girls would clamor for a One-Eye versus a dragon tale before heading off to the dreamlands for the night. So he knew he had to choose his words carefully, here in the crowded top of this tower. He went to one knee and spoke to her as sweetly as he could, even though he was nearly panting for air.

"I beg forgiveness, milady. I was directed here by your steadfast guardian, below. I do not wish to impose on your Excellency."

The dragon only smiled at him, each gleaming white tooth as tall as the slamming doors now far below him. She leaned back and rested her shining, clawed front paws on her pink belly. The piles of gold, jewels, and precious metals crinkled and crunched to adjust to her weight.

The Prince risked a look around. The round room was packed with chests and trunks overflowing with riches, and the floor was littered with loose coins and scattered rubies. But unlike most dens of dragons he'd seen in his life, the walls bore no dusty tapestries or priceless artwork. The walls were smooth, black, and unadorned.

"You admire my riches? I trust you did not come here to borrow a few trinkets?"

The Prince forced himself to look up at the dragon's glowing orange eyes. He'd seen jewels and gold coins before. A dragon this size, however, was a new experience.

"Of course not, milady. I'm here to save my kingdom."

Not until he said the words did the Prince realize how important his quest had become. His father's land would die if he didn't stop the poisonous black river trickling up out of here and spreading to the lands above.

"Your *kingdom*. So you're a king, are you? What might be your name?"

"I'm just a Prince, milady. Prince One-Eye," he added, tugging at his leather eye patch, wanting to tell her this quite badly. He realized, too late, of course, that you were never supposed to tell a dragon your name.

"Prince One-Eye. A lovely name. That is, a lovely *nickname*."

"Oh," he added, figuring the truth couldn't hurt him now, "and I want you to know. I'll help your friend down there get his tail back. That was, ah, sort of my fault, you see. But I lost the tail. For now."

The dragon answered with a quick puff of smoke from each nostril. He'd made her laugh. The Prince felt his courage inflate, and he took a step closer and pressed on, his curiosity getting the best of him.

"Milady. Why would a dragon as wondrous and powerful as you need all those doors in your tower?"

"Ah, you noble, chivalrous Prince. Such sweet talk. You have been trained well. Your mother would be proud."

The Prince smiled, but on the inside he was wincing. Mother, her Highness the Queen, had barely spoken to him in the past few months, ever since she learned of how he'd been slipping away from the castle to take part in the adventures of the Black Hoods. If she ever found out I was now *leading* the Black Hoods, I'd most likely not be a Prince anymore. Not even Dad's best explanation would be able fix that.

"I see I have struck a chord in you, my young knight. Please, let us not despair. I have much to show you. The doors I will explain in due time. But first," she said, lifting one razor-sharp claw on her left hand and pointing it at the wall to the Prince's right. "First, I want to show you something."

With a strange word that was somewhere between a dragon sneeze and a choking sound, the dragon threw a light blue spark across the room that hit the black wall with a sizzling sound. The wall shimmered, and then the blackness was replaced by a window.

"Let me show you the lost children of this Undercity, my Prince."

One-Eye saw a young boy in one of the flickering images, the youngster wearing short pants and a too-thin shirt, jumping across a blackened trickle of a stream at the edge of an overgrown forest. Easily two dozen, now three dozen images spread out and overlapped on the stone, each an image of a young child, alone, in varying stages of panic, excitement, fear, and devilment.

He looked away from the hypnotic series of images on the wall and saw the dragon begin to shift next to him. After just two blinks of his surprised, tired eyes, the Prince saw that the dragon had shrunk down to the size of a horse. Walking easily on her back paws, the dragon winked at the Prince and beckoned for him to follow her over to the images taking shape on the wall. She grew smaller with each passing moment.

What madness is this? he wondered, looking from the shrunken dragon to the multiple images forming on the wall.

"These," the dragon said, crawling up the Prince's leg and side until she made it up onto his shoulder, "are my lost children. I watch them and track their progress. Most of them end up here, eventually. To the top of this tower."

The Prince barely heard her. He was caught up in the image of a small blonde-haired girl, alone, walking through a gray neighborhood made up of dusty houses and barren lawns, on her way to a run-down old park. She was crying and walking fast. He saw an admirable determination in her short, fast strides.

"We have all been lost, once," the dragon whispered in his ear. "Some of us by no fault of our own. But now I can no longer reach them, to comfort them and guide them through my land. Someone has meddled in my duties."

The Prince couldn't get a good look at the dragon now, perched as she was on his shoulder, but he could feel her hot breath on his neck. Her tiny claws dug into his shoulders though his thick leather shirt, reminding him of how sharp those talons really were. A chill ran down his back.

We have all been lost, once.

"Who is she?" he whispered, nodding at the blonde-haired girl. She had stopped next to the roped-off section of a park where none of the swings or sand boxes were occupied. On the other side of the rope was a black river, growing wider with each passing second, just as the dragon had shrunk over time, until the water was too wide to see across. The Prince stepped closer to the wall, unable to believe what he was seeing.

He knew that girl.

At that moment, a misshapen shadow took shape on the dead grass in front of the girl. Trapped by the widening, pitch-black river in front of her, with no place else to go, she looked up with tearstained fear before the image of her winked out.

"What did you do?" the Prince demanded, his chest aching with fear and now anger.

"That is all I can show you of her, for now, my Prince," the dragon purred, smiling with a painful brightness, though she seemed lighter, somehow, and her voice held a tinge of tiredness. She flew off his shoulder and landed on a pile of silver coins. "You need food and rest from your travels. Perhaps, once you've recovered, we can watch more."

"Was that happening right now? Is this wall some sort of crystal ball?" The Prince knew he was using the wrong tone with the dragon, risking his life by addressing her so directly like this, but he'd never enjoyed seeing children suffer.

The dragon made no verbal answer, but her size and smoky breath were returning. She crunched across her gathered piles of gold and gems and began scratching in her nest like a dog digging for a bone. Soon she was bigger than a house again.

"Answer me, please," the Prince said, gaining control of his voice nearly too late to lessen the sound of his command. He was tempted to reach for his long-knife so he could feel its weight in his hand, but he knew he'd be just a mosquito trying to bite the dragon's hide. Violence was useless in this part of his story, and he needed her to tell him about those children.

Keeping his good eye on the dragon, who was huge once more, the Prince remembered something he'd been trying not to think about for ages. A digging dog. And a crystal ball.

As the dragon settled back into her torn-up piles of riches with a small groan, opening up her wings once and then wrapping them around herself again like a massive gray shawl—all the while never taking her glowing orange eyes off him—the Prince remembered striking his wolfhound out in the courtyard of the castle. Not for digging a three-foot gouge into the royal grass, but for not giving up what the shaggy beast had dug up in that hole.

For a strange, dislocating second, the image of his big gray wolfhound back at the castle was replaced by that of a fat, dark brown dog half the size of the wolfhound. The round dog was also digging in the ground, but in a place nothing like the castle grounds. Then the image of his wolfhound, jokingly named Daisy, returned.

Buried in a shoddy bag, the black object Daisy had dug up was round as a river stone, smoothed by years of water rolling over it, but with fine lines etched into it. He'd seen crystal balls before in distant lands—they were banned from the Queen's sight, so never had he seen one in this kingdom—but this black orb was the opposite of crystal.

When the hunting dog wouldn't give it up, the Prince had struck Daisy, repeatedly, and would've drawn a weapon on the growling dog if the King hadn't intervened. One of the King's workers had taken the ball from Daisy, ending up with a pair of bites on each hand. After his father had taken possession of the ball, the Prince only saw the strange orb once more before being forced to put it out of his mind.

He'd seen it in the hands of his mother the Queen. And it had done something to her. Changed her, in some way.

"Prince One-Eye," the dragon said from across the room, which seemed much smaller now that she was so much bigger again. Her voice was soft, almost gentle. "Surely that's not your real name. Tell me your *real* name, Prince."

The Prince wiped a traitorous tear from his eye as one by one, the images of the lost children flickered out of existence, leaving only black walls again. He was already forgetting the image of the young girl he'd seen. Had her hair been curly or straight? Dark or blonde? Whoever she was, he'd never get to know what happened to her, and it was breaking his heart. Far below them, a door slammed shut, once, twice, three times.

Noah.

Tell her your real name.

It's Noah.

He thought of his mother, the Queen, lit up with a sickly green light, her eyes wide with wonder and something else. Some emotion he couldn't quite understand.

We have all been lost, once.

Noah.

"That *is* my name," he whispered. "I'm the Prince. Prince One-Eye."

∽o∽

Some stories just did not have happy endings, no matter how hard Dad tried to save them, and those were the tales that he wished his father had never started.

This story was turning out to be one of those.

Everything got shaky when he was scared, and he always ended up thinking about other bad things from the past, making it even worse.

Today he'd not only remembered Dad saying the f-word to someone in the forest a while back, but he'd also remembered his mother, on the day she kept trying to figure out that black ball. The dragon had made him think of that day—what else would he remember today that he didn't want to?

He'd been playing in the fort he'd made, an old, flattened box from the new refrigerator covering the ground and all his best treasures and books within easy reach, when he'd heard Mom's footsteps above him. He knew it was her right away by the quick, light sounds her feet made on the wood above him.

He peeked through the special gap in the boards over his head and saw her with the ball in her hand. She held it out to old Mr. Herschel and asked him about it, explaining how she'd found it under some junk in the shed. But the old man wouldn't touch it, and he limped away as fast as he could.

The other old guy set down his pan of snap peas and asked Mom if he could hold it. Dun, everyone called him, but Noah rarely spoke to him. The guy was always watching him, like he was waiting for Noah to misbehave.

"Saw one of these once at a crack house outside Durham," Dun said, holding it up to his gray, wrinkled face like it was an apple and he was going to take a big bite. "Damnedest thing. Heavy. Think if you rub it the right way, it gives off some—Damn!"

Noah had been inching away from the gap in the flooring above him, not liking the sound of Dun's voice so close to him, when the green light spilled from the porch down onto him.

"Give it to me!" Mom had shouted, in a voice that Noah only heard when she was really angry. "Drop it, Dun!"

Above him, Mom took two fast steps closer to the old man, and then the porch above him went silent. Scary silent.

Noah peeked up and saw Mom holding the black ball up to her chest. The ball had turned bright green in her hands, covering her in its strange light, making her look like some kind of Martian from the covers of the old crinkly books Dad was always reading, but her green skin didn't bother Noah so much as the look on his mother's face.

She was smiling and looking down at the ball with a look of surprise, but also with a look that Noah hadn't seen in a long time. Not like this. Mom was looking down at the ball as if it were her favorite dessert, and she was going to eat every last bit of it herself, with ice cream. She was making a soft laughing sound with her mouth that gave Noah goosebumps.

"Mommy," he whispered, unable to stop himself as tears squirted from his eyes. "Mommy, stop it."

Mom's eyes widened as she started lifting the ball closer to her face, and then she finally blinked.

"Noah?"

The ball fell from her shaking hands. It hit the porch with a deafening thud right above Noah's head. Noah ducked and held his breath as it rolled off the porch. From the sound of it, the ball had landed in the grass next to the steps and then rolled downhill.

"What did you see?" Dun asked after a few seconds of silence. "Did you have a vision of the future, or something?"

Noah had clapped both dirty hands over his mouth, scared that he'd hurt Mom somehow by trying to talk to her. Hot tears spilled over his fingers, creating tiny rivers that cut through the dust and dirt on his hands.

"I think I need to go lie down for a little bit."

"Better do some research about that thing," Dun muttered as Mom walked off the porch. "Where'd you find it, anyway?" he called, grunting his way down the steps toward the discarded ball, but Mom was already in the house.

Noah had slipped closer to the crack to try and see more, but all he saw was Dun standing over the ball, rubbing his beard and shaking his head. He gave a decisive fart before he shuffled away down the gravel road toward the barn.

Noah was about to scoot out through the gap under the porch and try to find Mom when he saw a shadow hit the lattice in front of him. He held his breath and peeked out once more, this time at the front of the porch.

Julio stood there, alone as far as Noah could tell, and he held the black ball in his hand. He was staring at it, shaking his head as if he were disappointed with it, or maybe with Mom. Noah waited for the ball to turn green again, but all that happened was that Julio jumped and looked around suddenly, as if someone had walked up behind him and gave him a spark shock.

After looking around suddenly as if to make sure he really was alone, Julio swore a couple good words in Spanish, words he'd taught Dad and Noah a long time ago, when Mom wasn't around. Then he wrapped up the ball in his T-shirt and staggered off to his trailer, walking like the ball weighed a hundred pounds. Maybe two hundred. Noah never saw that ball again.

∽᳃∾

"My Prince, is that your friend down there," a soft voice said, knocking him out of his remembering, "making all that noise?"

The Prince took a quick breath and heard a horrible yowling sound, like a where-cat in the middle of night, looking for a fight or food. *Worse* than a where-cat.

"Elwood?"

From below them in the tower, doors began to slam, as if from closest to farthest. The loud explosions became softer, until they were almost too soft to hear. The Prince thought of falling dominoes. Boom boom boom on down the line until they reached the front gate, where he imagined Elwood sitting, licking dust off his big paws. Then the slamming came back, in reverse.

When the closest door below him slammed, Prince One-Eye made a move toward the ladder leading down.

"Slow down, there, Prince," the dragon said with a laugh in her voice.

Mommy, the Prince thought.

"Where do you think you're going?"

"I've got to go get my friend. We've got a job to do, ma'am."

The dragon was growing again, stretching and inflating like a balloon connected to one of those big gray tanks in the party store. Her green and black tail stretched out in front of him until it covered the opening to the hole leading down into the house of slamming doors. Elwood hollered even louder, far below them.

"I'm afraid your days of adventuring are over, son," the dragon said, blocking off the only exit. "You see, I need you here, along with the rest of the children. I don't want you to go and get lost again. I have a job for you, my Prince. A *quest.*"

As smoke and orange light filled the room at the top of this house, sending bright sparks off the gathered bits of glass (not jewels) and faded brown pennies (not golden coins), the Prince took a step back, feeling his courage evaporate.

Too much, he thought. I'm not a brave prince. I can't keep pretending I'm not scared. I want to *leave* this place.

He needed to get to Elwood, who was still howling far below them. He hoped the big cat wasn't hurt, but he had to admit that his reasons for wanting to get down to Elwood were more selfish than that—he simply didn't want to be alone like this anymore. But this dragon wouldn't let him.

Some hero I am, Noah thought, unable to move closer to the hole covered by the dragon's tail and attempt an escape to aid his four-legged friend. If Dad was telling me this story behind the counter of his store, with his old music playing all around us, I would've already asked him to stop and start over with a new one. One with a much better ending than this.

CHAPTER SIXTEEN:
WAITING FOR THE TOUR TO BEGIN AGAIN

He'd been driving for what felt like hours, through a flat suburbia of crooked houses and empty lots, following a white-grey strip of unforgiving concrete, yet during that time, he came across precious little that was familiar from his dreams. The only consistent feature was the blur of distorted cities followed by gaping, swelling landscapes speeding past his open car window, and the stink of burnt oil filling his nostrils. The dirty wind, warm as always—like the bad light, one of the few details that had matched his dreams— had dried his clothes and evaporated the last bit of moisture from his ankles, which heralded the return of the heinous itching from his don't-ask-how-many chigger bites.

Gil wasn't surprised that he didn't recognize this stretch of the Undercity. For one thing, this house-littered road he currently found himself traversing was much too straight. For as far as he could see ahead of him in the bad light, the damn thing never turned. Every other Undercity road he'd ever driven upon had been twisty as a pretzel, many of them turning back on themselves or hitting a hairpin turn with no warning.

So he drove, panic filling his mouth with greasy bile as the landscape began to close in on him; the purple-tinted mountains he remembered from too many interrupted nights were approaching straight ahead. He peered at the bluffs forming, big outcroppings of rock that started to replace houses in a random pattern. Familiar houses, twisted in nightmare dimensions that Gil chose not to look at too closely.

And just ahead of him, where the houses dropped away from the road, was a stoplight. Finally, he thought, an honest-to-goodness intersection. He rubbed the heel of his bare right foot against his itching left ankle—felt so good!—and pressed the brake, itching instead of downshifting, and something clicked. This intersection, the rocky outcropping, the twisting road that met this ruler-straight, unfamiliar road. He'd been here before. He must've approached this intersection from that intersecting road in a dream, and hitting the green light in his sleep, he'd never even stopped to look around.

Of course the stoplight was red for him, and though he'd yet to see another moving vehicle down here since climbing into the old Escort once more, Gil actually let his coughing old car come to a rest right at the white line. Safety first, and all that.

Now. Left or right?

He sat there in the driver's seat, itching and idling in front of the dust-flecked traffic light, which wasn't suspended from wires stretched across poles set into the ground, but hung instead from a single wire attached somewhere high above the road.

Made perfect sense, Gil thought, down here in the Undercity. He couldn't remember ever seeing the sky in his dreams, but he could see something high above him that gave the illusion of open air. Part of him knew, though, that behind that haze of nothingness where the stoplight cable disappeared was a rough ceiling of vines, dirt, and tree roots. Above that, the real world, full of tainted water, encroaching McMansions, and speeding trucks flying down Jones Ferry Road.

In the glow of the red light, Gil contemplated the road leading off to the right, which led down a snaky course and into a wooded park area. That was where the busty ladies with their oversized strollers would walk, no doubt. To his left was an equally curvy road, leading up to the dark-painted houses built into the purple-black mountainside, like manor houses for billionaire cavemen. He'd driven around and around that neighborhood of one-way streets and tall iron gates just last week in his sleep.

Maybe all my dreams were some sort of training for this day, Gil thought as he sat waiting, hoping no garbage cans or dumpsters would break loose and come rolling his way. Maybe part of me knew something like this was going to happen all along.

Or maybe I really *am* going crazy, and this is all part of my final hoorah. Gil sighed. Crazy or not, so long as I find Noah, he thought, I don't care.

There was a con at work here, he figured. A fix. Someone stringing him along, bad as he'd done to his two buddies ways back in his sophomore year at Apex High. His first con. He'd made off with a months' worth of fast-food-job salaries from both Stan and Marty Pins after convincing them that their two starting guards on the basketball team were shaving points as part of a complex high school sports gambling ring. Gil was the middleman, or so Stan and Marty thought, placing the bets with their French-fried cash, skimming a good four hundred bucks off their losses for three games before Marty caught on and broke Gil's nose for it. Stan was more forgiving; he asked Gil to show him how to keep a straight face and be convincing, and they'd been tight ever since.

Those were the days. Gil had been trying to perfect the role of a grifter ever since, intoxicated and addicted by the rush of breaking rules. He just wanted that smoothness, that confidence. Making the easy money was secondary.

And now, look where all those hours of palming twenties, working the numbers, and outright lying got me. Sitting at the crossroads, no idea which way to turn. Was it my fault the Martys and the F-Ts of the world made it so damn easy?

At last, the light for the intersecting road turned from green to yellow. Gil could hear them click as they changed.

He gazed off to his left and saw distant cars moving down the road, and even a pedestrian or three. Civilization. He decided to take that road, figuring he'd be able to track Noah down better there than down in another forest. At least in that direction he'd be able to stop and question some of the people moving around in the area. Surely someone would know something.

When he looked back through his windshield, the stoplight facing him had clicked to green, his car was now leaning to the right, and a large, smelly man was sitting in his passenger seat.

"Despite rumors to the contrary," the man announced, "*nothing is amiss in the Undercity.*"

∽∘∾

Gil should have known that as part of this road trip, he'd end up taking on a passenger at some point. But he never could've predicted that he'd actually meet this man face-to-face.

When the man appeared, Gil nearly stood up in his seat, choking himself with the seat belt. He let the belt snap him back to his seat, then he pivoted and grabbed his passenger by the lapels of his smoking jacket.

"You son a bitch! Nothing's amiss? You about gave me a heart attack, how about that for amiss?"

When he didn't answer, Gil let go of the cool fabric of the other man's coat, nearly tearing it in the process, and bopped him in the sternum. His chest made an empty sound, like a metal barrel.

The big man sank back into his seat, his strangely pale eyes aimed straight ahead, a half-smile almost lost in the thick black goatee that took up a lot of real estate on his wide face. He looked as if he was waiting for the tour to begin again. Like he was on Pause.

Gil pulled back and just sat there, shaking and thinking, So *this* is what the Tour Guide to my Undercity dreams looked like.

"Been a while," Gil finally said. He gave his ankle a quick scratch without looking away. "I always figured you'd be older. Better groomed."

The Tour Guide sniffed at that, and cast his eyes down at the gear stick, as if to ask: Why aren't we moving?

"I get it. You don't talk unless the tour is underway, right? Okay, let's move out then."

Gil let out the clutch and aimed the car to the left, hoping the light wouldn't turn red on him again. This way had to be the best option; the trees in the valley down to the right surely had it in for him, as did all forests of late. He'd try his luck at finding Noah up this way.

"Not a great choice," the man next to him boomed, projecting his instantly recognizable voice as if he were at the front of a charter bus full of blue-hairs. "To the right offers endless insights into the history of our fine Undercity. Straight ahead, not so much. To the left, not at all. But please, be my guest. Continue along this path of yours as you choose."

"Asshole," Gil muttered, working hard to swing the car out of its left-hand trajectory and wheel it around a hundred degrees or so. "You could've just said 'Turn right.'"

Gil hoped one of the houses behind the curb in his peripheral vision hadn't transformed itself into a Mack truck rushing up the other road at him as his little car swerved and shimmied across the smooth concrete road. The light above them turned yellow.

The Tour Guide didn't respond, but made a simple "Hmmph" sound and held onto the dashboard with hairy hands, his thick fingers littered with silver and black rings embedded with red and blue stones. And then he began his tour.

∾oᴄ∾

"The initial losses in the Battle for the Undercity were the bridges. When the first bridge over the river collapsed, the wires of the suspension's supports snapping like straws, the elders blamed it on our enemies from above. They claimed it was yet another covert attack meant to break our people's spirits. If only the explanation were as simple as that."

Gil nodded along with the Tour Guide's words to keep his eyes from rolling. Always a good story with this guy, though he had to admit, being with him in person left a little something to be desired. His breath, for one. Gil didn't *want* to know what the guy had been eating recently. And something about his weight, even though he didn't look all that much bigger than Gil, was making his car lean to the right, throwing off the handling of this finely tuned automobile.

And he could've used some help with the handling of his car on this twisty strip of narrow road, a sharp contrast to the road he'd just been on. He'd already lost all sense of direction as they swerved their way down from the bluffs and into the moister, cooler air of the valley.

"*Insurgents*, they called them. Insurgents had to be the cause of the destruction: lone attackers slipping inside our border, bent on uncovering the mysteries of our fair city, and then stealing away again after cutting off any chance of pursuit. Why, just there off to the left you can see the grassy park where once stood our proudest cathedral, burned to the ground, no doubt by a foreign guerilla (or so we all thought). A horrible loss, but the new park built on its remains has indeed entertained its fair share of children."

Gil's shallow breathing hitched at that. He looked off to the left, quickly, following the angle made by the Guide's pointing finger. He was afraid to tear his gaze from the untrustworthy road ahead, but he was unable *not* to look. He saw no children playing in the converted park, no little blonde girls wandering alone.

He couldn't imagine any sort of Undercity church ever sitting there instead of the rows of swings and clusters of slides, all situated around oak trees wide as his car. He didn't dare think of what sort of religions were practiced down here. Reaching down, he scratched his left ankle, then the right.

"But then the engineers and scientists got involved, and we learned the true culprit of the devastation of our conduits over the river. So many of us were wrong." The Tour Guide sighed, a slow, smelly puff of air polluting the interior of Gil's car. He could tell the man was pleased with himself. "Ah. Ahead of us you'll see the mansion for the leading scientist of our time, the one with the palindromic first and last name. Please note the burnished metal siding on the third and fourth stories, and the plethora of cupolas and arches at the roofline. He considered himself a retro architect, but many simply considered him mad."

This was never going to end, Gil thought as the Tour Guide shifted in his seat with a scuffling sound. But every building, every alleyway, every dented gray motorbike—all of it was matching up with the burned-in memories from his dreams, easing some of the panic dammed up in his mind. He didn't dare reach down to touch the tiny throbbing bites on his ankles, not any more. They were getting close, he could feel it.

"But back to the history," the Tour Guide said, working up to his crescendo like an orchestra conductor. "Weeks, then months passed, and more of the bridges fell. The defenses to the Undercity were checked and fortified, though we were cut off and isolated, and our beastly protector had vanished. Ah, City Hall up on our right now. And after the final round of testing, deep in the labs without windows, the scientists made their verdict. We weren't under attack from above, but a battle was indeed underway. The most sinister sort of enemy was at work. For it was the water of the Undercity itself that was killing our bridges."

"The water," Gil repeated, feeling his skin turn cold. Bad water—a farmer's worst enemy. An enemy he'd been an unwilling host to on his land for the entire growing season this year.

High above, the lights began to fade again. Gil squinted through the grayness, easing his foot off the accelerator in this deserted borough of the city, then slamming on the brakes. He nearly stopped too late. He'd found the first ruined bridge.

You don't really appreciate the sight of true devastation until you have it pressed up right in front of you like this. You can really appreciate the details, like the broken timbers splintered like toothpicks from the rupturing of the bridge's infrastructure. You can stop and think about how that thick slab of wood, now broken, was once a tree pushing its way out from the ground, gentle but insistent, adding more and more layers with each passing year. And the bent and rusting metal that had once been shaped and assembled by welders. And the vast emptiness of the whole structure, how nothing but dead air now hangs where a bridge once stood, moving people from here to there without any apparent effort.

Gil wanted to get out and examine the bridge more, but the Tour Guide's cold hand kept him from pulling open the door. Good thing, too. Gil's side of the car was edged right up to the drop-off leading down to the river. That first step, Doc, it's a doozy.

Gil wanted to throw the car into reverse and back the hell out of here, but the immense nothingness of the missing bridge made something catch in his chest. Or maybe it was the now-familiar dust and tar odor of the narrow black river below them that was causing his palpitations. He'd seen water like this before, less than half a day ago.

The light faded even more, painting brown shadows on every object that stuck up from the river bank—bone-white tree trunks, rusted wheels, jagged flat-tire rubber, and unidentifiable bits of misshapen rot. More garbage, everywhere he looked, and the river seemed to be reaching up for it, spreading its diseased fingers up into the banks. What seemed at first to just be a trickle of a river had become ten, twenty feet wide.

Gil followed the track of the water down to what was left of the supports for the downed bridge, and even the concrete pilings and iron girders had been eaten down to the skinniest of stubs.

"I thought you said," Gil whispered, his gaze stuck now on the depthless black water rushing by almost half a football field below him. The water just kept coming, filling like a dammed lake. He swallowed and tried his creaking voice again. "I thought you said that nothing was amiss down here in the Undercity."

And then he saw movement in the rising water. Whitish-gray streaks of what seemed to be plastic at first, a foot long here, three feet long there. Rushing past him, caught in the hungry current. He counted easily three dozen of them before he realized that they all had faces. Black, oval eyes and round, open mouths.

"I did not lie," the Tour Guide said with effort, as if talking while the car was not in motion was painful to him. Gil stared, eyes wide, mouth dropped open, down at the translucent, limbless creatures rushing past in the water with only the tiniest hissing sound.

"*Nothing* is amiss in the Undercity. The dead and the lost no longer rest as they travel down the river that was supposed to lead to their final homes, and we cannot silence them any more. Even the beast at the heart of the Undercity, our protector, is powerless, either dead or missing. And so, my friend, nothing and *everything* is amiss."

The hissing grew louder as Gil held his breath, and he could now hear the individual voices inside that sound. All ages of voices, but the worst were the children's voices.

They were screaming.

◦◦◦

The last time Gil threw up was over four years ago, a pretty good streak, but today he was two for two with the puking. So long toast and coffee. Hello dry heaves. He'd poked his head out of the window just in time, but he still managed to coat the side of his Escort with his own personal slime. At least the sound of his retching covered up most of the screaming. Most of it.

"Just drive," the Tour Guide hissed, his deep voice tight. His cold hand was still on Gil's arm, and he began to squeeze.

"Yeah," Gil said, fumbling for the keys. He looked down at the floor, checked the cup holder, dug into his damp pockets, and began to pant with panic before the Tour Guide released his hold on him and turned the key for Gil from where he'd left it, still in the ignition.

"Yeah, let's drive."

Gil didn't even look at the road or pay attention to where he was going. He just moved, first in reverse, almost backing over the edge, and then into first, second, third, fourth, and finally fifth gear, away from that damn not-bridge. They headed out of the city, the wind rushing into the car, and as they picked up speed going up and down the brown hills leading away from the city limits, Gil thought about the voice that made him lose his stomach.

A tiny female voice that rose up from the others in the crowded, polluted river. He'd recognized this voice within all those other rushing voices, though he'd never heard it before. She said no words, just cried out in an unending syllable of horror and fear: "Daaaaaaa . . . "

"Just drive."

The Tour Guide's rich, rolling voice filled the car as they left the raised land next to the river and descended once again, this time into a valley of green, tree-infested parks interrupted by annoying traffic circles.

The rare bird collector lived there before the virus wiped out all his collection. The aging actor held court in that tall Victorian for decades, a different party each night. The children once filled this playground, before the water turned bad and the dead remained restless.

Gil's reeling, exhausted mind couldn't help but listen to the Tour Guide, and he let himself get taken in by the stories and the shifting history of the place. In all the months he'd dreamt of this place and heard that voice, he'd never listened to the same story twice. Even if the Guide was simply making all this shit up, at least it was original shit, and Gil was always a sucker for a well-told tale.

He listened and drove and tried not to hear her voice, calling out to him. All the itching on his ankles and legs came to a stop when he heard that voice. Sophie. It had to be her, calling to me. And she was lost.

The Guide's anecdotes made him think of his own stories about the Prince that he'd made up for Noah on the fly.

Why did I start those, anyway? he wondered. Was it after Noah watched the "Lord of the Rings" DVDs with his Middle-Earth-obsessed friend from second grade that rainy afternoon this past spring? Or was it the lack of good books for a smart kid Noah's age?

Something moved inside the trees of the latest park, the first sign of life Gil had seen since the Tour Guide invited himself into his car.

"Noah?" Gil whispered, hitting the brakes. It couldn't be. Could it?

The car shuddered as he shifted from fourth to second gear. The Tour Guide went silent next to him, just sour breath and a grunt or two, holding onto the dash again. The road curved suddenly, and by the time the car stopped, the figure was gone, as if it had just winked out of existence. Too tall to be Noah. About the size of the half-man, actually.

"Bendy men," The Tour Guide said at last. The car was ticking like a windup clock. Gil had stalled it, trying to stop so soon. Either that, or they were out of gas.

"What?"

"One of the bendy men in there. Original denizens of the Undercity, before they were drummed out of here for their indiscretions and made unwelcome. Keep going, my boy. Nothing to see here. Just hope they don't—"

The rest of his sentence got ambushed by a series of flatulent roars as a trio of dark blue pickup trucks burst through the trees in front of them, aimed at Gil's stalled Escort.

He got the car started on the second crank, panicking as the trucks grew bigger with each second. They ate up the undergrowth and took out small yellow-leaved trees with their massive black bumpers. Behind the wheel of each truck was a man with a face easily three feet long, distorted as hell, and in the bed of each blue pickup were at least fifteen children. Screaming kids.

"I'd head on out of here if I were you," the Guide said.

Gil turned on him then, glaring at the Guide's dull eyes, a blue so faded they were almost white. Full of advice today, weren't we?

"*Would* you, now?" Gil gripped the wheel and forced his eyes to look only at the Tour Guide, not at the approaching nine tons of truck coming right at them in his peripheral vision. "Want to explain the story of these bendy men to me? Make it quick, while we have time."

"Go now, Gil Anderson."

Gil swallowed, not blinking. He pulled his foot off the clutch and let the car lurch forward in another stall. "Nope. Tell me a story, Tour Guide."

"The trucks, for God's sake! We'll die!"

"That's what this is all about, isn't it?" The trucks cleared the forest, caught traction on the stretch of open grass before the road, and lined up side-by-side, rushing at Gil's car. "A chance to tell stories. To escape reality."

Kids screamed and tried to hold on in the beds, some without luck. Damn my peripheral vision, Gil thought as he tried to grab the Tour Guide, but the man's slick suit slid out of his grip.

"To keep me away from my true job down here, finding Noah."

The Tour Guide was cringing inward, anticipating the kamikaze impact, but Gil wasn't buying it. Smoke and mirrors down here in the Undercity, all the time. He knew such things quite well.

"I don't know what—" the Tour Guide babbled, his voice no longer a baritone but inching close to a soprano. About sixty feet between the trucks, the bendy men, the kids, and the Escort.

"Get out." Gil knew he was right about this. All a diversion. Had to be. Thirty feet.

"The *children*," the Tour Guide whispered, his hand on the curved plastic of the door handle. "We'll lose all those children if you don't move."

Gil reached across, choking himself on his shoulder belt once again, and pulled on the door handle with the Tour Guide's fat, hairy fingers still in it. Three pickup engines roared, fifty-plus children screamed and began to fall to the asphalt. The Tour Guide grunted as Gil pushed him out of his car. The trucks filled the windshield in a wall of blue metal and elongated faces. The Guide fumbled out of his seat, feet kicking up and knocking the passenger door open wide.

The trucks were gone before the Tour Guide hit the road.

"Some story," Gil whispered, looking back at the road and the deserted park and silent forest beyond. "Wish I could've believed it, asshole."

He was talking to empty air. Just him, his car, and the road. And the trees of the forest, laughing at him in the non-wind of the Undercity. The damn trees.

"Screw you," he told the tittering pines.

He rubbed his face with a shaking hand. The kids in the trucks were just an illusion. The men with long faces? Hallucinations. And Noah hadn't been in any of the truck beds. He couldn't have been.

Because Noah wasn't here. Gil was in the wrong part of town altogether. The Guide was just trying to waste his time, get him off track. And he'd fallen for it.

He fired up the stalled engine at last, and it caught on the first try, just like the old beast always did. He knew where he needed to go now. He just hoped he hadn't lost too much time.

Accompanied by a whiff of burnt oil, Gil turned his car and stomped on the accelerator, pointing the car back to that intersection and the wrong turn the Tour Guide had helped him make. The little engine began to roar, while something under him broke loose. A coughing sound not unlike one of Ray's attack commenced, assuring Gil that he'd just lost the muffler.

If he listened closely, over the crashing sounds of the battered Escort and the rush of wind coming at him through his window, he thought he could hear the distant yowling of a deep-voiced animal, and the angry, pain-filled sound made Gil press down on the gas as hard as he could, until he was flying down the ever-curving road toward that sound, and toward the stoplight and the straight road that met it.

CHAPTER SEVENTEEN:
LIARS, RIVERS, GUARDIANS, GHOSTS

Far below, Elwood kept on howling, and Noah was starting to think that the big cat wasn't ever going to stop. The sad and angry sound of it got inside his head like a fire engine's siren in the middle of the night. Poor Elwood. Meanwhile, looming high above him, the dragon sat in silence, back to her usual big-sized self, watching something on her wall. Her tail sat firmly over the entrance to the ladder leading down. All of the other screens of lost kids had faded away except for a tiny, flickering rectangle. Noah couldn't see who was on that screen.

Still Elwood howled. Noah sank to the floor, rattling pennies and shaped bits of colored glass with his butt, and put his hands over his ears. It didn't help. Elwood sounded mad, but he sounded like he was hurt, too.

And then all of sudden, when Elwood *did* stop, Noah's heart almost stopped as well. After a few seconds of silence, he wished the old jaguar would start again. Even the doors far below him had stopped slamming.

"What did you do to him?" Noah whispered. At some point he'd moved about ten steps closer to the dragon, but he didn't remember doing that.

"Not a thing," the dragon murmured, smiling down at Noah with teeth the size of Noah's arm. "But your little friend Eric seems to have taken care of that big cat for us."

Something red-hot rose up inside of Noah's throat as he thought of someone hurting Elwood. That hot feeling felt too much like what he'd felt right after hitting Daisy that day, when his angriness melted away. Elwood was my 'sponsibility.

"You better not hurt him. You just better not. Tell your friend to stop. Tell that Eric kid to stop."

But the dragon was no longer paying any attention to Noah. She'd turned back to the tiny screen on the tower wall. Noah followed her gaze, not wanting to, but unable to avoid just one quick look. He walked around a pile of scrap metal and over an itchy pile of pink insulation that had fallen out of a busted-open cardboard box, and then he saw her again, the girl he thought he'd recognized earlier, the girl with the curly blonde hair.

"Go down and tell your friend Eric to stop, yourself, if you want," the dragon said in a bored voice. She rolled her big, log-sized tail away from the hole in the floor.

"Who is she?" Noah whispered in the continuing silence of the big house. The lack of sound was making his ears ring. All the doors below them must have been stuck closed, just like the door to the machine shed had been jammed shut.

"Just another lost child." The dragon shifted position on her pile of brown coins and glass and rusted bits of discarded metal. Noah thought he saw the world's biggest ball of aluminum foil in there underneath her before she settled back down. Some treasure she had here.

"Now." The dragon gave Noah an annoyed look that would've shaken most grownups, but he simply looked away. "Why are you still here, boy? You're free to go. Or are you feeling brave now? Ready to take on my quest after all?"

"But," Noah looked at the TV screen on the wall, rubbing his lips. "She's crying."

"Most of them do." The dragon peeked over at Noah for a second with a red-orange gaze. "It can't be helped. But why do you care so much about *this* girl? You saw all the others, hundreds of them here on my wall. Out of all the lost children, why her?"

Noah stared at the girl on the screen. She was walking next to a frothy waterfall that fell into a black pool three times as big as the blue swimming pool up the road at the fancy houses. The girl was lost, and he felt like he had to protect her. She was so small. And she was getting way too close to that black water. It looked deep, and wrong somehow.

"I don't know," he answered at last. "I just . . . I was lost too. Like her."

At last the dragon pulled her big head back from the tiny screen, and as she did, she began to shrink again. Noah had a hard time watching it happen, because her body became all bendy and messed-up looking (her face went all stretchy like taffy, and her claws went all twisty like those pictures of people who never cut their fingernails from Dad's *Guinness Book of Records*). But he didn't look away.

"Tell me why she's lost," he said to the dragon now perched on a rickety metal shelf covered in paperclips and used staples, half a room away. The opening to the ladder leading down was still wide open next to him, and Elwood and the doors were still silent below him.

I could make a run for it if I wanted to. That's what Prince One-Eye would do, without a doubt.

"A bedtime story, is that what you want?" Even though her body had shrunk, the dragon's voice remained strong and echoey, and her burnt-eggs smell still filled Noah's nose with every hot breath she aimed at him.

Being treated like a little kid made his face heat up, but he said nothing. *Be patient, kiddo*, the grown-up voice whispered in his head, sounding a lot like Dad. Thinking of Dad made Noah's fluttering heartbeat slow, and a wave of calmness washed over him like a dunk in a warm tub.

"I'll give you a story, little Prince Noah. And unlike those silly tales your father feeds you, this one is true, because it's about the

Undercity, and nobody who comes here can lie about it. I know, because this place is mine. I own it. I am its owner, as well as its guardian and protector."

The red light filling the dragon's eyes had spread, pushing away the angry orange glow from earlier, and her voice was growing softer, which should've calmed Noah, but instead it made him more nervous. He looked away from those angry eyes, and in the process saw the girl on the TV screen.

She stopped creeping closer to the waterfall pool, and she turned her face toward Noah, as if she could actually see him. He shivered from a sudden chill and looked back at the dragon.

"Everyone who finds themselves lost in the Undercity comes to visit me, eventually," the dragon began, easing back on her pile of fake riches. "I've been down here since the first cave was formed, hundreds of thousands of years ago. I'm old, Prince One-Eye Noah. Very old. Older than the hills, if you can believe it. Why, I was the one who helped *shape* the hills. I came here because I loved being alive, and I had to find sanctuary while my fellow dragons were dying in waves, in the aboveground lands, being killed by hunters and diseases. I found this place formed by dreamers and visionaries, shaped it with my own will, and made it my own. And then I began my most important task. One that would keep this place intact for me, forever."

The dragon shifted, and Noah jumped. She was full-sized again, and he hadn't seen it happening because her eyes had grabbed all his focus as she spoke.

"There's a river down here," the dragon continued. "You may have seen it. That is my river—I tend to it, make sure it flows through every portion of the Undercity, fed by the energy of the lost souls who make their way down here. But someone has polluted it. I have a pretty good idea who did it. Someone from," she pointed toward the smooth black roof with her head, which had swollen up to the size of Mom's little blue car, "up *there*. I'll be taking care of him next, you can be sure. As soon as I get out of this place."

Now that the dragon had returned to her big-ness, Noah could see the patterns of scars and wounds, most of them white with age, covering her green belly and slick black hide. Something big had, at some point a long time ago, taken a raggedy bite out of one of her wings. That must have hurt.

"Sophie," the dragon said, her voice almost a purr. "Would you like to tell Prince Noah about what I can do for you?"

Noah blinked, as if he were breaking free of a spell cast by the dragon (these sort of things happened all the time in Dad's stories, and he refused to believe those stories were stupid like this shifty dragon had said they were). Something made the air around him shimmer, and then he heard a tiny cough.

He turned, and the little girl from the TV screen on the wall was now standing in front of him, holding a tattered pink blanket. She used the blanket to wipe her glistening, tear-stained cheeks, but she didn't say a word.

∽◦∽

Noah could remember too many nights out on the front porch when nobody talked. Not that long ago, just last summer, Mom and Dad had laughed and chatted until long past Noah's bedtime. They let him stay up with them most nights, and Dad would get out the guitar he was trying to teach himself how to play. Noah had loved the way Dad kept trying and trying to get the sound right, plucking at the strings with his shiny green pick. Most times the notes came out sour in spite of his hard work. The best part was when Noah and his mom made up silly songs to go along with Dad's clumsy music, and they all got to laughing as night fell.

And then it just stopped, not last summer, but maybe the one before that. Mom and Dad would still sit together on the porch, but they weren't talking much and definitely weren't singing anymore. Mom looked different, smaller somehow, and her smile had disappeared. She brought piles of papers out with her to the rocking chair most nights, while Dad's stories became more boring and too easy for Noah to guess how they'd end.

Then Dad stopped telling them when Mom was around. Most nights Noah would just sit in one their laps for as long as he could stand sitting still, and Mom or Dad would just hold him tight and hug him. He didn't understand any of that, but he liked the feel of their arms around him, the warmth of their chest on his back, the flickering of his mom's or his dad's heart tickling him through his skin. He'd asked Mom about her belly just once, and after watching her face go all shaky, he swore to never ask her again.

"I guess she's shy," the dragon said, nodding at the blonde girl and puffing hot air through her tall nostrils. "Or maybe she's just not used to being around people anymore. Poor kid."

Noah wanted to go to the girl and give her the kind of hug his parents used to give him on those cool nights on the porch, but her face looked so scared he didn't want to risk it. He didn't want her running back into that TV screen. He knew such a thing was impossible, of course, but then, so were dragons.

"I'm Noah," he whispered instead. "I got lost too."

The girl flinched, as if not expecting him to be able to talk. Then she smiled, just a tiny flicker of her lips, but it was enough for Noah.

"I see the cat's got Miss Sophie's tongue," the dragon said from above their heads.

"Sophie?" Noah whispered. That name was familiar to him, but he couldn't figure out why, couldn't think straight with the dragon hanging over him and breathing her sewer breath on him. He looked up and around him and saw that the dragon's tail was blocking the exit hole again, just as he was entertaining thoughts of grabbing Sophie's hand and making a run for it.

"I have something," the dragon began, "that I need you two to do for me—"

As if on cue, something began whimpering outside.

"Elwood!" Noah turned to try and look the dragon in the eye, and he nearly fell over. She was just too big. "Let me go down and let him in, would you? Please?"

"Sorry. I simply can't do that. I'm not through with you." The dragon's voice softened a bit, and she shrugged her wings. "My story's not finished, you see. It's bad luck not to finish a story you've started. Didn't you know that? No? Well, then. I see you have a lot to learn, young man. I haven't even told you about the ruined bridges or the way the citizens went into hiding after the bendy men returned, have I? I wonder . . . " The dragon said in a tone that made it sound like she was thinking hard, but Noah wasn't buying it. This dragon was a big phony. "I don't suppose you know about ghosts, then, do you, Prince Noah?"

Noah didn't want to answer her, angry at the thought of Elwood being hurt down there and this lost girl now trapped in the tower with him.

"Ghosts haunt houses," he spat. "They're people who stick around after they're dead, just to scare people. Sort of like *you*."

"My boy!" the dragon laughed, spitting fire out of her nostrils. "Why, you're a little firecracker! Who would've known? I may be scaring you, but I am far from dead, unlike . . . "

As the dragon trickled off into laughter again, Noah inched closer to the girl, Sophie. She flinched away at first, then crept closer to him as well. He reached out and touched her hand, and a sudden shiver ran through him when he felt the coldness of her skin.

And then Noah stopped breathing. This was *Sophie*. He'd finally gotten to meet her, after all this time. His lost little sister!

"Now," the dragon said, no longer laughing. "Let me tell you two about ghosts and my rivers."

Noah exhaled at last. He was so happy and amazed at who he'd found down here that he didn't want to listen, but he had no choice. He held tight to Sophie's icy hand and let out the breath he'd been holding. It puffed in the air as if they were outside at Christmastime.

"Ghosts are funny creatures," the dragon began. "They think they know what they're doing, in the afterlife, but they're just like magnets, following whatever pulls them or pushes them away. Like bits of paper caught in the current of a river. And this place, my world, the Undercity, is filled with them. Ghosts. I made it that way. My river is like a magnet, and the Undercity is the in-between place between the land of the living and the land of the not. You know what a magnet is, don't you, Prince Noah?"

Noah glanced over at Sophie, feeling protective of her suddenly. He didn't want this story to give her nightmares, though he had a feeling he was going to have some of his own, soon, and most likely before he ever fell asleep tonight.

"Now. Your friend down there?" the dragon continued. "The big cat? How do you think he ended up down here? He's a ghost, you see, pulled here by you and his savage nobility to protect you. Poor jaguar must've died of old age, up there in his cage at that so-called Preservation Society. Preservation indeed!"

"You're wrong!" Noah burst out. "I let Elwood in here! I opened the door myself. He's not dead. He's *alive*."

The dragon paused in her story, looking a tiny bit annoyed at the interruption. "Can you prove that?"

"If he's a ghost, how come he's hollering? How can he get hurt if he's dead?"

"Good question," the dragon said, sounding surprised. "Maybe he just doesn't realize he's dead yet."

"But that doesn't make sense." The cold from Sophie's hand was traveling up Noah's fingers, up his hand and to his wrist, and he felt something even colder touch his heart as a bad thought entered his head. "And . . . but . . . does that mean that *I'm* a ghost, too?"

Once again, the dragon gave its best shrug.

Tears squirted out of Noah's eyes as he tried to find his voice. This was all wrong. It couldn't be.

"Listen to me," the dragon said. "Stay down here. You can explore and play Prince all you want. Then you won't have to worry about anything, like growing up." She turned her car-sized head to one side, giving a quick look at the silent little girl next to him. "Or dying, like the others. All you need to do is find the man who trapped me here. He's using his dirty brand of magic to hide himself and his cursed dog from my surveillance. Touch his hand for me and I'll take care of the rest."

Noah wasn't following the dragon's twisty words anymore. He kept thinking about growing up, and wondering: Did *ghosts* grow up?

He hated having to do it, but he felt like he had to do just that to face up the dragon and her lies. The problem with growing up was that you usually had to be mean to people.

"Elwood!" he shouted, pointing his face at the hole half-covered by dragon tail. "Just bust through the doors down there. Come inside and get away from whoever's hurting you."

Noah almost laughed at the distant "Mrowr?" that came from over three stories below the tower. It sounded as Elwood was asking him, "Are you *sure*?"

Noah swallowed, his dusty, dry throat aching already from yelling. "It can't hurt," he added. "I mean, you're already dead, right?"

Before Noah could finish his sentence, something big crashed into the house. He could about picture it—Elwood covered in dust, maybe even bleeding from Eric attacking him, backing up to the edge of one of the crooked porches to get a run at the door, tail dipping in the dusty lawn, and then throwing himself at the door. Three times he hit it, and on the fourth the door sounded like it exploded.

All the other doors sprang to life below them, opening and closing and creating a crazy drumbeat that nobody could dance to. Within fifteen seconds and hundreds of door drumbeats, something was scrabbling up the metal rungs of the ladder, and Noah was surprised to see not Elwood, but the tail-less salamander climbing up into the tower.

Alexander was now about the size of his dog Daisy, and he jumped from the top of the ladder and landed with a clatter onto a plastic bin of pennies. He was whining and panting for breath, and as the green and black critter ran past, Noah could've sworn he said in a shrinking voice, "Forget about me tail, mate. I'm outta here."

Short seconds later, Elwood the jaguar followed the cowardly salamander through the hole cut into the tower floor. He was covered in gray lawn dust and bits of bright red blood, and his white teeth were bared. His spots had stretched themselves into black lightning bolts zigzagging across his back and chest. He threw himself up and out of the hole and landed on a rare, bare spot of wooden flooring with a furious roar. Noah held tight to Sophie's hand, and the girl made no sound, not even breathing.

Where is she? Elwood's voice shouted inside Noah's head. *She has some explaining to do.*

But the big dragon was nowhere to be found.

～∞～

"Door in the floor," Noah whispered, holding tight to the girl's cold hand. It felt like it should be a song, something to sing along with Dad's choppy guitar plucking. "Door in the floor, door in the floor, watch out for the door in the floor."

Much to his disappointment, Sophie didn't sing along.

Noah's improvised song drowned out most of the terrible sounds from the tower high above them, but not enough. He hoped Elwood would be all right up there, but he couldn't stay to help. Elwood had made him promise to leave and take Sophie. Thinking about leaving Elwood made Noah cry just a little bit again, but he had a kest to finish. This was the *real* kest, and it didn't have anything to do with the tail of a sneaky, cowardly salamander.

Alexander must have learned how to be a coward from the female dragon. Elwood had stood there in the tower full of fake riches, growling for her to come out, but she didn't show herself until Elwood had approached her bed of pennies.

Then she'd dropped on top of him from the ceiling.

Go! Elwood had shouted inside Noah's head as the big cat and the dragon rolled across the cluttered tower, banging into things and slashing at each other. Noah had seen more blood, and that made his stomach all queasy. Then the dragon had started to grow, and he couldn't see his jaguar friend anymore.

Elwood yelled at him inside his head: *Get yourselves out of this house! I'll take care of this nasty lizard.*

"Door in the floor," Noah whispered, trying hard to carry a tune in the chaos of the house. "Door in the floor, everywhere we go, a door in the floor."

Dodging opening doors exploding up from the floorboards—Noah could tell when the door was about to fly open now, because the doorframe would wiggle three times first—they hurried back to the front door of the house, or what was left of it. The front door had been knocked off its hinges, with no sign of Eric anywhere. Noah didn't want to go back outside, and when he heard the distant rumble of a car engine—the bendy men in their pickemup trucks, he knew—he assumed he had to try another way. He led Sophie to the bottom of the very first door in the floor, an unpainted brown door covered in splintered bits of wood from the front door. This felt like the right door.

Sophie squeezed his hand and looked up at him as he caught his breath in front of the door. Outside, a car or maybe a truck was rumbling closer. In spite of all this, most of the scaredness had left Sophie's face, and when she smiled up at Noah, his chills went away, too.

His fears dropped away when he looked at her blue-green eyes and baby-teeth smile.

"You're my sister," he said. It was not a question. "But . . . how old are you?"

The girl nodded, her blonde curls bouncing in her face, and held up two chubby white fingers. She kept her distance from the door in the floor, the one that Noah wanted to open.

Noah had a million questions for her, but the sound of the approaching car or truck—it really had to be a truck, Noah thought—outside was growing louder, and he could hear footsteps somewhere in the house, now that the slamming doors had fallen silent again. He hoped it wasn't Eric again. He heard another set of footsteps coming from the next room, scratchy sounds like a dog's paw's on the bare floor. And heavy, rattling breathing, he thought, but surely he was just 'magining that.

"Come with me?" This time it *was* a question, the hardest one Noah had ever asked, because he was afraid she'd say no, and he couldn't imagine not being with her, after just meeting her moments ago. "It might be dangerous, but at least we'd be together. I'd watch out for you. I'm your big brother."

The little girl looked at the door in the floor again, then she pointed upstairs, her smile gone.

"The dragon? I think Elwood is dealing with her."

Sophie shook her head, stamping one small, bare foot for emphasis.

"The *other* kids?" Noah had forgotten about them, all those TV screens of kids wandering alone. So many. It was like trying to hold onto too many playing cards in one fist.

He nodded and opened his eyes. "You're right. We have to help them. As soon as we find what's wrong with the water down here, we'll come back for the other kids. Okay? We can only do one kest at a time, 'kay?"

Sophie gave him a look like she didn't really believe that, and

Noah squeezed her hand. From high above, Elwood wailed one last time, a sad, pain-filled sound. From a room nearby, two different sets of footsteps—one animal, one human—were growing closer.

"Come along with me?"

Finally Sophie smiled and nodded. Bending down, almost laughing with relief, Noah tugged on the knob to the door in the floor. He jumped back just in time as the big slab of wood opened with a rush of air. The door stayed open instead of reversing course and slamming shut.

Door in the floor, door in the floor . . .

With his silly song running through his head and his sister's cold hand growing a tiny bit warmer in his own, Noah stepped into the black emptiness of the door in the floor, and they both disappeared into someplace other and beyond before the door slammed shut above and behind them.

CHAPTER EIGHTEEN:
AN OVERTLY RUDE THING TO DO

The houses in this part of the city were nothing to write, call, or email home about, Gil decided. Not even worth an instant message. They had big lawns, sure, which made them better than the all-house, no-yard properties going up down the road from his farm, but what good was a big-ass lawn if you couldn't get to it thanks to the four-foot-high curbs? No driveways, nothing to break up those low walls of concrete on either side of the road. And the grass had been gone a long time, replaced with dust that looked to be a foot or so deep.

It hurt his eyes to stare too long at any single house, but he figured that all of the dwellings must have been designed by an architect with either no depth perception or a very bad sense of humor. Probably both. He'd never seen so many faux-Victorian houses with so many windows in the wrong place, or so many doors resting crookedly in their frames. Not even in his Undercity dreams. This was new territory.

A door slammed shut inside a drunk-looking gray house off to his left. Gil hit the brakes and let the noisy Escort skid sideways to a stop, kissing the tall curb. Something about the sound of that door—hell, any door slamming—made him pissed. Such an overtly rude thing to do, swinging a door full-force into its frame. Not that he was feeling defensive or angry at this point.

And this was as good a place to stop as any, what with the front door missing from this house, torn from its hinges from the looks of it.

Gil didn't trust that dusty lawn, so he climbed onto the dented trunk of his old beloved car, leaned back as far as he could, pausing for the tiniest of seconds, like an oversized hood ornament on the wrong end of the car. And then he surged forward, up and over the roof and hood, making dents with each heavy placement of his bare feet, gathering speed, and used the high curb as his launching pad.

When he hit the dust and started to sink, he wasn't surprised. He just plowed forward toward the middle porch with the broken-down door.

No, Gil thought as he sank down in dust to his crotch, I'm not offended by a door slamming. Not at this point. But I'm tired of being toyed with and manipulated. He let his anger propel him through the seething dust. He tried not to think about his son walking in this foul pit of a front lawn, but he'd never been one to have much control over his thoughts.

Needless to say, it was really, *really* bad timing for Ray and his damn dog to show up on the porch above Gil, with the half-man hovering a few feet behind them in the broken doorway.

Slam! And slam again. At least a dozen doors before Gil stopped counting. And they all sounded like they came from inside this house. So rude.

Ray stood back a few steps, watching Gil plow through the dust, which was now up to Gil's belly. The smug look on his neighbor's wrinkled, sun-burnt face carried Gil to the edge of the porch, even as something snapped at his ankles. He was pretty sure that wasn't a chigger, nipping at him down there.

"Do you think you're going to stop me?" he said to Ray. He'd crossed the lawn in what felt like no time, never taking his eyes off Ray and his companions as he reached the uneven bottom step of the small front porch. "Because I've about had it with you, Ray."

On the porch was a small pile of dust from the yard, and in that dust was a perfect sandal print, as well as an empty mint wrapper.

Whirly Brand Mints, the label said. The same kind of mints Gil kept in a bowl in his store.

Noah, Gil thought as he pulled himself out of the yard, shedding dust like a swimmer dripping water. He may still be here. And so may the person or creature who broke down this door.

Ray answered Gil by moving backward, deeper into the house, herding the half-man and Bullitt before him. Ray's heavy feet clomped onto a thick wooden door set into the dusty floor inside the house. Gil followed. Still the old man said nothing, which was unnerving as hell.

Gil stepped through the shattered frame of the front door and into a room stupid with doors. On the floor. Doors on the floor. Everywhere.

"Nice place you got here, jokers," he said, but his words were drowned out as the doors in front of him flew open in succession, starting with the one at his feet, the lower edge of the plain brown door almost taking him out at the knees before it slammed back shut again. Whiff-pause-slam. Whiff-pause-slam. Over and over again. A pile of doors, all of them a different shape and make, right here in this room. Screen, metal, wood, even a mirrored glass door.

Had Noah seen that one? Gil wondered. He would've liked it. Though I have no idea how it didn't break, he thought, as the glass door slammed again.

"Should we—" the half-man began, but Ray cut him off with a wet clearing of his throat. More doors opened and slammed shut in this room and the rooms surrounding them. Bullitt whimpered and dodged a closing door, paws clattering madly on the dusty, uncarpeted floor like hail beating the tin roof of Gil's store.

Then the room went silent, and Gil could think again.

From the sound of the slamming coming from upstairs—and the place had to be at least three stories, if not four—the place was riddled with doors. Hell, Noah could've walked through any of these doors. How was this supposed to work?

Ray, Bullitt, and the half-man spread out and let Gil walk a few more steps into the front room. He noticed that each one of them stood in front of the room's three open doorways leading deeper into this madhouse. No doors in the walls, of course. All the doors were at Gil's feet. No way was he going to walk on top of one of them. He stuck to the bare floor and kept waiting for an opening. Literally.

"Say something, old man. At least apologize for setting me up like this. Or was this all part of your master plan? Even me diving into that pool of water back in the cave?"

"Now *that* was stupid," Ray muttered, his voice surprisingly tight. "And I sure didn't see it coming, I give you that. You're lucky we caught up with you again. You don't need to be going off on your own down here. You don't understand this place."

"Look, you need to let me by. I know my boy has been here. I can smell him, for Christ's sake."

The half-man began to say something in his birdy voice, but Ray stopped him again, this time with a quick, cutting gesture. So that explained the Undercity pecking order, Gil thought.

He gave the half-man a big shit-eating grin, thinking: *Peon*. I feel your pain. Used to be one myself.

Ray coughed and blew his nose farmer-style onto a door below him. "I'll tell you what I can." He sighed and reached down as if to pet Bullitt, but the dog was six feet away, guarding his doorway.

Ray sighed. "I first came here when the Finley-Thompsons found the portal to the Undercity. Damn thing was right there on their farm. Didn't know there was one on mine, too. No, that woulda been too easy." Ray's breath became choked for a moment, as if his phlegm-filled lungs couldn't keep up with his confession. "This was all . . . years ago. Way before you guys. The F-Ts letting me come down," he coughed, eyes widening with pain. "All part of the deal."

"Deal?"

The half-man giggled from Gil's left, standing at a distorted angle above a door that had just slammed shut. He flicked a sheath of loose skin free from his forearm and giggled some more. Gil ignored him and glanced at Bullitt on his right, quivering on his skinny haunches like he was outside a rabbit's warren, waiting for the signal to dive in and start eating baby bunnies.

Something odd about the way the dog's sitting there in the dust, Gil thought, but I can't tell just what it is.

As he turned back to Ray, he froze. He saw tiny sandal prints in the dust of the floor ahead of him, just to the left of Ray's big boots. Something began poking him from inside his pants pocket as he looked at the two sets of prints, one heading toward the doorway where the half-man stood, and another set that went most of the way to the door in the floor closest to Gil, possible walking toward it, if he could figure out those damned oval prints. Coming or going? He had to be sure.

"What deal?" Gil asked, just as Ray began to wheeze. He needed Ray to keep talking so he could figure out those tracks, but it looked like it was close to the hourly phlegm-fest.

"We all made our deals with the devil," the half-man said, scratching his crotch. He nodded his loose-skinned, too-narrow head at Ray, who was still coughing. "Now we got to pay 'em off. It all started going bad, right about when the lady and the mister moved away, and smart guy here started cutting deals—"

"Shut up," Ray gasped between barking explosions. Gil thought he heard something from high above, an animal sound louder than a growl, quieter than a shriek. "Give me . . . a minute . . . "

Gil laughed, thinking of what the half-man said, and then slapped at whatever was poking him from his pockets.

"Even the *dog* made a deal with the devil?" Gil watched Ray drop to his knees, each cough louder than the last. His hands were quickly coated in dust from the floor.

Gil stuck his hand into his pocket and pulled out the pocket liner, trying to get rid of whatever he'd let slip in there. He didn't dare look down to see what he'd shaken out, not with Ray and the half-man coming unglued in front of him.

"That's what you get," the half-man tittered, enjoying Ray's torment, "when you dig in the wrong person's garden. Even the dog."

"Shut . . . up!" Ray managed from his knees. "I'll kill you . . . myself . . . if you don't . . . shut . . . up!"

"Garden," Gil muttered, watching the doors in the floor open up around him once again in waves of wood, glass, and metal. At his feet, he saw something tiny, smaller than a pencil, just a few inches from his bare foot and one of the many doors in the room. The damn salamander tail. He'd almost lost it. He bent down to pick it up, all the while trying to get Ray to talk more. That tail was trying to tell him something.

"Is that what this is about? This Gardener you've been going on about?"

"You wish it were that easy," the half-man said, kicking shut the door that had popped open next to him. The skin from both of his bare arms now hung loose in flaps, though none of it touched the floor. The meat of his skinless arm was gray and bloodless. "You'll never know what we were gonna do, what with the river going bad and the bridges all destroyed, and the dragon bitch locked up. Nope-nope. I tell ya—"

"What?" Gil's voice rose to a shout. "God damn it, Ray—"

"That's it," Ray whispered in a hoarse, clogged voice. "Bullitt . . . *Attack.*"

The dog moved so fast Gil swore he could feel Bullitt dive into *him* before he heard the sound of his paws scrabbling across the doors and the floor. He'd been watching Ray, though, unable to stand looking at the half-man moving and bending the light with his distorted body. What he saw first was Ray's finger, pointing not at Gil but at the half-man, followed by a fawn-colored streak of greyhound shooting across the room.

The heavy sound of dog meeting half-man echoed in the big room as if all of them were standing in a hollowed-out cave, and they both went down in a tangle of long limbs, fur, flapping skin, and elbows. They rolled right over Noah's dusty tracks leading out of (or was it into?) the room, stopping only when they landed on the mirrored glass door. For an instant the door held, then it gave way with a wicked shattering sound.

Bullitt and the half-man dropped through the opening the broken door made, accompanied by long, silvery shards of glass, sucking a large portion of the air in the room with them.

Gil stumbled and went down on one knee, holding tight to the tiny tail caught between his finger and thumb as he fought being pulled toward the open doorway. And then the horizontal glass door was simply *there* again, intact, and the air returned to the room, along with the stink of diesel exhaust and dust.

"Shit," Ray said. He pulled himself back to his feet, wobbling slightly and wheezing. "That was a good dog. I'm . . . all out now. This damn plan better pan out, for fuck's sake."

Gil's mind was as unsteady as Ray's legs. The half-man he could handle. The house full of doors, the underwater pools, the sheared-off bridges, the black river of lost souls (or whatever they were), even Ray's master plan and his healed chigger bites, all of that he could handle. But what he was having trouble with was the dust on the floor.

"Now you've got . . . to go, Gil," Ray gasped, just a few feet—one door's length—away. Gil could smell Ray's sweat and the too-sweet scent of his hair pomade. "For your own good."

"Just a second." Gil lifted the quivering salamander tail like MacBeth and his ghostly dagger, waving it once at Ray before pointing it at the floor. "Just one second, old buddy."

The dust. A good inch of it covered the floor of this room like fine snow. The stuff should've been scattered everywhere with all the activity this room had seen in the past few minutes, including that sucking wind that had accompanied the departure of Bullitt and the half-man. But Gil could still see Noah's tracks, clear as day, and Ray's big lined bootprints.

What he couldn't see in the dust was any trace of the half-man's shiny black boots, or Bullitt's paws.

Gil almost looked down at his own bare feet to check out the path he'd made in the dust behind him, but he was afraid of what he'd see. If there weren't any footprints down there, he'd just give up and let his mind finish unhinging itself.

The dead no longer rest . . .

He thought the Tour Guide had just been full of shit. But he'd been telling the truth. At least, his version of it.

"This house," Ray said. His calm, clear voice made Gil jump. Ray gave Gil a quick smile, like the kind the old Ray would've done. "It's a nexus. Nobody else was supposed to find it, Gil. But who should find it but you and your damn snot-nosed brat." Ray winced. "Sorry. Noah's a good kid. Just too nosy."

"You are so full of shit," Gil muttered, still thinking about the dead, something he'd been avoiding doing for most of the past two years. "Were they even *here?*"

Ray stared at Gil blankly as the animal noises from above began again, two different creatures from the sound of it, as if they were back at each other's throats after taking a quick breather. Gil heard the hiss of the door in the floor next to him opening and grabbed it by the edge as it shot open, only to pay for that mistake with a hand full of splinters when it wrenched itself out of his grip and slammed shut.

"Who?" Ray asked. Something about the dull look in his eyes made Gil's skin prickle. Ray was apparently off in his own little world right now.

"Bullitt. The half-man. Look down, man. They didn't leave any tracks."

"You don't want me to be completely honest with you, neighbor. *That* knowledge will play games with your mind. Believe me. I've been through all that, got the scars to show from it. Most of 'em on the inside, from my lungs to my inner eyelids." He shook his head again. "I tried to warn you and the Finley-Thompsons both. This place is too powerful for people who don't feel the call and take it seriously."

Gil swallowed hard, feeling the weight of too many lost seconds turning into lost minutes inside his head. Noah was slipping away from him while he stood here jabbering with Ray, just one more Undercity delaying tactic. But he had to know something.

"How did Bullitt die?"

Ray shuddered and narrowed his eyes.

"And don't say he died falling through the glass door just now. The dog left no tracks on the floor. Ray. He's a ghost, isn't he? I have a pretty good idea how the half-man died, and I can guess why he's hanging around this area, haunting it. I've read enough horror novels to get that. I can deal with that. So tell me how your dog died."

"You've gone out of your mind," Ray spat.

Something creaked behind Gil, a tiny settling sound he blamed on the battle still going on high above. He knew he should've turned and checked it out, but he was too intent on figuring out what Ray had just said.

"What about Rocky? I saw her get hit by that truck three months ago. She was dead, Ray."

"Don't bring that up now." Ray's face went purple as a bruise. Something shifted high above them, and Ray ducked, as if expecting a giant clawed hand to reach down and slash him. "Don't you dare throw that in my face now," he hissed.

"Don't you hold out on me now, not after all this." Gil pressed his lips shut and forced himself to stop and think. He thought about the way Ray had treated the half-man.

"*He* did it, didn't he? That skinny freak. The half-man killed Bullitt. Way before they both fell through that door. When, Ray? When did it happen? When did you start hanging out with your dog's ghost?"

"You don't want to know—"

"Don't start that shit. Just start talking. Tell me what you've gotten into down here, and what sort of shit you've gotten all of us into as a result, old man."

"No," he said in a soft voice. "Not me. *You're* the one who's gotten us all into this, Gil. You moved right into it, right after you stole the place from the Finley-Thompsons. Interrupting everything I'd set up."

Ray made a beckoning motion with his big hand, and Gil took a tentative step closer, then another, until he was at the crossroads of four different doors, three wooden and one screen. He made sure to stand in a clear spot on the floor where he wouldn't get nailed by any of the doors, which had all gone silent. The salamander tail wiggled once, twice in Gil's pinched fingers, and then went still.

"The Undercity got its hooks in me years ago. First I used the door in the machine shed on your property—the F-Ts didn't even know about it. Then I realized I had one of my own. Some days I'd end up here, other days I'd get stuck at that cave. Pretty soon I was coming down here all the time. Every time I had to make my own way back home, and I'd go almost crazy with fear, convinced I was lost. I always brought Bullitt with me, and he helped me get back home each time, even after he died. I kept coming back, just to see something new here. And there was always something new, even in the places I thought I'd figured out and mapped in my head. The whole place is shifty like that. Bendy. But powerful. It called to me, Gil."

Bendy men in pickemup trucks, a voice said inside Gil's head. He shuddered, looking at Ray and his dark, squinting eyes. Surely the old man had lost it, jumping through portals with his ghost dog, looking for power.

"I saw some wild stuff down here," Ray continued, "stuff you wouldn't be able to imagine in your wildest dreams." Gil's snort of sarcasm was lost on the old guy. "Dead people coming back to life, ghosts pretending to be alive, people breathing one second, then just bags of bones the next. And don't even get me started on the way the roads all turn in on you, twisting and bending and leading you exactly right where you started."

Bendy men, bendy men . . .

"And the children," Ray said, his voice breaking as if he were about to begin hocking up a lung again. "Those little kids, trying to get home. They're the worst part of this place. I've heard there's someone down here who gathers up all the lost children, gets them to do whatever he or she—or it—wants 'em to do." Ray shook his head and gave me a mournful look. "It's awful. Using those kids for their own purposes . . . "

"Do you mean there are *more*?" Gil said, sensing a trace of fakery in Ray's sad tone. He remembered looking down at the river from next to the broken bridge, hearing the screaming voices. "More lost kids?"

"There's one now!" Ray shouted, pointing at something behind Gil, and Gil fell for it, all the way. He twisted, off-balance, and looked, just as a small human cannonball rolled into his legs, taking him out at the knees and sending a fresh spike of pain into his bad hip. The salamander tail slipped out of his hands as he threw his arms in the air and struggled, unsuccessfully, to regain his balance.

The last thing Gil saw in this section of the Undercity was the dusty, tear-streaked face of the bully boy from up the road, laughing at him from the floor.

Eric, you sneaky little shit, Gil thought as he fell, vision going red with pain from his hip, while Ray's coughs peppered the air. Does your mom know where you are?

And then he passed through the horizontal screen door.

∽੦∾

Gil had always wished that his Undercity dreams would've taken the same low level of importance as the silly stories about heroes and their adventures did that he told to Noah. A fun way to pass the time, maybe, but nothing too lasting. He'd be able to just enjoy them for their weirdness, then forget all about the imagery and foreboding and get some damn sleep. No haunting images and strange undercurrents of significance.

But no. He had to attach *meaning* to the dreams. Some Freudian shit. Every element in the dream, from the car he was driving to the people he'd tried to avoid looking at, to the distorted houses and swollen factories he encountered. If he wasn't thinking about these things while he was trying to sleep, he was remembering details pronounced to him in the Tour Guide's voice about the history of people long ago who died strange deaths after living lives of bizarre misadventure.

It was pretty easy to obsess about this stuff instead of dealing with his regular life and the pain that came from falling away from Melissa in the past two years, along with his sense of dislocation back home, sixteen miles from everywhere.

All of this flitted through Gil's head as he fell through the screen door—without actually feeling the door break away under him— and dropped through a swirling tunnel of light and regurgitated faces and images from his past that made the one time he'd dropped acid look like bad night of cheap fireworks.

This was no flashback. I'm not dreaming this.

He saw the house he lived in as a kid, but it was burning orange with a hungry flame. He saw the pale, wrinkled faces of his grandparents glaring down at his as if he were a five-year-old robbing from cookie jars. He saw Melissa and Noah, huddled together under a tarp to ward off dark brown pellets of hail. He saw Ray, hands over his mouth, eyes so wide he thought they'd explode. For one heart-stopping instant he saw a tiny newborn baby, her skin bluish-gray instead of beet red, a splash of black water on her perfect cheek. More images on top of that—kids he'd known growing up, loved ones he'd lost or forgotten. Each image flashing by hit him like a fist to the stomach or two fingers to the throat.

Surely this wasn't my life passing before my eyes, Gil thought, and then he hit the hog waste lagoon.

Back on his father's tobacco and soybean farm in eastern North Carolina, the neighbors on either side of them had lagoons like this. The stink was ungodly, the pools of waste acres-wide and filled with the sludge deposited by thousands of hogs, nightmares of pollution just waiting to fill wells and rivers used for drinking water. Surely the last place on earth Gil would want to end up.

He sank into the warmish, thick sludge, the lagoon stretching around him as far as the eye could see. He couldn't even make out the walls of the cave he was in, just the acres and acres of brown pig shit and urine stirred together, along with any other toxins that may have leeched their way through the battered topsoil and crops to add another layer of poison to the mix.

His legs had sunk to mid-thigh when he landed, and now he was in it to his waist. He couldn't even kick his bare feet in this muck. If he'd had anything left in him to throw up, the stench would have made him do so, but all Gil could do was dry heave and look around, desperate to find a way out.

Tears filled his eyes as he realized how desperately tired he was. He hadn't slept a complete night without interruption in months. For almost two years, really. Ever since . . .

He was sunk in to his chest now. Nowhere to go but down.

Somehow Ray had arranged all this, Gil realized.

Maybe it was his tears, or maybe it was all just a hallucination, but when Gil looked around him again, he understood where he was.

He saw the pumps, so many of them, and so far away that they were no bigger than a fingertip in the distance. He could see the tiny trails of exhaust leading up from each one, tiny pencil lines of smoke. If he held his breath for a moment, he could hear the tiny engines chugging away, coughing like his dog-loving neighbor liked to do on an hourly basis.

Was this the source of the foulness flowing into the water of the Undercity, infecting it all, including the river? Was this the power Ray was talking about?

Gil lifted his chin up from the slime trying to coat it with a sickening caress. The rest of his body was blessedly numb. He saw the tributaries of waste created and urged on by the pumps, pushing the filth away from this central holding area, spiderwebbing out from here, making its way out into the rest of the Undercity waterways.

Spreading to my family, Gil thought. My *world*. Ray had wanted me to see this before I died, the bastard.

Gil cried out his son's name, once, and then he had no other choice. He sealed his mouth shut and inhaled as much air as he could into his nostrils, nearly choking on the foul reek.

As the filth covered his nose and closed eyes, another name entered his head, a name he and Melissa had chosen for the child they'd lost two years ago, a name filled with so much unrequited love and pain-filled regret that simply thinking it caused his body to convulse in agony.

Sophie.

The name lit a light inside his blackened world, for just a moment, even as his heart skipped a beat and the foulness closed over his head, and he sank deeper into his nightmare.

I get to see you soon, Sophie. At last.

CHAPTER NINETEEN:
INTO THE REALM OF
STIMULUS AND RESPONSE

For the first time in years, Melissa wasn't trying to assess her current situation and generate an immediate evaluation. There were no symptoms to address, no maladies to remedy with careful steps and thoughtful analysis. Today had moved way beyond that, into the instinctive, non-thinking realm of stimulus and response. No sense in fighting it any more.

The logical part of her brain had tried to absorb and process all that she'd seen in the past hour, but at right about the point when she dropped through the tiny gap of Ray's portal and landed in the dripping tunnel with the spongey floor, she'd felt like a tiny switch had been thrown. She was truly out of her element. The tunnel led to a low, circular room with doors for walls and cobwebs for a ceiling.

After picking a door following a good ten minutes of arguing, they entered a winding, unlit passageway, with Smoot and Billie sniping at each other every step of the way. Melissa had just kept on walking and watching, letting the groupmind of her search party guide all of them.

Finally, they staggered through the darkness into a smooth-walled cave that opened up onto this gray, dusty world. Another ten minutes of searching was lost as everyone wandered in circles, looking up and down, trying to figure out how this place was possible.

And now they stood at a clearing at one end of a broken bridge that had once spanned a black river fifty feet below, the water easily a hundred feet wide and giving off a sulfurous stench.

Melissa kept thinking how much Gil and Noah would have loved every minute of this little adventure of hers, this twisted fairy tale. For her, though, she felt closer and closer to screaming at the other people around her with each step she took away from her farm and land. All she could do was clamp her mouth shut and focus on doing whatever it took to get her boy—*both* her boys—back.

"Look, Butch," Smoot was saying, as everyone either peered down the vine-choked ravine or gazed in wonder at the chopped-off bridge. "We gotta do what the ball says. I *know* I saw it pointin' a little green laser beam of light down this street—" he aimed a thick finger at the road ahead of them, parallel to the river "—right before it went out again. So that means we haul ass down that street next to the river. I don't see the reason for your confusion, honey."

Melissa gripped the tiny oak in her hand, something she'd been doing almost non-stop in the past hour. The tree gave her a concrete link to the world above, regardless of the circumstances in which she'd found it. As Billie hissed something at Smoot, Melissa looked down at the river with a shiver of vertigo. On either side of the black water, an explosion of bright yellow vines had taken root, covering the ground like snakes. Trapped inside the vines were bits of plastic, metal, paper, and other garbage. She touched the slick ropey material holding her hair back. It was like kudzu. Undercity kudzu.

She felt a sudden chill. Undercity. Where did I learn *that* name?

"Hold on one second. What do you know about that ball, old man?" Billie stood with her big arms crossed over her chest, her long gray hair mottled with cobwebs and sweat like the rest of the group. "Who says we should trust it? It hasn't helped us yet. I already lost a tit to radiation. I don't want to lose anything more."

"I know a little somethin' about them balls," Smoot said. "Let's just say there's more than one, and this one is back in the place where it came from. They come up out of the land like bits of shrapnel pushing out of a soldier's ten-year-old wound. The ball's our best bet. Even if Paco here don't seem to know how to use it yet."

"Smoot," Melissa said, tearing her gaze away from the water of the river before it hypnotized her, and before Billie could retort. "If you knew something about the ball, why didn't you say something earlier? Like when Julio was knocking himself out trying to figure out which door to take in that cave full of cobwebs?"

"Pain in the ass," Dun muttered from ten feet away, where he and Herschel were picking and digging at the broken edge of the bridge.

"Got to be systematic about this," Herschel added, tweaking a long, bent piece of metal stretching out over the abyss two feet from him. If they weren't moving quite so slowly and groaning every time they bent down to get a closer look at something, the two elderly men could've been mistaken for a pair of twelve-year-old boys out exploring an abandoned house.

"Crazy old coots," Smoot muttered next to her, earning another dirty look from Billie.

"Well?" Melissa said, glancing at Smoot but growing impatient now. Three times on the way to this bridge, the ball had given out a flashing beam of light, each one so fast Melissa had never been sure she'd actually seen anything. They'd been following the direction of each beam, but that had been an easy choice; the road had been straight and unbroken, so there'd been no other way to go, until now.

Melissa knew that Smoot wasn't going to answer her or the others with anything other than a shit-eating grin. Billie stepped away from him with effort, blowing out a sudden exhalation like a horse after a sudden gallop, and they went to stand next to the two old men on the ruined bridge.

Back the way they'd came was nothing but gray shadows and a narrow street of sticky asphalt. The doorless buildings on either side of that street had kept them from seeing anywhere but ahead of them, leading them to this cleared space giving way without rhyme or reason to the river and its ruined bridge.

"Melissa," Julio said, materializing next to Melissa so suddenly she took a quick step away from him. "You should watch this."

He held up the black ball again, just as he had in the room walled with portals. This time the ball was turning in his hand, and Julio wasn't turning his wrist or doing anything else to make it spin.

"I am thinking only of Noah," Julio said, and Melissa looked over at him. His face was serene, peaceful as a quiet Sunday afternoon, and she believed him. "The ball will find him. I know this."

Just go with it, Melissa told herself. Don't examine it too closely. Maybe he's onto something.

The gray lines etched into the sides of the sphere began to make swirling designs as it spun, and then that familiar green light bubbled up from the lines, converged in a tiny ball of light, and shot out and away from Julio in a finger-tip-thick beam. The beam just missed Herschel, whose back was to them, and crossed over the gravel drive leading up to the bridge. It traveled down the concrete-white road running parallel to the river—Smoot grunted in triumph at that—before bending off to the right. From asphalt to gravel to concrete, the green beam traveled down a street bordered with absurdly tall curbs, then went out.

Melissa had somehow not noticed that part of this strange underground city before. As if it had just popped into existence, thanks to the black ball. She reminded herself to breathe.

"That's *it*, Papa," Anna said, pulling Billie closer in her excitement. "Down there. Noah's there. It's where all the lost kids end up."

Melissa looked away, back at the bridge, just for a second imagining it stretching out in front of her instead of sheared off at both banks. How many feet and cars and bikes had once crossed that span? When did it fall?

At least with the bridge out she didn't have to consider crossing that wicked stretch of water. From somewhere ahead of her, maybe in the exact same direction the ball had pointed them, a familiar smell was tickling her nose in spite of the rotten-eggs odor of the river. She took a few steps closer to the concrete road and smelled it even more strongly. It was something she hadn't smelled in years: Motor oil and burnt plastic.

"Let's get moving," Smoot said. "The ol' ball has spoken, I'd say."

"Do you hear that?" Billie said, moving away from Smoot and walking next to the fading green beam from the black ball, careful not to get too close. "Sounds like doors slamming."

Herschel extricated himself from the twisted metal. "This bridge had to have been bombed," he said. "I think we walked into a war zone down here."

"Hurry up!" Anna said, waving at everyone from the other side of the gravel road leading to the bridge. "We're almost there!"

"Wait," Melissa said. Everything was happening too fast, and everyone kept talking all at once. "Just hold on," she said, but Billie and Smoot, followed closely by Julio, were already moving away from her, walking onto the concrete road as the green light faded completely from the ball. Dun and Herschel looked at her, gave her identical shrugs, and followed the others.

Pushing down the instinct to chase after them like a lost little kid herself, afraid of being left all alone down here, Melissa walked slowly onto the road of crushed rock that led to the bridge. Off to her right, the gravel road ended abruptly after about a hundred yards—a football field—at the closed door to some sort of garage.

"Some road," she whispered. "Ends up in two dead ends."

From far below, as if trying to answer her, a low wailing sound rose up from what seemed like the depths of the river. The sound was sad, like the wind on a winter day, but with a mix of anger and frustration in it as well. Like a child who can't yet talk, but knows how to *scream*. Not a child, but a baby.

Sudden, unwanted tears blurred her vision, and Melissa lost sight of the bridge and the gap ahead of her. She took a step forward, blinking hard until she could see straight, but she couldn't locate the source of the sound. Already it was fading. She took another step onto the wrecked bridge, feet tapping on the bits of warped wood and twisted metal before she put her weight down.

Nothing. She couldn't see anything below her but black, smelly water.

Who had been crying like that? The voice had been familiar, younger than Noah. Like something from a dream—

A hand grabbed her upper arm.

"Melissa," Julia hissed. "*Ten cuidado*, please!"

With a sudden intake of breath, Melissa looked down and saw that the toes of her shoes were dangling over empty space. One more step, and she'd be gone. Gripping the small wooden tree tight in her hand, she stepped back onto the gravel, away from the bridge.

"This way," Julio said, watching her closely from under the brim of his Bulls cap. She could see the fatigue and worry etched there in the tiny wrinkles at the corners of his dark brown eyes.

"Thanks," she said. Her legs went rubbery for a second, thinking about the five-story drop into that bad water. Without saying anything more, she and Julio followed the tracks that their fellow searchers had left in the dust of the white concrete of the new road Julio's ball had found.

They stepped silently down the road as it narrowed to a three-foot-wide gap between cement barriers. Julio let her push through the opening first—yet another portal, she thought—and once she'd passed through it, she saw nothing but crooked houses protected by curbs as tall as Noah.

But at her feet, in the white dust of the concrete road, she could see the faint twin tracks of a small-wheeled car. The track wavered erratically, as if the car had simply rolled forward after the emergency brake had let loose. She looked both ways, but couldn't see any cars on the long stretch of road. The light here was dim, as if lit with just a pair of evenly spaced, forty-watt light bulbs.

For a good two minutes, she and Julio followed the tracks of the car mingled with the trudging footsteps of her search party, the stink growing in her nostrils until she wanted to sneeze with each breath. Like walking in fog, she could only see thirty or forty feet in front of her in the weak gray light, and all she could hear was her and Julio's soft breathing and muffled footsteps, churning up dust.

Finally, as they caught up to the others huddled together next to one of the tall curbs, she saw the source of the burnt-oil smell. She knew that odor: someone's old beater had left an oil stain in the road fifty feet ahead of her, just like Gil's old Escort used to do, all over their garage floor. The stain was in front of a rickety, leaning, four-story monstrosity of a house whose front door had been broken in. Violently.

This was it. Melissa sucked in a dusty breath and patted Julio's arm. They'd been pulled here sure as if the house was a magnet and they were all wearing metal shoes. Noah had to be here, along with Gil. She could almost feel their presences.

As the others pulled themselves onto the high curb in front of the house, only to stand perched there like oversized birds, Melissa looked down at the Rorschach-like oil spill on the road. It looked like a map of their land, with dust motes stuck into it to symbolize where their house and buildings stood, almost engulfed in the black liquid. Flooded in darkness, or polluted water.

"What the hell?" she whispered. The map reminded her of Ray's map from up in his shed, and she wished now she would've folded it up and slid it into her pocket. She'd left it sitting on the floor of Ray's shed, along with his little day planner.

Before Melissa could call the others over to examine the map, she saw sudden movement ahead of her. Julio stepped off the curb and onto the front lawn. He immediately sank down to his knees.

"Keep going," Smoot shouted. "Don't stop now, Chico, or you'll never make it!"

"Papa!" Anna cried out, lunging after her father. She hit the dust and sank to her belly. Julio spun, still sinking, and grabbed for Anna and the curb behind them. The black ball slid out of his grasp and fell clanging to the concrete road. Anna clung to her father's arm until they were both out of the dust and back on the curb once more.

Melissa watched all this, with no reaction other than the dulling chill of fear—horror—spreading up from her gut and coming to rest in the middle of her chest. She was thinking of the car that smelled just like the stink left in the heavy, unhealthy air of this place, and she was also remembering something Gil had said to her, just this morning. He'd been half asleep, stumbling his way out of the bedroom in the darkness, pre-coffee.

"Wish I could find the keys to that old Escort," he'd said.

He hadn't mentioned the Escort since it had stalled out on them for the last time five years ago, and they'd donated it to charity. This had been right after Noah was born and she'd insisted he give up the car. A rolling deathtrap, she called it.

Maybe I just dreamed it all, Melissa thought as something tapped against her left foot and a dull rumbling sound filled the air. Gil's not sleeping well, which means I'm not sleeping well, thanks to his tossing and turning. She never seemed to get good and asleep enough to have dreams anymore.

She looked down and saw the black ball resting against her shoe. It had found her again, just like that day on the porch, when it covered her with energy and made her nauseous all day.

The low rumbling had risen to the sound of an engine. A car engine, Melissa realized.

"Gil," she whispered, looking back and forth on the street. There weren't any sidewalks down here, just that ridiculously high curb on either side of the road, so she and her friends were completely exposed here. The others were dusting off Julio and Anna up their four-foot-high perch, and Smoot had turned her way.

The engines—more than one, now, she could tell—were coming toward them from the opposite direction in which Melissa and the others had walked.

They sound like trucks, not cars, she thought, shoving the tiny tree back into the pocket of her shorts. Blue pickemup trucks. I'd seen them this morning on the farm. Hadn't I?

Unable to stop herself, ignoring the roar of the pickemups coming at her, Melissa bent down and touched her finger to the oil staining the street, then pulled back when the oil map evaporated, leaving just a shadowy outline on the concrete. She rested her hand on top of the ball without thinking about it.

"Gil," she said, unable to hear her own words. "What the hell is *happening* down here?"

Then the three blue trucks arrived, hauling Gil's Escort behind them like burly guards manhandling a feeble prisoner, and Melissa never learned the answer to her whispered question.

വൗ

If she had the strength, Melissa would have launched the black ball like a fastball at Smoot's head. This was all his doing, after all. He'd come along to make sure everyone kept to his script, his plan.

The blue pickup trucks sat idling like growling dragons less than ten feet away from her and the rest of her dusty party. In the other world, high above, Melissa had always felt annoyed by these pickups and their jangling mufflers and black-tinted windows. She'd figured they were being driven by a bunch of teenagers or a renegade landscaping company. Noah always called them pickemup trucks. The last thing she'd expected was to see them again down here.

"Everyone stay back," Smoot said, leaping down from the curb with a surprising amount of agility for a man his size and age. He walked out in front of the middle truck. This was the one with Gil's Escort dangling like a caught fish from a hook above its king-sized bed. "*I'll* handle this."

When she saw Smoot's confident smile and heard him call out a light-hearted "*Que pasa*" to the drivers of the truck, Melissa reached for the black ball next to her, still resting on the road. She was going to need it, even if it made her vision go green and turned her stomach to mush again. Smoot had turned on them, and they needed every advantage they could get.

"So why won't they get out of their damn trucks?" she whispered to Julio.

Sitting on the curb, Julio shrugged at her, creating a cloud of dust around him. He was listening to Smoot, wincing occasionally, most likely from Smoot's mangled Spanish.

"He thinks they are his friends," Julio whispered. Billie grunted, her face red with betrayed anger. "He told them he's glad they finally made it. That he's got some work for them to do." Julio's face tightened as he strained to hear what Smoot was saying. "And that their money would be paid to them soon."

"Traitor," Dun hissed from where he was sitting on the curb, head in his hands.

"I knew it," Billie said.

Herschel was looking up at the house, oblivious to Smoot's chatter. "What are the odds," he said, as if to himself. A door slammed somewhere inside the leaning, motley house.

The ball began to turn in Melissa's hands as she followed Herschel's gaze up toward the house. She saw something move inside the broken doorway, along with a fluttering pair of blinds in a mismatched window higher up. Holding tight to the ball, she moved closer to where Herschel stood next to the curb. But she couldn't go any farther, not with Gil's old car back from the dead. Was Noah in there, behind the tinted windshield of one of the pickemup trucks?

"He's telling them all about us," Julio said.

"That does it," Billie said, pushing away from the curb. "I'm kicking his ass, right here in front of his illegal alien employees."

No sooner had Billie taken two steps when the doors to all three trucks swung open, propelled by long white arms. Impossibly long arms.

"Hold on, now," Smoot said, forgetting his Spanish. "Y'all just settle down, y'hear?"

Gil's not here anymore, Melissa realized as the drivers and passengers of the trucks unfolded themselves. And neither he nor Noah were in those trucks. These men—*bendy men*, a voice not unlike Noah's whispered in her head—were not human. Their arms and legs were like tubes, stretched out of proportion, and she had trouble seeing their faces. Her head began to ache, just looking at their distorted bodies and oval heads.

"Everyone back in the pool," she said, pulling herself up onto the high curb. "Smoot's on his own."

The others paused only for a second, frozen by Smoot's voice, going from confident drawl to panicked bluster to something else. Fear-tinged anger.

Julio got to his feet next to her, holding tight to Anna as they balanced on the six inches of curb. The house seemed much too far away.

"I'm sorry," Melissa said. She remembered how fast he and his daughter had sunk into the dust. "We've got to get to the house. We can't stay on the road. We're targets there."

Julio nodded, shielding Anna with his body as Smoot began to scream behind them. The old man was buying them some time, at least. "Let's go, then."

Melissa, with the two elderly men on her right, and Julio, Anna, and Billie on her left, took a quick breath of stale Undercity air—there's that name again, she thought—and then jumped off the curb into the gray dust of the lawn in front of her, the black ball pointing the way at last with a beam of green light that shot over the dust, onto the middle porch, and through the open front doorway. The front door had been shattered, Melissa could see now.

I've done stupider things, she thought as she landed in the dust and immediately began to sink. But not many.

CHAPTER TWENTY:
FALLING, BUT NOT ALONE

Noah was glad his sister was with him as he fell. This was a day when he'd been *with* someone, then alone, then with someone, over and over again. The alone times always were the worst. The bad stuff kept happening when he was alone, like falling into the hole, getting lost down in the darkness as soon as he walked through the magnet door, and tiptoeing through the door-filled house on his way to see the dragon.

Now at least he could squeeze Sophie's hand, even if her fingers were cold, and feel a tiny bit braver as they both dropped through the door into a tunnel of spinning lights worse than the strobe lights in the haunted house Dad had taken him to last year.

Sophie's here, Noah told himself, and she needs me to take care of her. She needs me to be brave.

"Close your eyes," he shouted to her as they fell. He saw more of those flat TV screens all around them—maybe they were causing the flashing lights, he thought—and on one he'd seen stuff on fire and people screaming. Old people, like the ones who worked with Mom on the farm. Other screens had even worse images, like people falling out of speeding cars or jumping from crumbling buildings or sinking in gray quicksand.

"Don't look, Sophie."

The fall took his breath away after that, and he held tight to his sister, his own eyes squeezed shut as well. They fell for what felt like forever, and then they landed, soft as jumping off the bottom step of the porch.

Noah touched the cold dirt floor under him, smelling grease in the warm, heavy air. It wasn't the good smell of grease, like when Mom made bacon and Dad cooked up waffles to go with them, but old, nasty, French-fry-smelling grease. The stuff that always made Noah want to take a bath after smelling it for too long. Mom never took him to the place Dad called Mickey D's or even a Burger King, and on the few times Dad had snuck him into a Chick Fil-A or the greasiest place of them all, Time-Out Chicken in Chapel Hill, Noah had always felt a bit sick after chowing down on a fried sandwich and hot, salty fries. But they tasted so good, going down.

At last Noah opened his eyes. Like a reminder of the kest he had to finish, another nasty stream went past Noah's feet, flowing uphill through the tunnel they'd dropped into. The walls were smooth dirt, while the floor was squishy as cheese. The tunnel itself was wide as a car. The greasy stream gave off a strange heat, and it ran up the middle of the tunnel, drawing a wavering line between Noah and his sister. A weak gray light lit up the tunnel about half a football field away from them.

"Watch out," Noah whispered, trying to keep Sophie from stepping into the warm, greasy river, but it was too late. She'd inched closer to him and, in the process, she'd gotten her toes wet. Just like that, the miniature river snagged her and she was half-running, half-stumbling up the tunnel, caught in its current. She didn't even scream.

"Sophie!" Noah took off after her, scared she was going to take a bad tumble and hit her head. At the same time, he couldn't figure out how the tiny stream no wider than his hand was able to pull her away like that. "Jump out of it! It's not that big!"

Within three more seconds, Sophie was at the top of the tunnel, the stream running uphill, and Noah was running so hard he kicked right out of his sandals. The hill was steeper than it looked, and soon he was gasping for air.

"Jump, Sophie!" he shouted with the last of his breath, and just at the edge of his vision in the tunnel, her small form lit by the gray light far ahead of them, he saw his little sister lean hard to the left, and then fall out of the backward river.

"Oh no," Noah panted, his bare feet slapping on the packed dirt beneath him.

After what felt like an hour of hard running, a stitch digging itself into his side and spreading upwards toward his armpit, Noah made it to his little sister's side. This place just kept getting bigger, somehow. Sophie lay on her back, eyes closed, hands resting at her side. She wasn't moving.

"Sophie," Noah whispered, crying tears of pain and frustration. He'd just met her, and now she was dead again. "Sophie, wake up."

Waiting for his baby sister to draw a breath or open her eyes, Noah stopped breathing himself and listened. He'd heard something, far above him. A low rumbling sound that grew louder, then went away. He looked up and saw, not ten feet above him, a round black disk embedded in the dirt. The gray light was coming from this disk, slipping though the five holes punched into it.

"Manhole," he whispered, squinting up at the disk and the light.

As soon as he spoke, he heard Sophie move on the ground below him. With a sudden head rush, Noah looked down and saw his sister sliding across the soft dirt floor toward the greasy river again.

Her eyes opened at last, and she mouthed Noah's name, along with a word that could only be "Help!"

Noah dropped to the floor and wrapped Sophie in his arms. The river was still pulling at her, like a magnet. He pushed away from the river, on his hands and knees, always keeping himself between Sophie and the polluted water.

He was almost ready to give in when his reaching hand hit something cold and metal, and he latched onto it with all his remaining strength, keeping Sophie close in the grip of his other arm. She slid forward a tiny bit, headed for the water again, and then she stopped. She felt like a baby doll in his arms, cold but shivering.

They were safe. For now.

"What's happening?" Noah whispered, and he heard the scaredness in his voice. "Why can't you stay out of the water?"

Sophie just closed her eyes and shook her head, as if to say "I don't know."

Noah wished she'd talk to him, but for some reason he understood why she didn't. She didn't know how. And she'd never learn how.

"It's okay," he whispered, feeling just a tiny bit like Prince One-Eye again. "I've got you now."

He felt something start to hurt in his right hand, and he looked at the piece of metal he was squeezing with it. He didn't dare let go. It was part of a ladder, he realized, with more metal pieces above it and below it. One led up to the manhole and what might be the real world, away from the Undercity. The other led down, through a round hole in the floor that Sophie had almost fallen into. The trickle of river dripped down through that hole.

Now that he'd caught his breath and wasn't fighting to keep his sister out of the river, Noah could smell the stink of something dead coming from that hole. Lots of dead things, actually.

"Oh boy," he said. "I think I know which way we have to go, Sophie. But I'm not crazy about it."

Noah felt even more like a character in one of Dad's Prince One-Eye stories. What would Dad say here, in the story? Something like, "You have to go down, as far down as you can go, before you can go up.'"

Down it was. Going up wouldn't do them any good. Up there was the forest, nothing more. Here was the bad river he'd been looking for. Noah didn't dare let go of Sophie, so he half-walked her, half-dragged her to the rim of the hole and sat her up there, careful not to touch the water next to him or let her fall forward into the nothingness.

"Want a horsey-back ride?"

The smile that his sister gave him as an answer gave Noah the last burst of strength he needed to carry Sophie down the wet rungs of metal into the deepest section of the Undercity he'd seen so far.

"Don't be scared," he said to his sister, leaning away from the dripping water from the greasy waterfall next to them. "I'll tell you a story on the way down."

⌒o⌒

Noah told himself he was not going to look down, even as he felt the cave open up all around him, a too-warm breeze tickling his skin and the smell of grease and rot filling his nose.

Starting with one of his favorites, Noah told Sophie about Jack and the beanstalk. This time, though, the golden goose didn't holler for the giant while Jack was on his way down the stalk. The goose just held tight to his back and told Jack which handholds were best for climbing.

Noah paused in his story to catch his breath. He was dying to look around, aching to itch his nose, but his arms started shaking, so he kept on creeping down, the metal rungs cold and slick under his hands and bare feet.

After what felt like hours, he made it to the wet, spongey surface of the cave. With both feet on the unsteady ground, Noah realized he couldn't let go of the last rung of the ladder. In his 'magination, or maybe it was actually real, he felt like the wall that held the ladder going back up would rush away from him and leave him stranded in the middle of this vast open place.

With one hand still locked on the metal rung, his sister still clinging to his back like a baby monkey from one of Mom's Discovery Channel shows, Noah took his first real look around.

He and Sophie were in a wide open wasteland.

The cave was so big that he couldn't take it all in with one look. He had to look back at the ladder leading up the side of the cave wall, and the weak light and dark water trickling down from the room high above them, much farther away than he remembered. Did I really climb down that far? He'd counted maybe fifty rungs in the ladder, but what he saw above him had to be closer to a hundred, maybe more.

No wonder my arms hurt, he thought. Going back up was not going to be fun.

In a way, this wide open, uninhabited wasteland seemed to contain the entire aboveground world, but with everything reversed or flipped. Noah saw trees, but they were buried upside-down, so their roots stuck up in the air. Sludgy black rivers moved around the trees, creating slow whirlpools spinning in the wrong direction. Clumps of mud rose up out of the rivers like islands, but they would sink whenever Noah looked at them for more than a second.

And covering everything, floating in the water, coating the tree roots, was garbage. Broken bottles, soggy cardboard, paper, rusty metal, bent plastic. The smell was worse than the stink coming from the dump Dad had driven him past one day a few weeks ago. The place had made Dad really mad, for some reason. Noah was starting to understand why, now.

This was the *real* Undercity, Noah realized, feeling Sophie squirm on his back. This was what this place was really like.

The polluted cave went on forever, starting at this ladder and spreading, filled with countless rivers of pollution running backward. Far off in the distance, Noah could see tiny puffs of green, but even as he watched, the blackness crept up on one patch of grass and covered it, killing it and turning it black as well. The Undercity was spreading like spilled milk on the tiles of the kitchen floor.

Sophie's arms around his neck had grown so tight that Noah could barely breathe. At the same time, he could feel her legs dangling on his back, kicking him softly as she hung there. He had to let go of the ladder to keep from losing his balance and stop Sophie from sliding off into the mucky water now covering his bare feet.

As soon as he lost contact with the metal, the wall did exactly what he'd feared it would do—it rushed away from him so silently, like a magic trick, that Noah wondered if it had ever been there in the first place. At least the stinky waterfall went away as well when the ladder disappeared.

"Don't touch the water!" he hissed at his sister, whose toes were inches from the muck. She'd been wriggling ever since he put his feet down on the surface of the cave, as if it hurt her being here. Still she said nothing, but he could hear an occasional grunt or puff of air on his neck and arms.

The size of this place was making Noah's head hurt. It felt wrong to him, not just the impossible depth and width of the place but the switched-up colors of the place.

He'd spent one rainy Saturday last month looking at pictures with Dad and Julio and Julio's kids, and he'd found an envelope filled with black strips of film. When he held one of them up to the light, he could see the black smile of a white-faced Julio. All the colors were reversed in that picture. Dad called it a negative. And that's what this place was—a negative of the world up above.

"Please stop squirming," Noah hissed. He inhaled and nearly gagged on the smell. "I've got to figure out which way we need to go, okay?"

Careful not to put his bare foot down on glass or anything else sharp, Noah turned a slow circle, taking in the garbage-strewn basement to the Undercity. He heard another rumbling sound fill the air, high above him, but when he looked up, he couldn't see the roof of the cave anymore. Just blackness.

He was just starting his second circle when one of the hands around his neck lost its grip.

"Sophie? You all right?"

He looked up and saw his sister's hand, pointing at a clump of flipped-over trees. On the other side of the tree, almost completely buried by black plastic bags that were in the process of spilling their guts everywhere, Noah could see a small patch of green grass poking out above the surface of the dark water.

"That's it, isn't it?" Noah began picking his way through the warm water and garbage, biting his lip in concentration. Sophie patted him on the back and held tight to him, hardly squirming any longer. She'd managed to find something still alive down here, something that hadn't turned brown or started to rot.

Noah retold the story of Jack and the beanstalk as he walked, starting off with the seeds tossed out the window and the stalk rising up outside his house the next day. Lucky for Jack he got to go up instead of down like me, Noah thought.

He looked for the island of green ahead of him, lost it for a panicky moment, and then his sister pointed it out to him again. Getting closer.

Noah had always wondered about the goose that laid golden eggs. Did you crack open the eggs and eat them and sell the shells? Or was it solid gold? If that was the case, well, poor goose. That had to hurt. He hoped the goose was happy with Jack and his family, now that the giant was gone.

Coming around the pile of trees, he kept watching for someone or something to jump out at him, but nothing living seemed to come down here, just him and Sophie. She felt lighter than ever, even though Noah was dog-tired.

Just a little bit farther, he told himself.

He pushed his way through a waste-high creek of garbage-filled water that reminded him, not in a nice way, of the dusty yard high above them. Noah pulled himself up onto the square patch of grass his sister had found for him and threw himself up the last few feet until he was resting on his belly on the grass, sinking the tiniest bit into its muddy surface.

Somehow this grass had stood up against the pollution of the Undercity. Something strong was holding it together. Noah could feel it under him, almost like a tiny pulse. His spirits lifted, just touching this healthy, living piece of this underworld.

And that was it, of course. It all came back to Jack and the Beanstalk—the magic seeds! That was why he came down here.

Just as he was about to ask Sophie where to dig, he realized that she'd slipped off his back. She stood a few feet away, at the very center of the small, shrinking island of green, and her feet had sunk into the ground to her ankles. She pointed at the ground in front of her, smiling and crying at the same time.

"No!" Noah shouted. "Stay, Sophie! Don't go away now! You're my *'sponsibility*."

Sophie just shook her head and wiped away her tears. She pointed once more at the ground in front of Noah.

Dig.

Noah felt like his heart would crack open, but he nodded.

"Okay," he whispered, blowing her a kiss with his filthy hand as she sank farther into the muck. He'd never reach her.

"Thank you, Sophie," he added, tears spilling from his own eyes, turning this inside-out, upside-down cave into a blur of browns and blacks.

And then Noah dropped to his knees on the last patch of grass left in this underground place, and he began to dig.

CHAPTER TWENTY-ONE:
DEAD AGAIN, FOR THE FIRST TIME

I knew what it was like to be dead.

I'd been dead for half of my twenties and a large portion of my thirties. The farm was what resuscitated me and pulled me out of my rut, my day-to-day misery. The farm, and my son, of course, and Melissa too. But ultimately it was the idea behind the farm—the dream of creating it and raising our kids there—that rescued me from the dead landscape of fluorescent lights, gray cubicles, and climate-controlled air.

I knew a guy there at the corporate campus who hadn't seen the sun in fifteen years. He worked long days during the week, and whenever I had to work on the weekend, he was there, fixing and improving the server farms. The guy had a little place of his own set up in a windowless corner of the long, endless hallway that was the server room—a fridge and microwave, piles of quarters for the vending machines, a nasty yellow-looking cot next to the oldest, loudest of the racks of data-crunching machines. He claimed he slept better in that chilly room with all the humming and buzzing, better than he'd ever slept with his ex.

I found out that he'd sold his house years ago and rerouted all his mail to his work address. The crazy bastard actually did live at work. Probably never saw the sun. What the hell? And why? He surely made three or four times as a permanent employee than what I was pulling down as a lowly contractor.

But that was the life he chose for himself. He probably never thought about whether he was alive or dead.

And that's when I knew I had to get out. That sort of crazy was contagious. Happens when you let your work become your world.

My world. I'd lost my grip on my world the day we lost Sophie.

She wasn't supposed to be sick like that. All the OB-GYN tests had come back negative, all the physicals except that last one had been without a hitch. We'd done everything right, though Melissa would only blame herself in the days and weeks after that awful delivery. Still the universe found it necessary to humble us and take our baby from us.

God damn it, it wasn't fair.

I knew what it was like to be dead, and I knew too what it was like to see death, the nightmare of all parents come to fruition. Seeing her tiny, motionless body that day, pulled from Melissa's belly as part of the c-section we'd planned weeks earlier, broke something in my heart and in my brain. Living in that damaged state was far worse than being dead had been.

And now it was over, thanks to the Undercity.

∝

Under the surface of the worst, foulest lake imaginable, Gil could feel himself shutting down. Dying, again. All alone.

He sank deeper, arms tight to his chest, legs numb from the pressure of the sheer volume of waste pressed against them, and waited for it to end. He'd failed, just like all his schemes and plans had failed before. Foolish quests and wasted plots.

But just as he was ready to give in and stop fighting the panic and pain, right before he simply let go and inhaled the foulness surrounding him, he realized he was no longer alone. And he was able to breathe.

A petite, white-haired woman had joined him under the surface of the lagoon. She was sitting in a little pocket of air, toking on the fattest joint Gil had ever seen, smiling at him like the Buddha as she held in the smoke. It was Missus Finley-Thompson.

When he leaned forward, breathing hungrily as something wet dripped off his face, she jammed the j right into Gil's mouth. He greedily sucked in the herbs along with whatever oxygen he could get inside her impossible little bubble of air, blessed air. And he didn't even cough. Not bad for a guy who hadn't had the wacky weed for over a decade.

He exhaled and told himself he wasn't even going to ask her what she was doing here. He knew he was most likely dead, just like she no doubt was. He'd failed.

"Can't believe you found me," she said in her raspy voice, rubbing a hand over her short-cropped hair.

The bubble was sinking, slowly.

"I think you know why I'm here, Missus F-T. I have to find my boy."

"This is the last place I'd expect an environmentalist like you." She coughed out a laugh. "Mr. Organic. Hope you enjoyed *our* farm all those years. Smooth-talking land-grabber."

"I'm not sure I appreciate your tone," Gil shot back. "Where's Noah?"

Missus F-T answered by plucking the joint from his mouth. He'd forgotten it was even there. Honest.

Gil's head was already going light from that lone toke of cannabis. Tying to get his bearings, he looked down at himself and saw that instead of muck and filth, he was covered in a fine coating of condensation, as if he'd just passed through a mist of clean water instead of thirty feet of waste.

That little transition, Gil thought, did not bode well for me and my grip on reality and mortality.

"'Fraid you'll have to deal with my tone," Missus F-T snapped as they continued to sink. She did not offer him another tote. "At least for a few minutes longer. I mean, this *is* my place you've intruded upon. For the second time."

The woman floating in front of Gil had the wrinkles and weary expression of a woman a decade past mandatory retirement age, except for her eyes. Maybe it was the pot, or the diminishing supply of oxygen in here—Gil could see the shit swirling around outside, as if they were in a see-through bubble—but her eyes were just as focused and fierce as Melissa's when he'd told her Noah was lost again that morning. She could tear a hole in you with that gaze.

And she had yet to answer his question.

"Tell me about Noah, Missus F-T, and I'll be out of your hair."

The petite woman waved at him with an "in a minute" gesture and got busy with the last bit of her joint. That thing had gone up fast, and her little bubble was turning translucent from the exhaled, sweet-and-sour pot smoke.

It *did* feel medicinal, Gil thought, remembering Ray's crazy histories. It also was making him a bit crazy. He'd been searching for too long today, been through too much. He wasn't able to stop his tongue from flinging more sarcasm her way, like a shit-throwing monkey.

"I see you've been keeping up with this place you've got here, just like you did with your old digs. What the hell did you guys grow in that lake on the farm before we moved in there? Mutant sea monkeys from the back pages of old comics? That mess took a year to clear up."

He trailed off as Missus F-T sucked in most of the air left in the bubble and lifted herself up just the tiniest bit in preparation for what felt like a good, long-winded speech. Gil decided to head her off at the pass.

"And what'd you do with Mister F-T?" he began. "Did you stuff him down in the dust of those front lawns up there? Was that him grabbing at my ankles up there? Or did you give up on him and hook up with your Herb-ology buddy, good ol' cough-up-your-lungs Ray?

Come on, you can tell me. It's just you and me down here in Never Neverland."

That almost got her. He saw the twitch in her face, a new set of crows-feet around her eyes that appeared like magic. And then she regained control, and the wrinkles went away.

"You really don't understand what I went through to get you here, do you? Or why I brought you here in the first place."

"Nope," Gil said, going to one knee as their bubble rocked suddenly and stopped. "Let's go up to the farm and you can tell me about it, why don't we?"

Either we've hit the bottom of this lake of shit, he thought, or I'm about to wake up. Neither opportunity appealed much to him.

Missus F-T took another breath, one so deep Gil felt the bubble shrink even farther. Then she began to talk.

"You were the one who talked us into leaving. We tried not to come back. You made moving away from here sound so appealing, so right. You made us think we needed you to buy it from us, someone who'd develop strong ties to the earth—what's forming under it and what's growing on top of it. You and your wife fit the bill. Even Ray approved, once he got over the fact that we'd be moving. But the mister didn't want to stay away. First he'd drive by the place, once or twice a day, and then he'd be slipping into the forest and getting some of his old friends to meet him there for their research and exploration. Losing this place killed him."

"Old friends," Gil said. He stayed down on one knee, unable to get up much higher. "Like Ray," he added. "And some messed-up homeless dude with some serious skeletal issues?

"That was two of them. Two of many. Ray was easy to rope into our schemes to get the land back, once I got him to work for me in exchange for clearing his lungs most of the time. Just cost me a couple plants and some sleight of hand."

Gil nodded sagely, thinking that Ray most likely had more control in this relationship than Missus F-T realized. The old man had some serious connections to the Undercity; you could see it in his eyes when he talked about the place.

Missus F-T continued. "Now, your friend you brained with the shovel took a bit more work, getting him to cooperate—he was so *dense*—but it was worth the effort, having a minion right under my thumb like that. Then the mister up and died on me, before we could get our land back. If only my vines had taken root down here faster. Pity."

"Wait a minute—" Gil gasped. The air in the bubble was about used up. He could feel it in the ache forming behind his eyes and the ringing in his ears.

"No," Missus F-T said, glancing at something just over Gil's right shoulder that took all his willpower not to look at as well. "I'm through with you now. Plus," she added, "*They're* here for you. My vines make the water a magnet for them, and I promised them they could have you."

Turning his head at last to look at who'd arrived behind him felt like the hardest act in his life Gil had ever performed, at least the most difficult task he'd yet faced today. He'd already heard them hissing, drowning out the ringing in his ears. His vision, already pink at the edges as it always did when he was mad, was turning a deep red color.

In spite of his discomfort and hopelessness, he could still smell it. The tangy scent of a con, in progress.

Someone was trying to fuck me over, Gil thought. This isn't about Missus F-T's revenge, as much as she may think so.

At last he made his neck tendons twist enough so he could see the new arrivals. The hissing grew louder. He should've known they'd be here, but he still flinched in surprise and gasped up the last of his air. Tiny white bodies, heads made up mostly of black eyes. Lost souls, needing warmth, no doubt. Trapped somehow by the vines feeding off the Undercity rivers.

"I promised them I'd let them have the person responsible for their recent . . . discomfort. I've been telling them about you for a while now. They didn't think you'd ever get here."

Missus F-T leaned close and gave Gil a wide-eyed grin, kissed him on the lips with a dull smacking sound, and then the bubble burst.

Even though his eyes were jammed shut as the tons of filth dropped on him once more, Gil could see the army of pale, black-eyed wraiths drop on him, screaming. Easily a hundred of them, moving through one another to get at him. Filled with a final burst of spastic, desperate energy, his lungs burning for air, he kicked and fought and struggled against the dozens of tiny hands gripping him, but all he succeeded in doing was injuring his bad hip again and opening up a new kind of pain in both shoulders.

They lifted him up so fast he stopped caring about not having any air in his lungs. Con or no con, he just wished now that it would all be over. Because despite the crud in his ears and the pain in his failing body, he could still hear their screaming. They were mad with pain and rage.

He let them drag him up and away from the bottom of the lagoon and into the foul air above it. Gil inhaled and exhaled twice before they reached the roof of the cave housing this heart of darkness being pumped out everywhere. They didn't even pause there, but kept going up, through solid rock. Gil didn't worry. This trip was over. He was ready to go back home.

He closed his eyes and took another shallow breath and hoped Melissa and the others had had better luck at finding Noah than him.

∽○∾

Noah dug as quickly as he could, fingers straining through the warm, heavy mud, but his sister was sinking faster than he could dig. She was slipping away from him, all because he had to finish this kest of his.

"Slow *down*," he said, tears squirting from his eyes in frustration. "Don't leave, Sophie!"

Sophie just nodded at him as her belly disappeared under the surface of the unsteady island of green in the vast black lake.

"What do I do with it when I get it?" Noah had to lean down over the hole he'd opened up and pushed with all his strength. He dug in with his bare toes for traction and clawed with his fingers mercilessly into the hardened layer of dirt under the black mud.

Sophie pointed upwards, toward the fading bits of sunlight high above them.

The earth was cool in his hands now, and Noah risked a glance at his sister. He could see *though* her, he realized. The muddy grass touched her chin and crept up her jaw. He could see the last patches of green down here slip under the influence of the hungry black water.

He snagged something with the tip of a bloodied finger. "Hold on," he said, afraid to look at Sophie as the mud covered the lower half of her face. "I've got something!"

Just before the mud and dying grass obscured the rest of her face, Sophie's blue eyes went wide. Her head nodded, then she went down, her blonde hair trailing after her like a kite's muddied tail.

Noah worked at the mud surrounding the tiny, warm ball in the ground, nearly three feet down, until he felt it give. He gripped the object—it was a seed, he could tell, like an acorn without its little fuzzy cap—tight in his fist and dove over to the spot where his sister had sunk into the mud. With his free hand he dug as hard as he could, but the warm mud she'd passed through was quickly thickening and turning cold.

Before Noah could cry out once more, he smelled something. Something fresh for a change. He looked down and nearly fell over. The grass under him was coming back, and the ground had become firm and solid. The green was spreading out around him like water spilling out of a huge barrel. Even the mud on his hands was drying and flaking off.

Around him, the changing Undercity began to rumble once more.

Noah thought about dropping the seed, just giving up, but he couldn't ignore the way his own hands and arms had been wiped clean of the dust, mud, and filth that he'd accumulated on this crazy day. He felt better, too, stronger, just from holding the little seed. It had a tiny pulse of its own, stronger than when he held two fingers on the inside of his own wrist like Mom had taught him. The seed had been lost and buried down here, he realized, and now he had to get it up to sunlight and fresh water.

And the best place for this seed, in Noah Anderson's opinion, was on Dad's farm.

Unable to even see the spot where Sophie had sunk into the mud, Noah turned and ran, tears of hope and loss warping his vision. He couldn't even see the wall with the metal ladder that had pulled away from him earlier, but he followed the last hints of light slipping in from high above, still thinking about his lost sister.

The water got her, he thought, just like it did in the tunnel. There's no way I can help her anymore.

As Noah ran, the blackness receded in front of him as if the seed in his hand was a green flashlight that lit up everything it touched with life. The stink of motor oil and plastic was being replaced by the clean smells of grass and vegetation. Noah ran faster, upwards, his path opening up before him as the seed pulled him toward the light.

"Why didn't they tell me?" he whispered, barely able to make a sound, he was so out of breath.

He ran, blinded by tears, unable to enjoy the rebirth of the Undercity taking place all around him.

"Noah," a small voice said, making Noah flinch and look around, even though he knew whose voice it was. "I'm okay. I have to go help someone else now. Someone who needs me."

"But," Noah said, slowing down and wiping his eyes. "Will I see you again? Ever?"

"Don't stop, big brother," Sophie said, and her name for him filled Noah with a final burst of energy. "Finish your kest, okay?"

Noah began running, and not far ahead of him he could see a vast wall opening up in the murky light. At its bottom was the opening to a tunnel. On either side of him, the trees had righted themselves, some of them even flipping back over as he drew closer, replanting themselves as the garbage surrounding them disintegrated with tiny puffs of smoke.

"And I'll see you again," Sophie whispered inside his head, accompanied by a spooky hissing sound that grew louder with each running step Noah took. "Somehow."

∞

I'm doing it again, Melissa thought, her mouth full of dust. I'm letting myself think of her again, and that's something I vowed never to do. Yet even as she half-walked, half-swam through the deep, dust-filled front yard, a name kept drumming itself inside her head like a cadence.

Sophie. Sophie Anderson. Baby Sophie.

She lifted her head and saw on the middle porch ahead of her—an indeterminate distance away from her in this shifty, poorly lit landscape—a man who looked suspiciously like their neighbor Ray. He was waiting for her on the porch, leaning forward, hands on knees, as if eager to see her sink into the dust along with the others. Ray the dog-killer. The husband-distracter. Possibly the child-abductor. Melissa focused on his bullet-shaped head and broad shoulders, letting her anger propel her as she swam one-armed through the thick, grasping dust.

Sophie. Baby Sophie.

The name was stuck on endless loop in her head, not even stopping when something bit at her bare legs in the clinging, sucking dust under her.

The fact that Ray had put in an appearance down here didn't even surprise her much. She kept expecting Gil to show up at any second as well, but you could never count on Gil to do anything you expected him to do. She just hoped Ray hadn't done anything to hurt Noah. Or Gil.

She didn't dare look behind her to where Smoot had been facing down the strange bendy men. With the frenzied sounds of the others struggling and fighting their way through the dust behind her, she couldn't hear his booming voice anymore. She wasn't sure if that was a good thing. At least not for Smoot.

Sophie, Sophie, Sophie. She kicked and pulled her way through the dust, the ball tight against her right side.

Her eyes were too full of dust to properly blink anymore, and more bits of what might have been bone and other unknown objects kept poking her legs and torso. She watched Ray slip back inside the house with a troubled look on his face, as if amazed that all his neighbors were making such good progress across this dusty moat protecting his crooked castle.

Mommy's coming, Noah. And Sophie. Sophie.

She was fifteen feet away when the little shit Eric from up the road replaced Ray up on the front porch. Was the whole neighborhood down here? Were the trophy-wife moms and ten-hour-a-day white-collar daddies inside, sipping lattes and scotch?

She paused—sinking immediately to her chest—when she saw that Eric was armed with doorknobs. He flung two at her, narrowly missing her head with his first throw. Melissa moved the black ball to her left hand and caught the second one. Treading dust, she returned the doorknob to Eric at full force, clipping him neatly on the forehead. He fell over with a thump, and Melissa made it to the front porch a few seconds later in an adrenaline-aided final surge.

"What the hell were you thinking?" she gasped to herself, checking to make sure she hadn't killed him. "He's just a kid."

To her relief, he was still breathing, and the other members of her search party were right behind her. She grabbed Julio's forearm and helped him and Anna up onto the porch. Spluttering and swearing, Dun made it next to the crowded porch, followed by Herschel, fat circles of dust sticking to his face and arms like polka dots. Billie pulled herself onto the bottom step of the porch and waited there, glaring into the house.

"Did I see that bastard Ray here a second ago?" she said.

Melissa could only nod from where she sat, bent over Eric. His mouth was dirty with what looked like the remnants of some candy mixed with dust.

"Typical man," Billie said, pushing past Melissa and the others so she could get into the house. "Let me take care of that good ol' boy, once and for all."

"Just wait—" Melissa began, but Billie was already inside the front door. "Damn. Everyone else stay here, okay?"

With a warning glance at the remaining searchers crowded onto the porch, followed by one last look out across the lawn that she immediately regretted—the bendy men stood in a line next to the curb, long arms folded across narrow chests, all of them watching and waiting, with no sight of Smoot anywhere—Melissa got up and followed Billie into the house.

The place had doors built into the floor, just like the two portals she'd discovered this morning. But these were full-sized doors, the real things, not the narrow little half-sized doors up in the sheds. At least three different sets of footprints crisscrossed the flooring next to the doors, and the house around her was eerily silent. She couldn't see Billie or Ray anywhere, though she did hear a door slam high above her, accompanied by a rumbling sound, almost like a growl.

Thinking of Noah, calling to mind the photo of him in the snow from last winter, with Gil's boot in the corner of the picture, Melissa held up the ball. It began turning again, giving off a soft green glow. The light narrowed itself into a beam, and she watched it roam around the room.

It stopped on a plain metal door, painted black. Her hands were shaking so badly that the ball drew strange symbols made of green light on the door's smooth, horizontal surface.

"I should wait for the others," she said, but she was already bending down for the knob. In the narrow strip of floor between the black door and an old-fashioned screen door sat a tiny black and green stick no larger than a child's pinkie finger. Something itched at Melissa's memory, looking at that object, but she couldn't figure out why. She gripped the knob to the black door and twisted it.

"Wait!" a voice cried, gravelly and panicked, from deeper inside the house. "Melissa, wait!"

She ignored the voice and the approaching footsteps. With the glowing black ball held tight against her belly, she hauled the metal door up and open. A damp wind rose up from the other side of the door.

Once more into the breach, she thought, feeling her Caesarean scar flare up, itching. No more waiting around.

From the corner of her eye, she saw a shadow fill the archway across the room for her. Instead of turning to see if was Billie or Ray, she closed her eyes and let herself fall forward through the open door in the floor.

༄

Melissa opened her eyes just an instant later to find that she was now standing up again, though she'd never felt her feet hit the ground.

Instead of the house, though, she found herself in a black cave, facing a pair of orange-tinted eyes as big as TV screens. The stink of burnt toast mixed with sulfur filled her nose, and she did her best not to topple over backward from the sudden changes buffeting her senses, especially her vision.

There was a *dragon* in front of her. Just like the beasts in one of Gil's stories.

You've got to be kidding me, she thought.

With that thought, she moved, instincts taking over. Her arms shot out like a point guard making a pass, and she launched the black ball at the snout of the huge creature in front of her.

The dragon snatched the ball from the air with a tiny twitch of its big head, bit down and turned the ball to powder. Flecks of green-glittering debris dusted the creature's brilliantly white, extremely long teeth.

"Thank you for returning that," the dragon said in a voice that was one step away from sounding human, and female, at that. "I assume the Gardener sent you. This looks like her handiwork. Now I'm *really* going to have to get out of here and find her."

"The Gardener? I don't know any Gardener."

Melissa's voice was barely a squeak, but her initial shock had worn off enough for her to attempt an assessment of the situation: she was still alive, surprisingly, and she was in a giant, windowless cave filled mostly with a dragon, but also another scurrying creature she could hear off to her left. Something small, climbing over the tall piles of gold and gems. What looked like a bright orange leopard or jaguar skin lay against the far wall, stained in places with dark blood.

"Go ahead," the dragon said. "Take a look around. But don't lie to me about your friend the Gardener. She's the one who uncovered these black orbs from my trove and took them aboveground, handing them out to her friends the bendy men. Lie to me again, and I'll see how bendy *you* can get."

Melissa stood up straight, arms at her side, and looked up at the dragon. She swallowed hard before talking.

"I'm telling you. I have no idea who this Gardener—wait. Oh, shit."

Ray's map. Melissa remembered it now, seeing it as clear as if it were right in front of her, instead of lying abandoned somewhere high above them in his shed, next to his portal.

"What would you say if I told you," Melissa began, remembering the scribbled words on the map she'd rescued from the vine-choked living room of Ray's trailer. "Let me get this right: 'The Gardener plots revenge from the bottom up, kids and all.'"

The dragon edged closer, all brimstone and smoky breath and narrowed orange eyes. "*Where* did you hear that?"

"Nowhere," Melissa said. "I read it, though, on a map, a long way from here." She looked up at the dragon, who seemed to have shrunk the slightest bit as it leaned over her. The cave was losing some of its luster as well, and some of the gold seen from the corner of Melissa's eye looked more like stacks of nickels and pennies.

"How do you know Missus Finley-Thompson?" Melissa asked the dragon. "And Ray?"

With a puff of gray smoke and a shrug of its—*her*—scaly shoulders, the dragon said, "If you mean the wheezing man with the sacrificial dogs and his little sidekick who calls herself the Gardener, why, I've never met them."

With a flick of her gray wings, which had been so tight to her side that Melissa hadn't noticed them until that moment, the dragon reared back and gestured at a bare black wall. The wall lit up with rows of rectangular screens, each one showing a different scene, so poorly lit and dusty that Melissa couldn't see anything significant.

"I've never met them," the dragon continued, "but I've seen them here in my land far too often for my tastes. The Gardener's plants are literally a thorn in my side, polluting my rivers, turning the water black. Her vines thrive down here, growing madly, choking out all the green."

Melissa felt a sudden urge to remove the Undercity vine holding back her hair, as if it were fishing line hooked in her, dragging her to this place. The dragon, still talking, didn't seem to notice Melissa's discomfort.

"Those vines turned my rivers into traps. And its foul magic made prisoners of the lost souls that come here, to my Undercity. My lost children. Children I'd vowed to protect and lead to their final homes. So I pulled some strings and maneuvered some minions to get the right people down here to help me. And now, here you are. You and—apparently—your whole family."

"Why us? Why don't you leave this tower to deal with these people on your own?

Melissa was gazing not at the dragon but at the multiple screens, searching for a five-year-old boy and a thirty-six-year old man, afraid she'd see more black water and dust instead.

"Hell," Melissa added. "Ray's no threat. The guy can barely breathe."

She couldn't see anyone familiar on the screens. The abrupt silence from the dragon made her skin suddenly turn cold.

"You ask too many questions," the dragon said, stepping around a spill of scrap metal that minutes ago had looked like stacked sheets of silver. "A guest shouldn't behave in such a way. A hostess like me might be insulted."

Melissa found herself on the verge of apologizing, but her bitch voice beat her to the punch. She'd been through way too much to get stuck here, listening to a deluded dragon whine.

"I'm not here to bother you or get caught up in your feuds with Ray or this Gardener woman. I have a son who's lost, and unless you can find him in one of your screens, I'd best be going."

As Melissa spoke, she slipped her hand into her pocket and pulled out the tiny figure of the oak tree. The tree had been poking in her leg, branches biting into her like tiny teeth.

"Look," she added, opening up her hand. "I'm just trying to find my child." She took a sudden breath, thinking of that name again, the name she wasn't supposed to think of. "My *children*."

If dragons could gasp, that's what this one did. "Where did you find that?"

Melissa looked down at the tiny figure in her hand. The tree was almost glowing white in the weak light of this murky cave. It was just a carving of an oak tree, wasn't it? What did it matter?

Suddenly afraid she'd walked into a trap, she inched back, knocking over a stack of coins. She swallowed and said slowly, "Next to the portal up above us, on my land."

"You found it? Buried in the ground, perhaps?"

Melissa nodded, then looked the dragon in the eye.

"Want it?"

The dragon was immediately suspicious. "You're just going to *give* it to me?"

"Sure," Melissa said. "So long as you let me walk out of here. I have a task or two left to do yet today, and *I'm* not afraid to leave this tower. Deal?"

The dragon winced, then nodded.

"Great." Melissa tossed the tiny oak tree up to the dragon, who caught it between two claws with a happy hiss. She puffed a thin funnel of flame onto the tree until it was nothing but white dust.

"One more portal closed, forever," the dragon said.

Below them, as if to reiterate that point, a door slammed, echoing through the tower, and Melissa remembered her vision from earlier that morning, in the kitchen: the tiny voice, calling out for help, and the oak bursting into flames that turned the forest orange.

"This was from the Gardener's portal, I assume?"

Melissa shrugged. "I guess, if we're talking about the same woman. I found it in the machine shed on our land. We found another next door—portal—at Ray's."

The dragon sniffed. "Oh really? That scheming bastard. That would explain a lot. Lovely." The dragon leaned close to Melissa, one eyebrow raised. "From one mother to another," she said, as more doors slammed below them, "you'd better get yourself through one of those portals down there while there's still time. Doesn't matter which one, so long as you go through focused on where you need to be. The doors connected to your portal up in your world are closing, now that you've given me this tree. Connections are being broken. Hurry now. Things are going to get noisy down here soon."

Melissa nodded, scrambling awkwardly across the junk filling this cave, which was looking more like a cluttered attic than a dragon's lair. The hole in the floor was just a few more feet away.

"All I ask," the dragon said, as if an afterthought, "it that you destroy that other carving for the wheezing man's portal. Do that, and I'll make sure you find your way out, unhampered." The dragon rumbled low in her belly. "I'll take care of that portal's owner soon enough."

"Speaking of," Melissa said from the second rung of the metal ladder, feeling cool, dusty air blow up her bare legs, as doors continued slamming below her, "Ray *is* downstairs."

The results of her words were instantaneous, and destructive. The big green-scaled beast started flinging herself at the walls of her cave in a determined attempt to break free of this prison, once and for all.

Melissa half-climbed, half-slid down the ladder, desperate to get out of there as. It wouldn't take long for the dragon to get loose. So Melissa opened the first door in the floor she saw, not caring where it took her, only knowing she had to get out of here and find those who needed her most, and she dropped through that doorway like a skydiver leaping from a plane.

CHAPTER TWENTY-TWO:
BIRTH DAY

Welcome to the afterlife, Gil thought as he opened his eyes and took his first breath in what felt like ages.

Inhaling deeply, letting it out slowly, he stood on unsteady legs under flickering gray light. His mad flight through the air had ended abruptly, and the strange beings that had pulled him here had dropped him and then apparently disappeared.

The weak light from high above shone on what had to be the last unbroken bridge of the Undercity. Yellow vines crept up the sides, growing over the surface of the bridge even as he watched. Black water crept up the tall, narrow supports. This bridge was not long for this world, either.

He was all alone for a long moment, the only sound his shallow breathing and his timid footsteps in the dust, and then he saw her.

Gil had no idea how time flowed in dreams, or, for that matter, how it passed when you're no longer alive. So he shouldn't have been surprised to see her at this age, walking toward him across the slightly swaying span of the vine-ridden bridge, even if she'd never really been born. How old would she have been, if she had lived?

He tried to say her name, but his tongue stuck to the roof of his mouth. Just the simple act of breathing again had made pretty much every other function of his body stop working on a voluntary basis.

As she reached the end of the bridge, the bridge finally cracked under the weight of the vines. Starting at the midpoint, it dropped away, pulled apart by the vines to drop into the black water hundreds of feet below. Gil couldn't move to save her from falling; his body was no longer following his brain's orders.

But the little girl never fell.

"*Two,*" a small voice whispered inside his head, sweet as the tinkling of piano keys. "Today's my birthday. I'm *two.*"

"*Sophie.*" The name tore a hole in his throat as he said it.

"Yes. And you're my daddy." The last chunk of bridge dropped out from under her feet, but she never moved, didn't even bat an eye. Her curly blonde hair was speckled with dirt, and her round cheeks were flushed red. Blue eyes. Milk-white baby teeth.

She was so small, so precious. Hanging there in the air, no more than five feet from him, Sophie looked down at the river far below her, with a shudder, then her gaze returned to Gil.

He inhaled, held it.

"You . . . you died, baby."

Gil slapped a hand to his mouth hard enough to bring tears from his eyes. Of all the times my mouth has reacted before my brain, he thought, this was truly the worst. I am a damned fool.

"I know, Daddy. But here I am." She clapped her hands, smiling wide. "And guess who else I got to meet?"

Gil hunkered down so he could meet her, eye-to-eye. His arms ached for her, but she remained out of reach, standing on the air two feet over where the bridge ended.

"You're so beautiful. So . . . perfect. Baby Sophie."

He was rewarded with a blush, a rush of pink to his lost girl's already rosy cheeks that made him reel on his feet. How was that possible? Did ghosts blush?

"Noah, Daddy. I got to meet Noah! Pay attention, okay?"

Gil dropped to the ground then, his bad hip and both knees betraying him.

Sophie nodded. "He was here, and he found the seed that bad lady stole from our farm and hid down here. The seed that's gonna clear up the river again for us and kill all her nasty weeds."

Gil was bawling now, relief and loss and fatigue taking over. This was our lost Sophie, and she'd seen Noah. He was here.

Sophie was still talking. "We couldn't get where we needed to go, you see, in that river. We just kept circling and circling in that awful water. Circling, and screaming."

"Noah," Gil said, the name almost as painful to say as hers had been. "Is he . . . dead?"

"He's a *hero*," she said, ignoring his question. "Just like Prince One-Eye in your stories. And he knew you'd be down here looking for him. He finished his kest. But now, before you go, I want to show you this. What you and Noah have done."

She was pointing down at the river, easily half a mile below them, receding somehow, almost hidden by the evil yellow Undercity kudzu, decorated with garbage and bridge debris. Gil shook his head, not wanting to see the souls caught in the current again. Or hear the screaming again.

"It's *gone*, Daddy." The hint of impatience in Sophie's voice made him think of Melissa, and he smiled. She was her mother's daughter, that was for sure. "The hurting's over. None of us are screaming anymore, because the river's clean again. You distracted the Gardener lady long enough to let Noah dig up the seed. The vines are already starting to die. See how it all works, now, silly?"

"The Gardener?" Gil squinted at the vines below him, which indeed appeared to be turning brown and flaking apart. "I thought that was someone my neighbor Ray dreamed up."

"You were just talking to her, Daddy. Under all that pig poop. I don't know *how* you held your breath so long before you got down there. And the dragon lady will take care of Ray, now that Mommy talked to her. You'll see."

"Mommy? She's down here too?" Gil reached out over the emptiness of the non-bridge. "How can you know all this, Sophie?"

"I'll give you two guesses," she said, and leaned forward to kiss him on the nose.

When Gil reached out to pull her closer to him, she was gone. And he had leaned too far over the edge, about to fall over into the river below him.

Everything stopped—his forward motion, the flow of the river, his wild gyrations as he struggled to get his balance back—and in that instant of frozen panic, like being on Pause, Gil looked down at the clear water of the river. Nothing was trapped in it, and even the browning vines and garbage lining the sides had receded.

The water was so clean and so clear that Gil could see the white and black rocks on the bottom. In the river, translucent figures danced and played under the surface of the clear water. Playing, not screaming and writhing in agony, and maybe even laughing. Yes, he was sure they'd been laughing. And then they were gone.

And then he was falling forward, unable to stop his forward momentum.

"Hold *on*," someone said, gripping the back of his pants by the belt and tugging him back onto solid ground. "I've got you," she said, and of course Gil recognized her voice.

Melissa.

They both fell back onto the dirt road leading to the ruined bridge. Gil felt speechless, unable to compute all he'd seen and heard just now.

"What the hell were you doing?" Melissa said from the ground next to him, her words angry but her tone all wrong. She sounded as if, well, as if she were glad he didn't topple over the edge into the abyss, for a change.

Gil pulled his wife up with him and wrapped his arms around her. He held her tight, ignoring the ominous rumbling sounds all around them, as if the Undercity was experiencing some sort of seismic event. All he cared about was the feel of Melissa's body against his, her heartbeats and breaths matching his own body's mad rhythms. As the shifting sounds above and below them grew louder, Gil reluctantly let her go.

"How did you get here?" he said.

"Where is he?" Melissa asked at the same time, and then she added, "You don't want to know how. The whole story'd take too long. Let's just say it involves Ray and a dragon. So—Noah?"

Hand in hand, following the river, moving quickly now, they began to hurry back to the surface. Gil didn't care if his wife thought he was nuts, or if the Undercity shifted on him and they had to walk forever. He just started talking, and it felt so damned good.

"Let me tell you all about it," Gil said. "The whole story. Then you can tell me about any dragons you may have met. Deal?"

∽o∾

Noah found most of his neighbors waiting for him on the curb in front of the house of slamming doors. He'd let the seed show him the way back, lighting up the black rot and yellow vines surrounding him. He felt like he'd been walking forever.

And now he was back to the road in front of the crooked house, and they were sitting around next to the high curb, next to three crumpled-looking blue pickup trucks. He saw Julio, Anna, Herschel, Mr. Dun, their neighbor Billie, and even Ray, who was missing his air tank. They were all covered in dust and giving Ray the evil eye. Noah couldn't see Eric anywhere.

Maybe they're waiting for *me*, he thought, and then a rumble filled the air, shaking the ground in the process.

Noah walked up to Herschel and Dun, who were looking up at the dark windows in the tower of the house. Nothing moved up there, and Noah was afraid to go back inside and look for Elwood. He'd heard a purring sound in his ears right before he left the dark heart of the Undercity, and he knew Elwood was resting now, his kest to protect and guide complete.

"Where's my mom and dad?" Noah asked, and the two old men nearly fell over.

"Noah!" Julio said, leaping down from the too-high curb and scooping him up into his arms. "Your mama's in there, looking for *you*, hombre. I guess your papa is in there too, somewhere. I hope."

"Really? I knew they would be. I just . . . " Another rumble, louder than thunder, filled the air, and Julio rocked back on his heels, almost dropping Noah onto the concrete road.

"We need to get moving," Noah said. He noticed that Mr. Dun and Herschel stayed close to Ray, as if he were a prisoner or something. "This place is going away, soon. All the doors will be closing on us, I think."

"Noah," Julio said as they began hurrying up the street, following Noah's lead. "Bobbie found this inside, next to one of the doors. Does it belong to you?"

He handed Noah a small green sliver the length of a pinkie finger. The salamander's tail.

"Thank you," Noah mumbled, unable to believe this tiny thing had cause so much trouble.

Seed in one hand, tail in the other, with tears filling his eyes, Noah led everyone up the street, back to the door with Dad's magnet on it. It was an easy journey now that he knew the way, except he couldn't stop the tears from slipping out of his eyes.

Julio and Anna tried to talk to him, to ask him why he was crying, but he refused to tell them why. He felt both mad and sad, thinking about his little sister. They never *told* him.

"This is how I got in," Noah said when they reached the door leading back to the cave and forest beyond. He ran his hand down the smooth, unrusted surface of this side of the door. "But there's no handle."

"Try this," Mr. Dun said, pulling out a tiny carving of a greyhound. As soon the old man held it up, Noah heard Ray gasp, then something exploded back up the road behind them.

"Where did you . . . get that?" Ray said, his voice choking. A second later, Herschel and Billie went flying as Ray grabbed the tiny dog out of Mr. Dun's hand. Ray had run off ten steps back down the concrete road before Noah could even turn and figure out what had just happened.

When he did look back, he saw Ray keel over, coughing, with the tiny dog held tight to his chest. He was swearing so hard Noah felt his ears burn. And then a shadow fell over Ray.

"Don't look," Julio said. He tried to block Noah and Anna's view with his body, but Noah still got a glimpse of a big green-scaled foot reaching down from the sky to take Ray and his little wooden dog away. Ray was coughing too hard to scream.

"Let's get out of here," Billie said, pulling Julio and Noah and Anna to the door. The world was falling apart behind him. On a whim, Noah poked the salamander's tail into the door, hoping to hear the clicking of gears as the door unlocked itself again. But all that happened was the tail got stuck in the door. When he pulled on it, the door silently swung towards him.

"Go!" Billie and Julio shouted at the same time, and they all pushed through the door. As soon as Mr. Dun and Herschel slammed it shut behind them, the metal door disintegrated, leaving only solid rock. The place had sealed itself up tight.

"The tail," Noah said. "I left it behind, again."

With one last rumble that ended in a low booming sound, the Undercity went silent on the other side of the door.

"I'm glad we got out before you did that," a tired voice said from behind Noah. "I'd just like to know how that durn tail fell out of my pocket."

Dad.

Putting the image of that huge clawed foot grabbing his wheezy old neighbor out of his head, Noah spun and dove into his father's arms, still gripping the seed tight in his hand. Mom was right there next to him.

"Dad! I didn't think I'd see you again, ever. You or Mom!"

After a long, long time of enjoying the feel of Dad's arms around him, along with Mom's touch on his back, Noah remembered that he was supposed to be mad at them both. As they walked out of the cave and up through the tunnel and into the forest again, Noah showed his parents the seed. It was growing warm in his hand, almost hot.

"This is what I found in there. What *she* helped me find. Sophie. Why didn't you tell me?" he whispered. He could feel the hot tears running down his cheeks now, and he didn't try to fight them anymore, now that everyone was safe. Everyone but *her*. Noah stopped walking so he could look them both in the eyes. "Why didn't you tell me I had a sister?"

While Dad looked down at the seed that Noah had found, Mom came closer, resting her hand on Noah's back in the dark forest. She was covered with dust, and Noah knew she'd been swimming in the lawn with the others.

So many stories to tell from this day, Noah thought, but the one he truly needed to know wasn't made up. After all he'd been through, he needed to hear the truth.

∽∘∾

"Sophie," Melissa said at last. The word both tore her heart and began the process of healing that open, unacknowledged wound inside her. "We lost her," she said, her voice breaking. "She got sick inside of me, and . . . she died, Noah."

"She died," Noah repeated in a whisper.

"I'm sorry," she said. "We didn't tell you, because I—we—thought you were too young. She . . . Sophie was never born, Noah. I lost her."

Gil took her hand, shaking his head gently. "No. She was just . . . *lost*. We did all we could, Melissa. It's not your fault."

Noah gave them both a look that made Melissa more ashamed for hiding Sophie from her big brother than any other misdeed she'd ever done in her life, even the way she'd treated Gil in the past two years. She'd been so angry, and she'd never realized the extent of it. Even having Gil close to her had hurt too much. It all hurt too much.

"We have to plant this seed," Noah said, pointing at the edge of the forest, where their land began. "There. Right now."

Gil nodded at the same time as Melissa. She took his outstretched hand, and put her other hand on her son's shoulder. The three of them found a place at the edge of the forest and began to dig with their fingers. Once she saw the dirt embedded in the nails of Noah's hands, Melissa wouldn't let Noah dig any more.

At last, when the hole was deep enough, Noah dropped the seed in, covered it, and then wiped the tears from his face. He rubbed them into the dirt covering the seed. Melissa looked at Gil for a long second, then she nodded, and they did the same. Tears were easy to come by today.

Seconds or minutes or days passed—how long, Melissa would never know—but even before she'd had time to sit down and rest, something green and small began to press its way out of the soil.

None of them were about to leave here until they had seen this through. No more running, Melissa vowed. No more denial.

The others from her search party had wandered away, still silent from the shock of their journey and all they'd seen, including Ray's death. The three Andersons remained together in the weakening daylight as they watched the earth, waiting.

Soon, their patience paid off. Tiny green tendrils pushed their way through the cooling ground, surrounded in a white haze. Melissa watched her daughter's spirit rise from the earth, green and dancing. Sophie was the little girl she'd always imagined—beautiful and happy, fat-cheeked and smiling. Sophie's blue eyes never looked away from Melissa's eyes as the girl turned and spun and danced for her mother.

"I'm so sorry," Melissa whispered, tears again spilling from her eyes and splashing onto the ground. "I'm sorry I won't be able to be your mommy. And for not being able to let you go the first time. I'll miss you. Goodbye, sweet baby Sophie."

"Thank you, Mommy," Sophie whispered. "Now stop hurting yourself about it, okay?"

And at last, as Sophie turned and danced off into the other trees in the forest, leaving behind her tiny oak shoot still growing taller, Melissa felt herself begin to accept their loss at last, and start to heal.

༺ོ༻

I watched them both from a few feet away, feeling the part of my heart that had been boarded up and off-limits begin to open up again, after far too long. Darkness crept into the forest around us, but I had no fear of either any more. With Noah heavy in my arms, I pssted softly at Melissa until I got her attention. She wiped her eyes and face and crept next to us, hesitating just long enough to about break my heart.

"Please," I whispered. "Sit with us."

After the longest five seconds of my life, Melissa did.

Noah nodded off to sleep in my arms, safe and secure in the thought that Mom and Dad were right there with him. As for me, well, I was looking forward to my first unbroken night of sleep in years. I'd sleep right here, next to the forest, if I had to.

This is why we bought this farm, I thought as I looked around at the trees of the forest, the trickling stream at my feet now running clear. This is how the land brought us all together again. I inhaled the clean smell of nature and took in the scents of my returned son and wife and the last traces of my daughter's spirit, greedily imbibing the different scents and essences until I felt like I'd explode from it all.

You can forget all the rest. This is the only story worth telling, the only story that matters.

Printed in the United States
137345LV00002B/6/P

9 780809 573158